And he di meant to dc didn't knov revenge when he couldn't seem to make her do anything—but he couldn't take *this* any longer. He couldn't stand it.

"I'm not empty inside," Chase blurted out, gravel and steel in his voice, and she jerked in her seat as if he'd smacked her. He hated himself as if he really had.

"What?"

But he was already crossing the room. He was already right there, looming above her, so obviously brutal and dangerous, and yet she still gazed up at him in a kind of wonder. Like she saw all the things in him he'd stopped wishing were there a long, long time ago.

Like she was as much a fool as he was.

"It's much worse than empty in here," he gritted out. "It's murderous dark, vicious and wrong, and there's no changing it. You should have run away from me when I gave you the chance, Zara. You should have understood that it was a gift, and I don't know that I'll hand you another one."

VOWS OF CONVENIENCE

Bound by duty!

The Whitaker name was once synonymous with power, wealth and control. But with the family business facing certain ruin, and its reputation turning into dust, the Whitaker siblings need to make the ultimate sacrifice to safeguard their futures…

HIS FOR A PRICE

Following the death of Mattie Whitaker's father, a merger with Greek tycoon Nicodemus Stathis's company will go a long way towards fixing her problem—but Nicodemus's help comes at a price…

October 2014

HIS FOR REVENGE

Chase Whitaker is playing his own dark game of revenge against Zara Elliot's father, the chairman of his board. He plans to replace him—but he has no defences against Zara's unstudied charm and natural beauty…

December 2014

HIS FOR REVENGE

BY

CAITLIN CREWS

Published in Great Britain 2014
by Mills & Boon, an imprint of Harlequin (UK) Limited,
Eton House, 18-24 Paradise Road, Richmond, Surrey, TW9 1SR

ISBN: 978-0-263-25033-6

Harlequin (UK) Limited's policy is to use papers that are natural, renewable and recyclable products and made from wood grown in sustainable forests. The logging and manufacturing processes conform to the legal environmental regulations of the country of origin.

Printed and bound in Spain
by Blackprint CPI, Barcelona

Caitlin Crews discovered her first romance novel at the age of twelve. It involved swashbuckling pirates, grand adventures, a heroine with rustling skirts and a mind of her own, and a seriously mouth-watering and masterful hero. The book (the title of which remains lost in the mists of time) made a serious impression. Caitlin was immediately smitten with romances and romance heroes, to the detriment of her middle school social life. And so began her life-long love affair with romance novels, many of which she insists on keeping near her at all times.

Caitlin has made her home in places as far-flung as York, England, and Atlanta, Georgia. She was raised near New York City, and fell in love with London on her first visit when she was a teenager. She has backpacked in Zimbabwe, been on safari in Botswana, and visited tiny villages in Namibia. She has, while visiting the place in question, declared her intention to live in Prague, Dublin, Paris, Athens, Nice, the Greek Islands, Rome, Venice, and/or any of the Hawaiian islands. Writing about exotic places seems like the next best thing to moving there.

She currently lives in California, with her animator/comic book artist husband and their menagerie of ridiculous animals.

Recent titles by the same author:

HIS FOR A PRICE *(Vows of Convenience)*
UNDONE BY THE SULTAN'S TOUCH
A SCANDAL IN THE HEADLINES
(Sicily's Corretti Dynasty)
A ROYAL WITHOUT RULES *(Royal & Ruthless)*

Welcome to the world, Baby Haslam!

CHAPTER ONE

ZARA ELLIOTT WAS halfway down the aisle of the white-steepled First Congregational Church she'd always thought was a touch too smug for its own good—taking up a whole block on the town green in the center of the sweetly manicured, white clapboard village that her family had lived in since the days of the first Connecticut Colony way back in the 1630s—before the sheer insanity of what she was doing really hit her.

She felt her knees wobble alarmingly beneath her, somewhere underneath all that billowing white fabric that was draped around her and made her look like a lumbering wedding cake, and she almost stopped right there. In front of the hundreds of witnesses her father had decided it was necessary to invite to this circus show.

"Don't you dare stop now," her father hissed at her, the genial smile he used in public never dimming in the slightest as his wiry body tensed beside her. "I'll drag you up this aisle if I have to, Zara, but I won't be pleased."

This constituted about as much paternal love and support as she could expect from Amos Elliott, who collected money and power the way other fathers collected stamps, and Zara had never been any good at standing up to him anyway.

That had always been her sister Ariella's department.

Which was how this was happening in the first place,

Zara reminded herself as she dutifully kept moving. Then she had to order herself not to think about her older sister, because the dress might be a preposterous monstrosity of filmy white material, but it was also much—*much*—too tight. Ariella was at least three inches taller than Zara and had the breasts of a preteen boy, all the better to swan about in bikinis and gravity-defying garments as she pleased. And if Zara let herself get furious, as she would if she thought about any of this too hard, she would pop right out of this secondhand dress that didn't fit her at all, right here in the middle of the church her ancestors had helped build centuries ago.

It would serve her father right, she thought grimly, but it wouldn't be worth the price she'd have to pay. And anyway, she was doing this for her late grandmother, who had earnestly believed that Zara should give her father another chance and had made Zara promise to her on her deathbed last summer that Zara would—but had left Zara her cottage on Long Island Sound just in case that chance didn't go well.

She concentrated on the infamous Chase Whitaker—*her groom*—instead, as he stood there at the front of the church with his back to her approach. He looked as if he was drawing out the romantic suspense when Zara knew he was much more likely to be concealing his own fury at this wedding he'd made perfectly clear he didn't want. This wedding that her conniving father had pushed him into in the months since Chase's own larger-than-life father had died unexpectedly, leaving Amos a distinct weakness in the power structure of Whitaker Industries that he, as chairman of its board of directors, could exploit.

This wedding that Chase would have been opposed to even if Zara had been who she was supposed to be: Ariella, who, in typical Ariella fashion, hadn't bothered to turn up this morning.

Zara had always prided herself on her practicality, a vastly underused virtue in the Elliott family, but she had to admit that there was a part of her that took in the sight of her waiting groom's broad, finely carved shoulders and that delicious height he wore so easily and wondered what it would be like if this was real. If she wasn't a last-minute substitute for the beauty of the family, who had once been breathlessly described in Zara's hearing as *the jewel in the Elliott crown*. If a man like Chase Whitaker—worshipped the world over for his dark blue eyes, that thick dark hair and that devastatingly athletic body of his that made women into red-faced, swooning idiots at the very sight of it, to say nothing of that crisp, delicious British accent he wielded with such charm—really was waiting for *her* at the end of a church aisle.

If, if, if, she scolded herself derisively. *You're an idiot yourself.*

No one, it went without saying, had ever described Zara as a gemstone of any kind. Though her much-beloved grandmother had called her *a brick* once or twice before she'd died last summer, in that tone women of Grams's exalted social status had only ever used to refer to the girls they considered *handsome enough* and even *dependable* instead of anything like *pretty*.

"You're so dependable," Ariella had said two days ago, the way she always did, with that little smile and that arch tone that Zara had been choosing to overlook for the better part of her twenty-six years. Ariella had been putting on her makeup for one of her prewedding events, an exercise which took her a rather remarkable amount of time in Zara's opinion. Not that she'd shared it. "I don't know how you can bear to do it all the time."

"Do I have a choice?" Zara had asked, with only the faintest touch of asperity, because the way Ariella had said *dependable* was anything but complimentary, unlike the way Grams had said it back when. "Are *you* planning to step up and be dependable at some point?"

Ariella had met Zara's gaze in the mirror, a bright red lipstick in one languid hand. She'd blinked as if amazed by the question.

"Why would I?" she'd asked after a moment, as light and breezy and dismissive as ever, though her expression had bordered on scornful. "You're so much better at it."

That had obviously been a statement of intent, Zara thought now, as she moved closer by the second to the man at the end of the aisle. Who wasn't waiting *for her.* Who, given a choice, wouldn't be there at all.

Zara was glad she was wearing the irksome, heavy veil that hid her away from view so that none of the assembled onlookers could see how foolish her imagination was, which would no doubt be written all over her face. The curse of a natural redhead, she thought balefully. Hair that she only wished was a mysterious shade of glamorous auburn instead of what it really was. *Red.* And the ridiculously sensitive skin to go along with it.

But then she stopped thinking about her skin and the things that might or might not be splashed across it in all those telling pinks and reds she couldn't control, because they reached the altar at last.

Amos boomed out his part of the archaic ceremony, announcing to all that he gave away *this woman* with perhaps an insulting amount of paternal eagerness. Then she was summarily handed over to Chase Whitaker, who had turned to face her but managed to convey the impression that he was still facing in the other direction. As if he was deeply bored. Or so mentally and emotionally removed from this absurd little exercise that he thought he *actually was* somewhere else entirely.

And Zara remained veiled, as if she was participating in an actual medieval wedding, because—as her father had reminded her no less than seventy-five times in the church lobby already—Chase needed to be legally bound to the family before this little bait and switch was discovered.

“How charming,” Zara had said drily. “A fairy tale of a wedding, indeed.”

Amos had eyed her with that flat, ugly look of his that she went to great lengths to avoid under normal circumstances. Not that waking up to find oneself in the middle of a farcical comedy that involved playing Switch the Arranged Bride with her absentee sister’s unknowing and unwilling fiancé constituted anything like *normal.*

“You can save the smart remarks for your new husband, assuming you manage to pull this off,” Amos had said coldly. As was his way, especially when talking to the daughter he’d called *a waste of Elliott genes* when she’d been a particularly ungainly and unattractive thirteen-year-old. “I’m sure he’ll be more receptive to them than I am.”

His expression had suggested he doubted that, and Zara had decided that one smart remark was more than enough. She’d busied herself with practicing her polite, “just married to a complete stranger” smile and pretending she was *perfectly fine* with the fact Ariella’s dress didn’t fit her at all.

Because what girl didn’t dream of waddling up the aisle in a dress that had been cut down the back to allow her breasts to fit in it, then held together with a hastily sewn-up strip of lace she was afraid her stepmother had ripped off the bottom of the church’s curtains?

Her soon-to-be husband took her hands now, his own large and warm and remarkably strong as they curled around hers. It made her feel oddly light-headed. Zara frowned at the perky boutonniere he wore in his lapel and tried not to think too much about the fact that her father clearly believed that if Chase got wind of the fact that it was *Zara* he was marrying, he’d run for the hills.

The arranged marriage part was no impediment, was the implication. Just the fact that it was to the less lovely, less fawned over, much less desirable Elliott sister.

It wasn't until she heard a strange sound that Zara realized she was grinding her teeth. She stopped before her father—glowering at her from the first pew—heard it and did something else to ensure this marriage happened according to his plans. Zara really didn't want to think about what that *something else* might entail. Switching one daughter for the next should really be at the outer limits of deceitful behavior, but this was Amos Elliott. He had no outer limits.

The priest droned on about fidelity and love, which verged on insulting under the circumstances. Zara lifted her frown to Chase Whitaker's famously beautiful profile, so masculine and attractive that it had graced any number of magazine covers in its time, and reminded herself that while this situation might be extreme, it wasn't anything new. Zara had always been the mousy sister, the dutiful sister. The sister who preferred books to parties and her grandmother's company to the carousing of a hundred idiotic peers. The quiet sister whose academic aspirations were always swept aside or outright ignored so that Ariella's various scandals and kaleidoscopic needs could be focused on instead. She'd always been the sister who could be relied upon to do all the unpleasant and responsible and often deadly boring things, so that Ariella could carry on with her "modeling" and her "acting" and whatever else it was she pretended to do that kept her flitting about the globe from one hot spot to the next, answerable to no one and spending their father's money as she pleased.

Stop thinking about Ariella, Zara ordered herself sharply, when Chase slanted a dark look her way, and she realized she was squeezing his hands too tightly.

She loosened her grip. And she absolutely did not allow herself to think about how warm his hands were, how strong and interestingly callused and yet elegant, holding hers in a manner that suggested his gentleness was only a veneer stretched thinly over a great power he didn't care to broadcast.

She definitely wasn't thinking about that.

Then it was her turn to speak, in as even a voice as she could manage, expecting Chase to tear off her veil and denounce her in front of the entire church when the priest slipped in her name instead of Ariella's, so quickly and quietly that she wasn't sure anyone even heard it. But he was too busy concentrating on something just to the right of her gaze—and again, she got the sense that he was ruthlessly holding himself in check. That doing so took every ounce of the obvious and considerable strength she could feel in him as he slipped the necessary rings onto her finger.

That, or he was as drunk as the faint scent of whiskey suggested he was, and was trying not to topple over.

He recited his own vows in a low, curt tone, that accent of his making each word seem that much more precise and beautiful, and when it was done, when Zara had slid his own ring into place, she felt dizzy with relief and something else she couldn't quite name. Was it really that simple? Had she really squeezed herself into an ill-fitting dress she couldn't zip up and a blindingly opaque veil and pretended to be her sister? For the singular purpose of trapping this poor man in one of her father's awful little plots, because this had seemed like *the chance* her adored Grams had advised her to give Amos before she wrote him off forever?

"You may kiss the bride," the priest intoned.

So it appeared that yes, she had.

Chase sighed. Then he paused, and for a moment, Zara thought he was going to decline. *Could* he decline? In front of all these people? In any possible way that wouldn't make her look unwanted and unattractive besides?

She didn't know if she wanted him to kiss her or not, if

she was honest. She didn't know which would be worse: being kissed by someone who didn't want to kiss her because he felt he had to do it, or *not* being kissed by him and thereby shamed in front of the entire congregation. But then he dealt with the situation by reaching over and flipping her veil back, exposing her face for the first time.

Zara held her breath, cringing slightly as she braced for an explosion of his temper. She could *feel* it, like the slap of an open fire much too close to her, and instinctively shut her eyes against it. She heard an echoing sort of gasp from the front of the church, where someone had finally noticed that glamorous Ariella Elliott was looking markedly shorter and rounder than usual today. But Chase Whitaker, her unwitting groom and now her husband, said nothing, despite the roar of all that fire.

So she braced herself, then opened her eyes and looked at him.

And for a moment everything disappeared.

Zara had seen a million pictures of this man. She'd seen him from across the relatively small rooms they'd both been in. But she'd never been this close to him. So nothing could possibly have prepared her for the wallop of those eyes of his. Dark blue, yes. But they were the color of twilight, moments before the stars appeared. The color of the sea, far out from a lonely shore. There was nothing safe or summery blue about them. There was a wildness about that color, a deep, aching thing that she felt in her like a restless wind.

And he was beautiful. Not merely handsome or attractive the way he appeared in photographs. Not ruggedly lovely in some stark, masculine way, like dangerous mountain peaks were pretty, though he was decidedly, inarguably male. He was simply *beautiful*. His cheekbones were a marvel. His hair was a rough black silk and his brows were a great, arched wickedness unto themselves. His wide mouth made her feel much too warm, even flat and expressionless as it was now. And those stunning, arresting eyes, the blue of lost things, of shattered dreams, tore through her.

It took her a moment to register that he was staring down at her, incredulous.

And—as she'd already figured out from that blast of temper that she could still feel butting up against her like a living, breathing thing—he was very, very angry.

Zara went to pull away, not in the least bit interested in remaining this close to *that much* temper, but her new husband forestalled any attempt to escape with the hand he curled around her neck. She imagined it looked tender from a distance. But she was much closer, and she could feel it for what it was. Threat. Menace.

Fury.

No matter that a bright hot burst of flame danced from the place he touched her and then throughout the rest of her. No matter that a shiver rocked through her or that she felt as if her whole body *woke up* at the sensation of that hot, male palm against the nape of her neck. Her lungs felt tight and her throat ached. Her knees felt wobbly again, but for a very different reason than they had before.

And then Chase Whitaker, who had been quite clear that he'd never wanted to marry anyone and wouldn't have chosen her if he had, bent his head and pressed his perfect lips to hers.

It should have been awkward, Zara thought wildly. Even violating.

But instead, it was like her entire body simply…sizzled. Her lips felt seared through, and she felt herself flush what she knew would be a revealing, horrifying red. She felt that simple press of his lips everywhere. In her throat. In that ache between her breasts. In her suddenly too-tight nipples. In that hard knot in her belly, and worse, in the sudden molten heat below it. Chase lifted his head, his remarkable eyes darker than before, and she knew he saw all of that betraying color.

And worse, that he knew what it meant.

There was something taut and electric between them then, something that sparked in the air and then moved inside of her, setting off alarms and making her feel that she really might collapse in the first faint of her life, after all. Like the archaic, bartered bride she was impersonating today. *Maybe that would be a nice little vacation from all this*, a small voice inside her suggested, while everything else she was or ever had been drowned in those dark blue eyes of his.

And then he looked away and everything sped up.

There was applause, then organ music, then the murmuring of several hundred scandalized guests who'd finally caught on to the fact that Chase Whitaker, president and CEO of Whitaker Industries and one of the world's most beloved playboy heirs, had just wed the wrong Elliott daughter.

Zara found this as unbelievable as they did, she was certain, but she didn't have time to reflect on it. Chase was holding her by the arm—in a manner that made her feel rather more like a prisoner than a bride, and yet, somehow, more cherished than when Amos had done the same thing—and they were starting off down the aisle again. She saw her father's smug face as they strode past him. She saw her stepmother dabbing at her eyes, and thought that ditzy Melissa might in fact be the only person in the church who'd found the ceremony moving, bless her. She saw longtime neighbors and old family friends and the speculative expressions of a hundred strangers, but the only real thing was that hard arm that held her next to his impossibly lean and chiseled body.

And then there was silence. Chase marched them out of the church and down the steps into the searing, brutal cold of the December afternoon, then directly into the back of a waiting limousine.

"Home," he grated at the driver. "Now."

"The reception is actually here in the village, not wherever your home is," Zara said, because she was incapable of keeping her mouth shut.

Chase had thrown himself into the cushy leather seat beside her and when he turned that furious, incredulous gaze of his on her again, it was like being burned alive. She felt charred.

He stared at her. Moments passed, or maybe years. The car drove off from the church. The world could have exploded outside the window, for all she knew. There was nothing but that wild dark blue and the leftover heat where his mouth and his palm had touched her skin, like he'd branded that contact into her flesh.

Then the car jolted to a stop at a light, Chase blinked and looked forward again, and Zara decided she'd imagined that awestruck, spellbound, *on fire* feeling. It was the oddness of the situation, that was all. It was Ariella's ridiculous dress, cutting into her like a corset from hell, making it difficult to breathe. There was no reason at all to feel that despite everything, she'd never been more alive in her life than she was right now, in the back of a limousine headed God knew where with an angry, beautiful stranger.

"Oh, I'm sorry," she said, because they might as well make the best of it. It was what Grams would have done. "I don't think we've ever met." She smiled as politely as she could at this man, her brand-new husband, and stuck out her hand. "I'm Zara."

He was trapped in a nightmare, Chase thought, staring at that outstretched hand in stunned, outraged amazement. There was no other explanation. For any of this.

"I know who you are," he grated, and when he didn't

take her hand she merely dropped it back in her lap, looking wholly unperturbed. Exactly as she'd looked in the church, when he'd been glaring at her fiercely enough to burn holes through her.

Except for when you kissed her.

But Chase shoved that thought away, along with the image of her flushing that intriguing shade of scarlet in the wake of that kiss he still didn't know why he'd given her, and scowled at his bride instead.

The truth was, while he'd recognized who she must have been because she'd been ushered up the aisle by his nemesis, he couldn't remember if they'd ever met before. He wasn't sure he'd have known her name even if they had, just as he wasn't sure why that made him feel something like ashamed. He had a vague memory of her in a black dress that had fit her much better than the gown she wore today, and a flash of red hair from across a table. That was it.

Every other interaction he'd had with her family had involved her pain-in-the-ass father and blonde, brittle Ariella, who was apparently even more useless than he'd already imagined she was. And his imagination had been rather detailed in its low opinion of her.

"You tricked me," he said then, trying to gather his wits, as he'd been noticeably unable to do for some time now. Since Big Bart Whitaker had died six months ago, leaving him neck deep in this mess that got bigger and deeper and *swampier* every bloody day. Since he'd had to give up his life in London and come back to the States to take his place as president and CEO of Whitaker Industries, where he'd done nothing but clash with Amos Elliott—the driving opposing force on his board of directors and the bane of his existence. And now his father-in-law, for his sins. "I could have you up on fraud charges, to start."

Zara Elliott did not look alarmed by this possibility. She

was awash in masses and masses of a frothy, unflattering white fabric, like a foaming and possibly furious marshmallow had exploded from every side of her while her quietly aristocratic face remained serene. But her eyes—her eyes were a bright, warm gold. The color of late afternoons, of the sun dripping low on the winter horizon.

Where the hell had *that* come from? He must have had more whiskey for his breakfast than he'd thought.

"I'm three inches shorter than Ariella and at least two sizes larger," she said. "At a conservative estimate."

Her voice was smooth and warm, like honey. She sounded, if not happy, something like *content.* Chase didn't know how he recognized that note in her voice, given he'd never felt such a thing in his life.

So that was why it took him a moment to process what she'd said. "I don't follow."

"Was I tricking you or were you not paying very much attention, if you couldn't tell the difference the moment I set foot in that church?" She only smiled when he scowled at her. "It's a reasonable question. One we can ignore, if you like, but which a judge may dwell on in any hypothetical fraud trial."

"This hypothetical judge might well find himself more interested in the marriage license," Chase replied. "Which did not have your name on it when I grudgingly signed it."

Her smile only deepened. "My father imagined that might cause you some concern. He suggested I remind you that the license was obtained right here in this very county, where he's reigned supreme for decades now, like his father, uncles, grandfather and so on before him. He wanted me to put your mind at ease. That license will read the way it should before the end of the day, he's quite certain."

Chase muttered something filthy under his breath, which had no discernible effect on her composure. He leaned forward and rummaged around until he found the half-drunk bottle of whiskey in the bar cabinet and then he took a long swig of it, not bothering to use a glass. That sweet, obliterating fire rolled through him, but it was better than the numbness inside of him, so he ignored the scraping flames and took another hefty swig instead.

After a moment, he offered her the bottle. It only seemed polite, under the circumstances.

"No, thank you." Also polite. Scrupulously so.

"Do you drink?" He didn't know why he cared. He *didn't* care.

"I like wine, sometimes," she said, as if she was considering the matter in some depth as she spoke. "Red more than white. I'll admit that beer is a mystery to me. I think it tastes like old socks."

"This is whiskey. It doesn't taste of socks. It tastes of peat and fire and the scalding anticipation of regret."

"Tempting." Her soft mouth twitched slightly in the corners, and he decided the whiskey was going to his head, because he found that far more fascinating than he should have. He couldn't recall the last time a woman's naked mouth had seemed so *riveting*. He couldn't recall the last time he'd noticed a woman's mouth at all, save what it could do in the dark. "How much whiskey did you have before the ceremony?"

He eyed her for a moment, then eyed the bottle. "Half."

"Ah." She nodded. "I thought you might be drunk."

"Why aren't you?" he asked, not caring that the dark rasp in his voice gave away far too many of the things he needed to keep hidden.

"Sadly, that wasn't on the list of options I was given when I woke up this morning and was informed Ariella had flown the coop." Her impossibly golden eyes gleamed with something almost painful Chase didn't want to understand, but her voice was still perfectly cheerful. It didn't make any sense. "I had to fight for a single cup of coffee in all the panic and blame. Asking for something alcoholic would have started a war."

He felt something very much like *ashamed* again, and he didn't like it. It hadn't occurred to him that she might find this marriage as unlikely and unpleasant a prospect as he did, and he didn't know why something in him wanted to argue the point. Like it made any difference who wanted what. They were both stuck now, weren't they? Just as her father had intended.

And it didn't matter to him which Elliott sister was stuck with him in Amos's handiwork. It made no difference to his plans. No matter what Zara's mouth did to his peace of mind.

Chase decided he didn't particularly care for any of these thoughts and took another long pull from the whiskey bottle instead. Oblivion was the only place he truly enjoyed these days. He'd considered permanently relocating there, in fact. How hard would it be to lose himself entirely in this or that bottle?

But he never did it, no matter how many nights he'd tried. Because the fact remained: the only thing he had left of his father, of his parents and his family legacy, was Whitaker Industries. He couldn't let it fall entirely into Amos Elliott's greedy hands. He'd already compromised and merged companies with the man his father had considered a better son to him than Chase had ever been. He couldn't sell it now. He couldn't step aside.

He couldn't do anything but this.

Chase took another drink from the bottle, long and hard.

"Where is your sister?" he asked, with what he thought was remarkable calm, under the circumstances.

Those golden eyes cooled considerably. "That's an excellent question."

"But you don't know?" He let his gaze track over that face of hers, her pale skin blending into the white veil that billowed around her, reminding him of a bird's plumage. He found he was fascinated by the fact her voice remained the same, so unassailably polite, no matter what her gaze told him. Her mouth bothered him, he decided. It was too full. Too soft and tempting. Especially when she smiled. "That's your position?"

"Chase," she said, then hesitated. "Can I call you that? Or do you require that your arranged brides address you in a different way?"

He let out a short laugh, which shocked the hell out him. "Chase is fine."

"Chase," she said again, more firmly, and he had the strangest sensation then. Like this was a different time and there truly was an intimacy to the use of proper names. Or maybe it was just the way she said it; the way it sounded in that mouth of hers. "If I knew where Ariella was, I wouldn't have shoehorned myself into this dress and married you in front of three hundred of my father's closest friends, neighbors and business associates." She smiled at him, though those impossible eyes were shot through with temper then, and he understood that was where the truth of this woman was. Not in her practiced smiles or her remarkably cheery voice, but in her eyes. Gold like the sunset and as honest. "If I knew where she was I would have gone and found her and dragged her to the church myself. She is, after all, the Elliott sister who agreed to marry you. Not me."

He watched her mildly enough over his whiskey bottle, and noted the precise moment she realized she'd devolved into something like a rant. That telltale color stole over her cheeks, and he watched it sweep over the rest of her, down her neck and to parts hidden in all that explosive white. He found he was fascinated anew.

"No offense taken," he said, forestalling the apology he could see forming on her lips. "I didn't want to marry either one of you. Your father demanded it."

"As a condition of his agreement to back you and your new COO, yes," she said. "Your new brother-in-law, if I'm not mistaken?"

"Nicodemus Stathis and I have merged our companies," Chase said, as thinly and emotionlessly as he could. "And our families, as seems to be going around this season. My sister tells me she's blissfully happy." He wondered if Zara could see what a lie that was, if that was what the slight tilt to her head meant. If she knew, somehow, how little he and his younger sister Mattie had talked at all in the long years since they'd lost their mother, much less lately. He shoved on. "Your father is the only remaining thorn in my side. You—this—is nothing more than a thorn-removal procedure."

That was perhaps a bit too harsh, the part of him that wasn't deep in a fire of whiskey reflected.

"No offense taken," she said, her voice as merry as his had been cool, though Chase wasn't certain he'd have apologized, if she'd given him the chance. Or that she wasn't offended, come to that. "I'm delighted to be of service."

"I know why Ariella was doing this—or why she said she was all right with it," Chase said then, bluntly. "She quite likes a hefty bank account and no commentary on how she empties it. Is that a family trait? Are you in this for the money?"

Did he only imagine that she stiffened? "I have my own money, thank you."

"You mean you have your father's." He toasted her with his bottle. "Don't we all."

"The only family money I have came from my grandmother, as a matter of fact, though I try not to touch it," she replied, still smiling, though that warm gold gaze of hers had iced over again, and Chase knew he should hate the fact he noticed. "My father felt that if I wouldn't follow his wishes to the letter, which involved significantly less school and a lot more friendly games of things like tennis to attract his friends' sons as potential boyfriends-slash-merger options, I shouldn't have access to any of his money."

"Your sister makes defying your father her chief form of entertainment," Chase said, focusing on that part of what she'd said instead of the rest, because *the rest* reminded him of the many steps he'd taken to make sure that, while his father might have employed him, Big Bart had never supported him. Not since the day he'd turned eighteen. And he didn't want that kind of common ground with this woman. "She told me so herself."

"Yes," Zara said calmly, her gaze steady on his. "But Ariella is beautiful. Her defiance lands her on the covers of magazines and the arms of wealthy men. My father may find her antics embarrassing, but he views those things as a certain kind of currency. In that respect, I'm broke."

Chase blinked. "I'm very wealthy," he pointed out. "In all forms of currency."

"I didn't marry you for your money," she said gently. "I married you because this way, I can always remind my father that I sacrificed myself for him on command. To a wealthy man he wanted to control. Talk about the kind of currency Amos Elliott appreciates." Her mouth shifted into that smile of hers that did things to him he didn't like or understand. "He isn't a very nice man. It's better to have leverage."

Chase felt caught in the endless gold of her eyes then, or perhaps it was the near-winter afternoon outside the window that seemed to be some kind of extension of them, the sun brilliant through the stark trees and already too close to the edge of night.

"Are you looking for a nice man, then?" he asked quietly. From somewhere inside himself he hardly recognized.

"It would be difficult for you to be a worse one than my

father," Zara replied in the same tone. "Unless it was your singular purpose in life and even the briefest Google search online makes it clear that you've had other things to do."

Was she being kind to him? Chase couldn't fathom it. It made something great and gaping hinge open inside of him, too near to all that darkness he knew better than to let out into the light. He knew better than to let anyone see it. He knew what they'd call him if they did. He called himself that and worse every day.

Monster. Murderer.

He had blood on his hands that he could never wash clean, and this woman with eyes like liquid gold and the softest mouth he'd ever touched was being *kind* to him. On the very day her vicious father had lashed them together in unholy matrimony.

"I sold my own sister into her marriage because it benefited the company. I sold myself today." His voice was colder than the December weather outside. Colder than what he kept locked inside. And all those things he hid away swelled up in him then. Those memories. Those terrible choices. The day he'd lost his mother on that South African road where he'd made the choice that defined him, the choice that he still couldn't live with all these years later. To say nothing of the truth about his relationship with the father he felt he still had to prove himself to, even now, when Big Bart Whitaker would never know the difference. "You'll want to be careful, Zara. I'll ruin you, too, if you let me."

She studied him for a moment, and then she smiled, and he didn't know how he knew that this one was real. Even if it felt like it drew blood.

"No need to worry about that," she said quietly. "I won't."

CHAPTER TWO

THE HOUSE WAS like something out of a Gothic novel.

Zara had to fight to conceal her shiver of recognition from the man who lounged beside her in the black mood he'd worn throughout the drive.

"Cold?" he asked. Chase's voice was polite on the surface, but his gaze was a wilderness of blue and almost liquid, somehow, with a kind of sharp heat that speared straight through her. And none of it friendly.

"Not at all," Zara said, though she was. "Your house isn't the most welcoming place, is it?"

Gothic, she thought again. She'd read significantly more Gothic novels than the average person and not only because she was writing a master's thesis on the topic. On some level she should have expected she'd find herself in the middle of one. It was the only thing her absurd wedding day had been missing.

"It's December." Chase's voice was as cold as his estate looked in the beam of the limousine's headlights. Barren and frozen as far as the eye could see. "Nothing in this part of the country is welcoming at this time of year."

But it was more than that. Or it was her imagination, Zara amended, which had always been as feverish as the rest of her was practical. The old stone manor rose like an apparition at the top of a long, winding drive through a thick and lonely winter forest of ghostly, stripped-bare trees and unfriendly pines coated with ice and the snowy remains of the last storm. Several inches of snow clung to the roof above the main part of the house, and each of its wings glittered with icicles at the gutters, though the sky above tonight was clear. Thick and almost too dark, but clear.

She tried to imagine the house festooned in spring blossoms or warmed by the summer sun, and failed. Miserably.

For the first time in her life, Zara questioned her addiction to Daphne du Maurier and Phyllis A. Whitney novels. They might have helped her through an awkward adolescence and paved the way toward what she hoped would become her life's work, but they had also made her entirely too susceptible to the dark possibilities lurking in a scary old mansion, a bridegroom she scarcely knew and whatever rattled around in the gloomy shadows of places like this.

"Are you sure you don't have any madwomen locked away in the attic?" she asked, appalled when her voice sounded more shaken than wry.

"Making me a convenient bigamist and you therefore free of this mess we're both stuck in?" he replied, smooth and deadly, and shocking Zara. She wouldn't have pegged him as a reader of *Jane Eyre*. Or a reader at all, come to that, when he could be off brooding beautifully somewhere instead. "I'm afraid not. My apologies."

Chase did not sound remotely sorry. Nor did he sound drunk, which Zara couldn't quite understand. She'd expected sloppiness when he'd continued to drink from that whiskey bottle throughout the drive, had braced herself for his unconsciousness and his snores. Instead, he simply seemed on edge.

More on edge, that was.

Maybe the place—and the man—was more welcoming in the daylight, Zara thought as diplomatically as possible as the car pulled up to the looming front entrance. Then again, it hardly mattered. She wasn't here to settle in and make a happy home for herself. She was here because Grams had wanted her to try. She was here because this proved, once and for all, that she was the good daughter. Surely this finally settled the matter. Surely her father would finally have to recognize—

"Come," her brand-new husband said from much too close beside her, his hand at her side and that disconcerting gaze burning into her as surely as that small contact did, and when she jerked her head around to stare back at him it was even worse. All that irrational, unmanageable fire. "I'd like to get out of these clothes, if you don't mind. And put this lamentable farce behind me as quickly as possible."

Zara couldn't keep herself from imagining beautiful Chase Whitaker without his clothes any more than she could stop herself from breathing her next breath. All that long, lean, smooth muscle. All that ruthlessly contained power—

Get a hold of yourself! she yelped inwardly.

And then she pretended she didn't see the way his eyes gleamed, like he could read her dirty mind.

Chase ushered her into the grand front hall of the sprawling stone mansion, adorned with art and tapestries and moldings so intricate they almost looked like some kind of architectural frosting, with what felt like more irritation than courtesy. He introduced her to his waiting housekeeper, Mrs. Calloway, without adjusting his stride and then marched Zara up the great stair to the second floor. Zara had the jumbled impression of graceful statues and priceless art, beautifully appointed rooms and long, gleaming hallways, all in a hectic blur as they moved swiftly past.

He didn't speak. And Zara found she couldn't. Not only was the house lifted from the pages of the books she studied, but now that she was *this close* to getting out of her horribly uncomfortable dress at last and, God willing, sinking into a very deep, very hot, restorative bath for about an hour or five, every single step that kept her from it was like sheer torture.

That and the fact that Chase was more than a little forbidding himself. It was that set way he held himself. Contained and furious, even as he prowled along beside her. It seemed particularly obvious in a place like this, all shadows and absence, empty rooms and echoing footsteps.

You're becoming hysterical.

When she felt like herself again, she was sure she'd stop thinking like this. *She was sure.* And then she'd fish her cell phone out of the bag she fervently hoped was in that limo and she would either listen to the host of apologetic messages Ariella should have left for her today, or, in their far more likely absence, call Ariella until her sister answered and explained this great big mess she'd made.

And then maybe all of this would feel a little bit less Gothic.

Particularly if she got out of this damned dress before it crippled her forever.

"Here," Chase grunted, pushing open a door.

Zara blinked. Her head spun and her heart began to race and her feet suddenly felt rooted to the floor. "Is this…?"

"Your rooms." He smirked. "Unless you planned to make this a more traditional marriage? I could no doubt be persuaded. I've certainly had enough whiskey to imagine anything is a good idea. My rooms are at the other end of this hall."

Zara thought she'd rather die than *persuade* him to do anything of the kind. Or anyone like him who would, she had no doubt, need nothing in the way of *persuasion* if she was lanky, lovely, effortlessly appealing Ariella.

Not that you want this man either way, she reminded

herself. Pointedly. She'd always been allergic to his type: basically, male versions of her sister. Younger versions of her father. Entitled and arrogant and no, thank you.

Despite that thing in her that felt like heat, only far more dangerous.

"Whiskey wears off," she said crisply. "And more to the point, I haven't had any." She brushed past him, determined to sleep in whatever the hell room this was, even if it was a cell and her only option was the floor. "This is perfect, thank you."

"Zara." She didn't want to stop walking, but she did, as if he could command her that easily. *You're tired*, she assured herself. *That's all*. "I'll be back later," he said, his voice dark and, yes, foreboding.

"For what? Persuasion? There won't be any. No matter when you come back."

He let out a noise that might have been a laugh, and the madness was that she felt it skim down the length of her spine like a long, lush sweep of his fingers.

There was no reason that she should have *felt* him the way she did then, like an imprint of fire, large and looming over her from behind, like he could cast a shadow and drown her in it all at once. And there was no reason that her body should react to him the way it did, jolting wide-awake and *hungry*, just like that.

"I'll be back," he said again, a low thread of sound, dark and rough, and she felt that, too. *Felt* it, like his hands against her skin.

She nodded. Acquiesced. It was that or succumb to panic entirely.

Zara waited until he closed the door behind her, then let out a long breath she hadn't realized she'd been holding. It came out in a kind of shudder, and she had to blink back all that overwhelming heat from her eyes.

Then she actually looked around her.

The bedroom suite was done in restrained blues accented by geometrical shapes etched in an elegant black, with a lit fireplace against one wall that was already crackling away and an inviting sofa and two chairs in front of it that begged for a book, a cozy throw blanket and a long, rainy afternoon's read. The bed was a cheerful four-poster affair, with quilts and blankets piled high and a multitude of deep, soft-looking pillows. It was a contented, happy sort of room, and it made all that Gothic fervor ease away, leaving Zara feeling overtired and foolish in its wake.

Her gaze snagged on the set of photographs on the mantel above the fireplace as she walked deeper into the room, all featuring pictures of a very tall, very recognizable black-haired girl, solemn dark eyes and an enigmatic almost-smile on her pretty face. *Mattie Whitaker.* Chase's infamous sister.

Zara read the tabloids, and not only when she was stuck in line at the supermarket. Mattie had been all over them recently for her "secret marriage" to "playboy Chase's greatest rival," which Zara didn't think could have been too terribly secret if there were all those pictures of Mattie and her harshly attractive husband gazing at each other in front of a glorious Greek backdrop. Just as Nicodemus Stathis couldn't possibly be the terrible rival the papers wanted him to be if Chase and he were working on a merger.

Shockingly, she told herself derisively, *the papers lie, as your entire life watching Ariella manipulate them to her benefit should have made you well aware.*

But it was Mattie Whitaker's bathroom she cared about then, not the marriage Chase had claimed he'd sold his sister into. Or what the tabloids might have made up about it.

"That," she said out loud as she headed for the far door across the bedroom, "will be something Mattie and I can bond over across the table at Christmas. Our delightful forced marriages, whether secret or not."

She lost her train of thought and let out a sigh of delight instead when she walked inside and found the bathtub of her dreams waiting for her, vast and deep enough for a group of people, placed before high windows that looked out into the silken night.

Bliss.

Zara turned on the tap greedily and dumped a capful of the foaming bath salts that sat on the tub's lip into the warm stream. Then she ripped that veil straight off her head, not caring that it tugged at her hair. That it *hurt.* It came off with a clatter of hairpins against the floor, and Zara moaned out loud in stark relief as she massaged her way over her abused scalp, pulling out the remaining pins and letting her hair fall free at last.

Now it was time to deal with that torturous dress. The water poured into the bath behind her as she tugged and pulled, twisting herself this way and that as she tried to free herself. It was far more difficult than it should have been—but Zara was desperate. She yanked even harder—

And then at last she heard a glorious tearing sound, the fabric finally gave—and she yanked it all off, kicking the tattered remains away as the dress fell to her feet in a voluminous cloud. At first, she hurt *more* than she had before. Her breasts ached, and she could see the angry lines the built-in corset had left all over them and her belly, red and pronounced because she had the kind of skin that showed every last mark like a neon billboard.

And because the dress had been made for her sister, who better resembled a starving gazelle and had needed that corset to create the illusion of the cleavage she didn't have rather than tamp down any existing breasts.

It was such a relief to be free of that hideous torture device that Zara's eyes filled with tears. But she refused to indulge them, not here in this too-Gothic mansion with the whiskey-pounding, possibly dangerous husband she'd never met before the ceremony. Not when she didn't know that she'd stop. Not when the wedding was only the latest in a long stream of things she could probably cry about, if she let herself.

Not here. Not tonight. Grams had maintained her stiff upper lip to the very last of her days. Zara could do the same with far less provocation.

She toed off the white ballet flats she'd worn all day—thank goodness she and Ariella wore the same size shoes and she hadn't had to make like one of Cinderella's unfortunate stepsisters and hack off a toe to fit into them—and shimmied out of the very bright, screaming red thong panties she'd worn beneath it all. The only thing in the whole, long, strange day that was hers.

Zara couldn't control the deep, atavistic sigh she let out when she slipped into the bath at last. The water was hot and the bubbles were high enough to feel decadent without being so high they became a problem. She piled her hair—wild and thick and incredibly unruly from a day in pins and scraped into submission beneath that veil—up on top of her head in a messy knot as she tried to picture glamorous, couture-draped Mattie Whitaker lounging in this bathtub the way she was now. Mattie Whitaker, who was a good deal like Ariella in Zara's mind—one of those effortless girls, all long, slender limbs; hot-and-cold-running boyfriends; and the ability to float through life without a single care.

Zara's life had been charmed in its own way yet was significantly less *gleaming*, despite the fact she, too, was an Elliott. She'd failed to look the part from birth and hadn't ever managed to act the part, either, despite the thousands of lectures Amos had delivered on the topic. Even when doing so would have been in her best interests.

Well. She'd acted the part today, hadn't she? She'd done

it. *I did what you asked, Grams*, she thought then. *I gave him one last chance to treat me differently.*

She shut her eyes and leaned back against the smooth porcelain, breathing in the jasmine-scented steam as she tried to expel all the tension of the day from her body. As she tried not to think about what had happened earlier in that church. Or what might happen later, because who knew what the expectations were in a situation this twisted? Or what she'd got herself into, marrying a man who was not only a total stranger, but who'd turned up to his own wedding half-drunk and entirely furious, and that had been before he'd seen the switch.

Zara didn't know how long she sat like that, the water cascading all around her, the jasmine heat like an embrace, soaking all the red marks from the vicious gown away into the ether and her headache along with it. She was lazily contemplating climbing out of the bath and investigating the possibility of dinner when she felt a shift in the air. Everything simply went taut, her skin felt too tight, and she reluctantly opened up her eyes.

To find Chase leaning there in the doorway, looking dark and disreputable, lethally dangerous in a way that made the back of her neck tingle, and nothing at all like drunk.

For a moment Zara stopped breathing. Her heart gave a mighty kick against her ribs and then jackrabbited into high gear. Her ears rang as if someone had screamed, and her throat ached as if she was that someone, but she knew she'd done nothing at all but stare back at the man who shouldn't have been there.

She needed to say something. She needed to *do* something. But he was so beautiful it hurt, even more so now that he'd changed out of his wedding suit and was something far more elemental in bare feet that defied the weather beneath a soft-looking button-down shirt he hadn't bothered to do up properly over a pair of jeans. And his dark blue eyes seemed wilder than before, remote and with that aching thing at once, like some kind of ruthless poetry. She didn't know what lodged in her chest then, only that it was much too sharp and alarmingly deep.

"Shouldn't you be passed out on a floor somewhere?" she asked, harsher than she'd meant to sound.

Maybe this was his version of drunken, idiotic behavior. She'd witnessed the bitter end of her parents' marriage over the course of too many drink-blurred nights, as they'd each got drunker and meaner. Ariella had sneaked out to escape it, while Zara had tried to hide from it in books where all the terrifying goings-on weren't usually real, in the end. She'd never seen the appeal of getting drunk since.

Though even that looked better than it should on Chase Whitaker.

"I'm not drunk," he growled at her. "Not nearly enough."

He shifted so he could prop one of those finely cut shoulders against the doorjamb, and she felt the way he looked at her like a touch. Hot and demanding. And she understood then, that what happened here would set the stage for the whole of their unconventional relationship, however long it lasted, and in whatever form. If he thought he could walk in on her like this, what else would he think he could do?

Zara had been raised on a steady diet of *no boundaries*. Her father was a tyrant. Her mother cared more about scoring her pound of flesh from him than her own daughters. The older sister she'd hero-worshipped when she was a kid turned nastier by the year. Ariella was on a crash course to becoming their father, a man who truly believed that he got to make whatever rules he felt like following that day by virtue of who he was and how much money and power he had.

Zara was fed up with *no boundaries*.

"You have to leave," she said, firm and direct. Unmistakable. "Now. I take my privacy very seriously."

"Are we not cleaved unto one?" Chase's tone was dark and there was something terrible in his gaze, mocking and harsh. "I'm sure I heard something about that earlier today."

"We are engaging in mutual thorn-removal, nothing more," she corrected him, using his phrase and not sure why it made that gaze of his get harsher. Wilder. Untamed in a way that made something deep in her belly coil tight. "And I may have married you, but I didn't agree to any kind of intimacy. I don't want any. That's not negotiable."

"Has anything about this been negotiable?" he asked, his voice almost idle, though Zara didn't believe it at all. Not when those eyes of his were on her, intent and arresting. "Because what I recall is your father parading your sister under my nose in a variety of questionable attire and telling me that he'd crush me if I didn't marry her."

Zara felt almost outside herself then, as if she was watching this interaction from a great distance. It was the way he'd said *questionable attire*, maybe, because it summoned Ariella as surely as if she was a genie in a bottle, and Zara wanted nothing more than to smash that bottle against the tile floor. If it had made any kind of sense, she would have thought what she felt was *hurt*. And something so close to *offended* it might as well have been the same thing.

"Is that what this is?" she asked with a coolness she didn't feel at all, not in any part of her, like that wilderness that he carried in him was catching. "You've been downgraded from the coveted main attraction to its much less interesting runner-up and you want to see the full extent of that downward spiral? Why didn't you say so?"

"I beg your pardon?"

Zara didn't let herself think it through. She slid both

her hands out to the high sides of the bath and then she stood up. Water coursed down her body and there was a howling sound inside her head, but she didn't take her gaze from Chase's.

Not for a second.

"This is it," she said, aware that her voice was shaking, and it wasn't with upset. It was more complicated than that. Challenge and disappointment and *fury*, and the fact that none of it made sense didn't make it any better. "Take a good look, because I'm not doing this again, and yes, it really is as bad as you fear. You married me, not Ariella. I'll never be any fashion designer's muse. I'll never be photographed in a bikini unless the goal is to shame me. No one would ever call me skinny and no one has ever claimed I was anything like beautiful. I'll never fast my way down to Ariella's weight and even if I did, even if I wanted to, it wouldn't matter. We're built completely differently."

For a moment—or a long, hard year or two—there was nothing but the sound of the water she stood in, still sloshing from how quickly she'd stood. And that pounding thing in her head that made her ears feel thick and her stomach churn.

Chase simply stared.

He was frozen in place, something she couldn't read at all stamped on his gorgeous face, making him look something other than simply beautiful. Something *more*. Something so dangerous and so intent, she felt it thud through her, hard. Then he blinked, slowly, and Zara understood that she cared a good deal more about what he might say next than she should.

Which meant she'd made a terrible mistake. As she so often did when she decided to act before she thought. Why could she never seem to learn that lesson?

"Yes," Chase scraped out into the close heat of the bathroom, in a hoarse voice that shivered over her like warm water but was much, much hotter, a match for that deep, dark blue of his gaze and as irrevocably scalding. "You bloody well are."

If she'd taken a sledgehammer to the side of his head, she couldn't have stunned him more.

She was so…pink. *So perfect.*

That was all Chase could think for long moments. She'd looked round and solid all draped in white as she'd been; stout and tented, like a gazebo. That's what he'd thought in the limousine, uncharitably. Perhaps *this* was his punishment.

Or, a sly voice inside of him, located rather further south than his brain, *she is your reward for all of this.*

It was hard to argue with that. She was a symphony of curves. Gorgeous, mouthwatering, stunning lushness, from the fine neck he could remember beneath his palm in the church in an almost alarmingly tactile manner to a pair of heavy, perfect breasts, plump and flushed from the damp heat yet marked by fine blue lines that reminded him how fair she was.

And nipples so pert they made his mouth actually ache to taste them. Chase was glad he'd happened to lean against the door, because he wasn't certain he could stand on his own.

Her waist was the kind of indentation that made him understand, profoundly, whole schools of art he'd never paid much attention to before, particularly with the breathtaking flare of her hips beneath, wide and welcoming and making that trim V between her legs all the more delectable.

He wanted to be there—*right there*—more than he could remember wanting anything. Ever.

All that and the riot of reds and coppers and strawberry blonds that she'd fastened atop her head somehow, the wet heat making tendrils into curls and spirals that framed her elegant face, making him as hard as a spike and incapable of thinking of anything for long moments but getting his hands in the mess of it, deep. Holding her still while he thrust himself between those perfectly formed thighs, plundered that astonishingly carnal mouth of hers, and happily lost what was left of his mind.

Chase was a product of his time, he understood then, and felt sorry for all the men his age. Like them, he'd always preferred longer, slimmer women by rote, preferably with the smooth leanness that spoke of countless years of deprivation. Women who wore clothes in ways that emphasized their narrow hips and the angular thrust of their collar and hip bones. Women who looked good in photographs, especially the kind that he was always finding himself in, splashed here and there in the harsh glare of the British press.

Women like Zara, he thought in a kind of daze as an ancient, primitive need he'd never felt before pounded through him, should never, ever be confined to anything as foolish as modern clothing. They should never be subjected to a dress like that monstrosity she'd worn today. They should never be contained in photographs that adored angles and punished soft curves. Not with bodies like this, like hers, that were made to be seen whole in all their primal glory. That were created purely to be worshipped.

She was branded into him now, he thought wildly, so red-hot and deep he might never see anything or anyone else again.

And he was so hard it hurt.

"Then we need never repeat this experience," she was saying, her voice a brittle slap against all that warm heat, and Chase was still knocked senseless. He couldn't follow what she was saying, not with his heart trying to kick its way out of his chest, so he stayed where he was and watched as she stepped out of the tub and yanked one of the towels from the nearby rack, wrapping that gorgeous body of hers away from view.

He wanted to protest. Loudly.

"You can go now," she said, her voice even more rigid than before, and when her gaze met his again, those miraculous eyes of hers were smoky with something bleak. "I trust it won't be necessary for any further object lessons tonight, will it?"

And Chase could think again then. With both his brains. More than that, he remembered himself and what he was doing, something he couldn't believe he'd lost track of for even a moment. He opted not to analyze that too closely. Not while the wife he didn't want was still within an easy arm's reach, her skin still pinkened and softened from her long soak, her warm golden eyes still shooting sparks—

He had to stop. He had to remember that whatever else she was, she was an Elliott. She might have proved herself far more interesting than her shallow, grasping, run-of-the-mill sister, to say nothing of *that body*, but she was still an Elliott.

Which meant there was only one way this could go.

"I appreciate the show," he said in a voice that made her jerk where she stood, as surely as if he'd hauled off and slapped her. Exactly as he'd planned, and yet Chase loathed himself at once—and he'd have thought he'd hit his maximum where that was concerned years before. *You always have somewhere lower to go, don't you?* He waited until the red blazed across her face, until her gaze turned stormy. "There's a private dining room on this floor, above the library. Follow the hall to the end and it will be the arched doorway in front of you. You've got ten minutes."

"And you will have to drag my dead body in there," she said, her voice stiff with a fury he could see all too plainly in her gaze. Fury and whatever that darker, harsher thing was. He told himself it wasn't his to know. That he didn't *want* to know. "As that is the only way I'll ever spend another moment in your company."

"Trust me, Zara," he said, his voice much too low and not nearly polite enough, things he didn't want to think about all over his face—or so he assumed from the way she stiffened in reaction, and not, he could see too plainly, because she was offended. "You don't want me to come back here and force the issue. You really don't."

CHAPTER THREE

CHASE WAITED FOR her in the small dining room, the place Big Bart had reserved for immediate family alone. There was a huge, formal dining room downstairs near the old-fashioned ballroom that now housed a grand piano Chase's mother had once played, and another medium-sized dining room that his father had used for smaller gatherings, but this one had always been off-limits. It was close. Intimate.

Exactly what Zara had indicated she didn't want.

His mouth twisted in derision, and Chase moved away from the window before he could look too closely at his own reflection there against the dark night beyond. He already knew what he'd see, and there was no point in it. There was nothing he could change now. It was done.

Going into that suite hadn't helped. It had only underscored the scope of his own failures. He'd never spent much time in his sister's rooms, not even when he and Mattie had been small and far happier. Not even *before*.

Even now, all these years after she'd moved out and despite what she'd sacrificed two months ago for the family and the company by marrying Nicodemus Stathis, he couldn't think about his sister without losing another great chunk of himself in all that guilt. It cut too deep, left him nothing but gutted and useless. It had always seemed a kindness to simply keep his distance instead. To let her grow up without the dark weight of the secrets he carried. To let Mattie, at least, be free.

Not that it had worked.

I'm guessing you don't wake up every night of your life screaming then, Mattie had said the last time they'd spoken. She'd sounded raw. Unlike herself. He'd been as unable to face that as anything else. A coward down to his bones, but that hadn't been news. *Calling out for Mum again and again.*

Chase didn't wake up in the night, he thought now as he found himself by the window again, looking out toward the Hudson River at the low end of the property even though he couldn't see it with the dark December night pressing in on all sides. Nightmares would have been beside the point. He carried his ghosts around with him in the light.

He never forgot what he'd done.

And neither had his father.

Maybe that was why Big Bart Whitaker had left his empire in such disarray. It was so unlike him, after all. Chase had always been Bart's heir, and because of that he'd spent the past decade working his way up the ranks until he'd achieved the VP slot in the London office. He'd never minded that his future had been so mapped out for him. He'd enjoyed the challenge of proving he wasn't just his surname, but a capable businessman in his own right, no matter what the papers intimated. Everyone had always assumed that he'd move from London to the Whitaker Industries corporate headquarters in New York and transition into his eventual leadership of the company. That had always been the plan, except it had never been the right time, had it? Bart had always had other things to do first. Chase had always found a different reason to stay in London.

The truth, he acknowledged now, was that they'd been a good deal more comfortable with each other when there was a nice, wide ocean between them.

Maybe the fact that Bart had left Chase to fend for himself wasn't a mistake. Maybe Bart had thought that if Chase couldn't hold on to Whitaker Industries against the tiresome machinations of Amos Elliott or the cash flow issues that the merger with his brand-new brother-in-law would solve, he didn't deserve it.

And Chase couldn't find it in him to disagree.

He'd forgotten where he was, he realized when he heard a light step on the old floors behind him and scented the faintest hint of jasmine in the air.

"I don't understand what this is," Zara said from the doorway, her voice tight. But she'd still come on time, he noted. "I don't understand what you *want*."

Neither did he, and that should have alarmed him. It did. But it also occurred to him that the only time in the past six months—hell, in the past twenty years—that he'd actually forgotten about that lonely stretch of South African road and what he'd done there, what he'd become and what that had done to his family, was when Zara Elliott held his gaze and did her best to confound him, one way or another. In the bath, yes. God help him, *the bath*. But in the limo, as well.

He didn't want that to mean anything. But he couldn't seem to ignore it, either. And that spelled nothing but doom for them both.

Chase turned, slowly, and felt a deep, purely masculine regret lodge beneath his ribs when he saw she'd dressed. *Of course she had.* Black, stretchy pants that clung to those marvelous hips and her well-formed legs and what looked like a particularly soft sweater on top, a bit slouchy and roomy, so that her softly rounded shoulder peeked out when she moved. Her wild, glorious hair was combed through and fixed neatly at the nape of her neck, and he wanted the other Zara back. That powerful, compelling goddess creature he wanted to taste. Everywhere. With his teeth. That stunning woman he had the agony of knowing was *just there*, now hidden beneath clothes that couldn't possibly flatter her as much as no clothes at all did. Nothing could.

This was his bride. His *wife*. His wedding night, some darkness inside him reminded him.

Good lord, but he was still hard.

"This is our marriage," he told her, his voice a grating thing, harsh and a little too mean. He thought she'd flinch again, but her gleaming eyes only narrowed.

"This had better also be dinner," she said as crisply as if she was discussing the weather of a distant city. And as if she'd put on a sheet of armor beneath her clothes. "Or I may collapse from starvation. And while I might view that as a handy escape from all this excitement, I doubt that's what you have in mind."

"I've never had an arranged marriage before," he said grimly as she moved farther into the room with a wariness she made no effort to hide, then perched on the edge of the chair nearest the door. "Perhaps nightly collapses are but par for the course."

She eyed him. "Arranged marriages are really quite stable," she said after a moment. "Historically speaking. More so than romantic marriages."

"Because the arrangements are so well orchestrated by fathers like yours? Lovingly and with great concern for the participants? Or because neither party cares very much?"

"The latter, I'd think," she said, ignoring the sardonic way he'd asked that, though he could see by that gleam in her gaze that she'd heard it. "In our case, anyway. Once you've overcome your shock at finding the wrong sister at the altar, of course."

Her gaze then was as arid as her voice, and Chase couldn't understand why he cared. When he knew he shouldn't.

"I was surprised to learn the notorious Ariella Elliott

had a sister in the first place," he said, with some attempt to make his voice less rough. "Somehow, that never came up in all those discussions with your father. Or in any of the articles I've seen about your sister over the years. Though there was no attempt to hide you at any of the dinners we both attended."

He still stood by the window, watching her as if doing so would lead to some grand revelation, and countered that restless thing in him that *wanted* things he refused to acknowledge by shoving his hands in the pockets of his trousers. Quite as if he worried he'd otherwise have to fight to keep them from her.

Zara smiled. It was a slap of perfectly courteous ice and told him a number of things he didn't wish to know about her.

"I don't date musicians or actors. I don't attend the sorts of parties that the paparazzi cover, much less stagger out of them under the influence of unsavory substances at ungodly hours of the morning. I like books better than people. None of that makes for interesting gossip, I'm afraid."

He regarded her with what he wished was a dispassionate cool. "What would the gossips say about you, then? Interesting or otherwise?"

There was something vulnerable about her soft mouth then, a darker sheen to her golden eyes, but her chin edged high and she didn't drop her gaze from his.

"Is this a little bit of friendly, husbandly interest?" she asked. "Or are you merely gathering ammunition?"

She wasn't at all what he'd expected. That turned in him like heat. Like need.

"Everything is ammunition, Zara. But only if you're at war."

A ghost of a smile flirted with her mouth then, and was gone in the next instant. "And we, of course, are not at war."

"This is our wedding night, is it not?"

She studied him for a moment, and he wished that things were different. That he was, to start. That she was anyone other than who she was. An Elliott and his wife.

"I'm writing a master's thesis in English Literature," she said after a moment. "My field of study is Gothic novels in popular culture. It's my father's opinion that I'd be better served getting a degree in something that made for better cocktail party conversation. Everybody has an opinion about *Romeo and Juliet*, for example. Why not study that instead of stupid books only hysterical women read?"

Chase was sidetracked from his own dark thoughts. "Your father has an objection to advanced degrees? Surely most parents would be proud." His own, for example.

"Academia is the refuge of the ugly and boring," she said, obviously quoting her father, and remarkably cool about it. It spoke to a long familiarity with Amos's insulting opinions, and Chase found he didn't like the idea of that at all. "While he acknowledges that it is thus a perfectly appropriate place for the likes of me, the fact remains that I'm *his* daughter. I ought to be a better bargaining chip. The kind of frat boy investment bankers he'd like to throw my way, because of who their fathers are and how such connections could benefit him, have no patience for women who think that much."

Chase could only stare at her.

Zara smiled, and it was even icier than before. "I'm paraphrasing."

He shook his head. "You must know that you are none of those things."

He didn't know why he'd said that. This wasn't a therapy session, and he was the last person who should have been offering advice to anyone. Zara's eyes chilled.

"I love being patronized," she said. "I really do. But I find it goes down a whole lot smoother with food."

And the fact was, this was war, and Zara was ammunition. That Amos Elliott was horrible to his own child shouldn't have surprised Chase at all. It didn't.

He had to stop pretending he was any different. That he was some kind of hero who could save anyone from anything. He already knew better, didn't he? He already knew exactly what he was. *Murderer.*

But this was about the future, not the past.

Chase rang for their dinner. Then he beckoned his enemy's daughter to the small table, took his own seat across from her and began the war in earnest.

"What are you doing in here?"

Zara jumped at the sound of Chase's voice, whirling around so the bookshelf was at her back and the mad beating of her heart as it tried to fly from her chest might not knock her down to the floor. She didn't know how she didn't scream—and then she saw him.

He stood a few feet away, dressed in the jeans, bare feet and casually buttoned shirt she'd learned he preferred, the messiness of his dark hair the only hint that it was an hour of the night when most people were asleep. He should have looked rumpled, but this was Chase Whitaker, so he looked *lethal* instead.

And the way he looked at her made everything inside of her roll up into a knot and *pulse*. She couldn't have screamed if she'd wanted to. She was too busy trying her best not to purr—and the fact that it didn't make sense that she should have this kind of reaction to a man she'd resolved she'd merely tolerate didn't make that knotted, pulsing thing ease.

If anything, it made it that much worse.

"I couldn't sleep," Zara said.

Unnecessarily, as her presence in the house's spacious, book-jammed library this long after midnight made that abundantly clear on its own. But it was better than surrendering to her traitorous body and making like a cat.

A December storm howled around the old stone house tonight, rattling the windows and making the floorboards creak ominously. Zara might have decided to keep her overactive imagination in check while she had to stay in this place but there was no sleeping through all of that.

So she'd crawled out of the soft, warm bed, pulled on the long, lush wool sweater she used as a kind of bathrobe, and padded down through the dark house to the library, where the fire was always blazing and the storm at the French doors made her feel cozy instead of vulnerable.

Quite the opposite of how her husband made her feel.

He studied her in that hooded way of his that made her feel like prey. And much too unreasonably warm for a night this close to full winter in upstate New York. In a drafty old stone house that might or might not have been haunted, the way old stone houses often were. *In your imagination, not in reality*, she reminded herself sharply—though it was the kind of two o'clock in the morning that blurred those lines.

Zara swallowed hard as she moved away from the bookshelf, clutching the thick, eighteenth-century novel she'd selected to her chest as she made her way back to one of the deep, comfortable leather armchairs that sat before the fireplace. She curled herself up in it, her legs tucked up beneath her, and told herself she felt better no matter what racket her heart was making.

She wasn't surprised when Chase followed, settling himself across from her with that curious grace of his that she was certain could hypnotize her, if she let it. *Could and would.* And then he fixed her with that same, unwavering blue stare of his that made every hair on her body dance in instinctive response.

It had been a strange week.

"Welcome to your honeymoon," he'd said that first night in that little dining room where he insisted they take all their meals. He'd lounged there, pushing the shockingly good food around on his plate as if he was too restless to eat—*or too drunk*, she'd reminded herself sharply—and he'd watched her. He was always watching her. Looking for something she grew more and more sure she didn't want to name, especially not after she'd allowed him to see her naked. *Stop thinking about that*, she'd ordered herself. Fruitlessly. "It will last the month. We'll spend it here, in seclusion, as happily married new couples do."

"All the happily married new couples I know spend their entire honeymoons on this or that social media platform, tirelessly documenting every moment of their bliss," Zara had pointed out. "It's a sign of the times."

"It is not a sign of our times." His gaze had gone even darker, if possible. "You will contact whoever you must to let them know that you'll be out of touch for the remainder of December. Holidays included."

"You mean my thesis advisor?" She hadn't understood why she was responding to him as if he had the right to make declarations about how she'd spend her time, or where. Why she'd been pretending this was some kind of normal conversation when it was not. When the specter of her ill-conceived nudity had hung before them as if there had been another version of her lounging across the small table between them, as naked as she'd been in that bathtub. "There's no need. The semester is nearly over and I completed all my coursework last week."

She certainly hadn't understood why she'd told him *that*. Why not go traipse around in dark alleys, while she was at it? Why not write *victim* in big, bold letters on her forehead? She'd then reminded herself that as she was not, in fact, a Gothic heroine, there was no need to worry what she told this man.

"And aren't you lucky that I did," she'd continued then, her annoyance at herself bleeding through into her voice, "or I'd have to tell you exactly what you could do with all your orders. I'm not your subordinate, Chase. I'm your wife."

"Thank you." His voice had been cool. Sardonic. "I'm unlikely to forget that."

Zara had interpreted that as a slap. She'd told herself it was a good thing. Bracing and necessary. This man was much too tempting, and she didn't need or want to be sympathetic to him. She didn't need or want to *want* him, either. She only needed to survive this marriage long enough to make her point to her father, in so doing honoring her grandmother's last wish. *Sympathy* for the likes of Chase Whitaker was unnecessary.

Lust was suicidal.

"Since you asked," she'd said mildly, still holding that thrilling blue gaze of his, "I envision a marriage as a union of like-minded partners. In this case, we both seem to want the marriage to do something for us. How delightfully equal that makes us, don't you think?"

His mouth had twitched. "Is that what you call it?"

"I don't know what kind of arrangement you had with my sister," she'd said, her chin rising, because she hadn't wanted to know what agreements he and Ariella had come to—much less how they'd come to them. "But you should know that I don't do very well with overbearing asses who try to dictate my every move."

"Save your father."

"One overbearing ass in a girl's life is more than enough," she'd said, and had even laughed as if she'd found the whole thing frothy and fun, like an adventure—when she adamantly did not. "And the sad truth is that I have a tendency toward seething rebellion. I'm telling you up front, so there are no surprises down the line should you decide to go all…" She'd waved a hand at him, encompassing that brooding, ruthless thing that spiked the air all around him. "Grouchy."

And she'd have sworn on a stack of Bibles that was laughter in those wild blue eyes of his then, in that small curve of his intoxicating mouth.

"I don't believe anyone has ever called me *grouchy* in all my life."

Zara had smiled. "To your face."

He'd sat there, looking as much discomfited as he'd looked amused, for what had felt like a very long time.

"There is a company holiday party of sorts on New Year's Eve," he'd told her, long after she'd decided he wasn't going to speak again, that they'd simply sit in that pretty little room tucked away in that vast, echoing house until they'd turned to dust. "It's an annual affair, though I haven't attended very often in the past."

Zara had nodded slowly, trying to work out his angle and seeing nothing but those unsettling blue eyes and all the secrets they held.

"I've been to it many times," she'd said. And each time, her father had trotted Ariella out like she were the spoils of war while he'd either ignored Zara entirely or had made her feel like an interloper. *And this is my younger daughter*, he'd said one memorable year. *She's got a face for radio and spends most of her life with it in a book, anyway.* Charming. She'd preferred the years her invitation had been "accidentally overlooked." "I can't believe you ever had something more exciting to do than waft about the Whitaker Industries offices all night, waiting for the year to end. You've been missing out."

"I've no doubt." He'd finally moved his gaze from hers, but only to toy with that ever-present glass of amber liquid before him, and it hadn't helped. Zara had still felt *caught*.

Held tight, like he was the spider and this was all a great web. "It will be our first appearance as husband and wife."

"I'm sure the grateful masses will pay us an extraordinary tribute," she'd said drily. "Particularly after our month of seclusion, the better to whet their appetites. We might as well be your British royalty."

He'd raised his eyes to hers then, and it had amazed her, the force of them, the *punch* of all that blue, as if she hadn't seen them a scant moment before. She'd wondered if she'd ever get used to it. Or if it would always be like that when she was near him. If he would always stun her.

"This time, wear something that fits you," he'd said.

And she'd stopped thinking about his eyes.

Now she sat there before him in all that brooding silence broken only by the crackle and pop of the fire within and the rush of the storm without, and Zara couldn't take it. She didn't like where her mind went when she was around him. She felt far too many things she didn't want to feel. This had never been about him, after all. It had been something she'd let her father sweep her into because she'd thought it might solve things between them the way Grams had wanted. Or—because she was a realist, down there beneath the part of her that heard a creak in a floorboard and thought *ghost*—give her a better bargaining chip with him. Chase himself had been an afterthought.

Funny then, that she'd thought a great deal about Chase and not at all about her father since she'd arrived here a week ago.

"Have you rung your sister?" he asked now.

It sounded like such an idle question. But it was somewhere in the neighborhood of two-fifteen in the morning, and if Zara had learned anything from this week in Chase Whitaker's presence, it was that he was very rarely idle. About anything. No matter the role he seemed to play in all the gossip columns.

"At this hour?" she asked. Stalling.

The twitch of his mouth indicated he knew exactly what she was doing.

"If I'm remembering your sister's habits correctly, this would be an excellent time to reach her," he pointed out. "She's almost certainly awake and about."

"Exactly how well do you know Ariella?" Zara asked.

Something like amusement, though it was too hard to be only that, gleamed in his blue eyes then, and she realized a bit too late that she'd sounded much too sharp. Sharp the way one might sound if she cared, when Zara knew full well she shouldn't. *She didn't.*

She wouldn't let herself.

"That sounds a bit loaded, doesn't it?" On another man, that might have been a smile. On Chase, it only made everything seem perilous. "I'm not sure that's a question I should answer."

"You're very interested in whether or not I've spoken to her," Zara pointed out, in a far more reasonably moderate tone of voice. "You ask me every day."

"She did stand me up at an altar," Chase said in that same deceptively casual voice, though Zara had to restrain her urge to shudder at the intensity beneath it. "That does tend to focus the attention. Or, at the very least, require some kind of discussion after the fact."

He shifted in his chair, calling attention to that rangy, athletic body of his. He was simply too beautiful. His was a kind of savage elegance, evident despite the way he lounged there as if he was something other than ruthless. There wasn't a single thing about him she trusted.

But she couldn't seem to look away, either.

"I'm not one of Ariella's priorities," Zara said after a moment, ignoring that softly singing thing inside of her, the pitched heat that felt like a ruinous melody from deep beneath her skin. That awful longing she refused to acknowledge. "She hasn't called me."

He continued to study her for a long moment, then he shifted all of that brooding focus of his to the fire, leaving Zara feeling simultaneously released and bereft.

Ariella hadn't called. Zara hadn't lied.

But she hadn't seen fit to mention that Ariella had responded to Zara's texts and voice mails with a text of her own. In her own sweet time. She'd written the day before:

This is like a coup for you. You should enjoy it while you can. It's not like there's any other way you'd date someone like Chase, is there?

That was her explanation for disappearing on her own wedding morning. That was her apology for leaving Zara to clean up her mess, and it was her thanks, too.

That was the only response Zara had got.

It was so typical that Zara had screamed. Into one of her pillows, facedown on that fluffy bed that belonged to another woman too much like her sister, who would never have received a text like that from anyone, and who would never, therefore, have had to deal with all its nasty undercurrents.

She'd told herself that she didn't care. That Ariella's obnoxious insinuations were designed to hurt her, which was precisely why she shouldn't let them. She'd focused on her work instead, reading several of the books on critical theory she needed to incorporate into the current chapter of her thesis and working on her ever-expanding bibliography.

But it was very late on a very dark night now, Chase Whitaker was the most dangerously beautiful man Zara had ever been this close to and it was like Ariella was standing right behind her the way she'd done as a mean-spirited teenager, whispering her little poisons straight into Zara's ear.

The arranged marriage Zara had been forced to undertake in Ariella's stead was a *coup*, because Zara couldn't expect to marry anyone under her own devices. Much less someone like Chase, who was *obviously* miles out of Zara's league. Zara could hardly dream she'd ever *date* someone like him. Ariella thought she should *enjoy it* because, of course, this must be like a fantasy brought to life for sad, lonely, fat and ugly Zara.

It didn't matter whether Zara believed these things. She was a twenty-six-year-old woman, not a sixteen-year-old, and she knew better than to listen to her nasty family members and their tired old refrains about who she was in their eyes. What mattered was that Ariella had become so much like their father that she'd felt comfortable spewing that kind of thing at her only sister in a *text*. Like she really and truly believed she'd done Zara a *favor*.

Zara realized she was scowling the same moment she felt the weight of Chase's attention again.

"Why are you always barefoot?" she asked quickly, because she didn't want to give him the opportunity to yank the truth from her. She hadn't liked how it had felt when she'd told him her father's feelings about her master's degree. It was one thing to experience her own family in all their dysfunctional glory. It was worse, somehow, to share it. Especially with a man like him. It was impossible to imagine him putting up with the same kind of nonsense. From anyone. "Have you lost all feeling in your feet? It's cold outside and this house is made primarily of old, drafty stone."

Again, that little crook in his lips that was his version of a smile that Zara found she liked—and looked forward to coaxing out of him—a great deal more than she should. Like it was their own personal version of happiness. Contentment. Newly wedded bliss.

You need to get a grip on yourself, Zara, she told herself then. *Right now. You'd be better off chasing ghosts down the hallways, and far more successful at that.*

"I've spent most of my life in England," Chase said. He sounded conversational—which was so unlike him that Zara viewed it as a personal victory. "It's cold here, but dry. It doesn't get in the bones in quite the same way."

"Didn't you grow up here?" she asked, startled. "I thought I was staying in your sister's childhood bedroom."

She couldn't define the expression she saw on his face then. As guarded as it was intent, that hint of any kind of easiness gone as if it had never been. She was certain he wouldn't answer her—and couldn't entirely hide her surprise when he did.

"This was my father's house," he said, sounding very careful, as if he was making his way across eggshells and glass, and Zara wished she could see them. Or help, somehow. "It was handed down from his grandfather, who built it to compete with the likes of the Rockefellers and all the other grand houses up and down the Hudson River. My parents used this as their primary residence, but I spent the bulk of my time in school in England. Mattie was here far more than I ever was. Especially after our mother died."

"I read about that." She'd scoured the internet, in fact, for every tidbit ever written about any member of the Whitaker family. She told herself she couldn't help it, that she was a researcher at heart, as her master's degree course proved. That she had no personal stake in any of it, that she felt *absolutely nothing* when she read this *Vanity Fair* article about his late mother, Lady Daphne, or that tabloid paean to his overly observed love life. Nothing at all. "I'm sorry."

She thought there was something hollow in his gaze then, something so broken it made her hurt, but told herself it had to be the shadows all around them. The hour. Those terrible songs that moved in her that made her despair of herself.

When he spoke again his voice was almost too low. "It was a long time ago."

"My mother isn't dead," she said. She didn't know why. "But she was never quite right after my father divorced her. Grief can take any number of forms, I mean. Even extraordinary selfishness."

He studied her, and Zara didn't know why she felt so *stricken* suddenly. As if everything had shifted all around them and gone somehow wrong.

"They say time cures everything," he said after a moment, but she knew—*she knew*—that he wasn't the least bit cured. That time did nothing for him but pass.

Around them, the library was a vast, high room, but tonight it felt small. Close. Like it was only the two of them in a cave somewhere, warding off the storm. It felt much too intimate.

And that was the last thing she wanted with this man, because Zara knew herself. She didn't do casual. She didn't *enjoy herself* in any of the ways Ariella had meant she should. She couldn't. She wasn't built that way—and this marriage wasn't built to last out the season.

But he isn't casual at all, a voice inside of her whispered. *He's your* husband, *no matter how you got to the altar. He is the very definition of* not *casual.*

It was amazing how tempting it was to listen.

But Zara knew better.

"I think it's time I tried to get some sleep," she said, her voice little more than a whisper. A small scrape against the warmth, the closeness, that look in his eyes and the things that surged in her like an answer she didn't want to hear.

Like that same song deep inside of her, changing her with every note.

His mouth crooked, and he watched her like he could see all of her confusion right there on her face.

Like it was a challenge. A gauntlet on the floor at her feet.

"Good night, Chase," she whispered, and then she fled.

CHAPTER FOUR

SHE WAS DRIVING him crazy.

Chase let her race from the room, glancing at the grandfather clock on the far wall and noting it was nearly time for his end of the workday call to Tokyo. He knew Zara thought he rattled around this house all night in some kind of drunken stupor. He encouraged it.

Just as he'd encouraged the British press to portray him as a pretty boy of no depth whatsoever, happy to whore himself around Europe and play at a corporate job in Daddy's company as it suited him. The great part about having discovered his own dark depths at thirteen, he knew, was that he'd stopped caring very much about any bad reputation he might have thereafter.

So there was no reason at all it should have bothered him that Zara Elliott looked at him like he might well be the very monster he knew he was. That she was the first one who'd ever looked at him as if she *knew*, as if she could see straight through twenty years of pretense to the truth.

What he didn't understand was why he wanted her all the more because of it.

"You are a twisted, terrible man," he muttered, glaring at the fire. But he already knew that.

He might have declared this a honeymoon, but that was mostly so he'd have some breathing room to prepare the counterattack that would rid him of his Amos Elliott problem at last. His merger with his new brother-in-law's company was moving forward as planned. Nicodemus and he had come to a number of agreements on key issues, which meant everything was falling into place, exactly as he'd planned in the desperate days when he'd realized he and his sister had no choice but to go ahead with these medieval arranged marriages. That it was the only thing that could save the company, and thus the two of them, too. Or their father's legacy, anyway.

Revenge was going to be more than sweet, Chase thought then. He knew he couldn't change the past. He couldn't undo what he'd done. He couldn't bring back his mother or be the son his father had deserved. But he could save Whitaker Industries. He could preserve the second great love of his father's life. And he could cut Amos Elliott down to size while he did it.

Zara was the key. But she wasn't behaving the way he'd thought she would. Correction: the way he'd thought her sister would.

He'd understood everything there was to know about Ariella Elliott within three seconds of meeting her. She'd shimmied about before him, all jaded eyes and come-hither lips, and he'd been as bored as if he'd actually dated her for months. It was one of the reasons he'd agreed to Amos's insane demands so easily. He knew her type. He'd met thousands of Ariellas in his day. Apathetic. Entitled. Awash in a sea of her own self-importance and buoyed in her narcissism by all her father's money and influence. He couldn't think of a single thing a woman like Ariella could do that would surprise him.

A long December locked up in this house with Ariella would already have gone differently. That first night in that bathroom would have ended in an entirely more physical manner, Chase was well aware. By now he could have moved on to other things, like the troweled-on compliments and feigned interest that would lead a woman like Ariella to talk. To talk and talk and talk, indiscreet and self-satisfied, secure in her misguided belief that any man she condescended to sleep with remained forever under her spell.

It would have been easy.

But Zara was nothing like her sister.

This Elliott sister required thought, and the more Chase tried to puzzle her out, the more he found himself remembering her standing in that bath, slick and warm and so stunning it still raced through him, hot and wild. And he had the very disconcerting notion that just like that night, if he touched her, he wouldn't be in control at all.

Not to mention his very real concern that if he tried to use her for information the way he'd planned to do with her sister, she'd know exactly what he was doing. He couldn't decide if he found that irritating or, much worse, arousing.

He heard her footsteps on the floor above him, moving down that long hall to her rooms, no doubt to lock herself away from him the way she should. He heard the storm outside the library windows, hurling itself against the side of the house like it wanted to fight its way in. His usual ghosts took up their positions around him, almost like old friends after all this time. His mother on that last day, laughing the way she'd always done, with her whole body and such easy, captivating delight. His sister the way she'd been back then, young and bright and happy, her little girl's voice singing a song he'd spent a lifetime trying to forget. His father when he'd still laughed so large, so unfettered, like he had nothing at all to lose, before the day that Chase had proved him wrong forever.

The worst thing about Zara was that she made him remember, if only for moments here and there, what it had felt like to be happy.

Unforgivable, he thought harshly.

Because this time, Chase knew exactly what he'd have to do to her, no matter that she was nothing like that terrible sister of hers who he wouldn't have minded using as a simple, effective tool to get what he wanted. This time, he knew what it would cost her when he did the thing he needed to do.

And the price he'd have to pay when he did it anyway.

Chase might have been the perfect Gothic hero, all brooding and dark and occasionally windswept as if to add to his mystique, but Zara spent a lot of her energy during the daylight hours making certain that the rest of this new married life was nothing like the books she studied. The house had a name, it was true, but no one invoked it in ponderous tones or acted like the house itself was alive and/or angry at its occupants.

"It's called Greenleigh," Mrs. Calloway, the housekeeper, had told her when she'd asked. "Just wait until spring and you'll see why. It's so pretty, with the lawns and the trees stretching out halfway to Poughkeepsie. The original Mr. Whitaker's wife's name was Leigh, so he named the place after her as a gift."

Zara was thrilled to discover that Mrs. Calloway was neither dour nor disapproving. She didn't waft through the house in shades of black, muttering alarming things about the past. Instead, she was a friendly older woman who bustled rather than walked, insisted upon decking the halls in as much Christmas cheer as it was possible to cram into one house and cooked like a dream. Her husband—who sang Christmas carols as he puttered about, in a surprisingly lovely tenor—had never been in Zara's presence without also being wreathed in smiles. They lived out in one of the guest cottages that dotted the estate and were more than happy to talk about their cheerful, well-adjusted children and their growing tally of plump grandchildren.

Despite first appearances and the slightest bit of hysteria brought on by impersonating Ariella, she group texted her three best friends from college, who lived all over the place these days and had been universally unimpressed to hear about her sudden wedding on the news, my actual marriage appears to be anything but supernatural.

A conviction that was not shared by the general public, insofar as the tabloids could be held to represent their views.

Society Shocker! they'd screamed that first week, right after the wedding. *Hottie Chase Spurns Ariella for Ugly Duckling Sis!*

And that was one of the more flattering headlines. When one week became two and neither Chase nor Zara appeared in public, they'd dropped any pretense of "flattery."

Ariella could have written those headlines herself, her friend Amy texted back staunchly from Denver after Zara shared the worst of them. They're as nasty as she is.

I suggest you ignore them, Marilee had chimed in from Chicago, and concentrate on that hot husband of yours.

I know I am, Isobel texted from Edinburgh.

Zara laughed out loud in her little sitting area before the fire, which had fast become her favorite part of her bedroom suite.

Relax, ladies, she texted back. It's not real.

But what worried her was how much she wanted it to be real. How much she wished and yearned and longed, like the sad little ugly duckling her sister and the whole world imagined she was already.

It was maddening. It was like being thirteen years old all over again, ungainly and insecure.

"Did I offend you in some way?" Chase asked at their usual dinner that night, cooped up in that tiny little room that seemed smaller all the time.

That was when Zara realized she was scowling at him. She forced herself to stop, to cast around for that polite smile she'd worn so easily before she'd met him. For years.

"Not recently," she said. "But I'm sure we need only wait a few moments before you remedy that."

And there was that little crook to those perfect lips of his that she spent more time fantasizing about than she should. Because she remembered all too well how they'd felt against hers in that church. The press of heat. The whisper of power in it. The way it had ricocheted through her body and lodged low in her belly, like a punch.

"No doubt," he agreed. "Mrs. Calloway tells me you were interrogating her about my ancestors again today. You need only ask me what you want to know, Zara. I'm a walking encyclopedia of all things Whitaker."

Zara had run into the housekeeper in one of the salons, dusting the forbidding portraits of old, steely-eyed men hanging there. Zara had grown up with a number of similar paintings in her father's rambling old house in Connecticut, many of them involving those silly Revolutionary War–era wigs she still couldn't take seriously.

"I very much doubt that the word *interrogate* was used," she said now. *So we both grew up surrounded by pompous portraits*, she told herself derisively. *That doesn't mean a thing. They aren't a bridge between you—they're paintings*. She really was pathetic, she thought, and sniffed. "And I'm not all that interested in your ancestors. I have far too many of my own. Also, I read your Wikipedia page."

He leaned back in his chair, looking as if he was actually enjoying himself, and Zara felt a warm sort of glow spill through her. Like that had been her goal all along.

Wasn't it? that traitorous little voice asked.

Chase was wearing a sweater tonight, a sleek, dark knit that was obviously soft as it pulled against th those shoulders of his and drew attention to the easy perfection of his physique. But he was more than simply *hot*. He exuded something raw and primal, something that kept her belly in a tight knot whenever she was with him. Something that made her breasts heavy and her core slick, and she'd never felt anything like it before.

She was an imperfect Gothic heroine, Zara knew. She wasn't chaste or virginal. She'd always thought she was as reasonably experienced as anyone her age, after the boyfriend she'd had for the last two years of college and the other one she'd had for about eighteen months before graduate school. Not too much, not too little. She'd thought she'd known what it was to want, to need, to *lust*, but she'd never met anyone like Chase before.

This—*he*—was something new.

It was like everything had been the same before she'd met him. Primary colors, bleeding one into the next, indistinguishable from each other. But Chase was rich, deep blacks contrasted by stark whites. Arresting. Incandescent. Moody. He was something deeper than what she'd known. Something *more*.

And it occurred to her that her friends—and even Ariella and all the mean-spirited tabloids—were right. This was an opportunity, and not one that came along very often. How often did a scholar of Gothic novels get the opportunity to spend this kind of time with her very own Gothic hero?

Zara knew she wasn't hideous. She'd come to terms with the differences between herself and the Ariellas of the world a long time ago—it had been that or simply suc-
mb to how wretched that gap made her feel. But even so,
Whitaker was not the sort of man she'd ever have
'd find herself with, under any circumstances.
who were more like her. Quirky. Brainy.
incandescent.

Capable of fading into the background instead of commanding the attention of the whole room by the simple virtue of entering it.

Chase was wild blue, uncontainable, and she was stuck with him for at least the rest of the month of December. After that party on New Year's Eve that was obviously important to him for reasons she doubted he'd share with her, she imagined they'd wash their hands of each other. *You'll have your life back*, she told herself fiercely to cover that odd little hollow feeling at the thought.

And in the meantime, she didn't trust him or his motives for this marriage or his seeming obedience to her father's wishes—but why did she have to? She didn't want *trust*. She didn't want to *date* him.

She just *wanted*.

It didn't matter if she couldn't do casual under normal circumstances. What was *normal* here? This marriage had an expiration date on it already. Casual or serious or neither—it would take care of itself.

"Careful," Chase said then, and Zara realized she'd been staring at his mouth. "I might get the wrong idea."

She put her knife and fork down on her plate carefully. Very carefully. She lifted her gaze to all that raw blue. She breathed in, then out, and told herself there wasn't any part of her that might regret this rash decision.

You might as well enjoy yourself after all, that little voice whispered deep inside her, *and not only because Ariella is absolutely certain you won't.*

She hadn't asked to be in this situation. She'd been pushed. Dragged up the aisle, in fact. Why not indulge herself? Why not view this strange marriage of hers as *research*—and why not get the most out of her primary source while she could?

Zara smiled at him. Her husband, at least for now. And the most beautiful creature she'd ever beheld.

"But what if I want you to get the wrong idea?" she asked as casually as if she was discussing the weather.

"I'm sorry?"

She let her smile widen. "Just because this isn't a traditional marriage, it doesn't mean we're obligated to overlook all the benefits of one. We can pick and choose, surely."

"Let me make certain I understand you." She couldn't describe that look in his eyes then. More than wild. Deeper than primitive. So hot she lost herself for a moment. So bold she wasn't sure she'd ever breathe again. "You're not talking about sharing my surname, I assume. Or the dispensation of property."

There was a time she might have hesitated. Gone for the indirect approach to suss out his interest before committing herself. Before *revealing* herself. And it wasn't as if Chase was remotely *safe*, which had been the only reason she'd ever risked such things in the past.

She had no idea what came over her, but she decided she liked it. Her last recklessly spontaneous act had been to show him her naked body. How could propositioning him be any worse?

"I'm talking about consummation, that most traditional of marital acts," Zara said very deliberately, and watched him go still.

Very, very still.

She leaned forward so that her elbows were on the table and she could keep her gaze steady on his. Even if the blue of it burned and the deep fire there made her whole body feel shivery and *alive* again. Alive at last, no matter how reckless this was. No matter if she'd live to regret it.

At least she'd live.

"I'm talking about sex, Chase," she clarified. "With you."

Zara didn't regret it the moment she said it—but she certainly felt it drop through her like a stone. Hard and swift. Impossible to take back.

She told herself she didn't want to.

"Say that again," Chase ordered her, his voice low and rough.

He still didn't move. But then, he didn't laugh, either. If anything, he looked...*electric*. She could see he hadn't even twitched, so it made no sense that he seemed bigger somehow. As if all of those things she'd sensed in him—that brooding power, that sheer, masculine *force*—were unleashed now, and crowded out the air in the room.

He was immense. Wild. And she'd never wanted anyone more.

Zara considered him for a moment while her heart executed some kind of frantic ballet inside her chest, and she was certain the heat she could feel sizzling between them and making it difficult to breathe was splashed across her face. Like a beacon.

She was as subtle as a searchlight and she wasn't sure she cared.

"Which part?" she asked, because she enjoyed the tussle. The clash and roll of wits.

And because she was stalling. Still.

"Come here," he growled at her.

She felt it everywhere, like a touch. Like that low, commanding voice of his was wired directly to all of her secret places, to all of that desperate hunger she'd felt since the moment they'd locked eyes in that church. And everywhere she felt the caress of it, so rough and so raw, she felt a heavy kind of ache.

Need.

"I don't take orders," she said instead of obeying him, spurred on by some demon thing inside of her she didn't understand.

His mouth curved, and it was a hard, compelling thing. A stamp of sheer maleness, sex and desire, and she had to let out a hard breath to absorb it without dissolving where she sat.

"You will." He sounded certain.

"Are you sure you're interested?" she asked, instead of doing what that melting thing inside her wanted her to do, which was hurl herself at him in total abandon. And then do whatever he asked her to do, again and again and— "I ask because I did stand in front of you completely naked and your response was to tell me I'd best be on time for dinner."

The curve of his mouth became a smile, the first real one she'd seen on him, and it was devastating. It should have been impossible, but he became even more beautiful. Even more powerfully *him*. The smile made a celebration of that perfect face of his, those wicked brows, that mouth. It made his eyes gleam a brighter shade of blue, the blue of whole, perfect summers, all there in that single smile.

It made him irresistible, and Zara was certain he knew it.

"I haven't forgotten," he assured her, and he shifted in his seat then, lounging there as if he was relaxed when she could see that he wasn't. That he was in the grip of the same tension that held her.

But now that she'd brought up that night in the bath, and all the demons and specters she'd summoned along with it, she couldn't let it go.

"I'm not my sister," she said, her voice tighter than it should have been.

His gaze slammed into her. "A fact, Zara, of which I am well aware."

"And I don't want anything like pity sex, thanks," she continued, and though the words left claw marks on their way out, she managed to say it in a brash sort of way. As if it didn't hurt.

"Pity sex?" He looked thunderstruck.

"No substitutions," she said expansively, smiling as if she was calm, though she could feel the heat on her cheeks that proved she was a liar. "No closing your eyes in the dark and pretending it's the other Elliott sister beneath you." She couldn't believe she'd said that, and from the way his eyes widened, neither could he. "Or on top," she continued, as if *more talking* would make it any better. "I mean, no need to consign anyone to any traditional gender—"

"Zara."

Thank God he'd interrupted. She felt so out of control it was like a kind of dizziness, except she wasn't at all worried she'd get sick. She was more worried she'd keep talking herself into complications and then what?

"Shut up," he said in that sexy growl of his, and she did.

He studied her, the way he always did, except this time it left a trail of fire and hunger everywhere his blue gaze lit.

"Come here," he said again, and it was a dark, starkly sexual command. It shivered over her like a touch. Like that press of his lips against hers on that altar. Like he wanted her this hungry. This lit up and on fire. His mouth crooked up again, and that was the only reason she didn't simply burst, she thought. "Quietly."

Then he settled back in his chair and waited.

And Zara understood that this was not the first time Chase Whitaker had made these demands of a woman. She had no doubt that he knew exactly what he was doing, that he'd tested out this sort of thing a hundred times before. On some level, she supposed she should have been horrified by that. Unnerved, certainly, by someone whose experience so vastly outstripped hers. Alarmed by the sheer *certainty* in the way he waited, with all of that brash male confidence, for her to do as he bid her.

She was sure she should have felt *something* other than that dark, glimmering thread that wound inside of her, tighter by the second, miraculous and real.

"What will I do when I get there?" she asked. Mostly to disobey his order that she be quiet.

He smiled again, and it was a dark, thrilling thing. It connected to that knot deep inside of her and pulsed. Long and low and hard.

"I'm certain you'll think of something, clever girl that you are," he murmured.

And she knew that most girls, clever or not, would stand and walk around the table. They'd take the opportunity to roll their hips, pout a little bit, give the man a show. Or anyway, girls like her sister would do that, because they always did. Zara had *seen* Ariella do it to this or that boyfriend over the years. And she considered it. She had a brilliant flash of herself standing before him, then sinking down to her knees between those long legs of his…

But Zara didn't want to be *most girls*. She didn't want to compete. She didn't want to be anything like Ariella.

Ever.

Once again, Zara didn't think. She leaned forward and pushed all their plates to the side. Then, without giving herself time to second-guess it, she pulled herself up and onto the strong oak table that she'd admired for its lovely polish as well as its sturdiness over the past two weeks and launched herself across it.

Her reward was the way he almost came out of his chair, then caught himself. The way his blue eyes went supernova and every one of those long, athletic lines of his body went taut.

"What the bloody hell are you doing?"

But he said it like he couldn't believe it was really happening, not like it horrified him.

And Zara laughed. Like launching herself to her feet in the bath that night, she hadn't thought this through. Unlike then, this felt good. It was good to move. To slide her hands out over the smooth wood in front of her, reveling in the tactile pleasure of it, like it was that ridged wonder he called his abdomen. To let her hair fall all around her like she was as wild as he was, yet sensual and distinctly feminine. To push forward, her knees on the table, all of her in motion, answering that howling thing inside of her. To *do something* with all that crackling electricity inside of her that she thought might incinerate her otherwise.

"I have no idea," she replied, and she hardly recognized her own voice. Thick and needy and powerful, somehow, all the same.

And then she was right there, her face before his. And he wasn't lounging in his chair anymore, like some dissolute playboy king. His face had gone hard and almost feral, his eyes glittering with need and that mouth of his a hard, gloriously male line.

She trembled deep inside.

And Chase didn't ask her any more questions.

He reached over and speared his fingers directly into the mess of her hair, his palms at her cheekbones.

She made a sound of need. Of sheer, unadulterated greed.

He laughed then, and it was a triumphant sound. Dark and profoundly masculine, and it rolled through her, hot and dry, and only fanned the flames higher. And then he dragged her mouth to his.

This was no press of lips like that silly ritual he'd adhered to in the church. This had nothing to do with her damned father. This was a reckoning. This was long overdue.

This was more necessary than breath.

It was a taking.

He ravaged her mouth. He took and he tasted, and Zara met him. Every stroke. Every angle of his jaw. Every thrust of his tongue. She lost herself in the exquisite perfection of his taste. Rough. Male. And the hint of whiskey.

She wanted to drown in him.

That wild electricity danced between them, slick and

mad. She couldn't find the right angle. He couldn't seem to get close enough.

Zara wanted him with an intensity that might have alarmed her, had she cared about anything but the sheer exultation of his mouth moving against hers. That heart-stopping taste, like something she'd once known well and had lost.

Like recognition, she thought.

Like home.

And she understood that she was never going to survive this man. But his hands tightened in her hair, he held her jaw where he wanted it and he plundered her mouth with as much consummate skill as greed, and Zara couldn't bring herself to do anything but kiss him back.

Again and again and again.

CHAPTER FIVE

Mine.

The word pounded through him with every deep, drugging taste of her. Like a drumbeat. Louder than his own heart.

Like this would never be enough. Like it had nothing to do with revenge.

Chase tore his mouth from hers, shoved his chair back from the damned table and then hauled her the rest of the way across it until she tumbled over his lap and he could arrange her there the way he wanted her.

Or one of the ways he wanted her.

"Better," he muttered when he'd settled her with her legs over his and her arms around his neck. Not astride him, not yet, or he thought he might explode like a teenager.

And then he claimed her mouth once more.

It was more than *better*. That lush bottom he'd lusted after in the bath was nestled up against the hardest part of him, urging him on. Making him feel more animal than man. Every time she shivered, he felt it like a stroke of her hand.

And the deeper he kissed her, the more she met him, the wilder it got. And the more she shivered.

Mine, he thought again, a primitive hunger that should have alarmed him surging through him. *My wife.*

He kept one hand tangled in that gorgeous fall of her

hair, that riot of reds, and let the other one explore the body that had haunted him night and day throughout this cursed week. All of those breathtaking curves, right there beneath his palm. All of that stunning lushness *right here* in his arms. At last.

He traced his way down the sensual line of her back, that he could *see* as if she still stood naked before him. She was wearing a clingy shirt made of a soft, sleek fabric that moved with her and made her curves that much more enticing.

He thought she might kill him. He wasn't sure he'd mind.

Chase wrenched his mouth from hers and followed the line of her neck down toward that soft shoulder visible in the wide neckline of her shirt, licking his way across the lightly scented expanse of her skin.

Zara sighed. It was a broken, needy sound, and he felt it in his sex. Like she'd leaned over and taken him deep in her mouth.

He thought he'd never been this drunk in his life. Completely and utterly intoxicated by this woman, so rocked he couldn't tell if he'd ever feel sober again. And he didn't think he cared.

"Chase," she said, and it took him longer than it should have to realize that was his name. That it was not only his name, but that she wanted him to stop what he was doing and listen. Or worse, *talk*.

"Quiet," he told her, and he thought he sounded fierce, but she laughed. "I'm busy."

"I can see that," she said, her voice shaking with laughter and lust, and something bright shot through him. Like a bolt of sunlight, and he didn't want to know what that meant. He didn't want to dig into it. He used his teeth against the gentle rounding that was her collarbone instead, and felt that quiver all the way through her.

"I don't know what you're used to here in these wild, uncivilized colonies," he continued, moving back up her neck, tasting her as he went, collecting those shivers of hers like pieces of gold he could hoard, "but I take my traditional duties rather seriously. I can assure you that I attend to them with diligence—" and he found the curve of her earlobe then, taking it between his teeth in a little scrape that made her breath catch "—and focus."

On that he shifted, dropping one hand to hold her hip and the other moving to cradle her face in his palm. Too-bright gold in her eyes and that carnal mouth of hers. His undoing.

"But—"

He didn't want to hear whatever she was about to say. He licked his way into her mouth instead, like she was his dessert. And she melted against him, like she thought so, too.

And then he simply kissed her.

Until he forgot why he'd ever thought he shouldn't. Until there was nothing in the whole world but the taste of her mouth, her hair all around them like a sweet curtain and the way she moved against him as she sat there draped over his lap.

Until he didn't know which of them was which.

She pulled her mouth from his, and Chase didn't know if minutes had passed, or years. Lifetimes. When he failed to care about that, too, an alarm went off in some dim, dark recess inside him, but he ignored it.

"Stop," she whispered when he moved as if to claim her mouth again. "Listen."

He stopped. It took a moment for that greedy hunger to loosen its hold on him. For that roar inside him—lust and need and that pounding thing that was his heart—to ease back enough that he was less primitive, more man again.

So close to that monster in him, he thought darkly. Capable of anything, even here.

That was so unpalatable that it took him another moment to realize he could hear someone outside in the hallway. Mrs. Calloway, no doubt, right on time to clear their plates and serve their actual dessert.

"I heard the door close," Zara told him, her golden eyes huge and her voice still a whisper. "I think she walked in first."

Reality was like a roundhouse kick to the face.

Chase gathered Zara up and set her on her feet, then stood, furious. Blackly, consumingly furious. At himself.

What the hell was he doing? How had he forgotten himself entirely—again? What had happened to his self-control—necessary for the plotting required here? But of course, he knew. It was Zara. That teasing lilt in her voice. That challenging glint in her eyes. That damned body of hers he thought might be the end of him in all those lush, gorgeous curves.

He stalked to the door and wrenched it open, nodding stiffly at Mrs. Calloway by way of bidding her enter. Then he had to stand there and suffer through the storm battering at him, in all its rage and blackness and the bleak things beneath, as she swept in the way she always did, chattering and smiling.

"Should have known better than to burst in unannounced on a pair of newlyweds," she practically sang. "Can't apologize enough!"

Chase's gaze slid to the brand-new wife he would not have referred to as a newlywed, given all those implications, and he simply froze.

Because she was smiling back at Mrs. Calloway, standing right where he'd put her as if she'd forgotten how to move. Her face was bright red with embarrassment and leftover passion. Her hair was a tousled mess that showed him—and, no doubt, Mrs. Calloway—exactly what his hands had been doing moments before. She'd crossed her arms beneath her breasts, and he doubted she realized how that emphasized them, how that drew his attention directly to those pretty nipples so obviously tight and hard beneath her shirt. Her mouth was faintly swollen from his, and she was *smiling* as if all of this was precisely what it looked like.

As if they were simple, run-of-the-mill, everyday newlyweds who couldn't keep their hands off each other. Nothing more, nothing less.

And it pierced him as surely as if she'd hurled a spear at him, as if it had bored a hole straight through him, how much he wanted it to be true in that moment. He could *see* it. What it would be like if they were those people. If, when the door closed, they would laugh and start all over again, basking in their shared closeness. Their happiness.

Whatever it was that people felt when they were crazy in love with each other and not in the least bit afraid to show it.

Chase had never felt it himself, nor anything close. He'd always dated forgettable women, interchangeable women. He knew they'd bore him before they went out on their first date, so he'd always chosen them for other reasons. How their presence on his arm might benefit him. Whether or not they photographed well. Some or other lust, though nothing like what had swamped him tonight. What still beat in him now, heavy and low, testing his control.

He knew what it looked like, though. That kind of love. He'd seen it a very long time ago in his own parents. They'd sparkled when they'd been together, as if they'd been plugged in to their very own electric current. They'd held hands. They'd each smiled bright and happy when the other had walked into the room. They'd glowed.

And then you killed all that, the cold judge who presided over the darkest part of him pronounced. Lest he forget who he was. Or what he'd done. *You killed her. And them.*

"Now I understand why you married so quickly!" Mrs. Calloway said directly to him as she headed back for the door, snapping him back into the moment with her knowing little chuckle. "Enjoy this, Mr. Chase. You deserve it."

She might as well have elbowed him in the face, this kindly old woman whom he'd known the whole of his life and whom he knew wished him only good. It was that much of a body blow.

Because Chase knew exactly what he deserved. And it certainly wasn't whatever romantic fantasy his housekeeper had cooked up in her head. Not to mention what he'd been spinning out in his own.

And then Mrs. Calloway was gone, shutting the door very pointedly behind her as she sang back over her shoulder that there was no need to worry, they wouldn't be disturbed again. Not tonight.

"How embarrassing," Zara said as the other woman's footsteps sounded on the hall floor, then faded away, in that same voice she'd used before, that he'd determined was her nerves in action. He shouldn't find it adorable, he was well aware, and the fact that he did made him hate himself that much more. "I don't think I've ever been walked in on in my life. I can't decide if I'm humiliated or oddly—"

"I'm glad she walked in." Chase cut her off. He didn't miss the way she stiffened, or the coolness that crept into that gold gaze of hers. He told himself he didn't care about that. Because God knew, he shouldn't have. "That was a mistake."

Zara studied him then, and Chase felt…outsized. As if his skin no longer fit the way it had before. As if he'd lost complete control of himself and all those terrible things in him had burst free, distorting him where he stood.

As if she really could see all of that darkness in him for what it was.

"I'm sorry you think so," she said after a moment, and he didn't care that he knew her better now than to believe that calm tone she used. That he could see a far darker truth in the gaze she dropped from his an instant later.

And if I can see that after two weeks and a kiss, he thought, *what can she see in me*?

Chase felt his hands tightening into fists and ordered himself to breathe. To open them again. To claw back some goddamned control. He wasn't thirteen anymore. He was twenty years older than he'd been then, and these days, he knew how to handle himself.

Or he had before Zara Elliott had catapulted up that damned church aisle and into his life, dressed like a gazebo and capable of destroying his composure with a single look.

He hadn't expected this, he thought then, as this wife he hadn't wanted frowned at the floor like that might bring her clarity. He hadn't expected *her*. This all would have been different if he'd been dealing with her sister, who was so unmemorable he couldn't summon her features in his own head. If this had been Ariella, he wouldn't have been set on fire like this, even now, like there was a blaze in him that nothing could dim. Like all she need do was reach for him and he'd forget himself all over again.

Chase hadn't responded to a woman like this in as long as he could remember—perhaps ever—and that awful little fact all but flattened him. It also opened his eyes, at last, to the danger he was in. He had to remember his endgame here.

She was Amos Elliott's daughter, and that meant he needed to *use* her. Not *succumb* to her.

"Let's be honest for a moment," he said, not bothering to sound polite.

Zara laughed, a rueful little scrape of sound that Chase knew would haunt him later. He could add it to his expansive collection of ghosts and regrets.

"That's not an opening sentence that ever leads anywhere good," she pointed out. "Much like, 'I want to talk' or 'no offense, but…' Nothing anyone wants to hear ever follows."

She smiled in a hesitant sort of way, as if encouraging him to do the same, but Chase refused to be amused by her. *He refused.*

"This isn't going to last," he said shortly. Almost aggressively, and he saw that register in the way her body went tight. Too tight. Her arms, still crossed over her middle, stiffened like she was hugging herself. "This marriage is a joke. At best, a convenient vehicle. I need to be certain that when its usefulness has passed, there won't be any lingering confusion."

"Lingering confusion?" she repeated. Her head tilted and her gleaming eyes narrowed. "You mean mine, I'm guessing?"

What absurd thing had she said before? *Pity sex?* Chase could use that.

"You will fall in love." He shrugged when her glare glazed over into something far more hostile. "It's inevitable."

"And why is that?" Her tone was sharp.

"Please," he said dismissively, and with enough condescension that she stiffened further with obvious outrage. "The truth is, I don't want the mess. It's not worth the bother for something as easily obtained and equally forgettable as sex." He waited until he saw her temper bloom in bright red splashes across her cheeks, then went for the kill shot. "I can get that anywhere, Zara. You must know that. Your sister offered me a blow job within five minutes of our introduction."

She paled, then splashed scarlet again. But she didn't

keel over, this wife of his he wished he didn't want the way he did, like a searing fire in his blood. He supposed that would haunt him, too.

"Anyone can get sex anywhere, Chase," she retorted softly, his name a slap. "And a blow job is Ariella's version of a friendly handshake. I'm sorry if you thought it was something special, just for you."

So he sighed, and raked his hands through his hair and made a show of not quite rolling his eyes.

"You can't imagine you're the first woman to throw herself at me, can you?" he asked, his voice somewhere between patronizing and the sort of beleaguered kindness that he knew would appall her, it was so much like pity. "You're simply the first I've happened to be married to at the time. And I appreciate the thought, Zara. I do."

Her face was even redder then, and her eyes were so dark he could hardly see their color. But she stood there before him, drawn up to her full height, and he had the impression she was utterly impenetrable then. Like she'd wrapped herself in steel.

It was impossible not to admire her. He didn't fight it.

"You're the most beautiful man I've ever seen," she said, and her tone made the skin at the back of his neck tickle, because it was anything but complimentary. "But you're empty inside, aren't you? A shell of a thing, dressed up in pretty clothes and those lonely eyes, but really no more than a ghost walking around in the daytime. Like this house. An obsessively well-maintained mausoleum."

"Or possibly," he drawled out, his voice flat because he didn't want to admit the accuracy of the hit she'd just leveled at him or investigate the damage it had left behind, "I'm simply not interested."

She laughed at him then, and even though he could hear the hurt in it, he couldn't see it on her face. She'd locked him out and he hated it.

But he had no choice. If he couldn't control her—or more to the point, himself, when he touched her—he'd have to keep her at arm's length and find a different way to get his revenge on her father. Even if it killed him.

He thought, just then, that it might.

"Of course you're not," she said, and he thought that might be pity on *her* face. It set his teeth on edge. "It's all right, Chase. No need to go to such lengths to be an ass. I got the message."

She started toward him and something kicked at him, some bright shock of panic that she'd touch him and prove what a liar he was, or maybe it was only a flare of hope that she would—but then he realized he was standing next to the door, and she wasn't headed for him at all.

He told himself that was relief he felt, like a block of concrete inside him.

"In future," she said when she drew even with him, with dignity in her voice and every beautiful line of her stunning body, "you can simply say that you've changed your mind. No need for all these theatrics."

Chase said nothing as she walked past him and out into the hall. Nothing as she closed the door behind her with a gentle, admonishing sort of *click* instead of a great slam that might have indicated that she was as wrecked as he was—and therefore might have made him feel better. Nothing at all as she walked off down the hall, leaving him to his emptiness and his terrible shell, the lonely eyes he avoided in his mirror, his great hulking mausoleum and the dark maw of his regret.

A lifetime's worth of regret, piling higher all the time.

And nothing left inside him but his ghosts.

It was Chase's British accent that had made it so much worse, Zara decided a few days later while she indulged both her dark mood and her restlessness with a long, cold walk around the Whitaker estate. So much more eviscerating than if he'd said all the same things but had sounded as if he was from Weehawken, New Jersey, instead. It would have been embarrassing and upsetting either way, but with that accent of his, he'd been *withering*.

It played on a constant, deeply cutting cycle in her head.

You can't imagine you're the first woman to throw herself at me, can you?

It's not worth the bother.

And her personal favorite: *your sister offered me a blow job within five minutes of our introduction.*

He hadn't mentioned whether or not he'd accepted. Zara shoved her hands down as far as they'd go in her bulky winter coat and stamped harder against the path as she moved, because the crunch of ice and snow and frozen earth was primitively satisfying.

And because she was pretending it was his face.

His beautiful, terrible face, and those lonely eyes the perverse thing inside her still wanted to make better somehow. She was more than simply an idiot, Zara thought then. She was bordering on actively, unforgivably self-destructive.

Is this what you had in mind, Grams? she asked the fading light around her.

She puffed out a long breath, watching the cloud of it disappear in front of her, and scowled up at the massive house that reared up on the top of the barren hill, a dark and imposing silhouette against the night that was coming in too fast on a winter afternoon like this one, two days before Christmas.

A smart woman would have left this place—this marriage—after that scene in the dining room, she was forced to admit to herself, and yet here she was. Stomping about the estate half-frozen on another one of her solitary walks that neither cleared her head nor solved anything. But it was better than sitting in that bedroom suite that had started to feel a bit like a cell, pretending to work on her thesis when all she could think about was the man she knew was lurking about the rattling old house somewhere.

No doubt plotting out new ways to humiliate her.

It's not worth the bother. Your sister offered me a blow job.

"The facts are simple," she told herself then, out loud, as if that might banish that vicious loop from her head. She nestled her chin a bit farther into her favorite scarf, still glaring at the house and the lights in the windows, the sparkling Christmas trees and the soft strands of lights along the drive that made it all seem far more welcoming than it was. "You literally threw yourself at this man, and he rejected you." Her words were clouds against what remained of the daylight, but punched at her like heavy fists. "After kissing you like he thought he might die if he stopped."

That was the part she kept mulling over. The reversal.

If he'd simply rejected her outright, it might have been different, or so she'd told herself in these dark, chilly days since it happened, while he'd avoided her completely and she'd had nothing to do but brood about it. Zara hadn't reached the advanced age of twenty-six without having had her share of rejection. It was never pleasant, was it? Had Chase simply declined her offer, she liked to think she would have gracefully swallowed any stung pride and carried on—

Yeah, right.

She would have been mortified. She would have suffered through the rest of that dinner and then gone back to her room and prayed for immediate death, so she'd never have to face him again. But when the melodrama had passed, she would have been fine. Embarrassed, but fine.

If he'd rejected her in that snide, patronizing way but

without any kissing, Zara was fairly certain she would have walked out of that dinner, packed her things, called for a cab and taken herself back home to the little cottage that had once been her grandmother's in a pretty little village on Long Island Sound, where she could bundle herself up against the cold, light her own fire and hunker down for the long holiday break in peace and quiet. Chase could stay rude and obnoxious all on his own.

Because there was actually no reason that she and Chase had to stay together under one roof. Zara's life had always been wholly uninteresting to the entire world—no paparazzi dogged her every step, no curious neighbors took pictures of her on the sly and posted them on the internet. No one cared where she was, so she could pretend to be anywhere, couldn't she?

It was the kissing and *then* the rejection that she couldn't get past.

And only partly because calling what had happened *kissing* might have been technically accurate, but didn't come close to describing the experience.

Zara couldn't sleep. Or she did, only to wake gasping and burning up from the searing force of her dreams, all of which featured Chase. She *felt* him, that rangy body of his all around her, hard and hot and ready. That mouth of his, wicked and seductive in turn. The way he'd pulled her off that table and into his lap, like she was as light as a feather and as easily plucked from the air and then placed wherever he'd wanted her.

She'd never felt anything like it.

And she could still feel it now, she thought crossly, starting to move again because her feet had turned to blocks of ice inside her boots. Her chest was tight. Her breasts simply hurt, heavy and aching, while she could feel the thrust of her nipples against the fabric of her bra, abraded more with every step. And even as she made her way across the frozen lawn, up that hill toward the house, she could feel that desperate, molten heat between her legs.

All this from the *memory* of his hands on her, of that incandescent kiss, of his mouth like a joy and a curse on hers.

And there was absolutely no way that she could have imagined that he'd been as bowled over by it as she'd been. No way she'd fabricated the thunder of his heart in his chest, the way he'd held her head and her face like he'd never let her go, or God help her, the way he'd taken her apart every time he'd tasted her. Tormented her.

Taken her.

No way, she thought. That had all been real, despite what came after.

Zara trudged up to the top of the hill and then stopped, frowning, when she saw him through the tall, bright windows. She'd come up the north side of sloping lawn and that put her outside the farthest part of the house, where there was an indoor pool, a greenhouse atrium and a fitness area she kept telling herself she'd visit one of these days to work off Mrs. Calloway's cooking.

Chase was in the greenhouse, in the wide, central part surrounded by an explosion of well-tended tropical greenery, and at first she thought he was dancing.

He was so graceful. Smooth, athletic movement, one motion blending into the next, and it took her long moments to understand that he wasn't dancing at all—he was practicing some kind of martial art. She began to see kicks and strikes in the fluidity of his movements. That ruthless, formidable power of his exploding into a stream of controlled, yet lethal attacks.

But mostly, she saw *him*. Stripped bare to the waist and gleaming with the force of his exertions. Those haunted blue eyes of his and a sexily unshaven jaw, his dark hair much too long to be anything but wild. That he was truly the most beautiful man she'd ever beheld struck her square in the chest. Like one of his kicks.

Zara told herself it was her scholarly nature at work here. She liked research. She liked the compilation of facts, as many facts as she could find, no matter if she used them all or not in her final thesis. She liked to gather them and analyze them, then make her arguments.

This, she acknowledged as if from afar, was why she avoided "casual." Because she wasn't any good at it.

You're not delusional at all, she assured herself as she pushed open the greenhouse door and walked inside, stamping the cold off her boots and pretending not to notice that Chase froze in the middle of all those bright green plants and impossibly summery flowers, like she'd stepped through a portal to a different season altogether.

For a moment, they only stared at each other, and Zara was certain she could feel the weight of all that feral blue pressing into her, like the sudden embrace of the warm, soft air. She could hear the harsh sound of his breathing over the riot of her own pulse. Her skin prickled everywhere. Her cheeks were so hot she thought they might explode.

Then Chase shifted, breaking the connection. He turned his back on her and walked—stalked, really, in nothing but those loose black trousers that only seemed to call attention to the stark power he wore in every inch of those smooth, hard muscles—over to one of those heavy boxing bags that hung from its own metal apparatus that reminded Zara of the game hangman. And then he started to hit it. And kick it.

Hard.

Zara pulled her gloves off, one by one, then the wool hat from her head. She unwrapped her scarf from her neck, and then she shoved it all into her coat pockets. She unzipped her coat and shrugged it off, then tossed it all into a nearby chair, and while she had the kind of buzzing sensation in her ears and at the back of her neck that told her

Chase was perfectly aware of her throughout this whole process, he didn't stop beating the crap out of that bag.

And for some reason she felt every blow. Like he was landing them against her heart.

This is utter stupidity, she told herself. *And yes, delusional.*

But she didn't do any of the things she should have. She didn't leave. Not the room, not the house. She didn't hightail it back to her own life and to hell with what Chase thought, or her father thought. She didn't check herself into a nearby psychiatric institution to determine what madness this was that made her care what happened to this man.

That was the trouble, of course. She did care. Because this *was* her version of "casual," however pathetic. Married and yearning and caring, despite everything.

Because he looked tortured. That was what that particular wildness was this evening, pouring from him, filling the room like a scent. Like he was tearing himself apart the harder he hit that bag.

Like he was fighting his own demons with every punch he threw and every kick he landed. Fighting for his life.

Your sister offered me a blow job, he'd said. No doubt in precisely the way Zara had imagined Ariella would do such a thing. Zara wasn't about to compete with that. But she could offer something else. Something that had more to do with that stricken, compelling loneliness that shone so brightly in those eyes of his than with sex.

She wandered a little bit closer and then sat down on the little sofa that had been pushed back almost into the wall of plants, perhaps to make room for what she'd seen before and thought was dancing. She kicked off her boots and pulled her feet up under her.

And then she began to talk.

CHAPTER SIX

CHASE DIDN'T HAVE the slightest idea what she was on about.

The monster in him didn't care. It wanted her under him, not across the room, and who cared what happened to her when his New Year's Eve plan went off as intended? When he finally took his revenge? He wanted her, full stop. Now that she was breathing the same air as he was again, making him tight and hard and feral that easily, he couldn't understand the way he'd shoved her away that night at dinner. Much less the distance he'd kept from her since, no matter how many times Ben Calloway sang those vaguely romantic Christmas carols in his direction.

This is why, he told himself coldly. *Because you have no control where this woman is concerned.*

But that dark thing in him—sex and grief and hunger and need, heavy and fierce deep down into his bones until he couldn't tell who he was without it—didn't care.

He was so much more monster than he was man, and it appalled him. It made him hit the damned bag that much harder. And the more she talked, settling in on that couch as if they were great old friends and this was *comfortable*, the more he hit. The whole world narrowed down into those two things, like it was all part of the same great rhythm—her lovely voice, rich and warm, and the starkness of the violence he could dish out against inanimate objects he knew were merely stand-ins for him.

He was simply the instrument that linked the two, he told himself. And somehow, that made him feel less monstrous. Lighter. Warmer, the way she was so effortlessly.

"I look like my grandmother," Zara was saying, as conversationally as if he'd asked her. "She was Irish and always described herself as 'feisty,' though I never saw her do anything that wasn't strictly proper in that very old-money, patrician way. My father loathed her. She'd always liked his older brother much better than him, but Uncle Teddy died young. So when I ended up looking exactly like her, Dad transferred all of those feelings to me." Then she laughed, and it cascaded over him, sunbeams and heat. *Damn her.* "Or maybe that's what I decided to tell myself."

Chase had thought he'd finally lost it when she'd simply *appeared* at that door, in a rush of cold air and the darkening winter sky behind her. He thought he'd finally started seeing things, not merely the collection of familiar ghosts who usually cluttered his head.

He didn't know what to do with that scalding-hot, very nearly bright thing that had wound tight in him when he'd realized she was real. She was *here.* And despite what had happened between them the last time—what he'd done to her, he was well aware, because he couldn't seem to handle her the way he would any other woman—she appeared to be staying.

It couldn't be hope. Not that. He'd lost the last of his hope when he'd been thirteen. This was something different, he told himself grimly.

Because it had to be.

Chase hit the bag with his hands, his elbows, his knees, his feet. He hit and hit and hit, so hard he could feel the shock of it blasting through him, promising he'd regret it later when this raging thing in him wore off—but that only made him go harder. Faster. What *didn't* he regret?

Why should this, or anything that happened here, be any different?

He could still taste her. It was making him crazy.

Crazier, that was.

"My mother always claimed she was meant to be a great painter, but I think that was something she said to differentiate herself from the rest of the socialites she ran around with who had no aspirations beyond their weekly manicures."

Zara's voice had gone wry. Rueful, like she was crinkling up that fine nose of hers as she spoke, no doubt rendering herself dangerously adorable—but he would be damned if he'd look. Chase shuddered, imagining it anyway, and the heat that always graced those lovely cheeks of hers.

She was killing him.

"I never saw her paint a thing, but she picked fights with anyone who suggested that and hid from all the things she didn't feel like doing in the little guesthouse out back she called her studio. She used to lecture us about independence and personal freedom, but when she and my father finally divorced she demanded a laughably huge settlement. She lives on it to this day in her so-called 'artist's retreat' outside of Santa Fe with her collection of predatory boyfriends." A low, husky laugh that ripped at his self-control. "She doesn't encourage her grown daughters to visit her there, mind you. Or anywhere else. Predatory boyfriends require certain levels of care, maintenance and careful lies, and grown daughters make that a challenge, apparently. She claims she's still grieving the end of her marriage and seeing us only makes it worse. It's been five years."

Chase shifted, jumped up and down on the balls of his feet for a moment to recalibrate, then struck out with his knee. *Thunk.* And Zara's pretty voice rose and fell in the background, as thick and insistent around him as the humidity in the greenhouse. Making him sweat all the same. More.

Making him wish he could mete out a little justice to the people in her life the way he could to his punching bag.

Because you're such a hero, a derisive voice taunted him. *The perfect dispenser of truth and justice. What a laugh.*

He shifted again, then hit the bag with his elbow, hard enough to maim a real person, if never quite hard enough to silence his own demons.

"Ariella was the crowning achievement of my parents' marriage," Zara told him. "When we were growing up they would dress us alike and coo over her, telling her how pretty she was, how perfect, how cute. She was exactly the child they'd both secretly expected to have. Blonde and lovely and charming. Instantly beloved by anyone with eyes." Another low laugh, but this one was rougher, and he felt it like claws across his chest. "I was not."

Chase realized that growling sound was coming from him, and bit it back. So hard he almost bit off his own tongue.

"They sighed about my hair," she continued as if she hadn't heard him. "Which, in fairness, was more orange than red at the time. They told me to stand up straight, to walk softly, to be more careful and much more quiet. They hated when I called attention to myself in any way. Of course, that could mean when I walked into a room. It was hard to figure out the rules. And then it was worse when we were teenagers, because it wasn't only my parents saying those things."

But she didn't sound remotely self-pitying. She sounded faintly amused and analytical. And Chase found that hurt him. It *hurt*. Like a shot to the gut.

The bag rocked back and forth in front of him, like it was a balloon.

"But that's adolescence, isn't it? It's all wretched, unless you're pretty like Ariella and calculating enough to take advantage of it." That laugh again, which he was beginning to think might lodge itself in him forever, like permanent opiates in his bloodstream. What was wrong with him that he liked that idea? "I knew my place was in a book and I liked it there."

Thunk. Thunk.

But God help him, those greedy little noises she'd made, sprawled in his lap, her hot mouth wild against his. They haunted him. They woke him in the night. They kept him from his work. They'd wedged their way into him and made him ache for more.

He *ached.*

"My grandmother had always counseled me to give my family another chance. To let them see the real me. And when Ariella disappeared, I was the only one who could help," she told him, and he heard the change in her voice then. How serious it became, suddenly. "Me, at last. I could do something of value for my father that no one else could. It didn't matter that I knew exactly what kind of man he is. It didn't matter that I knew how unlikely it was that he'd ever see me as anything but a problem to solve. I could do the crazy thing that Ariella had walked away from. I know how pathetic that sounds, but for the first time in my whole life, he needed me. So I did it."

Chase stopped hitting the bag. There was an edginess in him, gnawing at the base of his spine, rushing through his veins. He was…affronted, he realized. That Amos Elliott should have that kind of power. That this woman should have spent a lifetime desperate for that petty little man's approval. That she was three-dimensional, *real*, and not the sort of easily digested and quickly dismissed woman he'd been prepared to marry. There was no preparing for Zara. She'd disarmed him from the start.

And Chase was very much afraid he didn't know who he was without his weapons of choice.

He turned to look at her then, very slowly, and it was worse than he'd thought. Much worse.

She was entirely too pretty, but she was also so *cute*. He could have resisted a pouty display, a calculation of curves and presentation. He could have resisted that particular cultivated attractiveness that passed for beautiful in his circles, that he could hardly believe he'd accepted all this time now that he'd seen this woman's perfect, incomparable glory. Now that he knew what she hid beneath clothes that could never do her justice.

Zara sat cross-legged on the couch in dark corduroy trousers and a cocoa-colored turtleneck sweater, her hair in a careless sort of cascade all over her shoulders and not a strand of it *orange*, her warm, pretty eyes gleaming gold and soft. And that bloody mouth of hers that was the sexiest thing he'd ever tasted was so naked and so carnal, it was like she was begging him to take it. *Her.* Taste it all over again.

How could he defend against ghosts like her when she wasn't a ghost at all? When she was real and *alive* and here—*right here*—watching him with so much compassion in her gaze that it stunned him? As surely as if she'd landed a blow to the side of his head and left him spinning?

He had the disconcerting notion that she could see all the way through him, to all that suffocating darkness he carried within. And planned to keep talking to him until he accepted it. Until he surrendered to this inept bridge she was building between them with these stories of hers, like the two of them were at all the same.

He knew better.

Anyone else would have kept their distance from him

when he was like this, so obviously on the edge of unhinged. Chase knew that. And yet here she sat, looking wholly unintimidated, telling him these stories about her life. Making him *understand* her the way he imagined people did when they weren't the kind of broken he was. When they were getting to know each other in all those ways he assumed normal people must.

When they hadn't killed their own mother and knew better, therefore, than to risk any more bridges or connections. He knew how these things ended.

But there was something like a howl in him, long and deep and shattering. Chase hurt everywhere, from the bag and from her and from *this thing* he couldn't seem to banish. Much less control.

And he didn't know what he meant to do with this woman—he didn't know how to make her his revenge when he couldn't seem to make her do anything, but he couldn't take *this* any longer. He couldn't stand it.

"I'm not empty inside," he blurted out, gravel and steel in his voice, and she jerked in her seat as if he'd smacked her. He hated himself as if he really had.

"What?"

But he was already crossing the room. He was already right there, looming above her, so obviously brutal and dangerous, and yet she still gazed up at him in a kind of wonder. Like she saw all the things in him he'd stopped wishing were there a long, long time ago.

Like she was as much a fool as he was.

"It's much worse than empty in here," he rasped. "It's a murderous dark, vicious and *wrong*, and there's no changing it. You should have run away from me when I gave you the chance, Zara. You should have understood that it was a gift, and I don't know that I'll hand you another one."

Her eyes had gone wide, but her chin tipped up, in another show of spine and determination he couldn't understand. What was wrong with this woman? She saw too much, much more than anyone else he'd let near him in years—so why wasn't she afraid of him the way she should have been?

"So is this," she said. "Do you think I sit around and tell people my life story, Chase? In all its sad little details? I don't generally like to hand people ammunition when I know that sooner or later, they're going to use me as target practice."

He didn't deny it. He saw the knowledge of that in the way she tightened her lips, but she still didn't look away.

"I told you I would ruin you." He watched her swallow hard, and he didn't know what it was about that, why it flashed over him like a wave of heat. "You should have listened."

He sank down on his knees before her, fascinated by the way she flushed. By her slight jerk against the couch, as if she'd had to wrestle herself into submission to keep herself from leaping out of her own skin. He held her gaze as he leaned forward and stuck a fist on either side of her, one at each lush hip.

And then they were close again. Much too close. It was like baiting a tornado, daring it to touch land, and the roar of it filled him. *Need. Lust.* And that other thing that couldn't be hope, not even its battered and bruised cousin, but moved in him nonetheless.

"I listened." Her voice was only slightly breathy, but he felt it as if she'd taken him deep in her mouth. The ache. The sweet burn. "You were as hideous as possible, to be certain I would. But what I don't understand is why."

"I told you why. In detail."

His voice was grittier. Darker. And he was leaning over her, his mouth the scantest breath from hers, and she didn't have to call him a liar. She didn't have to say a word. He was proving it.

But this was Zara. She smirked at him.

"You told me *something* in detail," she agreed. "But I'm not sure I would call that little performance an explanation. Would you?"

Chase decided he might as well take this collision course he was on—that they were both on and he didn't understand how that had happened—to its logical conclusion. Or go insane.

More insane.

But he couldn't care about that the way he knew he should. She was so *lush* and she was breathing too hard, and he could see the flush of arousal tint her cheeks pink. He could smell the delicate scent of her skin, like gardenias and vanilla, and he felt it wrap around him like a noose.

Chase gave up. He stopped fighting and let the monster take control, dark and greedy and wild.

He leaned in and slammed his mouth to hers.

It was like fireworks. Everywhere.

Inside her, around her.

Zara couldn't breathe. She didn't care that she couldn't. She wound her arms around his strong neck as his hands wrapped over her hips and tugged her closer. She dropped her legs to either side of him, and he surged between them as if he belonged there, until she locked her ankles behind him.

And then they were finally plastered together, her aching breasts flat against the wall of his chest, like she'd been crafted to fit against him just like that. She could feel him between her legs, the smooth, solid heft of his finely wrought form, and she shook with a ravenous hunger she'd never, ever felt before. Sensation washed over her, blowing out all her circuits and then lighting them up again, leaving her shaking and greedy and as wild as he felt against her.

This wasn't a kiss. This wasn't anything so sweet.

This was possession. Raw and intense.

And she had never wanted anything more.

He tasted of salt and need, passion and demand. And she couldn't get enough.

"More," he muttered against her mouth, and then he pulled back from her.

This was when clarity should have asserted itself, Zara thought, as he took her legs from around him and set her feet back on the floor. But then he looked at her, that dark, impossible blue gone brilliant with need, and she didn't care if she survived this. She didn't care what happened next, so long as it did.

Just so long as he didn't stop this time.

It was as if he could read her mind. His surprisingly tough hands, more laborer than CEO, and she assumed it was the martial arts that made them that way, went to the waistband of her trousers. Zara's heart walloped at her, and her own hands met his there—but to help him or to stop him? She didn't know.

"Take them off." It was an order, and he didn't pretend otherwise. Not with that stark, nearly guttural tone of voice. Not with that shattering look in his eyes that didn't look in the least bit lonely now. They looked hot.

White-hot and focused directly on her.

Zara pulled open the top button of her trousers. Her mouth had gone dry, and she licked her lips before she thought better of it, and then her breath stuttered when his gaze moved to her mouth, dark and hungry.

"Did you accept?" she asked before she knew she meant to say something. It took a long time for him to find his way from her mouth, and he'd gone that much wilder when he did. He was taut and hard. She was almost shaking from the sheer insanity of being this close to him, this *hot*, this eternally *hungry*, and seeing the same reflected in every line of his beautiful face. "My sister's lovely offer. When you met."

He looked blank for a long, deeply satisfying moment. Then his expression went feral. Calculating in a purely sensual, ruthless sort of way that shouldn't have thrilled her as fully as it did, sweeping through her like light.

"Would it matter if I had?"

More than it should, she realized. She wished she hadn't asked.

"I've made it a strict policy to avoid going where Ariella has forged any kind of path," Zara told him, fighting to keep her voice smooth and even dry, though she wasn't sure she succeeded. "Be that a favored vacation spot, a neighborhood in a city, a room in the same house. A man. It helps avoid any confusion."

Chase laughed. It skittered over her skin, then lodged itself in all of her tender places. Her nipples thrust toward him. Her core tensed and then melted. She shivered. And he'd never looked so wicked, so dangerously sexy, as when he leaned close again and spread his hands out over her belly that she hadn't known until that moment had been revealed when her sweater rode up.

His palms were hot and faintly coarse against her skin, and he simply held them there for a moment, his gaze narrow and something like amused on hers, and she hated that he could feel her quiver. That he could feel the goose bumps that rose all over her at the fiercely possessive way he held his hands there.

She hated it. She thought she'd die if he stopped.

"Is this confusion?" It was a taunt, and so it shouldn't have worked through her like liquid heat. "Because it rather feels like something else."

"Like avoiding the question, you mean?"

He blinked, and as she always did, Zara got the impression she'd surprised him. That most people didn't speak to this man this way, as if he was something other than lethal and untamable. She wished she could read the light that moved through those eyes of his, then over his remarkable face.

He laughed again. Low and something like indulgent. Then, inexorably, as if he'd never intended to do anything but this from the start, he shifted closer. He twisted one hand around and stroked his way beneath her half-opened trousers.

Zara jolted. Chase knew exactly what he was doing. His fingers found her latest thong covering her and stroked inside, slicking through her folds and then holding her there for a molten instant, hot and wet and in his hand.

"Does it matter?" he asked again, low and too close to her ear, while his fingers began to move. Learning her. Testing her. Then thrusting inside her. "Do you mind where I've been?"

Zara's mind blanked out. There was nothing but the hard hand that wrapped around one hip and held her still and that other one, that wicked one that was breaking her apart with every slick, easy thrust. With the sure pressure of his palm against her center while he used two fingers to drive her up, then up further, then into dizziness.

"If I say yes, will you turn me away?" he whispered, daring her, and then he laughed again. "Right now?"

He did something magical with his hand, a hard, sweet twist, and then Zara was gone. Shattered, that easily and that completely. Thrown apart into so many blissful pieces she was terrified she'd never come back—

But she did.

Eventually, she did, and he was waiting. Watching. That heavy hand still holding her core, his blue eyes intent on her face and dangerously, heart-thumpingly wild.

"No," he grated at her, fierce and low. "I never touched your sister. She never touched me. I'm not a pig."

She was still shivering through the aftershocks, and she couldn't speak. She thought there was an echo still bouncing around the glass in this atrium, and she was terribly afraid it was her. Screaming. Possibly even his name. She watched his mouth twist and that darkness move over his face, and she felt the tension in him them, in all the places they touched.

"Chase…" she managed to say, though she didn't know where she meant to go afterward.

"I warned you," he muttered.

And then he moved again. He dispensed with her trousers in a certain, shocking economy of motion that had them down her legs and whisked aside before she could draw a full breath.

"I'm not a good man, Zara," he told her, but the look on his face was bright and greedy, and he was staring down at the scrap of multicolored lace between her legs. "But if I don't taste you, I think I might die."

And like that, the fire swept through her again, tossing her right back into the heat of it. His gaze locked onto hers as he moved, tugging her bottom forward until it was on the edge of the sofa cushion, then crouching down to press her thighs open with the breadth of his shoulders. Her hands were somehow sunk in the rough black silk of his hair, and she didn't know how that had happened or why she seemed to be completely incapable of letting go of him.

And she was trembling. Everywhere.

"I don't think this is a good idea," Zara whispered.

And he grinned at her, this stunning creature, all raspy jaw and wild blue eyes, his mouth so close to her core that she was sure he could hear the way her pulse beat there. Or taste it.

"I know it's not," he agreed.

And then he pushed her thong aside and licked his way into her.

Zara simply *ignited.*

Thought fell away. There was nothing but Chase and the hungry way he feasted on her. He used his tongue like a weapon and she was helpless before it. She shook. She broke apart. She spun and she spun, and he only pushed her higher. Further. Deeper.

And when she convulsed around him this time, she heard a high, keening sound, and she didn't care that it was her. She only wondered how the glass around them didn't shatter. How the night simply hung there outside the windows without rending itself apart.

When she could move, she found she was limp and soft, sprawled back against the couch with her legs where he'd left them, tremors still chasing themselves across her skin.

She smiled before she thought better of it, wide and sleepy, and only then did she really look at Chase.

He'd sat back, lounging on the floor before the couch in a lazy way that was belied by every tight, hard line of his body and the intent way he watched her. Ruthless and hungry. Waiting. There should have been some kind of power in sitting higher than him, Zara thought, but he was too formidable for that. She doubted it would matter if he'd knelt there before her with his forehead to the floor; he was the least docile creature she'd ever seen. She thought of great, wild animals then, all with that contained force and the same predatory gaze.

Chase didn't move. He watched. And the more the silence grew heavy, the more Zara felt it like a fist in her belly. Hard and impossible to ignore.

She struggled to sit up, then looked around for her trousers, feeling a whole spinning host of things she really, really didn't want to feel. She decided to ignore them. She picked up the tangled pile of corduroy from the floor and stood, stepping into them and pulling them back up.

And all the while he lounged there, reminding her of a great big, indolent cat. Except far less cuddly.

"Let me guess," she said when her trousers were fastened, her cheeks flared so hot she thought she might run back out into the cold outside to relieve them and she was reasonably certain her voice wouldn't quake when she spoke. "This was a mistake. You wouldn't want to confuse me, as that will make me tumble straight off the cliff and find myself violently in love with you. You can get sex anywhere, Ariella was hotter, you're not really that interested." She smiled again, but this one was sharp enough to leave marks. "See? I listen."

He lifted himself up from the floor and onto his feet in a single, smooth jump that made her blink. Then clench hard, deep inside. Lethal grace. Impossible beauty.

She was in so far over her head with this man it was a wonder she could breathe at all, and the worst part was, she could still *feel* him. That talented mouth of his, like he was still licking heat into the core of her.

"Come," he muttered, short and dark. *Pissed off*, if she'd had to characterize it.

"I have to tell you," she said, because she couldn't seem to help herself. "If this is all part of some plot to put me in my place by punishing me with oral sex, I have to say, it's..." She paused when his gaze slammed into hers, looking somehow amused and furious at once. She swallowed. "Working, obviously. I feel very, very punished."

He muttered something else she couldn't hear, though it moved over her like his hard, capable hands. Then he jerked his head, bidding her precede him out of the greenhouse and back into the main house. The halls felt drafty and cool after the close heat of the atrium, and she felt it slap against the flush she knew must have turned her bright red.

Chase stalked beside her, his face shut down and forbidding and those blue eyes glittering brighter than the twenty-foot Christmas tree that dominated the front hall. He escorted her in that same tense silence all the way up to her suite, then stopped.

"Thank you," she said brightly, only half-aware that she was poking at him. And then unable to stop herself when she realized it. "That was fun. Especially the angry walking through the gloomy house. I think that part was my favorite."

He shifted, making Zara aware that her back was to the door and he was very big, very male, and not looking at her in any way that a wise woman would ignore. Or poke at any further.

But as she had proved a number of times already in her two and a half weeks of arranged marriage with this man, she was anything but wise where he was concerned.

"I am going to have a shower," he told her, and she had the sense he was biting off each word carefully. Like he couldn't trust they wouldn't simply run away with him if he wasn't vigilant. Or like he was *this close* to acting on that dark heat she could see shading his gaze, turning that wild blue something nearer to slate. "A very cold one. And then I'll meet you for the evening meal, as usual."

"None of this seems to end well," she pointed out. "Maybe we should stop trying. There's no law that says we have to cohabitate, you know."

"Don't tell me any more stories, Zara." His voice was low. Not quite angry, though; it was too quiet for that—and somehow he was closer than he should have been. "You don't want to win me over. I'm no kind of prize, I assure you. More like something you'd be better off endeavoring to avoid at all costs."

But he reached over and took a long, red wave of her hair in his fingers as he said it, then stared at it for a moment too long as he wrapped the shining strands around his finger. He shifted that stare to her when he tugged, not as gently as he could have done. The stare or the tugging.

"Are you sure about that?" She was whispering as if it hurt, though it didn't. Or not acutely, anyway.

"I am." He let go of her hair, and Zara felt bereft when he stepped back, like he'd taken all the heat and light with him. It was gone from his gaze as if it had never been. "Utterly, painfully sure."

And when he turned abruptly and stalked off down the hall, she stood there for too long, watching him until he disappeared into his own rooms—and told herself that what she felt then was relief.

CHAPTER SEVEN

IT WAS RELIEF because it couldn't be anything else, Zara told herself staunchly as she marched inside her room and started peeling off her clothes. Certainly not longing. Or anything like disappointment.

You should be relieved that someone *in this absurdity of a marriage managed to keep his wits about him*, a caustic voice inside of her snapped. *What were you thinking?*

But that was the trouble. She'd never thought less in her life. Her brain didn't appear to be involved at all when it came to Chase—and Zara hardly knew how to process that revelation. Thinking had always been her refuge. Her escape. Her single and best weapon.

She kicked her trousers off and surveyed the damage—none of it in her thoughts, which careened madly this way and that and offered nothing in the way of solace. She felt tremulous and still a scalding kind of tender between her legs. Her knees seemed wobbly, as if she might topple over at any moment and then crumple to the floor like the turtleneck sweater she swept over her head and then dropped at the foot of her bed. Her breasts ached, her nipples still pushed out taut and hard, and she had no idea why she couldn't seem to control herself where Chase was concerned.

Or why some part of her didn't *want* to control herself.

"Whatever made you think you could wade in and handle him?" she asked herself out loud as she made her way to the sprawling bathroom suite and turned on the water in the large, glassed-in shower. It fell from two separate fixtures like rain. "You can't handle yourself."

Zara knew that if she worried over it too much more, she'd explode. So instead, she stepped into the shower and let the heat pound into her. She stood under the spray with her head tipped back and gave herself up to the water. She could have stood there forever.

There were far worse places to hide, if only from herself. Eventually, the water would run cold. And maybe by then she'd have figured out how she could ever trust her own judgment again. Maybe she'd even wash herself clean of all that leftover sensation—

But then the glass door opened, the cooler air gusting in from outside the stall like ice against her heated skin.

She jerked out of the spray, startled if not precisely surprised, as Chase stepped into the glass enclosure. Big and male, formidable and still so beautiful, even while he made the huge shower stall seem puny around him.

His face was drawn. Harsh and intent. His gaze burned. He still wore those exercise trousers of his, but he didn't seem to care when the hot water soaked them on contact.

Zara knew she should say something. *Do* something.

But instead she merely stood there, caught as surely as if he'd trapped her between his hands and held her fast. As no small part of her wished he would.

She took a deep, shuddering breath. It did nothing at all to calm her.

"I can't seem to help myself," he grated at her, sounding aggrieved and somewhat accusing. "I've broken every last one of my rules with you already."

Zara blinked. "I'm sorry."

She didn't know why she'd said that, when she was a great many things indeed and not one of them was *sorry*, but she knew that hard curve in his lethal mouth was all for her. Maybe that was all the *why* she needed.

"I believe you will be, Zara, and far sooner than you think. But we are both doomed here. Never doubt it."

He moved closer, taking more of the spray on his wide, strong shoulders, and Zara's whole world shrank down to this. *Him.* His reckless blue gaze. His hard mouth. His inky-black hair wet against his head. The water coursing down his long, lean torso, highlighting the flat, hard planes of his chest and the ridged abdomen beneath, all of it dusted with a smattering of dark hair.

That haunted, hungry look on his face.

Again, she didn't think. She slapped her hands against the wall of his pectoral muscles and ignored the jolt of heat that rebounded back into her palms, arrowing directly into her core.

"Don't start," she told him, fearless in her need. If that was what was pounding in her like a drum, incessant and much too loud. A hot, molten pulse. "Not if you plan to stop again. I can't take the whiplash."

He ignored her hands. He simply leaned toward her despite them, took her face between his callused palms, and then his mouth was on hers, deep and wild. All of that volcanic heat. All of that terrible, wonderful fire.

Zara wanted to do nothing at all but burn.

"I'm not going to stop," he said against her mouth, a gruff and hungry thing that shook all the way through her and lit her up, from sex to scalp and back again. "I can't. But I can't make you any promises about whiplash."

She was wet again, flushed and pretty and red. She was hot and slippery from the water, like a thousand fantasies. And she still tasted too damned good. It wound in him, kicking over barriers and knocking down walls, and all he could do was angle his jaw for a better fit and keep right on kissing her.

This was a terrible idea.

Chase knew it.

He'd known it when he'd stood in his own bedroom, trying to breathe deep and ignore the imperative voice inside him that urged him to turn around and go back to her. To finally get her beneath him, above him, whatever. To sink deep inside her and who cared how?

He'd known it with every step he took down that long hall, and he'd certainly known it when he stood there in that bathroom again, staring at the indistinct impression of her lovely naked body on the other side of the steamed glass. He'd watched her, head tipped back, arms wrapped around her middle, and he could have left then with her none the wiser. He'd stopped his forward momentum, after all. He'd thought better of what he was about to do, and he'd known, with every last fiber in his being, that it was a mistake.

And he'd still walked straight into that shower.

It was a terrible idea that he would deeply regret, he knew as he pulled back. He held her to him, that luscious body flush against his at last, her bright gold eyes slumberous, the water making her glorious hair dark beneath his hands. It was among the worst ideas he'd ever had.

But it didn't stop him backing her up until she was against the tiled wall and he was angling into her, holding her fast, pressing himself against the particular beauty of her heavy breasts.

"You should stop this now," he told her, gritting the words out, sounding almost as if he was angry. Maybe he was. "You should run while you can. You've no idea the things I'm capable of doing to you."

She blinked, and then her sunset eyes gleamed in a way that went straight to his groin.

"Perhaps we'd better stop, then," she agreed, her voice perfectly sweet but that clever slap beneath. The undoing of him, and he suspected she knew it. "The way you're carrying on, anything that follows can only be a disappointment, don't you think? There is such a thing as overselling, Chase."

"I'm trying to protect you," he growled. She didn't know who he was. She didn't know what he was capable of doing, what he'd done when he was still a kid—

She rolled her eyes. Evidently unimpressed.

Chase stared. He racked his brain and couldn't think of the last time anyone had dared.

"At this point I'm verging on bored," Zara said, moving her hips in a decidedly suggestive manner against him. He blew out a harsh breath between his teeth and tried to keep that great, dark thing in him leashed. "All you've done is stop when I want to go on and mutter dire threats about dark and terrible things you never quite name. Oh, and insult me. Lest we forget."

"You should be more wary then. I sound remarkably unstable."

"You don't know much about psychology, do you?" she asked, and her eyes were shining then, that little quirk in her lips so magnetic, so delicious, he didn't know if he wanted to lick it or test it with his teeth. "The single best way to get someone to walk down a dark and scary hallway is to moan and wail and issue a thousand warnings about how important it is they never, ever do exactly that."

"I am not a dark hallway," he told her. "But that doesn't mean I won't hurt you."

"Otherwise known as Pandora's box," she continued blithely. "At the bottom of which was hope, I believe. I think I'll survive, Chase. Assuming you ever stop with all the threats and warnings and dark mutterings and *do something.*"

His hands tightened. He fought a thousand battles inside himself and lost them all.

"Show me a little self-preservation, Zara. That's all I ask."

"I'm fresh out." But she stretched her arms up and looped them around his neck, arching all of those delectable curves into him, making him nearly shake with the effort of controlling himself, however tenuously. Her smile went wicked and shot through him like flame. "I'm beginning to suspect that you can't deliver."

He stared at her for a moment, then laughed.

It was a real laugh, and he wasn't sure when that had last happened. Her eyes were warm on him and filled with mischief, and the laughter moved through him fast, lighting him up and fusing with all of that need and hunger. Turning into something much more potent.

He was still laughing when he kissed her again, and it made everything that much more intense. It rocketed through him, turning him to fire. Making him wild. Desperate.

Finally, he slid his hands up the tempting curve of her waist and found her breasts. He tore his mouth from hers and looked down as he held them in his hands at last, and then he bent to pull one taut nipple into his mouth.

She moaned and bucked against him, and that made it better. He felt an answering bolt of lust in his sex. He learned the shape of her breasts, their texture, each proud ridge. He played with them, using his hands and his mouth and the faint edge of his teeth, until she was thrashing against him, her cheeks that scarlet he craved and her mouth soft and open.

Her skin was like satin, and he wanted to taste every inch of it. He pulled back from her, and her eyes fluttered open, dazed and soaked through with a delicious, decadent heat that he could feel roaring in every part of him.

"My turn," she whispered.

Chase let her push him back to the other wall of the shower and watched intently as she followed, pressing red-hot kisses along his neck and then lower to find and tease each of his own nipples. She kept going, sinking to her knees before him as she kissed and licked and tortured him, following the line of dark hair that led across his stomach and down beneath his too-wet, now much too heavy trousers.

Zara reared back on her heels and glanced up at him, and that tiny little smile curved over her mouth. She held his gaze as she reached out and shoved the trousers down over his hips, freeing him at last, and then she pulled them all the way to the floor of the shower.

Chase kicked them aside, but Zara was focused on him. On his sex, which was so close to her mouth it made it impossible for him to breathe normally.

"Finally," she murmured, which went straight to his head, far more potent than any whiskey.

She looked up at him again, and he felt his heart give a great kick inside his chest, and then she simply leaned forward and took his length deep in her mouth.

He thought he died.

Her mouth was hot and lascivious. Perfect. She reached out and took hold of him, using her hands along with her mouth and setting a lazy, devastating rhythm that Chase thought might be the undoing of him.

He had no intention of moving, but his hands sank into her hair, to keep himself grounded in the reality of her more than to guide her, and still she kept on, licking and sucking him, worshipping him, turning him inside out with every deft sweep of her tongue.

Maybe she wasn't the only one who should have been wary, he thought—

And then realized that he was an instant away from embarrassing himself.

"No," he managed to say, in a stranger's voice. "Not like this."

He hauled her up against him, slapping the water off with his free hand and then simply lifting her into his arms.

The effect on Zara, who had been nearly unflappable thus far in their brief acquaintance, was nothing short of electric.

She went pale, then stinging red, and her entire body went stiff.

"You can't *carry* me!" she hissed at him.

Chase frowned at her. He shouldered his way out of the shower stall, holding her high against him as he strode into the bedroom.

"Are you sure?" he asked. "Because I appear to be doing it."

"No, it's just— You can't— I'm too—" But whatever it was she wanted to say, she couldn't seem to get it out.

He stopped beside the bed with her still in his arms and studied her face.

"Had I known this was all it took to unsettle and silence you, I would have picked you up in the damned church," he said drily.

"You'll give yourself a hernia," she snapped at him, temper in her eyes and mortification splashed over her cheeks and down her chest.

And finally, the penny dropped.

Chase laughed. He placed her on the bed and climbed up with her, rolling them over to the center of the mattress so she was on her back and he could look down into that lovely pink face of hers. She was scowling at him as if she was furious, but he could see now what lurked behind it.

"You are perfect," he told her with absolute sincerity.

Her scowl only deepened. "I've told you before that I

don't like being patronized. I'll add to that the fact I *really* don't like it when I'm naked."

"You should always be naked," he muttered, shifting so he could press his mouth to the place where her pulse went wild in her neck. "Clothes do you a grave disservice. You have the body of a lost goddess and I intend to taste every last inch of it."

"Chase." Her voice was so taut, so constricted, he stopped what he was doing and looked up. Her eyes were big and too dark, and they searched his almost hesitantly. "I'm not the sort of woman men pick up and carry places."

He propped himself up on one elbow and traced a finger down her lovely neck, then around one breast, fascinated by the soft slope of it and the blush that stained her there, too. He could feel the shiver that worked through her, and it made the fire in him burn hotter.

"I didn't realize there was a particular type of woman suitable for lifting," he said. "They're not free weights or barbells, are they? But there are certainly a large number of weak men roaming about, it has to be said. I'm not sure they could pick up a scone if pressed to do so, much less a grown woman."

"I stood up in the bath on the first night I was here—"

"Believe me, Zara. That is not something I am ever likely to forget."

"—so that we could dispense with these games. I don't need the seduction routine." She frowned at him. "I know what I look like. I know what every woman you've ever been photographed with looks like. I know that by your standards, I'm a fat cow." Her chin lifted, and he almost believed that blazing thing in her gaze. Almost. "And don't you dare argue with me. I'm *fine* with it."

His brows rose, as much in amazement that she could be so wrong as any kind of challenge. "Evidently not."

"I'd prefer it if you'd stop pretending I'm interchangeable with Ariella," she threw at him. "It's demeaning to all of us."

He couldn't help himself. He laughed again, and she let out a sound that might well have been a curse and started to roll away from him. Chase moved over her, pinning her beneath him with his lower body and his hands on either side of her furious face, and made no effort to hide his arousal.

"Zara." He waited until she looked at him, her golden eyes too bright. "What terrible lies have you been telling yourself?"

"It's the truth," she whispered. "As I told you earlier. It was made clear to me a very long time ago."

He ran his thumbs over her marvelous cheekbones, studied the weight of the dark lashes that rimmed those gorgeous eyes of hers.

"You told me that your father is even more of an ass than I'd imagined, your mother is a rather sad narcissist, and I already know your sister is cruel and vapid," he said, and he didn't know himself then. He didn't understand where this was coming from, this patient thing in him that felt too much like kindness. *As if she matters*, a voice intoned, *and more than simply as an agent of revenge*. He couldn't acknowledge it. He refused. "Why should it matter what such people think of you? Why on earth should you accept what they call truths?"

She moved, some kind of restlessness or even panic, but she didn't try to shove him off her, and that same strange thing in him he couldn't bring himself to look at too closely called that a victory.

"I don't need the strange man I married, who I hardly know and who hasn't been particularly nice to me anyway, to tell me pretty little lies so I'll sleep with him," she rasped, emotion high on her cheeks and a matching heat in her gaze. "I came to terms with reality a long time ago. I might have a childish yearning to please my dead grandmother and my eternally disapproving father, but never fear, I'm aware of how problematic that is. And how unlikely it is I'll ever be successful. I certainly don't need you to pretend I'm beautiful on top of all that. It's insulting."

Chase felt something inside of him break free then. Dissolve, like ice in warm water, and he understood that the danger this woman posed was far greater and far deeper than he'd already imagined.

But he shut down that line of thought, because it could only lead to all those dark places he didn't want to visit. Not here. Not now.

Not when he still thought he might die if he didn't find a way inside her.

"You are beautiful," he said bluntly. "Stunning, in fact."

She made a furious sort of noise. "You're *ruining* this!"

"I beg your pardon?"

"I don't understand why this is happening to me," she said in a sort of moan, as if complaining to the ceiling above them. Then she turned that glare on him. "You're supposed to be the kind of man who somersaults in and out of random women's beds like you're auditioning for the circus. Why can't we just have sex? Why is there all this *talking*?"

He shook his head, astounded. Again. And that thing inside of him spread, gaining ground like he was the same as any other man. Like he could do this kind of thing without collateral damage. Without losing himself and destroying her—and everything else he touched—in the process.

But none of that mattered. Not now. Not while he was pressed against her slippery, naked body, at last. Not while he had the whole night to show her exactly how wrong she was.

He couldn't wait.

"I'm not going to argue about this, Zara," he told her, a low, dark thread of sound that he could *see* wind its way through her. "If you can't process the truth when it's offered, the least you can do is shut up, lie back and let me prove it to you."

She stared back at him. He smiled. "Now."

Zara meant to argue the point. But Chase merely shifted back and dropped his head to her breast, licking his way to her nipple and pulling it deep into his mouth.

And somehow, as the wildfire seized her, she forgot.

To fight. To make him admit that she was too big, too unattractive, too *much*, as she'd always been told. As she'd accepted she was, because that was the only thing that made any sense out of how she'd been treated her whole life.

She could still taste him on her tongue—the sheer, dizzying maleness of him, the strength and the soft steel. She hadn't wanted to stop, kneeling there before him as the hot water poured over them both, cocooning them in all that heated sensation. She'd wanted to keep going until he was as weakened by this madness as she felt. She'd wanted to drown in him, then do it all over again.

And then he'd picked her up like she was as light as air. Her whole world had shot straight out of its orbit that easily, leaving her hurtling through space and light-headed from the speed of it.

Chase shifted again, letting one hand smooth its way down over her belly to cup her femininity beneath, and Zara forgot all of that, too.

There was nothing but the way he kissed her, trailing fire and hunger from one breast to the other, then the valley between, making her breath catch. There was nothing but his clever hand at her very core, tracing her and teasing her, testing that proud center and then sliding deep inside of her, until she was thrashing beneath him, so close yet again—

"Look at you," he murmured in her ear, so dark and so

ruthlessly masculine she shivered. "I've never seen anything so beautiful in the whole of my life."

"Stop saying that," she managed to get out, but he was moving again. He settled himself between her legs, his heavy shaft taking the place of his fingers. And then he waited, propped up over her and poised at her entrance, while every part of her screamed and shook.

"When you stood up in that bath the first night, I lost the power of speech," he told her, and *his voice*. She thought it might ruin her, the way it moved in her and made her shake.

"I wish you would now." She tried to pull him in, her legs at his hips, her hands at his waist, but he only laughed and stayed where he was. "What kind of careless, selfish playboy are you? We should have had sex five times by now. This is like torture."

"I haven't begun to torture you," he assured her with that wondrous dark thing in his voice that swept over her like some kind of honey. "You won't have to wonder, Zara. You'll know. I'm quite inventive."

"Let's hope that in the meantime I don't die of boredom, then," she threw at him, and he laughed again in that maddening way that she thought might make her scream out her frustration in earnest—

And then he simply thrust into her, deep and hard.

Slick. Intense.

Perfect.

He was big everywhere but it didn't hurt, it simply made her *aware*. That he was deep inside her. As if he'd been made for precisely this. As if she had.

He wasn't laughing anymore. His chest was moving like he was running a race, and his beautiful face had gone stark with the same need that pounded in her. His blue eyes blazed with hunger.

He slid out, then thrust again, and they both groaned.

The whole world fell away. Chase moved over her, gathering her closer to him as he set a shattering rhythm. Zara dug her hands into his smooth, hard flesh and met him, stroke after stroke, surrendering herself completely. Letting the dark thrill take her over.

Letting him take her wherever he wanted to go.

And the irony was, as she met each glorious thrust, as they moved together in a new sort of grace they built there between them, she had never felt more beautiful in her life.

This is where you belong, something kept whispering, like a chant in her ear. *At last. Right here.*

Chase started to move faster. Deeper. He ran a hand down her side, then to the center of her need and circled it. Teasing—but he couldn't continue in that vein for long. She felt the shudder move over him and knew he was as torn apart as she was. As raw.

He pressed down hard, and she was lost. That easily.

She shook around him, crying out his name, and he drank it in with a feral growl against her shoulder. And before she could recover herself, before she could come back down, he dug beneath them to hold her bottom in his hands and cradled it.

Then he thrust into her. Harder. Deeper. Far more demanding and so good, so *perfect*, it threw her straight back into the dancing flames and then over that edge again.

And this time, when she fell off into that sweet oblivion, he followed.

Later, Zara came awake in a sudden rush, aware instantly that she was alone.

Of course you're alone, that nasty little voice inside her that sounded a great deal like her sister snapped. *What did you expect?*

She sat up slowly, almost afraid to take stock of what she felt in the aftermath. She shoved the great mess of her hair back from her face and looked around the room instead, absurdly—perhaps disastrously—touched by the fact he'd lit the fire before he'd left. It crackled and danced, throwing light all around, and its sheer exuberance made her feel better.

More like the creature Chase had claimed she was than the one she knew, deep down, she truly was.

It was a deep, inky dark outside her windows, and she wasn't at all surprised to see that it had got late. That it was Christmas Eve, technically, and she couldn't help her small smile at that. They'd come together twice more in that bed, rolling and laughing and driving each other mad, before she'd fallen into an exhausted slumber.

If it never happened again, she told herself stoutly, she'd be fine. *Perfectly fine.*

But she felt herself turn crimson anyway, her body calling her a liar. Or, worse, an addict.

She moved to the edge of the bed and pulled herself to standing with a hand on one of the four posts, letting her bare feet hit the chilly floor. Zara shivered and hurried her way across the cold expanse to her walk-in closet. She was reaching for her heaviest pair of winter socks when she heard the door open behind her in the main room.

Chase, she saw when she poked her head out of the closet. A scowling, half-naked Chase, who was holding a tray of food, which Zara found about as unlikely as she'd have found the appearance of a Christmas elf.

For a long moment, they stared at each other.

"Don't dress on my account," he growled at her, and then stalked over to the low table in front of the fire and slapped the tray down.

Zara pulled on the nearest things she could find—a pair of lounging trousers and a soft, cashmere sweater on top—and, after a brief and vicious internal struggle that was all about the vanity she'd thought she'd eradicated years before, the ugly socks, as well.

"You brought food?" she asked as she walked over to the couch where he waited, standing there in front of the fire and *glaring.*

"Is that a question or a statement of fact?"

"A simple *yes* or *no* would have sufficed, for future reference, Mr. Grouchy All The Time For Absolutely No Reason, Even On Christmas Eve."

"It's a shepherd's pie," he said, but there was that telltale crook of his lips. "Mrs. Calloway's personal recipe, which she's made for me since I was a boy. It's good."

And if he looked faintly astonished by the fact he'd told her something that could have been construed as sentimental—almost as astonished as Zara felt—he covered it with that disgruntled expression of his. She sat down gingerly on the couch, automatically crossing her legs beneath her and wincing slightly as she felt a distant pulling sensation that reminded her what they'd been up to all evening.

"You're hurt," he accused at once.

Zara started to roll her eyes, but caught the look on his face. It was more than bad temper. It was much darker. Raw torment, she would have said, and a frozen look in those blue eyes of his that resembled winter now, chilly and bereft.

She made herself smile instead, then let it turn wicked. "Only in the best possible way."

He continued to stand there as she busied herself with the meal he'd brought. She took off the silver covers and helped herself to one of the plates. And a big gulp from one of the bottles of artisanal beer he'd brought along with them, dark and bitter and perfect. Nothing like socks at all. By the time she took her first bite, he'd moved away from the fire and sat down in the chair at the far end of the table. Jerkily. As if he'd thought better of it but was doing it anyway. Zara thought of wild animals then. Hurt and hungry and physically incapable, despite their own fierce needs, of coming closer.

"I had a kitten when I was little," she told him without daring to look at him. "She was my one true love and stayed strictly indoors. One day I came home from school to find a screen knocked out and the kitten gone. I searched everywhere. I sang into bushes and called her name up and down the street and into all our neighbor's properties. Ten days later, while I was calling for her one evening, I heard her reply."

"While I'm fascinated, of course, by tales of lost kittens and little girls," Chase said in a thin voice that was about as far from *fascinated* as it was possible to be without hurting them both on the sharp edge of all that sarcasm, "I think I told you not to tell me any more of your stories, Zara."

She slid a dark look his way. He looked elegant and dangerous at once, lounging back in the prissy armchair and owning it, somehow. Making it as riotously male as he was. His black hair looked as if he'd raked his fingers through it repeatedly. His laughably perfect chest was still on mouthwatering display, and he'd chosen to wear nothing but a pair of pajamalike bottoms in a black silk that hung very low on his narrow hips. He looked like a lazy, wanton, half-naked king, supernaturally impervious to the weather and that much more attractive because of it.

He made her mouth dry. She took another pull of her beer and ignored the narrow look he was giving her from those demanding blue eyes of his, that, despite his tone of voice, had warmed slightly since she'd started talking.

"She was under the hedge down near the woods on the edge of our lawn," Zara said, and smiled when he sighed. "I had to lie on my belly in the grass and talk to her, and after a while, she finally crept out. Inch by inch, but she wouldn't come all the way to me. Eventually I was able to reach out and grab her, and her heart…!" She shook her head, remembering the heat of the little body in her hand and the surge of protectiveness she'd felt then, filling her up to near choking. "It was *pounding.* So fast. So hard. Like she was terrified of the thing she wanted most."

Chase was ominously silent. Zara didn't look at him again. She applied herself to the hearty shepherd's pie before her, relishing every bite. Mrs. Calloway had outdone herself—and she was so hungry she even ate the peas slathered in gravy, when she normally avoided peas. For a while there was nothing but the sound of cutlery against china and the pop and rush of the fire in its grate.

And then Chase's voice, that dark rasp with all its precise British intonation that made her nearly squirm in her seat, cutting through all of that.

"Am I to take it, then, that I am the lost kitten in this scenario?"

Zara bit back her smile. "A much bigger one, of course. And fierce. Very fierce and mighty and male."

He watched her as if he was a very big cat, indeed.

"And what do you imagine it is I want most?" he asked quietly. "Yet am too terrified to claim?"

Zara picked up her beer bottle, more to hold it in her hands and disguise their tendency to shake than to drink it.

"I can't imagine," she said.

But she had imagined it, of course. She had too much imagination when it came to this man, and none of it was likely to help this situation any. It couldn't make her feel less fragile than she did just then, no matter how hard she fought to pretend otherwise. And it certainly couldn't compete with the reality of what had happened between them, all of which seemed to play on an endless, erotic loop in her head.

Maybe that was what gave her the courage to square her

shoulders and ask the thing she really wanted to ask him instead, because it mattered so much more now. So much more than she was prepared to admit, even to herself. And not because he'd told her she was beautiful—but because she'd been tempted to believe he meant it.

Zara met his gaze and held it. "Why don't you tell me the truth about why you went along with this ridiculous marriage?"

CHAPTER EIGHT

FOR A MOMENT, Chase thought he'd turned to ice at last.

That he'd finally frozen straight through, even as some part of him thrilled to the notion that she could read him that easily, that completely. That she could see so far into him she already knew what he had planned for New Year's Eve. His revenge. At last.

But she couldn't, of course. She might compare him to a lost kitten here in this warm room in the light of a flickering fire, but he wasn't one. The only thing he had in common with a pet cat were claws, and his, he was well aware, were by far the more damaging.

"I'm sorry," he said when she continued to look at him in that same expectant manner that made him want to tell her whatever it was she wanted to hear, simply to make her smile—a wholly alien notion that should have petrified him. "It's still the same reason it was before."

"And I'm sorry, too," she said, as unapologetically as he had, which might have made him smile had he not understood how serious this all was, whether he wanted it that way or not. She couldn't know. He shouldn't want her to know. Her knowing would help nothing, change nothing. "But I don't believe it."

"It's not a matter of belief," Chase said, very distinctly, in his CEO voice that allowed for no argument, only obedience. "It's a matter of fact. When I took over the company after my father died, no one was pleased. They'd read too many tabloids and paid too little attention to my actual achievements. Creditors who were content to take my father's word that they would be paid in due course felt no such allegiance to me, and called their markers. I needed an influx of cash, so I agreed to merge with Nicodemus Stathis, a union my father had always championed. But Nicodemus's agreement came at a price."

Zara's gaze moved over him then to the framed photographs above the fireplace. "Your sister."

Chase wondered what she saw. Her father had sold her off in much the same way, hadn't he? Was that what Chase was to her—a man so like her own father they were well-nigh indistinguishable? The very idea sickened him, but there was no denying the fact that this particular shoe fit all too well. Perhaps to beat Amos Elliott, he'd first had to become him. The notion stung.

"My sister, yes," Chase agreed, his lips twisting as he tasted the depth of how much he hated himself for that. He'd tried to protect Mattie his whole life and then he'd sold her off like a piece of furniture to the man she'd spent years running away from. *How proud their mother would have been of him*, he thought derisively. "And before you ask, no. She didn't want to marry him. I made her do it."

"I saw pictures of their wedding in the papers, like everyone else in the entire world," Zara said in that light way of hers that managed to wedge its way into him, forcing that brightness into all the places he wanted it least. *He hated it.* He wished he could hate her, too. It would make all of this so much easier—it would make it what he'd thought it would be when he'd concocted this revenge plan in the first place. It would make everything so much less complicated. "I failed to see a single shot of you standing over her with a gun to her head."

Chase eyed her, torn between ending this conversation

in a way likely to please him most as it involved his mouth on hers, or by simply getting up and leaving as he should. He had no idea why he did neither. Why he continued to sit there before her, as if those golden eyes kept him fastened to the chair.

Maybe they did more than that, because despite everything, he kept talking.

"The other pressing issue was that your father wanted me removed from my position altogether, and of course, he greatly influences how the board votes on such things," he said instead of any one of the things he could have said that might have been safer. "He insisted I join the happy Elliott family in exchange for his backing off on his campaign to have me removed as president and CEO of my own company." And then temper crept in, because why was he doing this? She wasn't a confidante. She was a chess piece. "We've already gone over this, haven't we? I was faintly drunk at our wedding. I didn't black out. I remember the conversation we had in the limo."

"Yes," she said after a too-long moment, and he couldn't read the expression on her face. "We've discussed parts of this before. But there are ways around my father, surely, that don't require marrying a stranger."

"Are there?" He raised his brows at her in stark disbelief that she, of all people, would say such a thing, and she flushed slightly. He had a predictable reaction to that, which he ignored. Or ordered himself to ignore, more accurately. "And yet here we both sit."

"I have Daddy issues, obviously," Zara countered in that rueful way of hers that was his undoing. Every time. "What's your excuse?"

Chase let out a laugh, however little humor it had in it.

"I suppose I have Daddy issues of my own," he admitted.

He couldn't look at her then. He thought that warm gaze

of hers must have some kind of sorcery to it, and it was making him say things he'd never, ever said to another living being. He glared at the fire instead, determined to resist her, and to keep himself from saying another word.

"That's nothing to be ashamed of, Chase." Her voice was warmer than the fire. Brighter. *Dangerous.* "I think you'll find that all children of powerful men have issues one way or another, even in the happiest and healthiest of families. It's the natural order of things."

"My father and I were never close," he was astounded to hear himself say, as if he was the kind of man who shared confidences. Who *talked* about things to the women he bedded. Or at all, to anyone. Ever. "I was a grave disappointment to him in all ways."

"How can that be?" she asked, and there was no judgment in her voice. Nothing knowing or insinuating, nothing sarcastic. She simply asked. "You're his successor. You worked in his company and your job wasn't all for show."

"You have no idea if it was or wasn't."

"In fact, I do." There was no malice in the way she said that despite his tone, just that quiet confidence of hers that he found more and more addictive each time he heard it. "I'm an excellent researcher, Chase. I know what your job was in London."

"Nonetheless, he felt my exploits were not a credit to the family name," Chase said stiffly, unwilling to dig any deeper into what she'd said, because it sounded like excuses. And lord knew he was filled to the brim with those, wasn't he?

He hadn't been a successor to his father in the way she meant. He'd been the cause of his father's worst nightmare. No amount of self-imposed exile in his mother's country or quiet competence in the family company was penance enough for his sins. He knew that too well. He'd been living it for the past twenty years.

"Exploits?" Zara asked him mildly. "That sounds exciting."

"It was too exciting for my father. My sister and I spent far too much time in the tabloids for his peace of mind," Chase said matter-of-factly. And then he kept going because why not? He'd already said too much. Why not compound the error? "He preferred Nicodemus to me. He said many times that Nicodemus was the son he wished he'd had instead."

He heard her shift in her seat and didn't want to hear whatever she might say next. He didn't want forgiveness. He didn't want absolution. He deserved neither.

"And I agreed with him, Zara. After he died, the only thing left was the company. I would do anything to save it." He looked at her then, and he knew it was a cold look. Harsh. Another warning she should heed—but she didn't flinch. Of course she didn't. Not Zara, who was afraid of being lifted but not in the least concerned by anyone else's demons. "I have. I will."

She stood then, surprising him. Then he told himself it was a good thing that she had the presence of mind to stop this train wreck of a conversation. He couldn't seem to walk away, so she would have to do it for the both of them—

Except Zara didn't storm off. She didn't move her gaze from his. She simply walked to him as if there was nothing more natural in the world. Then she threw a leg over him and sat herself down astride his lap, looping her arms around his neck as if they'd sat like this a thousand times before. As if she'd been made just for him.

As if they *fit*, key to lock. Perfectly crafted for each other, from head to toe.

He groaned, telling himself he was annoyed even as his hands moved to hold her there, pressed up against his sex so he could feel her softness. *Annoyed*, he reminded himself sharply as he moved to balance her better, to help her slide in and press those stunning breasts of hers closer to him.

"Tell me more about the things you have to do to save the company," she murmured, looking down at him in a way that made him burn much brighter than that piddling fire beside them. White-hot. Deep. "Did you have to sacrifice your body?"

"I did," he said, a low rasp, and she grinned. It was wicked and lovely, a promise that seared through him, making him hard and desperate for her that quickly. That completely. "It was terrible."

"You poor thing." She rolled her hips, making them both catch their breath, and then she laughed, throaty and low and designed to make him lose his mind. It would have worked, had he still possessed a mind to lose. "Why don't you tell me all about it?"

He tilted his head back and she angled hers down, until their lips were only the scantest breath apart and her hair swirled around them, cocooning them in the fragrance of it, red and sweet. As perfect as she was.

Mine, he thought. He felt it everywhere. Like a prophecy punched into his skin. *All mine.*

Zara smiled and shifted even closer. "I have all night."

Chase grinned back at her then. He forgot all the reasons he shouldn't succumb to this. Why he shouldn't allow the situation to get any worse than it already was. Why he shouldn't blur all these lines that much further than they already had, and when he knew where this was headed. Where it would have to end.

Instead, he took her at her word.

Zara walked out of the shower the next morning feeling very pleased with herself. With life in general, come to that. Certainly with the long, dark, wild night she'd had with Chase. So pleased, in fact, that she was humming a little "God Rest Ye Merry Gentlemen" as she toweled off, which was why it took her longer than it otherwise might have to hear the other melody that kept intruding on her admittedly off-key rendition of the happy carol.

Her cell phone, she realized when she heard the voice mail chime go off a moment later. She started toward the bedside table where she'd plugged it in, frowning when it started ringing again scant seconds later.

And that frown only deepened when she saw the name on her display.

Dad.

Zara swallowed. She sat down on the edge of the high bed, wrapping the towel tighter around her while everything she'd been feeling moments before spiraled out of her, as if off into a puddle on the floor at her feet.

But you are not a coward, Zara Elliott, she told herself briskly, *whatever else you might be, and Grams asked you to give him a chance, didn't she*, and then she picked the phone up and swiped the button to answer it before she could think better of it.

"Hi, Dad," she said chirpily. "Merry Christmas Eve!"

"Spare me the holiday nonsense, Zara," Amos said in his typically blunt, rude way. "Christmas is for feeble-minded idiots who need an excuse to spend money they don't have."

Nothing ever changed with her father. On some level, Zara supposed she ought to take a kind of comfort from that. She found she couldn't quite do it.

"That attitude is likely to get you put straight on the naughty list, mister!" she pointed out in the same too-cheerful voice—and then remembered that there were a thousand reasons not to talk to her father that way.

One of them being the thunderous silence that followed, during which she shut her eyes and covered them with her free hand, imagining Amos's gritted teeth and evil expression as if he was standing in front of her.

"I expected to hear from you by now," he said after a moment, and Zara understood that this was a gift. More of a gift than she'd received from her father in a long while. That he was ignoring her suicidal attempt to tease him and she should be grateful.

Except she didn't feel grateful.

Something new and much too hot charged through her, making her feel reckless and invulnerable at once.

"Has our relationship changed in some way?" she asked, and though she couldn't seem to control her mouth the way she knew she should, she used a mild, calm tone. As if polite defiance would go over better. "The last time I called home to chat you told me you'd let me know when you wanted to talk to me, and not to try to insert myself where I wasn't wanted. I believe that was my freshman year at Bryn Mawr."

There was a stunned sort of silence. Zara felt her heart beat too hard in her chest and told herself that was excitement. Victory, not fear.

"I don't think you want to test me," he growled at her, his tone even nastier than before. "Not when there's so much at stake."

"You called me, Dad," she pointed out, and she was sure she could actually hear her father gnashing his teeth. There was probably something wrong with her that she enjoyed it.

"We're having the usual Christmas dinner tomorrow at the house," Amos told her in that vicious way of his. "I expect to see both of you. You can leave the attitude behind. It's time to see if my investment is paying any dividends, and if I think you're in my way, I won't hesitate to crush you. I hope you're hearing me."

Zara heard him. But she chose not to focus on that part of what he'd said.

"And by 'your investment,' am I to assume you mean… me?" she asked drily. "Honestly, Dad, compliments like that are going to give me a big head. I might turn into Ariella before the end of the day if you keep that up."

"I mean the connection to the Elliott family, not you," Amos belted at her, loud and rough. She held her cell phone away from her ear and could still hear him perfectly. "And you better not be playing these dumb games of yours with Chase Whitaker. You better believe I would never have involved you in this if it could have been avoided—"

"You mean, if Ariella hadn't run away, proving herself perhaps slightly less trustworthy than the daughter who showed up and walked down the aisle?" Zara asked. "Maybe?"

It was like she had no control over her own bravado. It was easier over the phone, of course, where she wasn't within arm's reach—but this was bordering on insanity, surely. Or it was brilliant and long overdue, depending on how she chose to look at it.

And she knew exactly where the confidence to talk to her father like this had come from. *You are beautiful*, Chase had said, and it moved in her like courage. Now, when she needed it most.

"You need to do what you're told for once," Amos hissed then in that cold, horrible way that still got to her. Even when he wasn't in the same room. "Don't make me adjust that attitude for you. I don't think you'd like it."

Zara was sure she wouldn't. And then she despaired of herself. Because this man wasn't worth the loyalty she felt to him and she knew it, no matter what rose-colored glasses Grams might have worn. She kept thinking there was something she could do to make him say, *"Oh, my bad, of course you're wonderful—what have I been thinking all these years?"* When she knew very well there wasn't. He was worse than all the villains she studied, and scarier, because he was real. Hell, she had no naïveté left when it came to him, and she'd still married a stranger because he'd wanted it. Was it bold to throw some attitude his way—or sad that she still answered his phone calls?

"Are you listening to me?" Amos sounded even angrier, and something like incredulous. Because no one ignored him, did they?

"The thing is, Chase has his own set of Christmas traditions," Zara lied, pressing her fingers to her temple to ward off the headache this phone call was summoning. "It means a lot to him. There's no way he's going to abandon them for me. And in fact, pushing him might cause more harm than good." She heard her father mutter something and pushed on. "But he plans to attend the Whitaker Industries New Year's Eve party. I think he wants to start a new tradition. I assume you'll be there?"

"You have one week," Amos snarled at her. "I better not go to that party on New Year's and find out you've ruined something that I've spent a lot of time and energy working on. I promise you, you will not like what happens if I do."

And then he hung up. With a slam of the landline he still used into its cradle, making Zara's ears ring in protest.

"Merry Christmas to you, too," she muttered, and put her cell phone back down on the bedside table. Then she sighed, low and long and deep.

She didn't let herself dwell too much on her father, or the horrible way he both spoke to her and made her feel. She also didn't torture herself with worrying about what consequences he might heap on her for talking to him like that when she knew perfectly well that he wanted to hear nothing at all from her but quiet obedience, if that. What would be the point? Amos was Amos. The only question was why she kept putting herself in a position where he could say those hurtful things to her.

This was for you, Grams, she told her grandmother silently. *But this is the end of it.*

She walked over to the closet and went inside, dressing on autopilot. When she was done, she'd pulled on a pair of cream-colored velvet trousers and a dark green Henley top, as if her subconscious refused to let go of the holiday spirit no matter what a dampening influence Amos had been. She combed through her damp hair and tied it in a low knot at the nape of her neck. There was a full-length mirror in the dressing part of the walk-in closet, and she stared into it, not seeing all the ways her body and Chase's body had come together in the night, so miraculous and beautiful, but seeing her father's scorn instead. Hearing Ariella's lilting, malicious laughter. The music of her whole life.

This is a coup for you.

No matter how many times Chase had told her she was beautiful, or even set about proving it, she still saw what they did. An awkward woman, nothing like skinny, who would never be anyone's first choice for anything. It was the same thing she'd always seen.

The difference was, this time, it didn't make her sad. It made her furious. At her father, her sister. At herself. At this absurd situation she never should have let herself get trapped in no matter how great the temptation to be vindicated, to honor the one family member who had treated her well, *to prove herself at last—*

But the thought that she might have missed out on Chase, however temporary this was, however long it took her to recover from it when it was finished, made her heart ache inside her chest.

And she decided that made it as good a time as any to find out how her husband felt about the holidays.

She found him in the office high on the second floor in the wing of the house Mrs. Calloway had told her housed a selection of guest suites and a separate entrance, should business associates require access to the Whitakers yet not be suitable to mix with family.

Chase was frowning down at the laptop open before him, sitting at the great desk that loomed large in the center of the room with stacks of open files before him and several serious-looking binders filled with more documents at his elbow. The only noise in the room came from his fingers tapping against the keys, and Zara found herself caught there in the doorway, watching all that quiet ruthlessness of his turned to the details of the work a man in his position must have to do all the time, but which she'd somehow never imagined him doing. Smiting minions with a glare, yes. Typing out emails like mortal men? No.

She didn't move or even breathe hard, but he knew she was there almost at once. She saw him frown in the same instant his fingers paused on the keys, and then that wild blue gaze was slamming into her from across the room.

The last time she'd seen the blue of his eyes, it had been dawn enough that there was a faint shimmer of a matching color in the dark night beyond her windows and he'd been thrusting deep inside of her.

Zara felt heat rush over her, staining her cheeks and making her body shiver into total awareness. Chase allowed only that tiny crook of his clever lips. She still felt it like the sun bursting forth after a long afternoon of rain.

Oh, the dangers this man presented. She was already as good as lost.

"Do you celebrate Christmas?" she asked, because the only other thing she wanted to talk about might involve her launching herself over that great big desk to get to him, and what if he'd only intended that to be the one night it had been? She couldn't face it. "I'm assuming you must, given the amount of holiday decorations all over this house."

"The Calloways celebrate Christmas," Chase said, sitting back in his chair and threading his hands together behind his head. He wore the kind of long-sleeved shirt that looked simple and understated and which Zara knew was therefore exorbitantly expensive. It couldn't possibly cling to his every gorgeous muscle like that if it wasn't. "They take today and tomorrow off, of course. My father and Mattie used to have Christmas here. My father called that 'roughing it,' because my sister did the cooking."

Zara would not have imagined that someone like Mattie Whitaker knew her way around a kitchen, but that was the least interesting part of what he'd said. She leaned one shoulder against the door frame.

"Your father and Mattie? Not you?"

That hard, terrible thing she'd seen several times before moved over his face then. He sat forward and dropped his hands, then stood in the same smooth motion, as if whatever it was he was thinking of was too harsh to take while seated.

"Not me." He studied her for a moment. "I prefer to ignore Christmas." It looked as if he fought with himself then; she could see it flash in all that stark blue, and she didn't know if he lost or won, but he continued. "I have since my mother died."

She felt stricken. "You were only a kid when your mother died."

"Yes."

"And you never came here and joined in with your sister and father?"

A barely noticeable pause. "No."

Zara nodded. She told herself he couldn't possibly see that swell of sympathy for the boy he'd been flood through her.

"You're in luck then," she told him. "I've just declared this the anti-Christmas."

"We don't have to declare it anything," he said in that

harsh way of his that should have felt like a slap, but didn't. Maybe because she could see that dark thing in his gaze. Maybe because she mourned for a thirteen-year-old boy who had lost too much. "We can continue to pretend it isn't happening, which I've found has worked marvelously for the past twenty years."

"You'll be happy to know that I declined my father's generous invitation to spend Christmas at his house," she said as if he hadn't spoken. "You're welcome. I've been to that Christmas dinner many times, and let me assure you, it's not as much fun as it sounds. It's a bit more like the Inquisition. Everyone ends up drunk, in tears or both. I believe it's my father's favorite day of the year."

"Yet I bet you show up every single year anyway," Chase said, and not in a complimentary way. "Dutiful and obedient to the bitter end."

"The point," Zara said loftily, "is that I've spent a lot of time hiding in the guest bathroom in the far part of the house imagining what a perfect anti-Christmas would entail."

Chase moved from around the desk then, that predatory gleam in his gaze that sent Zara's heart into overdrive.

"If it doesn't feature you naked and in my bed, I'm not interested," he said, and then he was in front of her, sweeping her into his arms and picking her up again, making her head swim.

This time, she didn't fight with him. This time, she smiled.

"I think that can be arranged," Zara murmured, and then his mouth was on hers and she didn't care what day it was. She just wanted him again.

And again.

And again, like there was nothing in the world but this. But him.

Them.

For however long it lasted.

* * *

Chase hated Christmas. He preferred to spend the whole of it working, and had spent years telling himself that he enjoyed it that way. England had always seemed to more or less shut down from roughly the fifteenth of December onward, and he'd had a whole half month to himself. He could hide away from the world and no one questioned it, as they were all too busy adhering to their traditions and Christmassing themselves half to death.

But whatever Zara called what they were doing, he found he liked it.

They'd spent most of Christmas Eve in his bed, which had suited him fine. Chase had dedicated himself to truly memorizing every last one of her gorgeous curves, and then they'd slept wrapped around each other. In a manner that Chase was opting not to question or even look at too closely, as he doubted he'd like all the alarms that set off inside him.

And now it was late on Christmas morning, and Zara was standing in the kitchens of Greenleigh, wearing a pair of his boxers, that lush little cashmere thing she'd worn before and an adorable pair of thick socks. Her hair hung about in an untamed tangle of red that reminded him of all the times he'd wrapped it around his fists or buried his fingers in it throughout the night.

And she was cooking him pancakes, like every domestic daydream he'd ever had about a family life he'd always known he didn't deserve.

"Chocolate chip pancakes," she told him over her shoulder. "Because this is the one day a year that sugar doesn't count. Well, maybe the second day, depending on your feelings about Halloween."

He could fall in love with her, he thought then, watching her fondly from the far counter with a mug of strong, dark coffee at his lips—

And then froze. Appalled.

Because, of course, he already had.

He felt that rocket through him. He felt the ancestral stones buckle beneath his feet. He felt everything he knew to be true about himself quake, then shift.

He felt.

Not that Zara noticed.

"The ultimate Christmas morning delicacy is, obviously, cinnamon rolls, but I couldn't find the right ingredients," she was saying, completely unaware what had happened right there before her. Completely oblivious to the seismic event that had knocked him sideways. She glanced over at him and laughed. "What? Everyone has a pastry preference, Chase. It doesn't make you less of a man to admit it."

And Chase couldn't help himself. He surrendered.

She fed him hot, gooey pancakes, sitting cross-legged on the gleaming countertops. She made him laugh more in the course of a single morning that he thought he had in a year. In twenty years. She was like a fountain of joy, and he wanted nothing more than to bathe in it—and he did.

Despite what was coming. Despite what he knew he would do to her before this was over.

He laid her out over that same counter and he feasted on her. Their mouths met, sweet from the chocolate and still too hot to bear, and Chase stopped holding himself back. He stopped pretending he could.

He took her in the library, stretched out on the rug before the fire, then again in one of those leather chairs. He propped her hands against the windows that looked over the river and took her from behind, reveling in the things their bodies could do together. Reveling in all the things he felt with this woman that he'd never felt before—that he'd never imagined he *could* feel.

And when he wasn't sunk deep inside of her, when she

wasn't moaning out his name, she talked. She told him of her Gothic heroes and their naive maidens. She told him of her college friends and the adventures they'd had, far removed from the merciless glare of the public. She told him what it was like to work on her master's at Yale and how she'd meant to redecorate her grandmother's cottage once it had passed to her but had found she couldn't bear to change a thing.

She cast that spell of hers with every word, pulling him deeper with every story, until Chase couldn't help but believe. That he was a normal man. That this was like any other love affair and would simply bloom and grow the longer they were together.

He believed that he could keep from hurting her. He believed that he was the man she seemed to see when she looked at him in that way of hers, with her eyes so warm they rivaled the sun and that pretty smile on her mouth.

Chase wanted to be that man more than he could remember wanting anything.

He slept with her and he woke with her, and it was very nearly dizzying, how quickly he became accustomed to both. To the scent of her hair, the sweet smell of her skin. To the soft weight of her against him in the night. To the scratch in her voice when she woke, and the way she frowned at him until she had her coffee.

He let himself believe, even though he knew better.

And then, soon enough, reality intruded in the form of a curt phone call from his brother-in-law and new chief operating officer, and their time was up. And Chase knew that while he would never forget these days he'd spent with the woman who should never have become his wife, they might also be the death of him.

It felt like a fair trade.

"We leave for Manhattan today," he barked out at her over the breakfast they'd taken to having in the private salon off the master bedroom.

"Today?" she asked, reasonably startled.

"Today." He sounded like an ass and he couldn't seem to stop himself. It was that or throw away all of his plans and collapse into her—but he couldn't do that. This wasn't about him. It was about the company. It was about the debt he could never repay. It was about revenge. He scowled into his own coffee and saw nothing but the deep, clawing murk of the past. "As soon as possible. Mrs. Calloway is packing your things."

He felt the way she looked at him, reproachful and watchful at once, but he knew better than to look her way. He'd melt. Again. Possibly for good, and then he'd truly be the failure his father had gone to his death believing he was.

"Then we'd better not linger," Zara said in that way of hers that would have made him laugh the night before. That should have made him laugh now, but he could feel himself changing. Growing his once-impenetrable armor back even as he sat there across from her in the elegant little room.

Reverting to form, something whispered inside of him.

When he looked at her, he knew his face was blank, and he told himself he was just as hollow within. And it was as much a lie as all of this pretending had been. A lie or a wish—what difference did it make? He was still the man he was. The monster hiding in plain sight, with all of that blood on his hands.

"This has been a lovely holiday," he told her, his voice chilly. "But we've only two days between now and New Year's Eve and quite a bit to accomplish." When she only stared at him as if he'd grown a new head, he let impatience seep into his expression. His voice. "Do you have a problem with that?"

He watched her shift in her seat. Her legs were folded beneath her as always and she'd pulled on one of his button-down shirts, letting the silk caress those mouthwatering curves of hers in all the ways he wanted to do. She looked edible. She looked like *his*, damn it.

But her marvelous eyes were turning wary and that wicked, carnal mouth was pressed into a too-neutral line, and this thing that never should have started was finished. Chase knew it. He welcomed it. It was time to move on.

So there was no reason at all it should tear at him as it did.

"Certainly not," she said quietly, and the Zara he knew had disappeared again, behind that cool, competent shell he remembered from their first, early days. "I believe you tasked me with finding a dress that fits me. We'd best get moving. There's no telling how long a quest like that might take."

And he told himself to get used to it when she stood up and walked away from him, because this was only the beginning. Who cared if he mourned? He was good at mourning.

This was the easy part.

CHAPTER NINE

AFTER THE ISOLATION of Greenleigh, Manhattan was a dizzying rush. All of that speed and sound, the whirl of so many lights and that pulsing energy that settled deep in the bones. Gusts of arctic winds swept through the concrete canyons and temporarily blinded Zara every time she turned a corner, no matter how well she bundled herself up against the chill.

And it was the change of scenery that was making her feel off balance and strange, Zara assured herself, and not Chase's abrupt change of demeanor since he'd announced it was time to leave for the city.

You knew this wouldn't last, she reminded herself as she walked through the famed marble lobby of The Plaza hotel, a New York City landmark and one of Zara's favorite places on earth. The Plaza was where Grams had stayed whenever she visited the city while she was still alive, and Zara had a thousand fond memories of meeting her here for tea and spending nights on the roll-out bed in the well-appointed sitting rooms of the various suites she'd stayed in. *It's your own fault if you imagined it might.*

Her friends wanted updates about her feelings. The tabloids had found her email and harassed her daily for any and all hints of something scandalous they could run. Her father left increasingly angry voice mails. And Zara had ignored all of them and spent the past two days sitting in the study on the bottom floor of the two-story suite Chase had declared was theirs for the duration, ignoring the elegant, iconic French decor and dutifully working on her thesis. When she hadn't been making the rounds to the Manhattan dress shops she could tolerate—meaning, the ones her sister didn't patronize—to find a dress that Chase might think "fit her."

Which might very well have been his restrained, very British way of telling you that you looked fat at your wedding, she reminded herself.

Not that she disagreed. But she wished he'd never said that. She wished a lot of things. It was as if that brief spate of Christmas cheer had never happened. As if it was all nothing more than the fevered fantasies of the Ugly Duckling Elliott sister who'd stolen her sister's man, as the tabloids now told it.

Until he came to her late at night, that was.

In the dark, Chase was tormented and possessed, and he took her like their lives depended on it. Zara half believed that they might. The Manhattan lights kept their bedroom bright, but he was always in shadow, always moving over her and in her like those increasingly dark dreams of hers, never showing her all those parts of himself she'd thought she'd come to know well in that big old house of his upstate.

It didn't take a genius to understand that Chase was coming undone, and that it no doubt meant this marriage was, too.

Zara made her way to the elevator and stepped inside, telling herself to be philosophical. Resigned to the inevitable, not saddened by it. She'd known the risks when she'd introduced the physical into this bloodless marriage on paper. She'd known that what happened between them would never, ever be anything but temporary.

There is absolutely no use crying over spilled milk, she

told herself briskly as the elevator rose toward their floor. *There never is.*

No matter that she was desperately afraid that she might have fallen in love with him. That was her version of "casual."

Her version of casual sucked.

She let herself into the large, airy suite dotted with huge windows that overlooked Central Park and let in so much winter light it nearly burned. She shrugged out of her coat and kicked off her boots, padding on bare feet down the hall, past the study she'd set up as her office while Chase spent his time at the Whitaker Industries headquarters several blocks south, and into the living room with its great, gold-rimmed mirror arching high above the marble fireplace.

And then stopped in her tracks when she heard a very familiar peal of laughter wafting toward her down the staircase from the second floor.

From the bedroom.

Zara stood stock-still, not believing her own ears. This was her vast swath of insecurities talking, surely, treating her to an auditory hallucination—

But footsteps followed the laughter, and she watched in a frozen kind of horror as Ariella sauntered into view.

Her feet appeared first, clad in ankle boots with her typical skyscraper heels that made no concession whatsoever to the fact that it was late December and the city streets were icy and treacherous. Then her long, skinny legs, shown to great advantage in a pair of dark leggings that hugged every lean inch of them. Then her teeny-tiny hips, wrapped in some kind of complicated metal belt that made them look that much more slight and narrow. Then her much-photographed torso, shown to great advantage in a dark blazer with a gauzy scarf tossed around her neck.

And then she was *right there* on the stairs leading down

from the bed where Chase had kept Zara awake until well into the morning—only hours ago, Zara couldn't help but think—all that carefully highlighted blond hair gleaming in the afternoon light and a self-satisfied smirk on her face as she saw who waited for her below.

She took her time. Ariella had always enjoyed a good entrance.

"Just look at you, Pud," Ariella trilled, using that awful nickname that had once been *Pudding* that she'd bestowed upon Zara for eating too much dessert one miserable summer. "What have you been doing all day? Digging sewers in the outer boroughs?"

Until that moment, of course, Zara had believed she looked good. Better than good. She'd tamed her hair into a concoction featuring a number of braids and collected it all in a big bun that she'd thought looked pretty and interesting at once. She was wearing a royal-blue sweater dress that she'd imagined made all of her curves sing. She'd been looking forward to gauging Chase's reaction to it, though she'd told herself several lies about that, as that felt slightly pathetic and needy. Still. There it was.

And she hated the fact that one snide comment from her sister made her doubt what she'd seen with her own eyes in her mirror that morning and in the dress shop she'd just left after finally finding the perfect New Year's Eve gown.

But she merely smiled, because it had been a long time since she'd showed Ariella that kind of weakness.

"Did you get confused, Ariella?" she asked, infusing her voice with concern. "I know dates and times and responsibilities aren't your strong suit. You were supposed to turn up at the church in Connecticut over three weeks ago. Not here at The Plaza today."

Ariella came to the bottom of the stairs, stopped with a bit of dramatic license and rolled her eyes.

"He's not really your husband, Zara. You're not that

delusional, are you?" She laughed when Zara only stared back at her. "Or maybe you are. I don't know how to break this to you—" and she made sure to smirk again, then let her expression turn lascivious and pointed at once "—but *Chase* doesn't seem to think he's very married."

The twelve-year-old inside of Zara reacted exactly the way Ariella wanted her to react to that insinuation—with horror and upset. Far more of both than was warranted, she understood, from something she kept trying to tell herself was "casual." But the rest of Zara was much older than twelve and had been dealing with Ariella for far too long to take anything she said to heart.

That Zara sighed. "Let me guess. You really don't like the fact that the tabloids are suggesting that I could steal a man from you."

"Because you couldn't!" Ariella spat at once. "The very idea is hilarious! *Look* at you!"

And then she waved her hand up and down, taking Zara in with the loopy gesture, making Zara feel tiny and hugely fat at once. As intended.

Zara locked that away. This wasn't junior high school, no matter how her sister behaved.

"Let this be a lesson to you, Ariella," Zara said very calmly. "When you run away from your own arranged wedding ceremony, someone else might be called upon to take your place. And the tabloids might draw their own conclusions."

Ariella glared at her, her hazel eyes narrowing. "You're loving this, aren't you?" she asked softly. "You've waited your whole, sad life for this kind of attention."

It was Zara's turn to roll her eyes. "Oh, yes," she said. "I love each and every demonstration of how little you think of me. It warms my heart. And it's always been my dearest wish to be neck-deep in one of Dad's ugly little plots. This is all a dream come true."

Ariella pursed her lips, then sashayed over to the long, ornate couch, sweeping up the long, black coat Zara had failed to notice was tucked away on the far side.

"Enjoy it while you can," Ariella advised coolly. Then she looked up, as if she could see past the gleaming chandelier and into the master bedroom suite above them, and smiled that smug smile of hers again. "I know I did."

Zara observed, as if from a far greater distance than simply the length of the sitting room bathed in too much sharp December light, that despite all the thousands of ways her sister had insulted and hurt her over the years, this was the first time she thought she really might haul off and punch her. Preferably right in her face.

But she knew better than to say anything—to give Ariella any more ammunition or satisfaction, especially if it could be construed as jealousy over Chase. She only crossed her arms over her front and waited as her sister took her sweet time buttoning up her coat and then pulling on her sleek leather gloves.

"I'll be sure to tell Dad that things are *finally* in check," Ariella was saying, sounding delighted with herself. "I know he'll be relieved. And I suppose I'll see you at the New Year's Eve party. If you still insist on coming."

"Chase wants me there," Zara replied, though she knew better than to engage like that. There was no winning a fight with someone who wasn't fighting for anything—whose single goal was to inflict pain. No winning and no point trying. But she couldn't seem to help herself. "And I am nothing if not a dutiful wife, Ariella. I find I've taken to the role like it was made for me."

Ariella didn't like that, Zara could see, and that just about made this whole scene worth it. Her pretty face twisted in something like disgust. Or maybe it was pure rage.

"It wasn't," Ariella said, and her voice was poisonous. "Like everything else, it was made for me, and you're the unwanted, unattractive backup plan. Too bad, Pud. But then, you can't imagine this was ever going to work out, can you?"

Her derisive laughter told Zara what she thought of that. And then she flounced toward the door, her ridiculous heels loud in the long hallway. Zara trailed after her automatically, leaving enough distance between them that she might—*might*—fight off the urge toward violence.

"I don't need an escort to find my way out," Ariella said as she opened the door and looked back over her shoulder. "I didn't need one on my way in, either."

"Don't be silly, Ariella," Zara replied, summoning up another smile, though this one was much sharper than its predecessors. "I'm making sure the door is locked. This is New York City. You never know what garbage might roll in off the streets."

Ariella looked surprised for a moment, but then she laughed in her superior way and closed the door behind her. And she was gone, leaving nothing but the faint scent of her perfume—a lovely bit of something citrus, of course, everything about her was calculated to be effortlessly lovely—behind.

Zara's hands shook as she threw the dead bolt, and she imagined that she could hear further peals of laughter from the hall beyond. Ringing in her ears. Taunting her. She gritted her teeth and turned back to the suite, glaring ferociously at the floor and her own feet in the tights she'd worn against the bitter cold outside. She ordered herself not to think about it. Not to give Ariella what she wanted. Not to succumb to that same self-hating madness that had chased her across so many years.

It didn't matter what Ariella had been doing here. It didn't matter what might or might not have happened between her and Chase. Because she might have the title at the moment, but Zara wasn't really his wife. She knew that. She *knew* it—even if her heart balked.

He was never yours, a caustic voice told her, harsh and true. *You can't lose something you never had to begin with.*

But when she walked into the living room, Chase was standing on the stairs that led up to the second story, staring down at her with a black look on his face and his wild blue eyes like a hard slap.

"Why the hell do you let her speak to you like that?" Chase demanded, incredulous, when that wasn't what he'd meant to say at all.

Zara stiffened, pulling herself up to her full height in the arched doorway to the hall and the door beyond, looking like a bloody queen in a soft dress that licked all over her the way he couldn't seem to stop yearning to do. The way that was driving him mad even now, when he entertained the foolish notion that he might protect her.

He, who would only hurt her, and well did he know it. It was laughable. But still, it worked in him, like need. Like madness.

"If there is a way to stop Ariella doing exactly what she wants, when she wants to do it, I've never discovered it," she said in a light, airy voice he didn't believe at all. "Did you fare any better?"

Chase scowled at her. "Is that an accusation?"

He watched her hands ball into fists and something very old and very tired moved over her face. It made that foolish thing in him that wanted so desperately to play the hero for her shift to full alert. It made him wish her sister were a man so Chase could have dealt with her as she deserved.

"We might be married," Zara said, her voice bland and cool and *he hated it*, "but I'd have to be a particular brand of idiot to imagine those vows meant anything to you. You're not required to keep any promises to me." Her gaze was dark and it hit at him. Hard. "Nevertheless, I'd like to think you're not stupid enough to sleep with Ariella when she's that obviously playing one of her games. No doubt at my father's urging." She shrugged. "But then again, the male libido makes its own rules, doesn't it? Or so says the history of the world."

Chase felt a muscle in his jaw tense, and he didn't know if he walked down the remaining stairs toward her to protect her—or make her pay, somehow, for thinking less of him when he knew that was what he should want. When it was no less than he deserved.

He should let her think he'd done exactly what Ariella wanted her to think he'd done. It would make everything easier.

"Of course I didn't touch her," he said instead, and there was no reason for it. Only Zara's lifted chin, her challenging gaze. Only that perfect mouth of hers and that stillness in the way she held herself that made him want to hold her instead. "She was here all of three minutes before you arrived, she was decidedly not welcome and I made no secret of that, and I've no idea how she wrangled a key from the front desk."

"Really?" Zara's voice was bone-dry. "No idea at all?"

He ignored that because there was a bleakness in her face then, and he couldn't stand it.

"Does she always speak to you in that manner?" he asked.

There was something he didn't understand in that hard gleam in her eyes, some truth he couldn't decode in the way she pressed her lips together, and she didn't answer him. She stalked deeper into the sitting room instead and didn't stop moving until she stood at one of the long windows.

"I'll take it that she does," he said to the fine line of her too-straight back. He wanted too many things that didn't make sense. To set her free, now, before he hurt her the way he thought he would. To gather her close and never let her go. To defend her. To help her. To change all of this before it swallowed them both whole. To believe that somehow, it wasn't already too late. "Zara, I don't want—"

"I suppose your family is perfect then," she said, and she sounded much farther away than she was, as if she'd catapulted herself out into all that winter sunshine and hung somewhere over the chilly expanse of Central Park. As if she was already gone. As if he'd already done the thing that would make her leave. His revenge. "No tensions, no arguments. No underlying darkness informing even the most banal of interactions. Just endless years of bliss and harmony. You're very lucky, Chase. But not everyone can say the same."

He didn't know what that was, that terrible thing that shook through him, an earthquake of devastation and determination, and it had too much to do with that bleak note in her voice. And that deep, black hurt where his heart should have died twenty years ago. Until Zara, he'd thought it had.

"I killed my mother."

Chase didn't know where that had come from.

For a stunned, breathless moment he thought he hadn't truly said such a thing, hadn't thrown it out like that, bald and ugly in the midst of this delicate, pretty room—that it was only inside his head, where it belonged, where it needed to stay locked up in the dark—

But Zara turned, slowly.

He didn't know what he expected to see on her face. Shock? Horror? Disgust?

She only held his gaze and waited.

And he hadn't wanted to blurt that out in the first place. He didn't know why he had. He wanted to turn and leave. To disappear into the cold embrace of this careless city and never return to this place, this subject, this woman with golden eyes who saw too much.

Instead, he moved a step closer.

"We were on holiday in South Africa. We'd been meaning to take a family trip that day, but my father was called away on some business thing or another, so it was only the rest of us." He bit out the words like they might fight back if he didn't, staccato and stern. As black as his soul. "Mattie and I were in the back. She was only little, and she kept singing this annoying song over and over. She wouldn't stop. I was cruel to her, of course, because I was thirteen and I knew there was nothing she hated so much as being called a baby."

He searched her face, but there was nothing. No reaction, no accusation. Just Zara, waiting. As if there was nothing he could say that was terrible enough to make her look at him any differently than she did then.

And he *wanted* her to know the truth, suddenly. He wanted her to see exactly who he was, so she'd stop looking at him like that. Like she had at Greenleigh, as if he was someone so much better than he was. Someone washed clean. Someone untainted by the things he'd done.

Someone worthy of her, the way he'd pretended he was for those too-few days.

"There was a man in the road," he said, his voice scratchy. After all these years, he remembered it so well. In such perfect, damning detail. "I teased Mattie about that stupid song until she hit me. My mother turned around—I remember her laughing—and then I saw the man standing there in our lane at the same time the driver did."

He shook his head, and Zara shifted, but only to fold her arms over her front in that way she had that made him envision her as the professor she'd told him she wanted to become one day, in the future when this odd little interlude of theirs was nothing but a dim, dark memory for her.

When she was free of this. Of him.

But at least she'd know exactly who it was she'd been

shackled to for so short a time. He could give her that gift. It could only help her forget him that much faster.

"There was a loud noise, like the tire going out," he said, and he realized as he did that he'd never said any of this out loud before. He'd never told this story. He'd never imagined he would want to tell it to anyone. "The driver swerved and didn't move again. He was shot, though I wouldn't know that until afterward."

Until Big Bart had told him the barest facts and instructed him to say nothing. Ever. To pretend it was an accident, for all their sakes.

"Oh, Chase," Zara breathed.

"When the car finally skidded to a stop, we'd tumbled all around. I ended up on top of Mattie. My mother was bleeding, and that was before they dragged her from the car." He was seeing more past than present then, but he saw the way her arms moved, her hands rising to cover her mouth, her eyes wide and dark with pain. "She looked right at me. She saw me. She was terrified." He swallowed, hard. "And then she told the men who held her that they'd killed her children, that her children were dead—and I covered Mattie's mouth with my hand and I held her down, so she couldn't see anything. I played dead." He stared at Zara, he mourned her, and then he said it. He spat it out, the words like poison. "And I did absolutely nothing when those men beat my mother before my eyes. Or when they shot her, too."

The room felt heavier then. Diseased, just as he was. As he must always have been, to do such a thing.

Zara didn't say anything for a long moment, and when she finally moved her hands from her mouth, all Chase could see was that too-bright warmth in her eyes. The same as always. Brighter, perhaps. He didn't understand it.

"How are you here?" she asked, her voice too quiet. "How did you survive?"

He didn't understand that question, either. "There was a passing lorry. The driver stopped and scared them off." He scowled at her. "That's all that you have to say? I did nothing. I was right there and *I did nothing*." He laughed, and even he could hear it was an awful, broken sound. "It's what I do."

"What should you have done?" she asked. There was no accusation there. No horror. It sounded like a simple question and it tore at him.

"I should have done what anyone would have done!" he raged at her. "I should have helped her!"

"How?"

She asked it so calmly. So easily. Chase felt his heart pound in his chest. Too hard. Too fast. He felt as if something giant and merciless had him fast in its grip and was tightening its hold. He felt suspended over a great abyss he couldn't even name. And all she did was stare back at him, her golden gaze so warm it made him feel scraped raw.

"Should you have abandoned your sister? What if she'd sat up and seen what was happening? What would those men have done to her?" Her voice was so calm, so cool, and Chase was sure that somehow, despite that, it was hacking him into pieces. He felt paralyzed. He felt inside out. And she only kept going. "Or perhaps you could have run out of that car and had those men beat you and shoot you in front of your mother first. Would that have been better?"

"You don't understand." He barely recognized his own voice, and he had no memory of moving, of closing the distance between them, but she was still before the windows and then he was, too. "You weren't there."

"No," she agreed. "But what you're describing—"

"I killed her as surely as if I shot her myself."

He didn't recognize his own voice, only the raw thing that the words left behind where his throat had been.

"Your mother wanted to save you, Chase," Zara said softly. Carefully, he thought, though her eyes were still so bright. "That's why she told those men you and Mattie were already dead, don't you think? Would you really undo her last sacrifice if you could?"

If the walls had started crumbling around them then, Chase wouldn't have been at all surprised. *He* was crumbling, collapsing, toppling into ash and dust, and the only thing he was sure of was that *she* was at the center of it. He wrapped his hands around her shoulders and pulled her closer, feeling outside his skin. Utterly destroyed.

"Don't you dare," he seethed at her. More monster in that moment than he'd ever been man. "Don't you dare forgive me."

Her lovely face crumpled in on itself, which he felt like a kick to his side, and then she smoothed it out somehow and offered him that smile of hers. *That* was like a kick to the head.

"Because you can't forgive yourself?" she asked. She reached up and took his face between her hands, as if he was only a man, after all. A broken, solitary man who couldn't possibly deserve all that light that beamed at him from her gaze. "Chase, you must know you couldn't have saved her. You were *thirteen*. There was only one of you, and someone had to take care of your sister."

Chase felt torn in two. He shook his head, breathing as hard as if he was running flat out through the streets of Manhattan. As if he was fighting off those ghosts that had haunted him for twenty years with his own fists, the way he'd dreamed he'd done. The way he wished he'd done.

"It doesn't matter how hard you train or how diligently you punish yourself or how completely you isolate yourself from the world," she told him, her voice so serious, her eyes so wide, tears he was stunned to understand were *for him* making gleaming tracks down her cheeks. "You can't change the fact that you're not the villain, Chase. You were a victim, too."

And he channeled all of those things inside of him, all that darkness, all those howling storms, into that dangerous heat that still moved in him—that always moved in him when she was near.

He couldn't answer her. He didn't know how. So he kissed her.

And he poured it all out. His anguish. His grief. The long years of hating himself, the separation from his family. All the things he'd called the monster in him. All the ways he'd made himself pay.

He poured it all into her, and she took it.

She took it and she reveled in it. When he went to strip that dress from her perfect body, she helped him. When he picked her up and walked her backward until she was up against the wall, she wrapped her legs around his hips and sank down onto him, sheathing him deep inside of her.

Like she was fluent in any language he might try to speak to her.

He put one hand flat against the wall, kept the other at her bottom to support her, and then he rode them both hard and wild and screaming into oblivion.

And it wasn't enough.

Nothing will ever be enough, something that felt like truth, like fate, whispered inside of him.

He was like a man possessed. He carried her up to the master bedroom and he took his time, licking his way across every inch of her lovely, flushed skin like that might bring any remaining secrets between them to the surface. Like that might heal them both.

Maybe it would, he thought. *Maybe it truly could.*

He lavished her with all the love and need and hope he'd carried around for too long, locked away so deep within him even he hadn't realized it was there.

"You're not to blame," Zara told him again and again, until it was like poetry.

He couldn't say he believed that, but he heard her. And the more she said it, the more those dark things in him yielded before the onslaught of all that glorious light.

Before *her*.

He ordered food at some point from the butler service that came with the suite and he fed her himself, like she was the queen he'd often imagined her. He took her into the spacious bath and soaked them both, muttering words he knew he'd regret later, but couldn't seem to stop from simply coming out of him, like she'd opened something up in him he'd never fully close again.

"I love you," he told her, fierce and foolish, while her tears still fell and mingled with the water all around them, like some kind of baptism he didn't deserve. "And you'll regret that, too. Trust me, Zara. You will wish you never met me, and you will curse the day you tried to heal me. The only thing that happens to the people I love is—"

"Chase," she said, twisting around in the bath and pulling his mouth down to hers. "Shut up."

He lost himself in her. He found himself in her.

And when he woke the next morning, she was draped over him as if she'd been expertly handcrafted to fit him *just so*. He brushed a hank of her fiery hair back from her face and almost smiled at the cranky little noise she made before burrowing into his chest, refusing to open her eyes.

He had never felt anything like this—a great wave of something too intense to name that swept over him, through him, into him. Nothing had ever felt like this before, in as long as Chase could remember. Nothing had ever been so *right*.

But it was New Year's Eve. Their time was up. Before

the clock struck midnight, no matter what happened with the company, he would lose her forever.

He knew he would. It was just as he'd planned from the start.

CHAPTER TEN

"If you'll come this way." The deferential young man who Zara knew was Chase's assistant politely indicated that she should follow him through the throngs of luxuriously dressed New Year's revelers, all of whom crowded into the Whitaker Industries ballroom high above Manhattan in their upper-class, expensive splendor. "Mr. Whitaker is gathering the board for a quick word before the ball drops."

"I'm not on the board," Zara said—stupidly. This man would know that already.

But she couldn't seem to help herself or the chill that rolled through her. Her hand clutched too hard around the stem of her wineglass, and she thought for a wild moment that she might snap it off. Then drop the whole mess of it on her own feet. Wouldn't *that* be elegant? Ariella—whose malevolence Zara was certain she could scent in the air, like incense—would love it.

Chase's assistant smiled. "Your presence was specifically requested."

Zara wanted to bolt. That was her first panicked reaction, and it ran deep, so deep that she shivered slightly and curled her toes hard into the too-high sandals she should have known better than to wear tonight. She wanted to leave this sparkling party, filled to the brim with so many fake smiles to her face and whispers behind her back, and run until everyone forgot, once again, that Ariella Elliott had a younger sister at all, much less that Chase Whitaker had married her.

It was the sandals that decided her. They were made for sauntering about like a woman with great confidence, not running away from the inevitable. She'd be more likely to trip and fall than make it out of this place, and she thought the humiliation of such a thing might actually kill her.

Pull yourself together, she ordered herself sternly.

"Of course," she said to Chase's assistant, and smiled coolly. "Lead the way."

And then she picked up the long, flowing skirt of her dress and followed him. He led her out of the warm, brightly lit ballroom and down one of the gilt-edged, darkwood-accented hallways that proclaimed the Whitaker wealth and status in unmistakable terms. It was quieter here, away from the crowd and the band and the anticipation of midnight. It made it impossible for Zara to be anything but all too aware that in every way that mattered, she was marching toward her own execution.

Which, funnily enough, made her think of a very similar forced march she'd made almost a month ago now, down the aisle in her hometown church.

At least this time, the damned dress fits, she told herself balefully, running her free hand over her hip and letting the smooth, pretty material soothe her.

It had been a very long day. Elastic and interminable.

Chase had been gone before she woke up, much later in the morning than she was used to waking, after such a torrid night. He'd left her instructions to meet him at his office that evening, and she'd had nothing to do but sit in that hotel suite and stew over...everything. By the time her dress had been delivered in the afternoon, she was in a state even the longest bath imaginable couldn't soothe. Yet somehow, despite her gnawing certainty that something terrible was about to happen, was *already* happening, the night had eventually fallen. The hours had finally passed.

And soon enough she'd found herself walking into Chase's vast, sleek CEO's domain in the corner of the top floor in the Whitaker Industries offices, and all of that waiting had felt like no more than an instant.

He was so beautiful, she'd thought, as stunned as if she was seeing him for the first time. Men like him were the reason formal wear had been invented, and the tuxedo he'd worn with such nonchalance made him look nothing short of edible, perfectly highlighting his lean, athletic form. His black hair had been a touch too long, his dark blue eyes had still been the color of lost things and winter seas, and she'd known then, what that mouth felt like when he whispered that he loved her, again and again, until her skin felt tattooed with it.

She'd felt marked. Claimed and entirely his—no matter that deep down, she'd known better.

"Have I mentioned that you're beautiful?" Chase had asked gruffly, his mouth a stern line and only the faintest gleam in that stunning blue gaze of his as he looked down at her. "Particularly tonight." His gaze had dropped, then heated to a hungry wildfire as he'd taken in what she was wearing. "Particularly in that dress."

"Well," she'd said mildly, "it fits."

It did more than fit. It was a marvel, and Zara had known it the moment she'd finally found it. The dress was a deep burgundy with contrasting red panels at the sides, flowing down from studded cap sleeves to the floor in a gauzy fall of fabric that hinted at her legs beneath. It sported a deep V in front that plunged down between her breasts almost to her navel, before being caught in a belt that cinched in at her waist and showed off her figure in a vaguely Grecian fashion. And that was the dress's true beauty: when she wore it, even when she'd tried it on in a tiny dressing room all by herself in a boutique on Madison Avenue, Zara felt the way she did when Chase looked at her.

It was a miracle in red. It made her feel like one herself.

He'd looked at her then for a long, heart-stopping moment, like he had nothing else to do for the rest of his life but that.

"Yes," he'd said, his voice that low rasp that had made her body prickle with heat, her core melt, her skin flush. "It certainly fits."

There hadn't been time for the need she'd seen in his gaze then, the white-hot surge of desire that had made her tremble when he'd taken her hand. He'd only offered her his arm and walked with her the way he had once before on that cold, Connecticut morning, only this time, he hadn't seemed at all drunk. Or furious.

If she'd allowed herself to think about it, she'd have said he seemed…as broken as he did determined, despite all the ground she'd foolishly thought they'd covered the night before.

I love you, he'd told her, again and again. The way he'd told her she was beautiful. And she was almost tempted to believe him, the way she had then.

But there had been no time for that, either. There had been Whitaker Industries employees and clients to meet as Chase's wife rather than Amos's problematic daughter. Speculation in all of those eyes she'd pretended not to notice, whispers everywhere she walked she'd pretended not to hear.

Even Chase's intimidatingly gorgeous sister, Mattie, who didn't look at all unhappily married to the ferocious-looking man who stood beside her, holding her waist in a protective, possessive manner.

"I can't believe Chase didn't invite us to your wedding," Mattie had said with a polite smile that Zara hadn't quite believed, though she'd dutifully returned it. "But then, the finer points of wedding etiquette seem to escape my brother, as I'm sure you've noticed."

"A Whitaker family trait," the alarmingly intense Nicodemus Stathis had said silkily from beside her, which had made Mattie's smile slip into something far more intimate.

More to the point, it had saved Zara having to reply. And Chase had muttered his excuses and moved them along to the next group of people they had to meet and greet.

"She doesn't know what happened that day," he'd rasped, his hand tightening on her back as they'd moved away. Zara's heart had seemed to contract in her chest. "My father wanted her to think it was an accident."

"Someday," Zara had said quietly, "you're going to have to tell her the truth."

He'd slid a dark look her way. "I can't imagine why."

She'd frowned at him. "Because it's her story, too," she'd said. "You shouldn't have to carry the weight of it by yourself, and she shouldn't have to stay out in the dark. It's not fair to either one of you."

"I can handle it," he'd muttered.

"Chase." She'd frowned at him, then remembered where they were and had forced her expression back to neutral. "You have a sister who would love you, I bet, if you let her. Not everyone can say that." And she'd finally admitted the truth that had surely been obvious to the entire world, but which she'd steadfastly refused to acknowledge her whole life. "I can't."

Chase had looked startled. Then something much darker. And there'd been no time for him to respond as she'd been certain he'd wanted to do, because there'd been this business associate, that connection. The business of his position, which meant hers, too.

"It's through here," Chase's assistant said then, opening

a door and reaching out to take her glass from her. She surrendered it a beat slower than she should have. "See that archway? The board room is just inside."

Zara murmured her thanks and walked on, feeling that cold panic again, starting from that knot in her stomach and radiating outward, because she already knew what was going to happen here, didn't she? Maybe not the particulars, but she'd known since she'd woken up alone this morning that this was all a goodbye. A long, painful, darkly passionate goodbye.

A long time ago they'd talked about ammunition. Target practice. *War.* How silly of her to think that what had followed rendered all of that moot. How terribly, inexcusably foolish.

It wasn't a surprise then, when she stepped into the magnificent glass-and-steel boardroom to find her father and sister talking quietly at one end of the long table. They fell silent as she walked inside, wearing identical frowns.

Wonderful, Zara thought, and ordered herself to smile. Even though it hurt.

Especially because it hurt.

She recognized most of the men arrayed around the table, all of them businessmen like her father, corporate and ruthless and sleek, no matter how merry the smiles they aimed her way. Not that it stopped her returning them, as if she was wholly at her ease.

And at the other end of the table stood Chase, with Nicodemus at his side. Mattie sat in one of the chairs that lined the far wall, an enigmatic curve to her mouth and her gaze on Zara.

"Excellent," Chase said, and she heard too much foreboding in his dark voice. Too much triumph and all that must mean. "Now we can start."

"Take a seat, Zara," her father barked at her.

But it all felt too fraught with peril. Too portentous and

strange, so Zara shook her head and folded her arms across her waist, leaning nonchalantly against the great arch.

"I'm fine right here," she demurred.

"Let's talk about you, Amos," Chase suggested in a voice she'd never heard him use before. His dark blue gaze touched hers, and it was like a flare of wild blue agony. Then he turned it on her father. "I was planning to make this the cornerstone of my speech at midnight in front of all our guests and esteemed members of the press, but out of respect for your daughter, I decided to make this more private."

"What the hell are you talking about?" Amos growled in that way that still made hairs rise on the back of Zara's neck.

"I'm talking about malfeasance," Chase said with cold precision. And no apparent attempt to disguise his own satisfaction. "A case could even be made for moral turpitude. I'm calling a vote to have you removed as chairman of this board, Amos."

"This is pathetic," Amos sneered as the other board members shifted and started murmuring to each other. "Do you really think this kind of childish attack will do anything but show us all how ill suited you are for your position? Your father must be spinning in his grave."

Beside Chase, Nicodemus shifted, thrusting his hands in the pockets of his trousers. Zara thought he looked like nothing so much as a bodyguard just then—a furious and capable bodyguard, whose attention was focused solely on her father.

"Those are serious accusations, Chase," Nicodemus said then, his rough, faintly accented voice cutting through the rising clamor in the room. "I assume you do not make them lightly."

Amos started to snarl something else, but Chase's voice overrode his, that cool, precise voice of his impossible not to heed.

"I do not," he said.

Then he turned, and it took Zara a dizzying, world-tilting moment to realize that he was looking straight at her. And then in a moment, so was everyone else.

"Zara," Chase said quietly, "why did you marry me?"

For a moment she couldn't speak. Too many things were tearing through her head, then falling like stones through the rest of her. *Ammunition*, she thought. It had always been heading here. Straight here. At last, she understood.

"Tell the truth, Zara," her father advised her in his usual, nasty way. It made her shudder.

But it was Chase she couldn't look away from. Chase, who had said he loved her. Chase, who had called her beautiful. Chase, who she'd known better than to believe. It wasn't until this very moment that she understood how deeply she'd wanted it all to be real.

Or how much she loved this man she knew, now, she really and truly could never have. Because he'd always been going to betray her exactly like this. There was no way this hadn't been his plan all along. It had all been about her father and this company, never about her.

This really had been target practice.

Her father shifted in his chair, managing to transmit his usual aggression from across the long room. Chase only stared back at her, all that wild blue unreadable. And Zara felt frozen in place. As if, were she able to draw this moment out as long as possible, if she could simply stop time right here and now, all the things she'd wanted to believe before she'd walked into this room could still be true.

"Way to draw out the suspense, Pud," she heard her sister say then, acerbic and amused. *Smug.*

And something inside of Zara simply broke. One moment it was there, and then it was gone, and she felt all the things in her that had frozen come back to life that quickly. Like the flip of a switch.

I'm sorry, Grams, she thought in that instant. *I tried.*

"I married you because my father made me marry you," she said, and she was surprised to hear how strong and smooth she sounded. As if she was either of those things. She tilted her chin up and pressed on, ignoring everything but that heartbreak of blue that gazed back at her. "He demanded that you marry his daughter so he could control you. And by extension, this company."

"And if I didn't?" Chase asked softly.

"He would remove you as CEO and president." She smiled faintly at her father's bellow of outrage. "He was quite clear about the consequences. I believe he said he would crush you either way."

"So help me, Zara—" Amos growled.

"I should say that, of course, I wasn't the first choice. He meant for you to marry Ariella. She makes for a much better conspirator. I'm really only any good with books."

Amos shot to his feet.

"This is nothing but lies," he snapped. "The two of them cooked this up. It's all a calculated maneuver to oust me—"

"You are ousted either way, old man," Nicodemus told him. "Between us, Chase and I now control seventy percent of this company. How do you think that will end for you, no matter what happens here tonight?"

"And why would I tell a lie that makes me look this pitiful?" Zara interjected then, tearing her gaze from Chase's and frowning at her father, wishing she felt as if she was seeing him for the first time—but no. He was the same man he'd always been. She simply wasn't the same woman. She had Chase to thank for that. "You've never treated me with anything but contempt, yet I married a complete stranger because you ordered me to do it. Because I had some fantasy that I could prove I was a good daughter. When the truth is, there is absolutely nothing I could ever do to please you. It took a forced march up an aisle and a monthlong marriage to a man you promised to my sister first, but I get it, Dad. I finally get it." She shifted, then looked back at Chase. For the last time, she thought, and so what if that tore her apart. She would survive that, too. Eventually. "Believe me, I get it."

And then she turned with all the dignity she could manage, whatever shreds of grace she'd ever had at her disposal, and kept her head held high as she walked away.

No matter that she left her heart there behind her, in pieces on the boardroom floor.

Chase caught up to her as she cut through the ballroom, the fastest way to the elevators.

He'd left the shouting to Nicodemus, knowing his brother-in-law was more than capable of handling the angry crowd and the necessary vote. By the end of the night—before midnight, if he had to guess—it would all be over. Chase would take his rightful place as chairman of the board and CEO. Nicodemus would become president as well as COO. And together they would usher Whitaker Industries into its next phase, as Big Bart would have wanted.

And Chase didn't care. His heart hurt, and he felt empty, and that didn't change when he took her by her arm and turned her around to face him. Because her eyes were all shadow and darkness, and he thought it might cut him in two.

"How can there possibly be anything more to say?" she asked, and she didn't sound like herself. She didn't sound like *Zara*. Her voice was brittle and harsh, as cold as her gaze. "Will you deny me three more times before the crowd sings 'Auld Lang Syne'? How biblical. Perhaps I should stone myself while we're at it, for a truly prehistoric feel—"

"Stop," he rasped, and there were too many people around. Too many avid gazes trained right on them, and he wasn't sure she'd go with him if he tried to move this conversation somewhere private. In fact, he knew she wouldn't.

He did the next best thing. He swept her into his arms and out into the middle of the dance floor.

She was stiff and furious, the hand he held in his a fist, but he didn't let go.

"Let me explain," he said. A low, desperate growl. "Please."

"No need." Her beautiful eyes were so dark as she gazed steadily back at him. "I understood all of that just fine."

"Zara—"

"You should have told me," she said, cutting him off, her voice less brittle but far more fierce. "There was no reason in the world you should have dropped that on me."

But, of course, that had been deliberate, too. Because she wasn't her sister. Because every emotion she ever had was written across her pretty face in all those shades of red. Her shock. Her humiliation when he asked the question, telling the truth before she said a word. Because she was obviously not the kind of woman who played the sorts of games everyone else in that room did.

"I see," she said when he said nothing, and she sounded beaten then. Lost.

Chase tightened his hand at the small of her back, and he forgot where they were. He forgot everything but Zara. His beautiful, noble Zara, who he'd ruined the way he ruined everything. Just as he'd told her he would do.

"I love you," he said because there was nothing else to say but that, no defense he could possibly offer, and she jerked as if he'd hit her. "And I warned you this would happen. This is what I do, Zara. I ruin everything I touch."

"We both live in the past," she said, harsh and low. "It's all we see. Your mother, my father. The horrible things my sister told me when I was a teenager. My grandmother, who already died. It's nothing but darkness. It's corrosive and blinding. It's a festering swamp."

Around them, people were chanting, and Chase realized that he and Zara had stopped moving.

"It's over now," he said. "It's done. This is the future. Here. Tonight."

"It's never over," she whispered. "It's never done. It goes on. It always goes on. It feeds on itself and consumes everything in its path. You know that as well as I do. You used it to your advantage in that boardroom."

"That part of it is over," he promised her. "There's only you and me now, and we—"

"There is no *we*," Zara said, very distinctive despite the clamor all around them, and despite the tears he saw well up in her eyes, making his chest feel so tight it was like some kind of pneumonia. "I like my Gothic terrors in books. I want to be able to trust the people in my life, not worry about the things they might be plotting. I want to be able to love the man who claims he loves me without worrying about his ulterior motives. I want better than this mess."

"Zara—"

"I want better than a man who would sell me out, Chase," she said, cutting him off as the first tear fell. "No matter why he did it."

Then the band started playing and the crowd cheered. The new year had begun, and Chase was nothing but a ghost, like the ones that had haunted him all this time. Zara had brought him back to life. And he'd killed that, too.

"Please," he said. "Don't go. Not like this."

But she only shook her head, her lips pressed tight together. Then she pulled out of his grip, and he had no choice but to let her do it. No choice in any of this, because this was his doing. Streamers and balloons poured down from above, there was kissing and singing and all the usual jubilation, and long after the crowd swallowed her up, long after she'd disappeared into the night, Chase still stood there.

He stood there a long time. Long after she'd left him. Long after the singing had turned to harder, drunker partying. Like if he stood there long enough, if he kept his vigil, it might bring her back.

When he knew the truth was, nothing could.

Zara saw the headlights flash through the windows of her cottage, interrupting the Jane Austen comfort reading she'd been doing on her very deep and comfortable chaise in front of the fire. She lifted up her head and frowned out toward the dark January night, wondering if someone had missed the turnoff for the public beach and found their way down her private lane instead—something that happened more often in the summertime.

She heard the slam of a car door and then, moments later, heavy steps on her front porch. Then a brusque, confident hand against the thick, old, sturdy New England wood of her front door. Zara didn't move. She stayed where she was, tucked up under a throw, scowling at the door. Maybe if she didn't make a single sound—

"I know you're in there, Zara," Chase said, loud enough that she could hear both that low rasp of his voice and the dark exasperation that colored it. "If not, I'll have to ring the fire department, as your chimney appears to be on fire."

She found she was up and on her feet without meaning to move, and she had no idea how that happened. Or how she found herself across the room with her hand on the doorknob. She caught herself there.

It had been four days since she'd last seen Chase. Since she'd turned and left him on that dance floor, unsure even now how she'd managed to walk at all when she'd been irreparably damaged by what had happened in that boardroom. And the truth was, she was still such a fool where he was concerned. She knew it. She could feel her body readying itself for him, as if nothing had happened. Even her idiotic heart beat harder, as if he'd never broken it so deliberately. So cruelly.

"Zara." His voice was so dark, so close. "I can say I'm sorry through the door, but it isn't the same, is it?"

She didn't mean to open the damned thing, but she did. And then he was standing there, right there in front of her. The porch light cast him in whites and golds, but that did nothing to mute the effect of those eyes of his that skewered her and made her ache immediately. He looked tired, she thought, though she hated herself for noticing. Tired and drawn, but then again, he was Chase Whitaker. Even his worst was remarkably beautiful.

And that terrible song that was him, only him, swelled inside of her.

"The door's open," Zara said as evenly as she could. "Apologize away."

His gorgeous mouth tilted up in one corner, and those wild, perfectly blue eyes lit with the sort of ruefulness she wished she could share. "Is this the part where I grovel, Zara? Is that what it will take?"

"That all depends on whether or not you feel you have reason to grovel," she retorted. She leaned against the door frame and pretended she didn't feel the icy blast of the wind that swept in from Long Island Sound and cut straight through her. She told herself it might keep her focused—less susceptible to him, somehow. "And that is between you and whatever passes for your conscience."

Chase's gaze darkened, but he nodded. "I deserve that."

This was worse, Zara decided. This was worse than what she'd been doing the past few days, which was figuring out the best coping mechanisms for living with a broken heart and the ghost of this man she seemed to cart around with her wherever she went.

Much worse.

"I already told you we don't need to do this," she said then. "I don't want to look back anymore. I'm finished."

She meant that. She'd said the same thing to her father and Ariella when they'd tracked her down here on New Year's Day, after she'd failed to respond to the approximately thirty-five thousand texts and voice mail messages they'd left her, all predictably abusive.

She'd opened the door to them, too. And she'd let them storm inside. Ariella had lounged about on the couch while her father had raged. It had gone on and on. Zara had simply stood in front of the fire and watched them both, wondering how she'd ever fooled herself into thinking there was anything there that could be saved. Or why she'd tried so hard to do the saving. *You're the only reason I tried, Grams*, she'd thought. *But no more.*

When her father had wound down, she'd smiled. Not, she'd imagined, a very nice smile.

"Okay," she'd said calmly. "I heard you. Now, please leave."

They'd both stared back at her.

"I don't think you understand the gravity of this situation," Amos had seethed at her. "I sank ten years of my life into Whitaker Industries and you handed it over to the enemy—"

"It's you who doesn't understand," she'd replied, cutting him off, which she knew happened rarely. "The only reason you're here is because you think I can do something for you. The only reason Ariella is here is because she feeds off cruelty. Neither of those reasons have anything to do with me."

"This is about our family," Amos had snapped at her.

"What family is that?" Zara had asked, and she'd known

she was doing the right thing, however overdue, because she felt nothing. No upset, no victory. Just an emptiness and her solid, bone-deep conviction that this had to end. "I'd love to have a family. My desire for one is what allowed all of this to happen. My loyalty to Grams, who you hated and Ariella ignored. But she's dead, and I shouldn't have to prove myself worthy of love you never give anyway."

"So melodramatic," Ariella had murmured. "This is about what happened at The Plaza, isn't it?"

"I used to hero-worship you, Ariella," Zara had said quietly. "Now I don't even know who you are."

Ariella had rolled her eyes, but Zara had thought that the lack of a toxic reply might have meant she'd hit a nerve. But that, too, hadn't mattered any longer.

"You listen to me, Zara," Amos had begun to say, all bluster and volume.

"No," she'd said very distinctly, and maybe it was the utter lack of fear she felt showing through on her face. She didn't know, but Amos subsided. "You listen to me for a change. We are done. If you want to regain your place at Whitaker Industries, you can figure that out on your own. I'm officially not interested."

"Are you choosing a man who would throw you to the wolves over your own family?" he'd asked as if astounded.

"Where do you think I learned how to survive being thrown to the wolves, Dad?" she'd asked coolly. "What Chase did felt like a warm bath in comparison."

"You'll regret this," Amos had promised her.

"No," she'd replied as they'd gathered their coats and stormed toward the door. "I won't. But if either of you ever do, you know where to find me."

The slam of her front door had sounded a lot like finality. But it had also sounded like freedom. She'd decided she welcomed both.

And now she stood before yet another wolf, and this time, she couldn't pretend that she was empty. She couldn't pretend she felt nothing. But she didn't want to let him in, either.

"You might be finished," Chase said now, his dark blue eyes searching hers. "But I'm in love with you."

Zara wanted to slam the door in his face, but she didn't. She turned abruptly and walked back toward the fire, fighting to keep all the things she felt from her face. She heard Chase step inside and close the door behind him.

"I knew there was no way I could get out of marrying your sister," he said without preamble. Zara scowled at the dancing flames in front of her and told herself she didn't want to hear this. But she didn't say anything that might stop him, either. "Your father had worked it all perfectly. I was vulnerable. The deal with Nicodemus was set to go through, but that only meant the company would be more powerful. Amos could still fire me from my own family legacy. And it's all I had left. It's all Mattie and I had of our father. It was the thing he loved most, save my mother."

She didn't want to melt. She didn't want to feel anything at all. She didn't want to imagine a terrified thirteen-year-old boy and how brave he must have been to try to save his sister on the side of that long-ago road, to stay quiet while he couldn't save his mother.

"And I believed I'd killed her," Chase said quietly. "I knew I had. It never occurred to me that there could be another way of looking at what happened. I'm still not sure there is, but thanks to you, there's doubt. There's the possibility that I'm not the murderer I've always known I was. But none of that was even a glimmer of possibility on any horizon a month ago, as I was set to marry Ariella."

Zara folded her arms over her middle and turned around then. She had to swallow hard. Chase stood just inside the door, still wearing his coat, ice and wet clinging to his black hair. He was all in black, except those eyes of his, and they were the clearest she'd ever seen them. No ghosts. No lonely seas. Just all that deep, dark blue. And he was looking at her like he never wanted to look at anything else again.

She had to bite her own lip hard to keep from going to him.

"I'd met your sister before. I'd certainly read about her." His mouth moved into something like a smile. "I've met a thousand women just like your sister, and I knew what I was getting into with her. It made it easy to come up with a perfect plan. But then you turned up. You looked ridiculous in that dress, and yet still, you were *you*. Zara. Undiminished by the dress, the wedding itself, your father. Like none of his dirt could touch you at all. You rose above it."

"That's absurd, revisionist history," she snapped, before she could think better of it. "You were drunk."

"Then you stood up in that bathtub," he said, his voice going hoarse. "And you brought me back to life, Zara. In that instant. But I'd set a course. I had a plan. And it had never occurred to me to factor in emotions. I wasn't capable of any, I thought, and certainly your sister isn't. But how could I have planned for you?" His mouth crooked again when she only stared back at him, stricken. "I can't imagine that anyone could spend any kind of time with you and *not* fall in love with you. I can't. I didn't."

"This isn't love, Chase." She ignored the wild cartwheels of her heart, her stomach. "This is guilt."

"I haven't felt anything but guilt in twenty years," he threw back at her. "I know the difference."

She shook her head hard.

"It's too late," she said quickly before she second-guessed herself. "I gave you everything I had and you chose to waste it by using me as a pawn in your little battle with my father."

"I regret using you," he said. His gaze slammed into hers. "But you hardly gave me 'everything,' Zara. You only told me that you might have loved me, that you wished you could have done, when you were leaving me."

"Was that the time to declare my love? Right after you'd showed me that yet again, the only time anyone pretends any interest in me at all is when they need me for their own ends?"

"You're making my point for me."

"I am doing no such thing," she snapped at him, and she didn't realize she'd advanced on him until his hands came up to grip her shoulders, and then it was too late. "I spent twenty-six years trying to work things out with my father. I'm not going to waste another day playing the same kind of games with a man who's just like him."

"Zara." Chase's voice was like gravel. "I'm not your bloody father."

"Tell me what the difference is!" she raged at him. She didn't realize her hands had curled into fists until she thumped them on his chest. "Tell me how I'm supposed to tell you apart! You both do nothing but use me, tell me whatever lies you think might make me do what you want, never giving one thought to what *I* might need!"

"The difference is, I'm here." His voice was low and commanding at once, and it cut through the storm in her, beating it back. He shifted, running his thumbs below her eyes to clear away a wetness she hadn't even known was there, and her heart clutched in her chest. "The difference is, I'm not going anywhere. I can't live without you, Zara. I don't want to try. The house is too big, the bed keeps me awake and it *hurts*. I don't care what it takes, I'll do it. Just come back to me. Let me prove that whatever happened over the past month, whatever happened at that damned party, *this marriage* is the one good thing to come of it."

She pulled back from him then, though she couldn't seem to step away, almost as if her bones had melted and she was stuck right there.

"You're not meant for someone like me," she told him, and he would never know how hard that was for her to admit. "I know that. If you don't know it now, you will. I'm sure the relentlessly negative attention from all those tabloids that adore my sister and yours will help."

Chase studied her for one of those too-long moments.

"This is what I'm talking about," he murmured. "Who gives a toss what the tabloids say? They're a soap opera—this is life. And you've spent much too long listening to petty comments from the likes of your sister."

"And yet, at the end of the day, you're the one who used me," she said quietly.

"Just as you used me, Zara," he pointed out gently. "To work out your Daddy issues. The only difference is that what I did was successful."

She scowled at him then, and he sighed.

"I have an idea," he said. "Let's decide that the rest of this marriage is ours. Just ours, starting now. No outside voices or influences need apply." His gorgeous eyes bored into hers. "Because they don't matter. They never will."

And she wanted to fall forward and trust that he'd catch her. She wanted to believe him this time. God, how she wanted that. But she shook her head again and moved back a step, because the truth was, imagination never got her into anything but trouble. Her heart was a liar. And if she didn't protect herself now, who would?

Chase reached over and took her hands in his, and then he dropped down before her. Onto one knee. Zara blinked. Then realized she'd stopped breathing.

"What are you doing?" she managed to ask, almost soundlessly.

"Zara Elliott," he intoned, and his eyes were the blue of summer skies, with only the faintest hint of shadows to mar them. "You've already married me. But I want you to be my wife. I want you to honor the vows you made to me when I was a stranger, and I want to dedicate myself to honoring the same vows I made when I'd had a little too much whiskey. I want to spend years sleeping in the same bed with you and waking there, too. I want to build a life from all the little pieces we stitched together in this past month. I want you to tell me stories, and I want to make more of our own. I want you to teach me how to love Christmas the way you do. I want to love you so well and so deeply that when you look back, you'll forget you ever doubted I could."

And Zara stopped fighting. She stopped trying to ward him off when he was the one thing she wanted, so desperately it actually made her shake. She couldn't help the tears that coursed down her cheeks then. She knelt before him, pulling her hands from his to hold his face. His beautiful face, and the far more complicated and fascinated man behind it.

"Chase," she whispered. "I do love you. I do."

"I know you do," he whispered back, *fierce and certain and hers*, she thought. *Finally hers.* "And we have all the time in the world to prove it."

And Zara would never know who moved first, but then they were kissing. Again and again, as if that was the only truth that mattered. That beautiful fire that was only theirs. That wild bright light that burned in both of them.

And would keep on burning, she thought then—holding him close, this man who had been her husband before he became the love of her life—forever.

Christmas Day, one year later...

"This has a certain, horrifying symmetry," Mattie said as she stood by the window in their father's office at Greenleigh that Chase had long since claimed as his own. "But if you order me to marry someone else, Nicodemus will have a fit."

Chase grinned, imagining the reaction his brother-in-law—a man he was beginning to consider a friend, even a good one—might have. One similar to his own, were anyone to suggest he marry someone other than Zara.

His Zara, who he loved more now than he'd ever imagined he could love anyone. He thought it grew by the day, making his shriveled old heart expand every time she smiled at him. And she smiled at him quite a lot.

She'd insisted they celebrate Christmas this year, and so they were. Dutifully, Chase had thought, at least on his part—but it was impossible not to succumb to the infectiousness of Zara's pure, unadulterated joy. That was true whether the subject was a book, a holiday or life itself. It had been her determination to reach out to Mattie that had created the bridge between Chase and his sister that, in his guilt, he'd never known how to build.

"Of course we're inviting them for Christmas dinner," Zara had said, and as she'd been naked at the time and moving her hips against his in a way designed to make him her slave, he'd agreed.

Though secretly, Chase knew he would have agreed anyway. Especially now that the family lawyer had produced that letter.

"Are you ready?" he asked Mattie.

She turned and looked at him, her expression serious. "How can I answer that? Is anyone ever ready for a message from beyond the grave?"

The letter was from Big Bart, their attorney had told

Chase when he'd delivered this letter only yesterday. And their father had left very specific instructions about when and how it was to be opened.

When they're both happy, were the words on the envelope.

"Apparently, the Calloways are the informants," Chase said now. "We've been deemed happy." He swallowed. "Is that right?"

Mattie blinked. Then smiled.

"Yes," she said softly. "I'm happy. You did a good thing, Chase. The truth is, I wish I'd married Nicodemus a long time ago."

It was another great weight from his back. He nodded. Then he held up the envelope. Mattie inclined her head, indicating that she was ready. Chase thrust his thumb beneath the sealed flap, opening it and pulling two sheets of paper forth, both written on in pen in Big Bart's distinctive hand. Mattie came to stand next to him, and with another glance at each other, they began to read.

> My dearest Chase and Mattie
>
> If you are reading this letter, I am no longer with you and more than that, I left you the same coward I've been all these years.
>
> The facts aren't pretty. Your mother's death was no one's fault but mine. She warned me a thousand times not to cross certain lines, but I didn't listen. I was Big Bart Whitaker. I knew best. Those gunmen were after me, not her—

"Gunmen?" Mattie asked in a horrified whisper.

"I'll tell you everything I know," Chase promised, his throat raw. "In a minute."

Mattie's eyes were too bright, but she nodded. And Chase felt better than he would have admitted a year ago when she moved even closer, like he really was the big brother he knew he'd never been to her. Maybe this was a new start, too.

—and I've never forgiven myself for not being there. For letting my sins catch up to the people I love most. I wish I could have told you both all of this. I wish I knew how. I wish I'd been the father you deserved, but the only way I knew how to be that man was with your mother's help. Without her, I fear I was nothing but a blowhard. Lost and no good to anyone.

I know you've both blamed yourself for that day in your own ways. I hope that this letter finds you truly happy, as you deserve to be. As your mother would have insisted you be. And I want you to know that while I couldn't save her or protect you from living through the terror of it, I could and did find the men responsible and make certain they, at least, paid for their crimes. I imagine the great hereafter is where I'll pay for mine.

But you, Chase and Mattie, have paid more than enough. My beautiful children. I couldn't be more proud of either one of you. I wish I'd been man enough to let you know that when it mattered the most.

Live. Love. Let the past lie where it should.

Be happy. I know you'll be better—you already are.

Dad

And when they finally emerged from the study, Chase felt like a different man. Weightless. Washed clean. He'd told Mattie everything he knew. They'd talked about their memories, their guilt. Their shared dismay over the distance in their relationship. Mattie wasn't the only one to grow a bit misty-eyed.

As they walked down the great stairs of Greenleigh together, Chase was sure he could feel all the usual ghosts around them. But this time, there was nothing but joy. And, finally, hope.

A great, bright future instead of the terrible past.

As they walked into the kitchens, they could see Zara sitting up on one of the counters, talking with great animation to Nicodemus, who looked as ferocious as ever, even as he listened closely to whatever it was she was saying. Zara waved her hands about, the light catching the rings she wore on her left hand—two that Chase had put there the day he'd married her, and the pretty band of yellow diamonds that reminded him of her eyes when she was happy, that he'd put there a month later. When he'd been able to admit he was in love with her.

Mattie laughed beside him, a sound that reminded him of the happy girl she'd been the last time he'd heard it. "What do you think they're talking about?"

"With Zara?" Chase grinned as Zara looked over and caught his eye, and her broad smile was still like sunshine, even inside. Even when she taught him every day how deeply he could love, and how fiercely she could love in return. How beautiful all of this was, if they were together. "It could be anything. Let's hope it's not the story of her bloody lost kitten."

Because that particular story was his.

And the truth was, Chase really had been terrified of the one thing he'd wanted most, and Zara had saved him, too.

* * * * *

Bailey wanted to say no. She desperately wanted to throw the offer back in his face and walk out of there, dignity intact.

But two things stopped her. Jared Stone was offering her the one thing she'd sworn she'd never stop working for until she got it. And despite everything else that he was—impossible, arrogant and full of himself—he was brilliant. And everyone knew it. If she worked alongside him as his equal she could write her own ticket. Ensure she never went back to the life she'd vowed to leave behind forever.

Survival was stronger than her pride. It always had been. And men having all the power in her world wasn't anything unusual. She knew how to play them. How to beat them. And she could beat Jared Stone too. She knew it.

She stared at him. At the haughty tilt of his chin. It was almost irresistible to show him how wrong he was. About her. About all women. This would be her gift to the female race…

"All right. On two conditions."

His gaze narrowed.

"Double my salary and give me the title of CMO."

"We don't have a Chief Marketing Officer."

"Now we do."

"Fine."

His curt agreement made her eyes widen, brought her swinging back around.

"You can have both."

She knew then that Jared Stone was in a great deal of trouble. And she was in the driver's seat. But her euphoria didn't last long. There was no doubt she'd just made a deal with the devil. And when you did that you paid for it.

Jennifer Hayward has been a fan of romance and adventure since filching her sister's Harlequin Mills & Boon® novels to escape her teenaged angst.

Jennifer penned her first romance at nineteen. When it was rejected, she bristled at her mother's suggestion that she needed more life experience. She went on to complete a journalism degree and intern as a sports broadcaster before settling into a career in public relations. Years of working alongside powerful, charismatic CEOs and traveling the world provided perfect fodder for the arrogant alpha males she loves to write about, and free research on the some of the world's most glamorous locales.

A suitable amount of life experience under her belt, she sat down and conjured up the sexiest, most delicious Italian wine magnate she could imagine, had him make his biggest mistake and gave him a wife on the run. That story, THE DIVORCE PARTY, won her Harlequin's *So You Think You Can Write* contest and a book contract. Turns out Mother knew best!

A native of Canada's gorgeous east coast, Jennifer now lives in Toronto with her Viking husband and their young Viking-in-training. She considers her ten-year-old book club, comprising some of the most amazing women she's ever met, a sacrosanct date in her calendar. And some day they will have their monthly meeting at her fantasy beach house, waves lapping at their feet, wine glasses in hand.

You can find Jennifer on Facebook and Twitter.

Recent titles by the same author:
CHANGING CONSTANTINOU'S GAME
THE TRUTH ABOUT DE CAMPO
AN EXQUISITE CHALLENGE
THE DIVORCE PARTY

THE MAGNATE'S MANIFESTO

BY

JENNIFER HAYWARD

Published in Great Britain 2014
by Mills & Boon, an imprint of Harlequin (UK) Limited,
Eton House, 18-24 Paradise Road, Richmond, Surrey, TW9 1SR

ISBN: 978-0-263-25033-6

Harlequin (UK) Limited's policy is to use papers that are natural, renewable and recyclable products and made from wood grown in sustainable forests. The logging and manufacturing processes conform to the legal environmental regulations of the country of origin.

Printed and bound in Spain
by Blackprint CPI, Barcelona

THE MAGNATE'S MANIFESTO

A big thanks to Rebecca Avalon of *Strip and Grow Rich*, the original stripper school, for taking me inside the life and mind of a dancer and helping me bring Bailey to life. I can't thank you enough!

CHAPTER ONE

THE DAY THAT Jared Stone's manifesto sparked an incident of international female outrage happened to be, unfortunately for Stone, a slow news day. By 5:00 a.m. on Thursday, when the sexy Silicon Valley billionaire was reputed to be running the trails of San Francisco's Golden Gate Park, as he did every morning in his connected-free beginning to the day, his manifesto was dinner conversation in Moscow. In London, as chicly dressed female office workers escaped brick and steel buildings to chase down lunch, his outrageous state of the union on twenty-first-century women was on the tip of every tongue, spoken in hushed, disbelieving tones on elevator trips down to ground level.

And in America, where the outrage was about to hit hardest, women who had spent their entire careers seeking out the C-suite only to find themselves blocked by a glass ceiling that seemed impossible to penetrate stared in disbelief at their smartphones. *Maybe it was a joke*, some said. *Someone must have hacked into Stone's email,* said others. *Doesn't surprise me at all*, interjected a final contingent, many of whom had dated Stone in an elusive quest to pin down the world's most sought-after bachelor. *He's a cold bastard. I'm only surprised his true stripes didn't appear sooner.*

At her desk at 7:00 a.m. at the Stone Industries building in San Jose, Bailey St. John was oblivious to the firestorm her boss was creating. Intent on hacking her way through her own glass ceiling and armed with a steaming Americano with which to do so, she slid into her chair with as much grace as her pencil skirt would allow, harnessed a morning dose of optimism that today would be different, and flicked on her PC.

She stared sleepily at the screen as her computer booted up. Took a sip of the strong, acrid brew that inevitably kicked her brain into working order as she clicked on her mail program. Her girlfriend Aria's email, titled "OMG," made her lift a recently plucked and perfected brow.

She clicked it open. The hot sip of coffee she'd just taken lodged somewhere in her windpipe. *Billionaire Playboy Ignites International Incident With His Manifesto on Women*, blared the headline of the variety news site everyone in Silicon Valley frequented. *Leaked Tongue-in-Cheek Manifesto to His Fellow Mates Makes Stone's Views on Women in the Boardroom and Bedroom Blatantly Clear.*

Bailey put down her coffee with a jerky movement and clicked through to the manifesto that had already generated two million views. *The Truth About Women,* which apparently had never been meant for anyone other than Jared Stone's inner circle, was now the salacious entertainment of the entire male population. As she started reading what was unmistakably her boss's bold, eloquent tone, she nearly fell off her chair.

Having dated and worked with a cross-section of women from around the globe, and having reached the age where I feel I can make a definitive opinion on the subject matter, I have come to a conclusion. Women lie.

They say they want to be equals in the boardroom, when in reality nothing has changed over the past fifty years. Despite all their pleas to the contrary, despite their outrage at the limits the "so-called" glass ceiling puts on them, they don't really want to be hammering out a deal, and they don't want to be orchestrating a merger. They want to be home in the house we provide, living the lifestyle to which they've become accustomed. They want a man who will take care of them, who gives them a hot night between the sheets and diamond jewelry at appropriate intervals. Who will prevent them from drifting aimlessly through life without a compass...

Drifting aimlessly through life without a compass? Bailey's cheeks flamed. If there was any way in which her life couldn't be described, it was that. She'd spent the last twelve years putting as much mileage between her and her depressing low-income roots as she could, doing the impossible and obtaining an MBA before working herself up the corporate ladder. First at a smaller Silicon Valley start-up, then for the last three years at Jared Stone's industry darling of a consumer electronics company.

And that was where her rapid progression had stopped. As director of North American sales for Stone Industries, she'd spent the last eighteen months chasing a vice president position Stone seemed determined not to give her. She'd worked harder and more impressively than any of her male colleagues, and it was generally acknowledged the VP job should have been hers. Except Jared Stone didn't seem to think so—he'd given the job to someone else. And that hurt coming from the man she'd been dying to work for—the resident genius of Silicon Valley.

Why didn't he respect her as everyone else did?

Her blood heated to a furious level; bubbled and boiled and threatened to spill over into an expression of uncontrolled rage. *Now she knew why.* Because Jared Stone was a male chauvinist pig. The worst of a Silicon Valley breed.

He was...*horrific.*

She forced a sip of the excessively strong java into her mouth before she lost it completely and slammed the cup back down on her desk. Flicked her gaze back to her computer screen and the "rules" on women Jared had also gifted the male population with.

Rule Number 1—All women are crazy. And by that I mean they think in a completely foreign way from us that might as well come from another planet. You need to find the least crazy one you can live with. If you elect to settle down, which I'm not advocating, mind you.
Rule Number 2—Every woman wants a ring on her finger and the white picket fence. No matter what she says. Not a bad thing for the state of the nuclear family or for you if you're already on that trajectory. But for God's sake know what you're getting yourself into.
Rule Number 3—Every woman wants a lion in the bedroom. She wants to be dominated. She wants you to be in complete control. She doesn't want you to listen to her "needs." So stop making that mistake. Be a man.
Rule Number 4—Every woman starts the day with an agenda. A cause, an item to strike off her list, the inescapable conclusion of a campaign she's been running. It could be a diamond ring, more of your time, your acknowledgment that you will indeed agree to meet her mother... Whatever it is, take it from me, just say yes or say goodbye. And know that saying goodbye might be a whole hell of a lot cheaper in the long run.

Bailey stopped reading for the sake of her blood pressure. Here she'd been worrying that the personality conflict she and Jared shared, which admittedly was intense, was the problem. The thing that had been holding her back. Their desire to rip each other apart every time they stepped foot in a boardroom together was legendary within the company, but that hadn't been it. No—in actual fact, he disrespected *the entire female race.*

She'd never even had a chance.

Three years, she fumed, scowling at her computer screen as she pulled up a blank document. Three years she'd worked for that egocentric jerk, racking up domestic sales of his wildly popular cell phones and computers… For what? It had all been a complete waste of time in a career in which the clock was ticking. A CEO by thirty-five, she'd vowed. Although that vision seemed to be fading fast….

She pressed her lips together and started typing. *To whom it may concern: I can no longer work in an organization with that pig at the helm. It goes against every guiding principle I've ever had.* She kept going, wrote the letter without holding back, until her blood had cooled and her rage was spent. Then she did a second version she could hand in to HR.

She wasn't working for Jared Stone. For that beautiful, arrogant piece of work. Not one minute longer. No matter how brilliant he was.

Jared Stone was in a whistling kind of mood as he parked in the Stone Industries lot, collected his briefcase and made his way through the sparkling glass doors. A five-mile run through the park, a long hot shower, a power shake and a relatively smooth commute could do that for a man.

He hummed a bad version of a song he'd just heard on the radio as he strode toward the bank of elevators that ran up the center of the elegant, architecturally brilliant building. When life was this good, when he was on top of his game, about to land the contract that would silence all his critics, cement his control of his company, he felt impermeable, impenetrable, *unbeatable,* as if he could leap tall buildings in a single bound, solve all the world's problems, bring about world peace even, if given the material to work with.

A gilded ray of brilliance for all to follow.

He stuck his hand between the closing elevator doors and gained himself admittance on a half-filled car. Greeted the half dozen employees inside with the megawatt smile the press loved to capture and made a mental note of who was putting in the extra effort coming in early. Gerald from finance flashed him a swaggering grin as if they shared an inside joke. Jennifer Thomas, PA to one of the vice presidents, who was normally a sucker for his charm, did a double take at his friendly "good morning" and muttered something unintelligible back. The woman from legal, what *was* her name, turned her back on him.

Strange.

The weird vibe only got worse as the doors opened on the executive floors and he made his way through the still-quiet space to his office. Another PA gave him the oddest look. He looked down. Did he have power shake on the front of his shirt? Toothpaste on his face?

Power shake stains ruled out, he frowned at his fifty-something PA, Mary, as she handed him his messages. "What is *wrong* with everyone today? The sun is shining, sales are up..."

Mary blinked. "You haven't been online, have you?"

"You know my theory on that," he returned patiently. "I spend the first couple hours of my day finding my center. Seven-thirty is soon enough to discover what craziness has befallen the world."

"Right," she muttered. "Well, you might want to leave your Buddhist sojourn by the wayside and plug in quickly before Sam Walters arrives. He'll be here at eleven."

Jared brought his brows together at the mention of the

chairman of the Stone Industries board. "I have nothing scheduled with him."

"You do now," she said. "Jared—I—" She set down her pen and gave him a direct look. "Your *document*, your manifesto, was leaked on the internet last night."

He felt the blood drain from his face. He'd only ever written two manifestos in his life. One when he'd started Stone Industries and put down his vision for the company, and the second, the private joke he'd shared with his closest friends last night after a particularly amusing guys' night out on the town.

It had not been intended for public consumption.

From the look on Mary's face, she was *not* talking about the Stone Industries manifesto.

"What do you mean leaked?" he asked slowly.

She cleared her throat. "The document…the whole document is all over the Net. My mother emailed it to me this morning. She asked what I was doing working for you."

The thought crossed his mind that this was all impossible because his buddies would never do that to him. Not over a joke intended for their eyes only…. *Had someone hacked into his email?*

He looked down at the wad of messages in his hand, his chest tightening. "How bad is it?"

Her lips pursed. "It's everywhere."

Thinking he might finally have taken his penchant for stirring things up too far, he knew it for the truth when his mentor and adviser Sam Walters walked into his office three hours later, Jared's legal and PR teams behind him. The sixty-five-year-old financial genius did not look amused.

Jared waved them into chairs and attempted a preemptive strike. "Sam, this is all a huge misunderstanding. We'll put out a statement that it was a joke and it'll be gone by tomorrow."

His vice president of PR, Julie Walcott, lifted a brow. "We're at two million hits and climbing, Jared. Women are threatening to boycott our products. This is not going away."

He leaned back against his desk, the abdomen he'd worked to the breaking point this morning contracting at his appalling lack of judgment in ever putting those words on paper. But one thing he never did was show weakness. Particularly not now when the world wanted to eat him alive. "What do you suggest I do?" he drawled, with his usual swagger. "Beg women for their forgiveness? Get down on my knees and swear I didn't mean it?"

"Yes."

He gave her a disbelieving look. "It was a *joke between friends*. Addressing it gives it credence."

"It's now a joke between you and the entire planet," Julie said matter-of-factly. "Addressing it is the only thing that's going to save you right about now."

The sick feeling in his stomach intensified. Sam crossed his arms over his chest. "This has legal implications, Jared. Human rights implications... And furthermore, as I don't need to remind you, Davide Gagnon's daughter is a charter member of a woman's organization. She will not be amused."

Jared's hands tightened around the wooden lip of his desk. He was well aware of Micheline Gagnon's board memberships. The daughter of the CEO of Europe's largest consumer electronics retailer, Maison Electronique—with whom Stone Industries was pursuing a groundbreaking five-year deal to expand its global presence—was an active social commentator. She would *not* be amused. But really...it had been a *joke*.

He let out a long breath. "Tell me what we need to do."

"We need to issue an apology," Julie said. "Position it as a private joke that was in bad taste. Say that it has nothing to do with your real view of women, which is actually one of the utmost respect."

"I *do* respect women," he interjected. "I just don't think they're always honest with their feelings."

Julie gave him a long look. "When's the last time you put a woman on the executive committee?"

Never. He raked a hand through his hair. "Give me a woman who belongs on it and I'll put her there."

"What about Bailey St. John?" Sam lifted his bushy brows. "You seem to be the only one who thinks she hasn't earned her spot as a VP."

Jared scowled. "Bailey St. John is a special case. She isn't ready. She thinks she was *born* ready, but she isn't."

"You need to make a *gesture,*" Sam underscored, his tone taking on a steely edge. "You are on thin ice right now, Jared." *In all aspects,* his mentor's deeply lined face seemed to suggest. "Give her the job. *Get* her ready."

"It's not the right choice," Jared rejected harshly. "She still needs to mature. She's only twenty-nine, for God's sake. Making her a VP would be like setting a firecracker loose."

Sam lifted his brows again as if to remind him how sparse his support on the board was right now. As if he needed *reminding* that his control of the company he'd built from a tiny start-up into a world player was in jeopardy. *His company.*

"Give her the job, Jared." Sam gave him an even look. "Smooth out her raw edges. Do not blow ten years of hard work on your penchant for self-ignition."

Antagonism burned through him, singeing the tips of his ears. He'd stolen Bailey from a competitor three years ago for her incredibly sharp brain. For the potential he knew she had. And she hadn't disappointed him. He had no doubt he'd one day make her into a VP, but right now, she was the rainbow-colored cookie in the pack. You never knew what you were going to bite into when she walked into a room. And he couldn't have that around him. Not now.

Sam gave him a hard look. "Fine," Jared rasped. He'd figure out a way to work the Bailey equation. "What else?"

"Cultural sensitivity training," his head of legal interjected. "HR is going to set it up."

"That," Jared dismissed in a low voice, "is not happening. Next."

Julie outlined her plan to rescue his reputation. It was solid, what he paid her for, and he agreed with it all, except for the cultural sensitivity training, and ended the meeting.

He had way bigger fish to fry. A board's support to solidify. His own job to save.

He paced to the window as the door closed behind the group, attempting to digest how his perfect morning had turned into the day from hell. At the root of it all, the abrupt end to his "relationship" with his trustworthy 10:00 p.m. of late, Kimberly MacKenna. A logical accountant by trade, she'd sworn to him she wasn't looking for anything permanent. So he'd let his guard down, let her in. Then last Saturday night, she'd plopped herself down on his sofa, declared he was breaking her heart and turned those baby blues on him in a look he'd have sworn he'd never see.

Get serious, Jared, they'd said. He had. By 10:00 a.m. on Monday she'd had his trademark diamond tennis bracelet on her arm and another one had bitten the dust.

He'd been sad and maybe a touch lonely when he'd written that manifesto. But those were the rules. No commitment. His mouth twisted as he pressed his palm against the glass. Maybe he should have given his PR team the official line on his parents' marriage. How his mother had bled his father dry… How she'd turned him into half a man. It would have made him much more sympathetic.

Better yet, he thought, Julie could devote more of her

time to controlling the industry media that wanted to lynch him before he'd even gotten his vision for Stone Industries' next decade off the ground. When you'd parlayed a groundbreaking new personal computer created on your best friend's dorm room floor into the most successful consumer electronics company in America, a NASDAQ gold mine, you didn't expect the naysayers to start calling for the CEO's head as soon as the waters got rough. You expected them to trust your vision, radically different though it might be from the rest of the industry, and assume you had a plan to revolutionize the connected home.

A harsh curse escaped his lips. They would rather tear him down than support him. They were carnivores waiting for the kill. Well, it wasn't going to happen. He was going to go to France, tie up this exclusive partnership with Maison Electronique, cut his competitors off at the knees and deliver this deal signed and sealed to the board at his must-win executive committee meeting in two weeks.

All he had to do was present his marketing vision to Davide Gagnon and secure his buy-in, and it was a done deal.

Spinning away from the window, he stalked to the door and growled a command at Mary to get Bailey St. John in his office *now*. He would promote her all right. But he wasn't a stupid man. He would leave himself a loophole so when she proved herself too inexperienced for the job, he could put things back where they belonged until she *was* ready.

His last call was to his head of IT. Whoever had hacked into his email was going to rue the day they'd crossed him. He promised them that.

Bailey had cooled her heels for fifteen minutes outside Jared Stone's office, resignation in hand, when Mary finally motioned her in. Her ability to appear civil at an all-time low, she pushed the heavy wooden door open and moved into the intensely masculine space. Dominated by a massive marble-manteled fireplace and floor-to-ceiling windows, it was purposefully minimalistic; focused like its owner, who preferred to roam the hallways of Stone Industries and work alongside his engineers instead of sitting at a desk.

He turned as her heels tapped across the Italian marble, and as usual when she was within ten feet of him, her composure seemed to slide a notch or two. She might not pursue his assets like every other female in Silicon Valley, but that didn't mean she could ignore them. The piercing blue gaze he turned on her now was legendary for divesting a woman of her clothes faster than she could say "only if you respect me in the morning." And if that didn't do it for you, then his superbly toned body in the exquisitely tailored suit and his razor-sharp brain would. He supplemented his daily running routine with martial arts, and there was a joke going around the Valley that it was no coincidence his name was Stone. As in All-Night Jared Stone.

Heat filled her cheeks as he waved her into a chair, his finely crafted gold cuff links glinting in the sunlight. She started to sink into the sofa, obeying him like his mindless disciples, before she checked herself and straightened. "I'm not here to socialize, Jared. I'm here to resign."

"Resign?" His usual husky, raspy tone held an incredulous edge.

"Yes, resign." She pushed her shoulders back and walked toward him, refusing to let the balance of power shift in his favor as it always did. When she was a few inches away from him, she stopped and lifted her chin, absorbing the impact of that penetrating blue gaze. "I'm tired of *drifting aimlessly* through this company with you lying to me about where I'm headed."

His gaze darkened. "Oh, come on, Bailey. I would think you of all people could take a joke."

She sank her hands into her hips. "You meant every word of that, Jared. And to think I thought it might be our personality conflict that's been holding me back."

The corner of his mouth lifted, the scar that sliced through his upper lip whitening as skin stretched over bone. "You mean the fact that every time we're in a boardroom together we want to dismantle each other in a slow and painful manner?" His eyes took on a smoky, deadly hue. "That's the kind of thing that gets me out of bed in the morning."

The futility of it all sent her head into an exasperated shake. "I think I've always known what your opinion of women is, but stupid me, I thought you actually respected me."

"I do respect you."

"Then why has everything I've done over the past three years failed to impress you? I was a star at my last company, Jared. You recruited me because of it. Why give Tate Davidson the job I deserved?"

"You weren't ready," he stated matter-of-factly, as much in control as she was out of it.

"In what way?"

"Your maturity levels," he elaborated, looking down his perfect nose at her. "Your knee-jerk reactions. Right now is a good example. You didn't even think this through."

Antagonism lanced through her, setting every limb of her body on fire. "Oh, I thought it through all right. I've had three years to think it through. And forgive me if I don't take the maturity criticism too hard after your childish little stunt this morning. You wanted to make every male in California laugh and slap each other on the back? Well, you've succeeded. Good on you. Another ten steps backward for womankind."

His hooded gaze narrowed. "I put women in the boardroom when they deserve it, Bailey. But I won't do it for appearance's sake. I think you're immensely talented and if you'd get over this ever-present need to prove yourself, you'd go far."

She refused to let the compliment derail her when he was never going to change. Pushing her hair out of her face, she glared at him. "I've outperformed every male in this company over the past couple of years, and that hasn't been enough. I'm through trying to impress you, Jared. Apparently the only thing that would is if I was a D cup."

His mouth tipped up on one side in that crooked smile women loved. "I don't think there's a man in Silicon Valley who would find you lacking in any department, Bailey. You just don't take any of them up on it."

The backhanded compliment made her draw in a breath. Sent a rush of color to her cheeks, heating her all over. She'd asked for it. She really had. And now she had to go.

"Here," she said, shoving the letter at him. "Consider this my response to your manifesto. And believe me, this was *draft two*."

He curled his long, elegant fingers around the paper and scanned it. Then deliberately, slowly, his eyes on hers, tore it in half. "I won't accept it."

"Be glad I'm not filing a human rights suit against you," she bit out and turned on her heel. "HR has the other copy. I'm giving you two weeks."

"I'm offering you the VP marketing job, Bailey." His words stopped her in her tracks. "You've done a phenomenal job boosting domestic sales. You deserve the chance to spread your wings."

Elation flashed through her, success after three long years of brutally hard work overwhelming her, followed almost immediately by the grounding notion of exactly what was happening here. She turned around slowly, pinning him to the spot with her gaze. "Which member of your team advised you to leverage me?"

If she'd blinked she would have missed the muscle that jumped in his jaw, but she didn't, and it made the anger already coursing through her practically flammable. "You want me," she stated slowly, "to be your poster child. Your token female executive you can throw in the spotlight to silence the furor."

His jaw hardened, silencing the recalcitrant muscle. "I want you to become my vice president of marketing, Bailey. Full stop. You've earned the opportunity, now take it. Don't be stupid. We're due at Davide Gagnon's house in the south of France the day after tomorrow to present our marketing plan, and I need you by my side."

She wanted to say no. She desperately wanted to throw the offer back in his face and walk out of here, dignity intact. But two things stopped her. Jared Stone was offering her the one thing she'd sworn she'd never stop working for until she got it—the chance to sit on the executive committee of a Fortune 500 company. And despite everything that he was—an impossible, arrogant full-of-himself jerk—he was the most brilliant brain on the face of the planet. And everyone knew it. If she worked alongside him as his equal she could write her ticket. Ensure she never went back to the life she'd vowed to leave behind forever.

Survival was stronger than her pride. It always had been. And men having all the power in her world wasn't anything unusual. She knew how to play them. How to beat them. And she could beat Jared Stone, too. She knew it.

She stared at him. At the haughty tilt of his chin. It was almost irresistible to show him how wrong he was. About her. About all women. This would be her gift to the female race…

"All right. On two conditions."

His gaze narrowed.

"Double my salary and give me the title of CMO."

"We don't have a chief marketing officer."

"Now we do."

His eyes widened. Narrowed again. "Bailey…"

"We're done then." She turned away, every bit prepared to walk.

"Fine." His curt agreement made her eyes widen, brought her swinging back around. "You can have both."

She knew then that Jared Stone was in a great deal of trouble. And she was in the driver's seat. But her euphoria didn't last long as she nodded and made her way past Mary's desk. There was no doubt she'd just made a deal with the devil. And when you did that, you paid for it.

CHAPTER TWO

BY THE TIME newly minted CMO Bailey threw herself into a cab twenty-four hours later, bound for San Jose Airport and a flight to France, the furor over Jared Stone's manifesto had reached a fever pitch. Two feminist organizations had urged a full boycott of Stone Industries products in the wake of what they called his "irresponsible" and "repugnant" perspective on women. The female CEO of the largest clothing retailer in the country had commented on a national business news show, "It's too bad Stone didn't put this much thought into how he could balance out his board of directors, given that the valley is rife with female talent."

In response, a leading men's blog had declared Stone's manifesto "genius," calling the billionaire "a breath of fresh air for his honest assessment of this conflicted demographic."

It was madness. Even now, the cabbie's radio was blaring some inane talk show inviting men and women to call in with their opinions. She listened to one caller, a middle-aged male, praise Jared for his "balls" to take the bull by the horns and tell it like it was. Followed by a woman who called the previous caller "a caveman relic of bygone days."

"Please," Bailey begged, covering her eyes with the back of her hand, "turn it off. Turn the channel. Anything but him. I can't take it anymore."

The cabbie gave her an irritated glance through his grubby rearview mirror, as if he were fully on board with Jared's perspective and *she* was the deluded one. But he switched the channel. Bailey fished her mobile out of her purse and dialed the only person she regularly informed of her whereabouts in case she was nabbed running through the park some night and became a statistic.

"Where are you?" her best friend and former Stanford roommate, Aria Kates, demanded. "I've been trying to get you ever since this Jared Stone thing broke."

"On my way to the airport." Bailey checked her lipstick with the mirror in her compact. "I'm going with him to France."

"*France?* You didn't *quit?* Bailey, that memo is outrageous."

And *designed* for shock value. She shoved the mirror back in her purse, sat back against the worn, I've-seen-better-days seat, and pursed her lips. "He made me CMO."

"I don't care if he made you head of the Church of England.... He's an ass!"

Bailey stared at the lineup of traffic in front of them. "I want this job, Aria. I know why he promoted me. I get that he wants me to be his female executive poster child. I, however, am going to take this and use it for what it's worth. Get what I need, and get out."

Just as she'd done her entire life: clawed on to whatever she could grasp and used her talent and raw determination to succeed. Even when people told her she'd never do it.

She heard Aria take a sip of what was undoubtedly a large, extra-hot latte with four sweeteners, then pause for effect. "They say he's going to either conquer the world or take everyone down in a cloud of dust. You prepared for the ride?"

Bailey smiled her first real smile of the day. "Did I ever tell you why I came to work for him?'

"Because you're infatuated with his brain, Bails. And, I suspect, not only his brain."

Bailey frowned at the phone. "Exactly what does that mean?"

"I mean the night he hired you. He didn't start talking to you because he detected brilliance in that smart head of yours. He saw your legs across the room, made a bee-line for you, *then* you impressed him. You could almost see him turn off that part of his brain." Her friend sighed. "He may drive you crazy, but I've seen the two of you together. It's like watching someone stick the positive and negative ends of a battery together."

She wrinkled her nose. "I can handle Jared Stone."

"That statement makes me think you're delusional.... Where in France, by the way?"

"Saint-Jean-Cap-Ferrat in the south."

"Jealous. Okay, well, have fun and keep yourself out of trouble. If you can with him along..."

Doubtful, Bailey conceded, focusing on the twelve-hour flight ahead with the big bad wolf. Admittedly, she'd had a slight infatuation with Jared when she joined Stone Industries. But then he'd started acting like the arrogant jerk he was and begun holding her back at every turn, and after that it hadn't taken much effort at all to put her attraction aside. Because she was only at Stone Industries for one thing: to plunder Jared Stone's genius and move on.

The master plan hadn't changed.

Traffic went relatively smoothly for a Friday afternoon. Bailey stepped out of the cab in front of the tiny terminal for private flights, ready to soak up the quiet luxury from here on in. Instead she was blindsided by a sea of light, crisscrossing her vision like dancing explosions of fire. *Camera flashes*, her brain registered. She was stumbling to find her balance, her pupils dilating against the white lights, when a strong hand gripped her arm. She looked up to see Jared's impossibly handsome face set in grim lines.

"Good God," she muttered, hanging on to him as his security detail forged a path through the scrum. "Do you regret your little joke now?"

"I regretted it the minute it was broadcast to the world," he muttered, shielding her from a particularly zealous photographer. "But basking in regret isn't my style."

No, it wasn't…although looking amazing in the face of adversity was. Because in the middle of the jostling reporters, acting like a human shield for her, he looked all-powerful and infinitely gorgeous. His fitted dark jeans molded lean, powerful legs, topped by a cobalt-blue sweater that made his piercing blue eyes glitter in the late afternoon sun. And then there was his slicked-back dark hair he looked like he'd raked his hands through a million times that gave him a rebellious look.

When you tossed in the pirate-like scar twisting his upper lip, you ended up with a photo that would undoubtedly make front page news.

A photographer eluded Jared's two bodyguards, stepped in front of them and stuck a microphone in Bailey's face. "Kay Harris called you a figurehead this morning on her talk show. Any comment?"

One hundred percent true. Bailey gave the reporter an annoyed look as Jared started to push her forward. She leaned back against his arm, stood her ground and ignored his warning look. "I think," she stated, speaking to the cameras that had swung to her, "Mr. Stone made an error in judgment he apologized for earlier today and that's the end of the matter." She waved her hand at the man at her side. "I work for a brilliant company that is on a trajectory to become the world's top consumer electronics manufacturer. I couldn't be prouder of what we've accomplished. And I," she forced out, almost choking on the words, "have the utmost professional respect for Jared Stone. We have a great working relationship."

The questions came at her fast and furious. She held up a hand, stated they had a flight to catch, and let Jared propel her forward, hand at her back.

"Since when did you become such a diplomat?" he muttered, ushering her through the glass doors into the terminal.

"Since you created that *zoo* out there." She came to a halt inside the doors, took a deep breath and ran a hand over herself, straightening her clothing.

Jared did the same. Before the airline staff could spirit them off, he squared to face her. "Thank you. I owe you one."

Her gaze flickered away from the intensity of his. Looking at Jared was like observing all the major forces of the world stuffed inside the human form—charging him with an energy, a polar pull that was impossible to ignore. She'd felt it that night he'd headed purposefully across that bar and ended up hiring her. But she didn't need it now. Not when she'd gotten used to avoiding it. Not when she had to spend twelve hours crammed into a private jet with him absorbing it all.

"It was nothing," she muttered. "Don't make me regret saying it."

"I'm sure you already do...." His taunting rejoinder brought her head up. The dark glint in his eyes reminded her that there was still a line in this détente of theirs. And she knew there was. She really did. She just couldn't help it with him.

"After you," he murmured, extending his arm toward the exit to the tarmac. She swished past him out the doors and up the stairs of the sleek ten-person Stone Industries jet. She'd been on it once before, the decor a study in dark male sophistication. An official boarded the plane for a cursory check of their passports, and Bailey settled into one of the sumptuously soft leather seats and buckled up.

They took off, the powerful little jet racing down the runway, leaving San Jose behind in a blur of bright lights. As soon as the seat belt lights were turned off, Jared unpacked a mountain of paperwork and suggested they rehearse the presentation. He wanted it perfect—was determined to rehearse until they'd nailed every last key message. Given that it was new material to her, it might be a long night.

It was. Their styles were completely opposite. She liked to wing it. Jared, emphatically not. Not to mention how intimidating he was when his passion for the subject took over. She could usually hold her own with the best of them, but he was too smart, too intense and too sure of himself to make it easy. So she resorted to her default mechanism of asking a million questions. Knowing the material inside out. What was the logic behind that statistic? Why were they making that particular point here? And wasn't this information coming too soon? Shouldn't they save it to drive the stake in at the end?

Four hours and four rounds of the presentation later, Jared flung himself into the chair opposite her and rubbed his hands over his eyes. "This isn't working. You are the queen of going off script."

"It makes it believable," she countered, sinking down into her chair. "I'm playing off you, taking your lead. You're the one who keeps losing the thread."

He gave her a disbelieving look. "*I'm* following the slides."

She blew out a breath as her head pounded like a jackhammer. "You are stuck on *process*. Try loosening up. It works beautifully. It's even better when I have an audience."

He dropped his head into his hands. "That idea scares me. Greatly."

She looked longingly up at the flight attendant as she came to hover by them with an offer of predinner drinks. "I'm having a glass of wine. I've earned it."

"Whiskey," Jared muttered to the attendant, then sat back and watched her from beneath lowered lashes. The *longest* lowered lashes she'd ever encountered. Divine, really.

He opened them. "What is it about falling in line you have a problem with?"

Bailey widened her eyes. "I fall in line when I need to. Witness the press a few hours ago, for instance."

"You are challenging everything I say," he growled.

"I'm challenging everything that doesn't make sense," she countered. "I haven't seen the material before. I'm an objective eye."

"It's *perfect*."

"It *would be* perfect if everyone in the world thought exactly like you. Davide Gagnon has a creative streak. You need to appeal to that side of him."

"An expert on him already?" he asked darkly.

"I did my homework." She tore open the can of cashews she'd brought with her and shoved some in her mouth. "What value would I be adding if I fell into line like a trained seal?"

His expression inched darker. "A lot of value right now, given that this is the only rehearsal time we're going to get. Davide is famous for his social lifestyle. You can bet he'll have things lined up every night."

She winced inwardly. Although her research had told her all about Davide Gagnon's lavish lifestyle and love of a good party that tended to include the who's who of Europe, and she'd packed accordingly, it was the type of lifestyle she abhorred. She'd seen too much of it when she'd danced in Vegas. The destructive things money and power could do. And although she'd been the girl who'd always gone home after the show rather than take advantage of the high rollers who'd wanted to lavish hefty doses of it on her, she'd seen—*experienced*—enough of it for a lifetime.

Focus on her studies, fast-track her business degree and get the hell out. That had been her mantra.

"Bailey?"

Jared was looking at her, an impatient look on his face. She blinked. "Sorry?"

"I was saying Davide has a fondness for blondes." He folded one long leg over the other and popped a handful of the cashews into his mouth. "I consider you my secret weapon."

Hostility flared through her, swift and sharp, spurred by a past she couldn't quite banish. "If you're suggesting I flirt with him, that's not going to happen. And I can't believe you would even say that considering that your reputation is hanging by a thread and I'm the only thing keeping it afloat."

He gave her a long look as the attendant set their drinks on the table. "I was asking you to charm him, Bailey, not sleep with him."

She gave him a black look. "Forgive me for misinterpreting. We women apparently don't have a use beyond securing ourselves a rich man and keeping ourselves within the style *to which we've become accustomed.* So I just wanted to make the point."

A muscle jumped in his jaw. "You were the one who just said I'd made my apology and bygones should be bygones. Perhaps you can walk the walk, no?"

"That was for public consumption." She pulled the glass of deep ruby-red wine toward her. "Know that in my head, my respect for you personally is at an all-time low."

His eyes darkened to a wintry, stormy blue. "As long as your professional respect is intact, I'm not worried about your personal opinion."

And there it was. The man who cared about nothing but his driving need for success. He was legendary for it and she couldn't fault it because she was his mirror image.

She took a sip of the rich, velvety red, her palate marking it a Cabernet/Merlot blend. "I am curious about one thing, though."

He lifted a brow.

"What *is* your real opinion of women?"

His sexy, quirky mouth turned up on one side. "If you think I'm answering that, you consider me a stupider man than I am."

'No, really," she insisted, waving her glass at him. "Utterly open conversation. I want to know."

His long-lashed gaze held hers for a moment, then he shrugged. "I think the science of relationships goes back as far as time. As far as the cavemen… We men—we hunt, we gather. We provide. Women want us for what we can offer them. And as soon as we can't, as soon as they get a better offer," he drawled, "we are expendable."

She was shocked into silence. Considering that her mother had been the only thing keeping her family afloat with her alcoholic father off work more than on, that seemed ludicrous. "You can't really mean that," she said after a moment. "It's crazy to lump all women together like that."

He lifted a shoulder. "I never say anything I don't mean. You wonder who's really in the power position, Bailey? Think about it."

She frowned. "What about women who can provide for themselves? Women who bring equal billing to a relationship?"

"It doesn't survive. There is *always* a balance of power in a relationship. And when a woman has that power, the relationship is never going to last. Women *need* us to dominate. To be the provider."

She stared at him. "That's ridiculous. You are impossible."

His white smile glittered in the muted confines of the jet. "I've been called worse this week. Come on, admit it, Bailey. A strong woman like you must like a man to take control. Otherwise you'd walk all over him."

A warning buzzed its way along her temple, signaling dangerous territory she wasn't about to traverse. She lifted her chin, met his magnetic blue gaze head-on. "On the contrary. I like to be in control, just like you do, Jared. *Always*. Haven't you figured that out already?"

His lashes lowered, studying, *analyzing*. "I'm not sure I have one-fifth of you figured out."

The air between them suddenly felt too hot, too tight in the close confines of the jet that pulsed with the powerful throb of the engines. She took a jerky sip of her wine. "Should we get back to rehearsing?"

"After dinner." He nodded toward her glass. "Enjoy your wine. Be social."

She searched for something in the safe zone to talk about and when that didn't materialize, pulled her purse toward her, searched for her lipstick and fished it out to reapply.

"Don't."

Her hand froze midway to her face. "Sorry?"

"Don't reapply that war paint. You look perfect the way you are."

Heat spread through her, confusing in its intensity. He'd probably used that line on a million women. Why it made her drop the lipstick back into her purse and reach for her lip balm instead was unclear to her.

Jared sat back in his chair, tumbler balanced on his knee, hand sliding over his dark-shadowed jaw. "There's never a hair out of place, Bailey. Never a cuff that isn't perfectly turned or posture that isn't ramrod straight even after four hours of rehearsing." He angled an inquisitive brow at her. "Why the facade? What are you afraid people might find out if you relax?"

She angled her chin at him. "I work in the male-dominated, testosterone-driven world of Silicon Valley. Men will walk all over me if I show weakness. You of all people should know that."

"Perhaps," he agreed. "Is that why you turn them all down? Let them crash and burn for all to see?"

She looked him straight in the eye. "That would be their stupidity if I wasn't showing interest. And *this* would be my personal life. Which doesn't have any part in this conversation."

"Oh, but it does," he said softly, his gaze holding hers. "We need to go into this presentation like a well-oiled machine. Know each other inside out, anticipate each other's needs, move together seamlessly until we are a well-orchestrated symphony. Trust each other implicitly so no matter what they throw at us we've got it. But right now, we're a disjointed mess. The trust is lacking, and I don't feel like I know the first thing about you."

A chill stole through her. No one *knew* her. Except perhaps Aria. They knew Bailey St. John, the composed, successful woman she'd created by sheer force of will. A female version of the Terminator…and not even bulldog Jared was going to uncover the real her.

Which necessitated an act. And a good one. She cradled her wineglass against her chest, leaned back in her seat and slid into the interview persona she'd perfected over the years. "Ask away, then. What do you want to know?"

Jared leaned back in his seat and took in Bailey's deceptively relaxed pose. He had no doubt from her evasive answers that she was going to give him only half the story. But something was more than nothing, and their disastrous rehearsals necessitated some kind of synergy. They weren't connecting on any level except to strike sparks off each other. Which might be fine, desirable even, in the bedroom, but it wasn't helping here with the board breathing down his neck, the press all over him like a second skin and the most important presentation of his life looming.

If he and Bailey walked into that room right now and did the presentation, they would go down like the Titanic. Slowly and painfully. Davide Gagnon might have handpicked them as partner, but it didn't mean they could afford to miss one detail about why he should work with them.

He took a long sip of his whiskey, considered her while it burned a comforting trail down his throat, then rested the glass on his thigh. "I was reviewing your résumé. Why the University of Nevada-Las Vegas for your undergrad? It seems an odd choice given your East Coast upbringing. Florida, right?"

She nodded.

"Did you win a scholarship?"

The closed-off look he'd watched her perfect over the years made a spectacular reappearance. "I'm from a small city outside Tampa called Lakeland. Population less than a hundred thousand. I wanted to go away to school, and UNLV had a good business program."

"So you chose Sin City?"

"Seemed as good a place as any."

"Did it have something to do with the fact that you aren't close to your family?"

"Why would you say that?"

"You never go home for the holidays and you never talk about them. So I'm assuming that's the case."

Her cool-as-ice blue eyes glittered. "I'm not particularly close to them, no."

Definitely a sore point. "After UNLV," he continued, "you did your MBA at Stanford, my alma mater, then went straight to a start-up. Did you always want to work in the Valley?"

She nodded. "I loved technology. I would have been an engineer if I hadn't gone into business."

"They're in high demand," he acknowledged. "Where did the interest come from? A parent? School?"

She smiled. "School. Science was my favorite class. My teachers encouraged me in that direction."

"And your parents," he probed. "What do they do?"

If he hadn't been watching her, studying her like a hawk, he would have missed the slight flinch that pulled her shoulders back. She lifted her chin. "My father is a traveling salesman and my mother is a hairdresser."

His eyes widened. Her less-than-illustrious background didn't faze him. The complete incompatibility with the woman in front of him did. He would have pegged her as an aristocrat. As coming from money. Because everything about Bailey was perfect. Classy. From the top of her glamorous platinum-haired head, to her finely boned striking features, to her long, lean thoroughbred limbs, she was all sophistication and impeccable taste.

"So no man, no family," he recounted. "Who do you spend your time with when you're not at work? Which is always..." he qualified.

"You should be happy I do that. It's why your sales numbers are so impressive."

"I like my employees to have a life," he countered drily. "Maybe you have a man tucked away none of us know about?"

"I have friends," she said stiffly.

"Pastimes? Hobbies?"

Silence. He watched her mind work, coming up with a suitable answer, not the real one. "I like to read."

"Ah yes," he nodded. "So home on a Friday night with a book in your hand? That sounds awfully dull."

"Maybe I import my men," she offered caustically. "Ship them in for a hot night, then send them home."

His mouth twisted. "Lucky guys."

"Jared..." She exhaled heavily. "Are you ever politically correct?"

"Hopefully this weekend, yes."

She smiled at that. "Is that enough information so we can move on to *your* fascinating backstory?"

"It'll do for now." He poured her another glass of wine, intent on loosening her up.

She shifted, tucked her legs underneath her. He kept his eyes off her outstanding calves with difficulty. "Is it true," she asked, running a finger around the rim of her glass, "that you got your love of electronics tinkering in the garage with your father?"

He nodded. "My father was an investment banker, but his true love was playing with a car's engine until the sun came down. I would go out to the garage and work alongside him until my mother made me come in."

She frowned. "You said *was*. Did your father pass?"

"No." He felt his defenses sliding into place like a cell door at Alcatraz, but opening up was a two-way street, and he needed to give, too. "He embezzled money from the bank, from his personal circle of friends, got himself in way too deep and tried to win it all back in a high-stakes game in Vegas."

Her eyes widened. "And they chewed him up?"

"Yes."

"I'm so sorry. I didn't know."

His mouth twisted. "It's not exactly in my bio. The bank did a good job of hushing it up, and only those close to it ever knew."

Her gaze moved uncertainly over his. Wondering why he'd told her.

"Trust," he said softly. "You shared with me. I need to

share with you. I meant what I said, Bailey. This is the most important presentation of Stone Industries' history. There are no second chances. We have to nail it. We have to trust each other completely walking into that room or we don't do it at all."

She chewed ferociously on her lower lip. He kept his gaze on hers. "You have to be all-in, Bailey."

She nodded. "I'm in."

His shoulders settled back into place, his relief palpable. "Good. Let's try to streamline that second section so it sings…"

She leaned forward to grab her notebook. "Ouch."

"What?"

She pressed her fingers to her neck. "I slept the wrong way last night. I've got the worst kind of kink."

She'd been struggling with it throughout their rehearsals, he realized. He'd thought her funny faces had been grimaces about the material but instead, she'd been in pain.

"Come here."

She looked blankly at him.

He held up his hands. "These are magic. Let me work it out so you can concentrate."

She shook her head. "It'll work itself out. Let's just figure that p—"

He got to his feet and pointed at the chair. "We need to nail this and you obviously can't concentrate. Five minutes."

She came then, taking the chair he'd vacated, as if she knew further resistance was futile. "Here," she told him, pointing to the spot. He sat down on the side of the chair, ran his fingers over her skin lightly, then with increasing pressure.

"Here?"

"Yes," she groaned. "Be careful. It's killing me."

"Trust, remember?" He set about working the immobilized muscles, on the outer edges first, loosening them up so he could find his way to the source of the pain. He felt her relax, let him in. But only so much. And he wondered how often, if ever, this woman allowed herself to be vulnerable?

I like to be in control, just like you do, Jared. Always.

Kink worked fully, he brought his hands down to her shoulders and started to work out the knots from where she'd held herself stiff from the pain. He expected her to protest. Say that was fine. But she didn't. And why the hell did he still have his hands on her?

The scent of her perfume filled his nostrils, light but heady. *Like her…* It made a fist coil tight in his chest. The air thickened around them, his hands slowing as he finished the job. She must have felt it too, this undeniable connection between them, because her breathing changed, quickened, a flush stained her alabaster skin, and she was completely pliable beneath his hands.

She wanted him.

Bailey St. John—queen of the brush-off—wanted him.

The vaguely shattering discovery took him to a place it wasn't wise to go. The woman every man in Silicon Valley coveted was not impenetrable. *No pun intended.* She was far from asexual as some had suggested jokingly, and perhaps bitterly. And it struck him that maybe he'd been avoiding working with her, promoting her, because he'd been afraid of *this*. Because they'd have to work hand in hand. Because he'd wanted to unravel the mystery that was Bailey St. John from the first day she'd walked into his office.

Correction. From the night he'd hired her...

His body tightened with an almighty surge of testosterone. Not particularly admirable, but there it was. And how had he not realized it sooner? Hadn't he learned this in grade school? You only fought with the girls you liked. And on a much more adult level, he realized he wanted

Bailey in his bed. *Under him* as he peeled back layer upon layer.

He would not be the one to crash and burn…

"Bailey?"

"Mm?" Her husky, pleasure-soaked tone rocked him to the core.

"I think I've figured out our issue."

"Our issue?"

"Mmm." He slid his fingers to the racing pulse at the base of her neck. "This."

CHAPTER THREE

BAILEY YANKED HERSELF out from under Jared's hands so fast she pretty much redid all the damage he'd just undone. Her hazy brain wasn't firing on all cylinders as she met her boss's glittering blue gaze, focused and intent, containing the same heated sexual awareness that had been fueling her unspeakable fantasy.

Hot and uncensored, it had been outrageously good...

"We— I—" She started to talk. Anything to deny what was happening.

Jared held up a hand. "There's only one thing that's called, Bailey: pure, unadulterated sexual attraction."

Her pulse racing, hectic color firing her cheeks, it was really pointless to deny it. But it would be insanity not to. "There goes your out-of-control ego again, Jared," she taunted, raising her chin. "You *antagonize* me, you drive me crazy, but you do not attract me."

His jaw hardened. The glitter in his eyes morphed into a spark of pure challenge as his *I am man*, chest-beating need to prove his masculinity roared to life. Her breath stopped in her lungs, her irrational desire to see what would happen if he did lose it mixing with her common sense to create a complete state of inertia. Then his dark lashes came down to shield his eyes, that superior control he exerted over himself sliding back into place. "I think," he said softly, "this is a case of semantics. Antagonize… Attract… Whatever you want to call it—it's an issue. And we need to figure it out if we're going to make this presentation work. If we're going to make this *partnership* work."

She pulled in a silent breath, using the reprieve to steady herself. To regain her equilibrium. He was right. *She* needed to figure this antagonism/attraction thing out before she made a complete fool of herself. Before she destroyed this opportunity she'd been handed.

"How about," she offered, with as cool a gaze as she could muster, "you try to be a little looser, go with the flow, and I'll pay more attention to the script? I'm sure even *we* can meet somewhere in the middle."

His mouth tilted up on one side. "It's worth a shot."

They dined on a delicious meal of filet mignon and salad, Bailey severely curtailing her consumption of the delicious wine so her head was clear. She'd made a serious mistake in ever thinking she could let her defenses down in front of Jared. In tipping her hand and revealing an attraction she hadn't even fully admitted to herself. But she'd learned her lesson. And she wasn't about to do it again.

Their final rehearsal wasn't perfect, but it was a heck of a lot better than their earlier attempts. She toned it down, made a concerted effort to follow Jared's lead, and they made it through in a fairly civilized way. Jared, being the generous soul that he was, gave her a couple of hours' sleep before they landed in the sparkling, glittering South of France.

Just how luxurious their trip was going to be was apparent when upon their arrival in the Nice airport, they were not met by a car, but a shiny silver helicopter flown by Davide Gagnon's personal pilot. He jumped down under the slowing, still-whirling helicopter blades, greeted them, stowed their luggage in the back of the aircraft, and took them on their way.

Their trip across the sun-kissed Côte d'Azur to the legendary Peninsula of Billionaires, in between Nice and Monaco, featured some of the most exclusive properties on the French Riviera. Bailey, who'd done the South of France on a budget in her backpacking days with Aria, was googly-eyed. Luxurious villas sat in secluded coves behind high cliffs that sheltered them from the wind. And the colors were glorious, brilliant fuchsia and purple-soaked gardens bordering the sparkling turquoise sea.

Jared gave her an amused look as she chatted with the pilot, extending her twenty-question strategy to him. It was presently a balmy twenty-one degrees Celsius, the pilot told them as he set the chopper down on the Gagnon property's private landing pad, expected to get much hotter over the weekend, just in time for film festival season in the South of France.

They were met outside the low, cream-colored sprawling villa that sat directly on the bay by Davide Gagnon's head housekeeper, who informed them their host was en route home from a business meeting and would greet them that night at the party. Until then, they were free to explore the grounds and beach and enjoy some lunch. Bailey forced some salad into her jet-lagged body, took one look at her oceanfront suite—situated directly beside Jared's at one end of a wing—and elected for a face-plant into the three-hundred-count Egyptian cotton sheets and an afternoon nap.

When she woke, the brilliant afternoon sun had faded into early evening, and a sensual pink-orange sunset was streaking its way across the sky. She yawned, padded to her terrace and watched as it deepened into a hot-pink fire laced with smoky gray-blue. She would have done just about anything to be able to sit there and enjoy the magnificent view with a glass of the wine on ice in her suite, but it was already close to six. She needed to shower, dress and face the jeweled, exquisitely coutured guests of Davide Gagnon in a half hour. And hope she had learned enough over the years to fake it so her lowbrow, uncouth roots didn't show through like an ugly weed in a sea of mimosa and lavender.

Put her in a boardroom matched against the world's nastiest deal-maker, and she was rock solid. Put her in a social situation like tonight, and she needed all her acting skills to survive. Etiquette training had only taught her which fork to use. Which wine to drink with what. It didn't make her one of them. And it never would.

She gazed out at the explosion of color in the sky and reminded herself parties like this were about working a room. If there was anything she'd learned as a dancer, it was that. How to get what she wanted out of the men who'd come to watch her so she could make a different life for herself. And tonight was no different. She needed to focus on the prize, Davide Gagnon. Use what she'd learned about him, what she knew of men like him, to convince him a Stone Industries partnership was his ticket to European sales domination.

Show Jared he'd been overlooking a valuable asset for a very long time.

Once she got over her nerves…

She reluctantly abandoned the gorgeous view and stepped inside. She might not be able to enjoy the sunset, but she *could* indulge in a glass of wine to ease the tension. Pouring herself a glass, she took it into the stunning marble bathroom, stepped under a hot shower, and systematically washed away the old Bailey and installed the new one in her place.

Wrapping herself in the thick, soft robe that hung on the door, she padded into the dressing area and ran her fingers over the whisper-soft silks and taffetas she'd hung in the wardrobe. But there was never any question as to which she'd pick. She pulled the just-above-the knee beaded champagne-colored cocktail dress from the hanger and slipped it on. The dress was the softest silk, hugging every curve with just the right amount of propriety. Sexy but conservative at the same time.

She surveyed herself in the floor-length mirror. There was nothing cheap about the woman who looked back at her. This was not the twenty-dollar designer knockoff dress that had once been the only thing she could afford. And it showed.

Working her hair into a smooth, shimmering mass of curls with a round brush and a dryer, she topped it with minimal eye makeup and gloss. Enough to highlight her features. She had just added a dash of perfume to her pulse points when a knock sounded at the connecting door. *Jared.*

She moved across the room, undid the bolt and opened the door. The sight of her boss in an exquisitely tailored black tux might have been more intimidating than the prospect of the evening ahead. From the tip of his slicked-back dark hair to his freshly shaven jaw and long-limbed masculinity, he was devastating.

Jared followed Bailey into her suite, her barefoot, wine-in-her-hand invitation to come in doing something strange to his insides. Her dress—what would you call it, champagne-colored?—hugged every curve as if it had been sewn onto her. Curves that could burn themselves into your memory if you let them. Her hair fell in smooth gold waves to her shoulders, one side pushed back with a diamond butterfly clasp. Her exquisite face held only the faintest trace of war paint. But she was the most beautiful woman he'd ever stepped foot into a room with. That he knew.

He attempted to divert his wayward thoughts with a thoughtful look down at the floor tapestry, and instead treated himself to a perfect view of her long golden legs, ruby-tipped toes sinking into the carpet. And felt himself lose the plot completely. If she'd been a woman he was dating, he would have skipped the cocktails entirely. Insisted she share her wine while they watched the sunset together, taken the dress off her with his teeth and made her come at least twice before they joined the others.

And that didn't take into account what he would have done to her after the night was over.

He would have had her until sunrise.

"Jared?"

He coughed and lifted his gaze to hers. "Sorry?"

A pink stain stole over her cheeks. "The gold or champagne shoes?"

He looked at the two pairs of sky-high heels dangling by her fingertips and decided either of them would make every man in the room tonight want to bed her.

"Gold," he muttered. "It'll contrast with the dress."

"Right." She tossed the other pair on the carpet, braced her hand against the wall and slipped the stilettos on. As his hormone-clouded brain cleared, he noticed the tight set of her face. The way her ramrod straight posture seemed to have pulled up another centimeter. How she picked up the glass of wine and downed the remainder with a jerky movement reminiscent of his father on the nights he'd had to attend the bank functions he'd never been comfortable with, except his drink had been scotch.

The chink in her armor confounded him. "Are you nervous? You know the plan. We find out Maison's strategy when it comes to the environment and we're all set. It's the last missing piece."

A stillness slipped across her fine-boned face. Indecipherable. "I've got the plan down, Jared. I'm fine."

He didn't buy it for a second. Her revelations on the plane had illuminated one thing about Bailey. She hadn't been born into this lifestyle. She did a good job making it look as though she had, but she hadn't.

He stepped closer, something about her vulnerability touching him deep down inside. "Don't you know?" he said softly, looking down at her. "You're always the most beautiful woman in the room, Bailey. *And* the smartest."

A small smile twisted her lips before she wrinkled her nose at him. "I'll bet that line works wonders for you."

"You have no idea." His answering grin was self-effacing. "But I've never meant it more than I do now. So be yourself tonight, and you'll knock them dead."

She studied him for a moment. Nodded. "We should go."

For what reason he didn't know, he braved her prickly exterior and wrapped his fingers around her delicate hand instead of offering his arm.

"Ready?" he asked roughly.

"Ready."

They emerged on the buzzing wraparound terrace of the villa, ablaze with light and laughter on the warm Mediterranean night, where perhaps close to fifty people had already gathered, cocktails in hand. As Jared cased the crowd, he noticed an Academy Award-winning producer to his left, a high-profile A-list Hollywood couple to his right, and wasn't that Roberto Something-or-other, the Italian film director known for his sprawling epics, straight ahead? The big personalities had, apparently, all made it into town.

He grabbed a couple of glasses of champagne from a passing waiter's tray and handed one to Bailey. Gagnon had spared no expense: a quartet playing in a corner of the large, floodlit deck, black-jacketed staff circulating like an efficient swarm of bees, and from what he'd heard, a well-known French singer slated to play later in the evening, purportedly a mistress to one of the French cabinet ministers. But Jared had only one goal in mind. To corner Davide Gagnon and get the information he needed to develop that final, crucial piece of strategy.

He did not miss the attention every man at the party paid to the woman by his side as he picked out Gagnon, placed a palm to Bailey's back and led her through the crowd. There were a lot of beautiful, stunning even, women at the party. Bailey outshone them all, glittering like a glamorous Hollywood icon brought forward to the present, outclassing even the real Hollywood A-listers in attendance if you were to ask his opinion. But in true Bailey style, she ignored them all and focused on their target.

Davide Gagnon detached himself from the group he was standing with and came toward them, his sun-lined, handsome, younger-looking-than-he-was face breaking into a wide smile as he took Bailey's hand and brought it to his mouth. "My pilot told me you were lovely," he murmured gallantly. "I think he erred on the conservative side."

Bailey gave their host a warm smile and returned his greeting. *In French.* In perfectly accented, lilting Parisian French that sounded so sexy Jared's jaw dropped open.

"I think I'm in love," Davide murmured, hanging on to her hand. "What are you doing with the most controversial man in the room, *ma chère?*"

"And the most brilliant," Bailey returned smoothly as she drew back, an amused sparkle lighting her blue eyes. "I'm with him for his brain."

Jared's gaze tangled with hers. She appreciated a lot more than his brain, he was sure of it. And he suddenly had the burning urge to make her admit it. Maybe it was the look of pure male appreciation on Davide's face. Maybe it had been the scene with the shoes. Regardless, it was out of the question. He had to be a good boy. He was on a very short leash with no room for error.

"You have an absolutely magnificent home," he murmured appreciatively, when Davide finally deigned to let go of Bailey's hand and offer him his. "Thank you for the invitation to join you."

"It only increased the desirability of my guest list," the distinguished Frenchman said in a wry tone. "Like you or hate you, they all want to meet you."

Jared caught the disapproval the Frenchman lobbed him loud and clear. "It was a personal joke that should never have been made public," he asserted.

"But it was," Davide drawled. "And now you've alienated fifty percent of the population."

Tension tightened his jaw. "It will blow over."

Gagnon's eyes glinted. "That's what Richard Braydon thought when his comments about the French were broadcast on YouTube." His gaze was deliberate. "It destroyed his business."

A fist reached in and wrapped itself around his heart. Gagnon could not have missed the business stories depicting him teetering on a high-wire when it came to retaining control of his company. His radical push in a direction few dared to go. The Frenchman's deal would push him over the edge one way or another, and Davide knew it.

"It *will* blow over," Jared reiterated harshly. "And when you see what we have in our marketing plan, you will not have any doubts, I promise you."

The other man inclined his head. "I expect brilliance from you, Stone. It's the wild cards you throw my way I'm not so sure about."

Jared gritted his teeth as Gagnon blew off the conversation and turned to introduce them around. Turned to introduce *Bailey* around, if he were to be accurate. With himself in Davide's bad books, she apparently was a more enticing draw.

He spent the rest of the cocktail hour deflecting conversation of his manifesto, which truly seemed to have struck a global note. Heartily sick of it and inordinately annoyed with himself, he was then seated next to Gagnon's daughter, Micheline, for dinner. Whether a joke or penance on Davide's part, Jared thought he'd died and gone to hell by the main course. Micheline had not let up over the soup and appetizers about how damaging his effort "to be cute" was to women. How much it denigrated everything she'd worked for.

By the time the Cornish hens came, he would have laid down on the floor and allowed her to stick needles in every part of him if she would have stopped. *Just stopped.*

Bailey, of course, had been placed beside Davide. She spent the evening chatting away to him in that perfect French he didn't understand so he couldn't follow their conversation. Apparently, she had lost her nerves.

Micheline glanced over at her father and Bailey, her thin mouth curving in a cynical smile. "She was a brilliant stroke of strategy on your part, Jared, no doubt about it. You know Daddy can't resist a beautiful blonde."

"She's extremely smart," Jared muttered. And annoying. *He needed* to be in on that conversation. But it didn't happen. Dessert stretched into liqueurs and no one moved. Finally, the French singer took the stage on the terrace, the band backing her up, and Jared seized the opportunity to grab his CMO.

"Care for a dance?" he requested on a slightly belligerent note, holding out his hand.

She nodded and excused herself from Davide's side. Jared's long strides ate up the distance to the dance floor set up on a corner of the balcony. He slid an arm around Bailey's waist, laced his fingers through hers and pulled her to him.

"When were you planning on including me in your little party?"

She absorbed that, absorbed his frustration, then sighed. "You told me to work him, Jared. That's what I'm doing."

"*Awfully* well."

She sealed her bottom lip over her top.

"When were you going to tell me you spoke French?"

"That was also on my résumé," she said pointedly. "Along with the fact that I speak Spanish and Italian."

"I have a feeling that résumé of yours isn't worth the paper it's printed on," he said darkly, inhaling that trademark floral scent of hers. Trying to ignore what she'd look like stripped of that dress, what his psyche had been working on all evening. "What other tricks do you have up your sleeve? Just so I have a heads-up."

Her perfectly arched brows came together. "I know it must be disconcerting that Davide's being a bit cool with you, but you can't blame me for that."

"I'm not blaming you, I'm wondering *who you are*. You whip out this perfect French I didn't know you speak then you're off talking about Plato over dinner."

"I studied that in college. He's Davide's favorite philosopher."

"Of course he is. He's also clearly besotted with you."

Her calm look hardened until she was matching him stare for stare. "I am using my brain, Jared. Something the women you consort with likely don't do. I can understand why you would find that hard to appreciate."

"*I* appreciate your brain."

"Right." She echoed his skepticism. "He's revealing a lot. I'm getting some good insight into how his brain works. I've run some ideas by him and—"

"You've *run some ideas by him?*" Fury twisted his insides. "I don't want you running ideas by him, I want you *sticking to the script.*"

Her lips pressed together. "He liked them. Loved them, in fact."

He kept a leash on himself as the urge to explode like an overdue volcano rolled over him. "Which ideas are we talking about? The ones in our presentation or your rogue *thoughts?*"

Hot color dusted her cheeks. "One of mine—the one about the kiosks in the yoga studios…"

He uttered a curse. "That is not in our plan. It is nowhere in our plan, nor is it going to be. You need to put a leash on yourself."

She lifted her chin, her blue eyes a stormy gray. "He loved the idea, Jared. He said it was exactly where his head was at. So maybe *you* need to open your mind. Use your imagination."

"I am using my imagination," he came back shortly, his gaze sliding over the dress, the *curves* every man in the room hadn't been able to take his eyes off of all night. "And I don't like where it's taking me."

She swallowed, a visible big gulp. "Do not do that. We are negotiating a business deal here, remember? Focus."

"I am focusing," he countered silkily. "Like every other male at this party, you have my complete attention in that dress. Now what are you going to do with it?"

Her eyes widened. Fire arced between them, swift and strong. It made his blood tattoo through his veins in a triumphant march. Sent heat lancing through his body. Bailey stared back at him like a deer caught in the headlights for a long moment. Then she blinked and stepped out of his arms.

"Walk away," she said softly. "You know the magazines are right about you, Jared. You're the one who needs a leash. You *are* out of control. You *have* lost your focus. You might think about getting it back. Think about what's actually going to win this rather than your own ego."

He stood there, hands clenched by his sides with the need to strangle her. She started off, then turned back with a final, parting shot.

"Green is only a peripheral strategy for Davide. He recognizes the importance to consumers, but he also knows they aren't willing to pay a premium for it. It's the price of entry."

She left before he could say anything. Wound her way back through the crowd. And he wondered if she was right. Was he out of control? Had he lost the thread? Because all he'd ever wanted to do was build a company that created great products. That made the impossible possible. But now that he'd done that, now that he was close to the pinnacle of success, he was doing everything but. He was glad-handing politicians, massaging a board's ego, weighing in on a marketing strategy he shouldn't have to worry about. About as far from the business of inspiration as you could get.

It was making him crazy.

He acknowledged one more thing before he bit out a curse and followed Bailey through the crowd. The yoga kiosk idea was brilliant. He'd thought that when she'd mentioned it, but final rehearsals weren't any time to be going off script.

Hell. He'd told Sam this would happen. He should have listened to his instincts.

Bailey spent the rest of the evening trying to manage the thundercloud that was Jared. She had the distinct feeling Davide Gagnon was administering a slap on the hand to her boss by giving him the cold shoulder, because there was no doubt that he respected Jared immensely.

She felt as if she was doing damage control on all sides. She also felt that she was the missing piece of the puzzle. The link between Jared's brilliance and Davide's creative side. Davide *loved* her ideas. He thought they were grassroots, buzz-inducing genius. And it made her feel just this side of cocky as she stood at the two men's sides for a last brandy as the crowd dwindled on the star-strewn terrace.

She felt *empowered.*

"My son, Alexander, has been delayed until tomorrow night," Davide updated them, pointing his glass at Jared. "Since he will be assuming the mantle at Maison upon my retirement next year, I want him to take the lead on this partnership decision. Why don't you enjoy the day tomorrow, meet Alexander at dinner and we can hear the presentation on Sunday?"

Jared, who had been raring to get the presentation nailed and over with, nodded congenially as if that were the greatest idea in the world.

"You're planning on stepping back over the next few months and transitioning, then?"

Davide nodded. "But I will still be very involved. My son is nothing if not ambitious and aggressive, but he'll need guidance." He shot Jared an amused look. "You'll like him. He likes to win as much as you do."

Jared smiled. "Not a bad trait." But his eyes were blazing with a plan. Four or five more hours of endless rehearsal? She almost groaned out loud at the thought. She might kill him first.

"I should say goodbye to a guest," Davide observed, "then I think I'm going to turn in. I'll see you in the morning for breakfast."

Bailey couldn't imagine anything better than bed. It was 2:30 a.m., her feet were killing her from the heels, she was jet-lagged, and the mental exhaustion of maintaining such a perfect facade all night, of using the French she hadn't practiced in years, had fried her brain. And then there was Jared, who moved silently beside her into the house like a quiet, lethal animal ready to strike.

She stayed quiet because taunting the animal was never a good strategy. And she'd slipped during that dance. Had gotten caught up in him for a split second before she'd walked away.

She didn't think that was helping their harmony.

The hallway stretched long and silent ahead of them. Jared stopped in front of her door, turned the handle and pushed it open. She came to a halt beside him, tension raking over her as she risked a look up at him. Latent, unresolved antagonism stretched like a live wire between them, Jared's penetrating stare making her shift her weight to the other foot. *Away* from him.

She pulled in a breath. "I shouldn't have said wh—"

Her heart sped into overdrive as he leaned forward and braced a hand against the wall behind her, his intent, purposeful look stopping the breath in her chest.

"Add the yoga idea to the deck, Bailey. Blow it out big and make it sing. And don't ever, *ever* run a strategy by a client without my approval first. Or you'll have the shortest tenure an executive at Stone Industries has ever seen."

He had removed his hand from the wall, stepped back and slammed his way into his room before her breath started moving again. She stood there, frozen for about five good seconds, then closed the door behind her. She backed up against the wood frame and finally let a triumphant smile curve her lips.

She had won. She had forced Jared Stone to acknowledge her ideas had merit. Not only had merit—they were going to present them to Davide Gagnon.

The smile faded from her lips, adrenaline pounding through her, licking at her nerve endings. Just now, outside that door, for a split second, she'd been convinced Jared was going to kiss her. Worse, for a fraction of that second, she had been unbearably excited by the idea.

Pulling in a breath, she wiped the back of her hand against her mouth. Since when had she become a fan of Russian roulette? Because surely that's what tonight had been.

With her own career at stake.

She might want to start thinking up alternative strategies.

CHAPTER FOUR

BAILEY WOKE UP full of "piss and vinegar" as her mother would have said, ready to attack the presentation, slot in her yoga idea and rehearse it until it sparkled. She pulled on shorts and a knit top, her mouth curving at the thought of her colorful mother. She may have limited her exposure to the family who'd turned her out when she'd started dancing, *stripping* as her father had bitingly referred to it, but it didn't mean she didn't have *some* good memories of her childhood.

She'd often spent Saturdays sitting on one of the worn, ripped leather chairs in her mother's hair salon rather than face the uncertain mood of her father—who could be even-keeled if he hadn't drunk too much that day, or downright mean if he had. She'd finish her homework, then sit fascinated as her mother's less-than-polished clientele talked about men, other women in an often catty fashion and anything else on their mind they felt needed to be aired. Eye-opening and illuminating conversation for a ten-year-old, to be certain. She'd made sure she didn't miss one juicy detail.

Unfortunately the glow hadn't lasted. As she'd gotten older, it was her mother's quietness she'd noticed. How she would listen but not talk much. Smile but not really. And she'd wondered if her mother knew what *she* knew. That her husband was not only a violent drunk who couldn't get over the loss of his high school football glory, but he'd also been unfaithful to her while on the road selling vacuum cleaners across the state. Bailey had answered one too many phone calls at home while her mother was working from a supposed "customer" named Janine not to put two and two together when her father subsequently ordered her out of the room and a hushed conversation ensued.

As a teenager, the glow had disappeared completely. What did it matter if her mother treated her to hot rollers on Saturday, if on Monday the clothes you wore to school were falling apart? When no one wanted to hang out with you because you were the epitome of poor *uncool?*

The memories floated in the window of her beautiful Cap-Ferrat suite, in blinding contrast to her current circumstances. She pressed her lips together, secured her hair in an elegant pile on top of her head, a hairstyle her mother would have called "hoity-toity," then made her way downstairs to join Davide and Jared in the breakfast room. The two men were discussing a trip into Nice to visit an art gallery. Davide stood, brushed a kiss across both of her cheeks and held a chair out for her. "Would you like to come with us, *ma chère*? The Chagalls are phenomenal."

"It's tempting," she responded, taking a seat. "But no thank you, I have work to do."

Jared murmured a greeting. She slid him a wary glance as she reached for the coffeepot. He was freshly shaven and annoyingly edible in a pair of jeans and a T-shirt that hugged his muscular chest and shoulders in all the right places. And more relaxed this morning if the softer edges of his face were anything to go by. She poured herself a full cup of the strong French brew. He'd probably been up at five doing his Buddhist meditation thing. Rumor had it he'd spent three months as a college dropout in India studying with a Zen master, and practiced it regularly. She'd even heard some of the engineers moan that Jared was on another tangent with his simplicity-inspired principles and they might never leave the lab with an end product if he didn't back off.

She removed her gaze from all that drool-inducing masculinity and focused on buttering a croissant. Rule number one when it came to her new strategy of handling Jared. No drooling. At all. Ignore him completely.

He and Davide took off to Nice in one of the Frenchman's vintage sports cars. Seduced by the spray of the waves and the chance to be outdoors, Bailey settled herself on one of the terraces overlooking the ocean, slid on some sunscreen and set to work building her slides.

By early afternoon, she had fleshed out her ideas into a compelling global strategy to catch consumers where they spent their free time. The kiosks to sell Stone Industries' wearable technologies—pulse monitors, odometers, fitness watches—onsite at yoga studios was only the first niche she was proposing. She added in examples of other health and fitness environments it could replicated in, reviewed the slides, then called it done with a satisfied nod.

This was her chance to shine. She'd forced Jared's hand in allowing her to include her ideas, now she had to make them worthy.

Turning her face up to the sun, she allowed herself a bit of downtime until the men came back.

Jared returned from Nice in his best mood of the week. He had bonded with Davide over their mutual love of art and managed to convince him that no, he was not dangling over the side of a cliff at Stone Industries with the board ready to cut him loose. He had also gone a long way to convincing him that there was little danger of long-term fallout from his manifesto with female consumers. People had short memories. Stone Industries would come out with its next big product and women would flock to it for its cool factor as they always did. And all of this would be a blip on the radar of a soon-to-be successful partnership.

The only thing that *was* messing with his superior mood was the email he'd gotten from his head of IT earlier this morning about the leak of his manifesto. It had literally stopped him in his tracks to discover after a cyber-chase of epic proportions, the email hack had been traced to the servers of Craig International. Which could only mean that Michael Craig, one of his most vocal critics on the Stone Industries board, was behind it. Had meant to bury him at a time of weakness. And for that, he decided, mouth set, stomach hard, as he went outside in search of Bailey, he would pay richly. He had never liked or trusted Michael Craig, had never felt they were playing on the same team. He would use this opportunity to get rid of him.

A growl escaped his throat as he headed toward the ocean-side terrace. You didn't mess with a man's lifeblood. That was way, way over the line.

He found Bailey on the terrace in a sun chair, laptop on her thighs, eyes closed, face turned up to the sun. Davide had gone on about how much he liked her on the drive to Nice. Not surprising after last night, but what *had* caught him off guard was that the collector of women, who'd lost his wife to illness at forty-five, had been focused not on Bailey's looks, but on her intelligence. Her creativity. He loved her—that much was obvious.

His mouth twisted as he surveyed her deceptively relaxed pose on the lounger, long legs kicked out in front of her. He had no doubt her mind was going a mile a minute under those closed lids. That she wasn't sleeping but strategizing. And a sour feeling tugged at his gut. He'd sidelined her. Put her aside as a problem he didn't have time to deal with when it was his attraction to her that had been the issue all along. It wasn't like him to put the personal before business, and he hated that he had.

She opened her eyes, the wariness he'd witnessed this morning making a reappearance. "Did you have a good trip?"

"I did." He sank into the chair opposite her and poured himself a glass of her mineral water. "I owe you an apology."

Her eyes rounded. "For what?"

"For underestimating you. For letting you languish in a role that was beneath you."

She pushed herself up in the chair, her gaze meeting his. "We haven't done the presentation yet."

"I've seen your ideas." He took a long swallow of the water and sat back, resting the glass on his thigh. "I was wrong about you. I should have given you a voice." He lifted his shoulders. "Maybe you were right last night. Maybe my judgment has been off. It's been a David-and-Goliath battle with the board."

She pushed her finger into her cheek, a slow smile curving her lips. "I think I'm just going to say thank you and leave it at that. Are you sure you're feeling all right?"

A wry smile edged his mouth. "As a matter of fact, I am. You got me thinking last night. In a good way."

A frown marred her brow. "I might have been a bit harsh."

He shrugged. "I needed to hear it. I haven't had any time to think lately, and that's when I get myself into trouble."

She pointed toward her computer screen. "Want to see my slides?"

He nodded. "I've heard Alexander is a stickler for detail. He likes to wade into the minutiae—a bit of a control freak. So I want to ensure all our ducks are in order."

They went through the slides. He loved the way she'd laid them out, made a few suggestions of his own, and in a feat that could be classified as the eighth wonder of the world, they did a perfect run-through.

Satisfied the presentation was as smooth and as flawless as it was going to get, he challenged Bailey to a tennis game. She wasn't half bad. What she lacked in skill, she made up for in determination. Which seemed to be her modus operandi. She'd used the incredibly sharp brain she'd been born with, worked brutally hard and taken herself places.

He studied her as he waited for her to serve, concentration written across her face. Pictured her slugging it out at the local café, serving coffee all evening to put herself through school. Selling fifty pairs of shoes a day at the local mall to secure her future. And he couldn't help but admire her.

There was a lot of substance to Bailey St. John.

Bailey was still on a high when she pulled on white capri jeans, a body-hugging tank and a gauzy sheer blouse over it for their dinner at sea. Alexander Gagnon, Maison Electronique's director of international development and soon-to-be CEO, had flown in by helicopter while she'd been showering, the whir of the blades deafening as he'd touched down with two of Maison's other senior marketing staff. Tonight they would get to know the three executives over dinner on Davide's yacht, in a trip up the coast to Cannes. And tomorrow they would present their ideas to the group.

Much more comfortable with the intimate choice of setting this evening, Bailey slipped on strappy, glittery sandals, spritzed on a headier perfume for nighttime and met Jared *outside* his door. A slow smile curved his mouth when he opened it, denting his cheeks with those to-die-for almost-dimples. "You aren't going to let me pick your shoes?"

She resolutely ignored the sexy indentations. "I had it under control tonight."

His gaze swept over her, smooth and all-encompassing. "You look like you're channeling Grace Kelly."

She shifted her weight to the other foot. "I'll take that as a compliment."

The hand he placed at her back to ostensibly guide her down the hallway burned into her skin. "Do that," he murmured, bending so his softly spoken words rasped across the sensitive skin behind her ear. He looked pretty gorgeous himself in casual black pants and a short-sleeved dark blue shirt that made the most of his eyes. But she'd keep that to herself.

A small powerboat was waiting at the dock to take them out to the yacht. All the others were already on board, the crew member told them, firing the motor. Bailey took it all in, eyes wide. Growing up on a swamp in Florida, she'd been around boats her whole life. She'd seen the cruise ships lined up in Tampa when they'd visited the city. But that was a world away from this. Davide's yacht was at least seventy feet in length, they were about to cruise to Cannes during film festival time, and it frankly seemed unreal.

As they neared the sleek yacht painted in the blue, white and red colors of the French flag, the powerboat slowed to a crawl. They pulled alongside the yacht and were helped aboard by crew members. The rosy sky descended low over them, the lights of Saint-Jean-Cap-Ferrat twinkling from the shore as she stood looking back from the deck. It was glorious.

Davide greeted them, then turned to introduce them to the three men beside him. She greeted the two marketing executives who had flown in from Paris, then Alexander Gagnon, a tall, distinguished male with dark hair and cold-as-flint gray eyes.

Her pulse flatlined as Alexander stepped forward. She teetered on her sandals and would have stumbled backward if Jared hadn't placed a hand to her back and steadied her. *It couldn't be. It could not be.*

Her gaze moved over him, hungry to prove herself wrong. But the cold, hard eyes that had studied her, eaten her up with an unflinching need to have her those nights in Vegas almost ten years ago, were unmistakable. And he didn't miss a beat.

"How lovely to meet you…*Bailey,*" he murmured, taking her hand to brush a kiss across her knuckles. "Alexander Gagnon."

Her breath constricted in her chest, a solid lump that threatened to choke her. She had never told him her real name. Had never told any of the men she danced for her real name. And now he knew it. She registered the fact with the almost hysterical need to turn around, jump off the boat and swim for shore.

Whether her body actually turned in that direction or whether Jared felt the shudder that went through her at the touch of Alexander Gagnon's lips on her skin, she wasn't sure. He released her for a moment to shake the other man's hand, then returned his palm to her back and kept it there. Alexander's gaze tracked the movement, then moved back to her face.

"I'm looking forward to your presentation tomorrow," he drawled. "Davide has been telling me about your great ideas."

Bailey's knees were shaking so hard she had to lean into Jared to keep herself upright. She felt his gaze hard on her, but kept hers focused straight ahead. Alexander was staring at her, waiting for a response. "Yes, well, we—" she stumbled "—we're hoping you'll like them."

"We know you'll *love* them," Jared corrected firmly, his palm pressing into her spine.

Alexander's lips twisted in a smile that didn't quite reach his eyes. "I've spent some time in the States. Davide mentioned you did your MBA at Stanford," he said to Bailey. "Where did you do your undergrad?"

He knew exactly where she'd done her undergrad. A fine sheen of perspiration broke out on her brow. Her voice dry, more gravelly than she'd ever heard it, she forced out, "At UNLV."

He snapped his fingers. "That must be it. I feel we've met before, but I can't place it. I've entertained a lot of clients in Vegas."

Every muscle in her body froze. The dark glitter in his eyes chilled her to the bone. "You must be mistaken," she rasped, finding her voice. "I'm quite sure we've never met."

Gauntlet laid, she lifted her chin. Alexander inclined his head. "My mistake, then."

She let out the breath she'd been holding. Requested a martini for the pure, unadorned hit of alcohol it would provide. Jared leaned down to her. "What is *wrong* with you?"

"I'm just not feeling…quite right."

His penetrating blue gaze ate through her. "A martini might not be the best thing, then. Let me get you some water."

"I'm fine," she said sharply. "It's probably just the boat. I'll get over it."

The martini helped. She sipped it, feeling the alcohol inject itself into her bloodstream, bite into the unreality gripping her. She had to find a way through this that didn't involve jumping off the boat and getting as far away from that man as she could. She had to pull herself together. *But how?* He had definitely recognized her. Her mind riffled through the options, desperately, not entirely clearly. She had to continue to pretend she'd never met him. Treat him as if he was just a business acquaintance. But it was just her luck that Alexander was seated across from her at dinner. And the red shirt he had on made it impossible to forget the last time she'd seen him.

She'd danced in her signature red lace dress and underwear as Kate Delaney that night at the Red Room—the highest-end strip club in Vegas, legendary for its beautiful women and sumptuous interiors. To wear red and dance last meant she was the owner's favorite, the most requested dancer of the week. Which wasn't unusual for her. She pulled in a ton of regulars who came to see her cool, untouchable beauty uncovered; to watch the sensual, erotic transformation unfold.

None of them could have known it was all an act for their benefit. That it was as far from the real Bailey as you could get.

Alexander Gagnon had sat in the front row that night. As he had every night for the past three. She'd felt his eyes on her, dark and unmoving. Despite the fact that there had been at least a hundred and fifty other men in the club, she had only been conscious of him. Of the tall, dark figure who had approached her each night to have a drink with him and whom she'd turned down flat despite the money he'd thrown at her, because there was something about the exquisitely dressed stranger with his thousand-dollar ties that said red light to her.

That night she had retreated to the dressing room, strangely affected by the intensity of the experience. The magnitude of the tip Alexander had left her. Her fellow dancers had showered and dressed in a mad rush to hit the town. Since she'd just been heading home to study for an exam the next day, Bailey had taken her time, sat at her dressing table and removed her thick, dramatic makeup. At some point she'd looked up to find the tall dark stranger standing inside the doorway. That all the other girls had gone. If you were to look past the dangerous edge to him that smoldered just below the surface, she would have called him inordinately handsome. Distinguished. But all she could smell was the scent of her own fear as she got to her feet, heart pounding.

"You can't be in here."

He'd lifted a brow. "Bruno owes me one. He gave us five minutes."

Her manager had let him in? "Get out."

He'd leaned back against the doorway, his gaze moving over her so slowly, so assessingly, she'd had to fight the urge to pull the edges of her blouse together. "After I give you my proposition, *Kate*."

She should have walked to the door then and had him thrown out, but she'd been afraid of him.

"You've rejected my requests to join me for a drink three nights in a row," he'd murmured, eyes glittering as he pushed away from the door and walked toward her. "I figured I'd try another strategy." She'd backed up until her behind was against the dressing table, trying hard not to show her fear. "I know you're a student, Kate. I'm offering you fifty thousand dollars for a night. Any hard limits, I'll respect them."

She had stared at him, shocked. Shocked that anyone would pay that much for a night with someone. Shocked that that person would be *her*. She was the woman men shoved money at in a dirty, covetous thrill. Not a high-priced escort.

For a second, for one split second, it had crossed her mind that fifty thousand dollars would cover her tuition and living expenses for the year. She could spend the days going to school and studying like a normal student. She wouldn't have to be exhausted all the time turning her nights and days upside down…snatching a couple hours' study before she passed out at night. She could leave the backbreaking pain of her four-inch heels behind. Just like that.

Then hot shame had flooded through her. *How could she even be considering it?*

She'd pointed to the door. "Get the hell out of my dressing room."

He'd just stood there. "Everyone has a price, Kate. Name it."

"That's where you're wrong." She'd walked past him to the door and flung it open. "I don't."

He must have seen the hatred burning in her eyes, because he'd left. Afterward, Bruno had denied involvement, then had been fired a few weeks later for stealing money from the club.

Alexander Gagnon had shown up for the next two nights to see if she'd changed her mind. It had been the hardest two nights of her working career, her ability to concentrate nonexistent.

"Bailey?"

Davide was frowning, eyeing her plate. "You didn't enjoy your meal?"

She looked up to see the waitstaff hovering by her side, ready to remove the seafood salad sitting practically untouched in front of her. "I'm so sorry," she murmured. "I'm just a little off."

"Perhaps you got too much sun today," he suggested in French. "You are so fair."

"Perhaps," she agreed. "I'm sure I'll be fine after a good night's sleep."

Jared hadn't taken his eyes off her the entire meal. It could have been because she didn't seem able to add any intelligent insights to the conversation, or alternatively, *ask* any valuable questions. Either way, it felt hard to breathe and she needed to escape.

She excused herself and made a beeline for the ladies' room. It was downstairs, off the opulent drawing room, done in royal-blue marble with gold accents. She pulled in some deep breaths, splashed water on her ashen face, then pressed one of the thick, luxurious hand towels to her face.

Could a nightmare actually come to life? Because this was hers...

She applied some lipstick and pinched her cheeks to give them color, but she still looked deathly pale as she left her sanctuary and headed back upstairs. She had just stepped on deck when Alexander cut her off at the pass.

"You've done well for yourself, Bailey." He leaned his arm on the railing and blocked the way back to the others. "Or should I say Kate? What *is* your real name?"

Bailey gave him a blank look, fighting to keep her composure. "I'm afraid I have no idea what you're talking about."

"You think I don't remember you?" He rested his gaze on her face, as chilling and unnerving as it had been that night he'd sat in the audience watching her. "I remember every curve, every dip of your mind-blowing body. How you seduced every man in that room and left them begging for more."

A fresh wave of perspiration broke out on her brow. "You have the wrong woman," she rasped. "And this is not at all appropriate."

"I don't think I do." He pushed away from the railing and took the last couple of steps toward her. Bailey's heart knocked against her ribs. A cool Mediterranean breeze flitted over her but she felt vaguely feverish. "I saw it on your face that night. You wanted to say yes."

"I don't know you," she bit out and started to brush by him. He curled his fingers around her arm and brought her to a halt.

"They don't know, do they?" His smoky gaze heated with challenge. "You've moved on. Gone to a great deal of trouble to put your past behind you…"

Yes. And she wasn't going back there now.

"Get your hands off her, Gagnon."

Jared's low, menacing command came from behind them. She twisted around and found him watching them, hands clenched by his sides, tall, lean body coiled like a cat ready to pounce. Her heart zigzagged across her chest, threatening to explode right out of it. *God, no. He couldn't know about this.*

Alexander lifted his hand from her arm and stepped back. "Cool your jets, Stone. We were just having a conversation."

Jared took a step closer until he was toe-to-toe with Alexander. "I don't particularly like the nature of it. And neither does Bailey from the looks of it. So perhaps we should all return to the table for dessert?"

Alexander stared him down, just for the fun of it, Bailey guessed semi-hysterically. Her airways seemed closed to oxygen. Alexander lifted his hands in the air. "Beautiful, isn't she? Can't blame you. Ask her about the sexy mole on her hip, Stone. It's quite something…or maybe you already know that?"

Bailey's heart sank into the deck. A trickle of perspiration rolled down her neck as Alexander turned and sauntered off. *He had not just said that.*

Jared's gaze moved over her face. It was the stillness, the absolute stillness about him that got to her. "What is he talking about, Bailey? And how do you know him?"

She shook her head, in full denial. "I don't know him." And that was true. She didn't know anything about him. *Except he was now the key player who would decide their fate in the biggest deal of her life. Of Jared's life.*

Jared stepped closer to her. "Then why are you white as a ghost? Why have you been off since the moment you saw him?"

Her brain swirled in a desperate attempt to make this go away. Heart thumping painfully hard against her chest, she looked up at him. "He is an obnoxious jerk who has mistaken me for someone else. I am not good with boats, Jared. Never have been. And I don't want to make it an issue for Davide, who has been kind enough to take us on this lovely sail. So I think we should get back to the others before he worries."

She brushed past him before he could stop her and headed back to the table where dessert was being served. Somehow she managed to spoon a few mouthfuls of the undoubtedly delicious chocolate mousse into her mouth. But she tasted nothing. How could she when the world felt as if it was unraveling around her?

Alexander's cool, unruffled composure across the table was utterly unnerving. As if they'd been trading old war stories rather than him throwing her past in her face.

The night thankfully ended an hour later when Davide, she figured, took pity on her and suggested they do a final nightcap back at the villa. He insisted she rest rather than join them, and Bailey didn't protest. She brushed off Jared's intention to walk her to her room. "I'm fine."

He came anyway, wearing a frown.

"I'll be back to check on you," he said when they'd reached her room, planting a hand against the wall and looking her over. "Are you sure you're okay?"

"I'm fine." She pressed a hand to her pounding head, which was making her feel distinctly nauseous now. "Don't bother. I'll be asleep."

He stared her down. "I'll be back in half an hour."

Bailey forced some painkillers down her throat with a glass of water and paced her beautiful, airy suite. The more she paced, the more her head pounded. The two lives she'd so carefully kept light-years apart for so long had just crashed together with debilitating consequences. And the chances she was going to be able to keep them apart any longer were slim. Alexander Gagnon had offered her fifty thousand dollars to sleep with him almost ten years ago. And now she had to face him, *to pitch to him* over a boardroom table?

What if she had to work with him afterward?

The trails of perspiration rolling down her nape made her feel hot, feverish. She had not spent years of her life building her reputation in the business world to let a man like Alexander Gagnon destroy it. To assume he knew what she was when she wasn't anything like that.

I remember every curve, every dip of your mind-blowing body. How you seduced every man in that room and left them begging for more...

Alexander's words, cutting, accusatory, washed over her. Suddenly she felt dirty, so dirty. Hands shaking, she ripped off her jeans and tops. Found her bathing suit, threw it on and took the back stairs to the beach. The sea was dark and strewn with moonlight. The surf was up, eating into the sand with swift currents. She ignored how the darkness made it look dangerous, walked into it and struck out to a place unknown. To a place where the past couldn't find her.

Jared knocked on Bailey's door forty-five minutes later. He'd nursed a final brandy with Davide and the others, fought the urge to put his fist through Alexander Gagnon's face and ultimately restrained himself. He didn't believe Bailey for a second when she'd said she didn't know him. She'd had a violent reaction the minute she'd seen him. He'd *felt* it.

They don't know, do they? You've moved on. Gone to a great deal of trouble to put your past behind you.

What had Gagnon been talking about?

He knocked again on the door, his mouth tightening. *Nothing.* He waited five more seconds, knocked again and turned the knob. The door was open, a table lamp flooding the drawing room with light. No Bailey. He strode across the room, pushed her bedroom door open and saw the bed hadn't been touched. Her clothes were lying in a heap on the floor, which raised his antennae because Bailey was obsessively, compulsively neat.

He walked out onto the floodlit terrace and found it empty. Scanning the grounds, he searched for her. On the beach below a flash of white in the water caught his eye. Bailey's pale skin in the moonlight. *There.* He stripped off his shoes and socks and went after her.

She was so far out in the waves, he almost dived in fully clothed. But her pace was steady and her strokes sure, so he waited her out instead, his heels sinking into the sand. When she reached shore, she headed toward her towel, not fifteen feet from him, but she didn't notice him at all.

He allowed himself to enjoy the view while she toweled off. He'd had his fair share of women in his life. Some would say gone through them much more carelessly than a man should. But he'd never seen a woman look so utterly…goddess-like in a bathing suit.

The spotlights on the beach rendered those never-ending legs of hers a work of art. The product of gently rolling hips, they were slim enough to look delicate, curved enough to be irresistible. His hungry gaze moved upward, over her slim waist and more than ample chest, the perfection of which made his mouth go dry. She might not be a D cup, but she was exquisite.

She reached up and pulled her hair back into a ponytail, squeezing the water from it. It threw her delicate, unforgettable beauty into perfect spotlight. She looked untouchable…*haunted*.

It reminded him why he was here. He started toward her. She bent over to dry her calves. Her mouthwatering backside was not something to be missed. The round, dark mark on the curve of her buttock wasn't either. He froze. It was unmistakably a mole. A mole Alexander Gagnon knew intimately enough to call out.

He was across the sand and in her face so fast it made

his own head spin. Bailey looked up, her pale face catching the moonlight. Her hands slapped the towel around her hips but he was faster, spinning her around and pointing at the mark.

"You lied to me," he snarled. "You don't know him but he knows about intimate marks on your body? What exactly is going on?"

She tried to twist out of his hold, but he was stronger, his fingers digging into her upper arms. Her eyes flashed dark, almost gray in the moonlight, contrasting with her chalk-white cheeks. "Get your hands off me, Jared. Or are you no better than him?'

He let her go then, fury singeing his nerve endings. "We are negotiating a deal worth tens of millions of dollars a year, Bailey. I want the truth and I want it *now*."

She took a step back. Wrapped her arms around herself. "I told you the truth. I don't *know* him. I met him once when I lived in Vegas. He came on to me, I turned him down. That's it."

"That's it?" He slapped his palms against his temples, biting out a curse. Seconds passed, three, maybe four. Then he pinned his gaze on her face. "How did he know about the mole if you turned him down?"

She went even paler. "There's nothing further you need to know that has anything to do with this deal." Her chin came up. "That's all I'm answering and this conversation is done."

His blood fired. Raced in his veins. And he realized his fury had nothing to do with the deal. He wanted to know why that snake had an intimate knowledge of Bailey's behind. "I don't think so." He took a step closer, and this time she didn't back up. She stood her ground, eyes flashing. "You turn every man in Silicon Valley down. You act like you are untouchable…and yet that arrogant jerk, *known for his womanizing*, has had his hands on you… I don't get it."

She stepped up to him, her heat fusing with his until they were in danger of a spontaneous combustion. "What's the matter, Jared? You can't stand that it wasn't you? That Mr. Manifesto has met his match?"

He raked his gaze over her. "You know what, Bailey? You're right. I can't. Because if it had been me, you wouldn't have walked away."

She opened those luscious lips of hers to say something not very nice. He kissed her before she made it there. And by God, she was the sweetest female he'd ever tasted. Hot, honeyed perfection he savored for about two seconds before she raised her hand to slap him. He caught it in his and slid his other behind her nape, tangling it in her wet hair. Changed the kiss into a persuasive, seductive assault on her senses. The kind that always, without fail, worked.

Bailey wanted to fight but somewhere along the way, somewhere along the edges of the soul-destroying assault Jared was laying on her, she found escape. *Needed* it.

When he cupped the back of her head and angled her to take the kiss deeper, she let him. Moaned her approval when he brought his tongue into play and stroked her deeply. He smelled insanely good and he tasted better. Of cognac and expensive cigars. And she wanted more of him. A lot more.

He muttered something under his breath. Slid his hard thigh between her wet, shaking ones and brought her closer. So close his heart pounded beneath her palm. His hand at her back dragged her against his chest, urged her softness against his hardness. Her cool, air-tightened nipples brushed against him through the fine material of his shirt, and the heat that flooded her core came hot and hard. Like nothing she'd ever felt before.

He cursed again and dragged his mouth down the column of her throat, pressing openmouthed kisses against her damp skin. "Bailey," he breathed. "Who is he to you?"

Reality hit her like the hard slap of the night waves to her face. He wasn't kissing her because he wanted her. He was kissing her because he wanted to *possess* her. *Just like all the others.*

She sank a palm into his chest and pushed. Caught off guard, he stumbled backward. His gaze flew to hers. "What the—?"

"You are all dogs," she hissed, legs spread wide, feet planted in the sand. "Fighting over what you want. What you think is yours."

He gave her wild-eyed look a wary glance. "You were as into that kiss as I was."

Her elegant blond brows came together. "And now I'm walking away. *Again*. You were wrong, Jared. You aren't any different than the rest of them. You're all the same."

She left him standing there, staring after her, his jaw practically on the ground. Why was she always thinking Jared was different when he so categorically wasn't? Maybe *she* was the one losing her sense of judgment.

CHAPTER FIVE

Jared had run the path around the rocky beaches of the Cap for fifty minutes before he gave up trying to figure out what had happened last night and pulled up into a walk, sweat dripping from his chin. Given the lack of information coming from Bailey, the only thing that *was* clear was that Alexander Gagnon, Davide's heir apparent and the man who would own the decision as to whether to link Stone Industries and Maison Electronique in a five-year strategic partnership, knew his CMO intimately enough to call out a mole on her behind.

The thought had his already-pumping blood charging through his veins. He scowled and swiped his T-shirt over his face. Bailey had said she'd met Gagnon once, he'd propositioned her, and she'd turned him down. So how would he know about the mole? *And why, in God's name, was that a more pressing question for him than what he was going to do about the changing dynamics of this deal and the impact on his future?*

He let out a colorful curse and raked his T-shirt over his face again. Why wouldn't Bailey tell him the truth? What could be so horrible about her past that she couldn't tell him? That Alexander would call her on? He'd seen that look before, the one on Bailey's face last night. It was the exact same one his father had worn when the hounds had closed in. When his inability to escape had become inevitable—when all of his carefully constructed lies had started to unravel.

His chest tightened. He did not tolerate secrets. What he *should* do was march up there and tell Bailey she either came clean or she was out. There was too much riding on this pitch…this deal, not to have complete transparency. But the fact was, she was his ace in the hole. Davide loved her and her ideas. So eliminating her from the pitch was a nonstarter.

A massive bird of prey flew in from the sea, its wingspan at least eight or nine feet across. His gaze followed it as it arced and headed inland. A vulture? It reminded him of Alexander the way he'd tracked Bailey with his eyes last night. It had been beyond the look men had when they coveted something. It had been something else entirely…

He turned toward the house, his mouth twisting in a grimace. He'd been right from the beginning. The mystery that was Bailey had a history. A history that could blow the lid off this deal if he didn't find out what it was and defuse it. *Now.*

He made his way up the stairs toward their rooms, refusing to let himself address the other lethal ingredient flavoring the situation: the heat that had exploded between them last night. It was one thing to acknowledge an attraction. Another thing entirely to act on it. Because when the cat was out of the bag, it was all too easy to do it again.

Out of the question.

He let himself into his room, picked up his cell phone and dialed the PI he used to track his father, just to make sure he was alive, every now and again.

Danny Garrison picked up after almost seven rings with a sleepy, "'Lo?"

"I need you to dig up everything you can on my CMO, Bailey St. John."

There was a rustling sound in the background. "You do realize at some point I do go off the clock?"

He looked at his watch on the bedside table. Eight a.m. He hadn't even thought about the time difference. "Sorry. But I need this yesterday."

"Considering it *is* yesterday for me,, no problem." Sarcasm dripped from his PI's voice.

"Focus on her time in Vegas. She went to school there."

"Am I looking for anything in particular?"

Jared stared out at the cerulean-blue sky. At the vulture that had looped back over the seashore looking for breakfast.

"Something she'd want to hide."

Bailey shrugged out of an orchid-pink silk shirt, her third choice thus far, and tossed it on the bed. Nothing, *nothing* felt right about this presentation happening in thirty minutes. Nothing had since she'd laid eyes on Alexander Gagnon and realized it was *him*.

She snatched the pewter-gray version of the same shirt off a hanger and tugged it on. She needed to walk into that room today and nail the presentation. Forget the past and focus on the future. But her churning stomach wasn't cooperating.

Her hands fumbled as she pulled the shirt closed and did up the tiny pearl buttons. Would Alexander play nice? And if he didn't was she now playing Russian roulette with Jared's future? With this deal? Could she afford to do that? Should she just pull herself out now and accept the fact that her past had caught up with her? Do the right thing?

Her fingers tripped over the buttons, making her curse and focus her concentration. Surely Alexander had better things to do than focus on a bruised ego. He had a major directional partnership to consider for Maison. A company to take the helm of. He would be all business.

The knot in her stomach said differently.

Maybe Jared would fire her first for the inexcusable things she'd said and get it over with.

She shoved the last button through the slippery material with a vicious movement. How could she have kissed him? How could she have done that of all things? She didn't *feel* lust like that for men. Didn't let them close enough to even inspire it because her father had taught her that men were dangerous, unpredictable. Better avoided.

The arrival of their once-a-month welfare check had sent her father on his infamous benders like clockwork, typically ending with him trashing their house and whichever one of them had particularly annoyed him that day. Her mother had shielded them from him when she could, taking the punishment and sending her girls to the neighbors, but that had only made them feel worse when they'd arrived home the next day to a fresh set of bruises on their mother's face.

Add to that her experience as a dancer, and complete abstinence had been her solution.

A sharp knock on the connecting door brought her head around. She tucked a stray hair back in her chignon, turned and walked over to open it. Storm cloud Jared was in attendance today, his blue eyes crackling with electricity. *All business.*

"You ready?"

She nodded. "Let me get my notes."

Her prep stuff was in a pile on the desk. She'd left the notes on top, ready to grab, but last night in her agitation she'd thrown another pile on there and they didn't seem to be anywhere as she riffled through them, flicking pages upside down.

"Bailey." She hadn't realized he'd moved until he was beside her, his hand closing over hers. She looked up at him, teeth tugging at her bottom lip.

"They're right here, I just can't—"

"*Bailey.*" He took the papers out of her hands and put them down on the desk. "Tell me what's bothering you. Who is Alexander Gagnon to you? We are *partners* in this. I need to know what's wrong so we can handle it together."

She brought her back teeth together before she blew this entirely and pulled her hand free to continue searching for the notes. "He is nothing to me. I told you that."

"Then why are you a total disaster?"

"I am *not* a disaster." She rounded on him fiercely, eyes flashing. "This is personal, Jared, and I won't have it brought into this."

His mouth twisted. "Were you there last night? Because I was. Alexander is now the deciding voice in this deal. He did not take his eyes off you all night and then he followed you to the washroom where he was extremely confrontational. So don't tell me it's *nothing*, Bailey. He is an issue. And I won't have it affecting this deal."

She sank her hands into her hips. "Then pull me out."

"*I can't pull you out.* Davide adores you. He loves your thinking."

She pressed her lips together mutinously. She would rather *die* than tell Jared she'd been a stripper. A man who thought so little of women he'd written a manifesto about their place being in the bedroom. She could only *imagine* how derogatory he'd be. It made her stomach curl. As did the thought that he wouldn't want her anywhere near this deal.

He let out a muttered oath, his gaze on her face. "Tell me it wasn't something illegal. Whatever it is you're hiding."

Illegal? She stared at him in disbelief. *What the?* The flare of anxiety in his eyes, the frown furrowing his brow, made it hit home. His father. Of course he would be afraid of scandal.... Her stomach lurched dangerously.

She wanted to tell him, to reassure him it had everything to do with her, but she could not.

She put her hand on his arm, her gaze imploring him. "It's nothing like that. It's a personal matter Jared, that's all. You need to trust me on this."

He stared at her long and hard. As if he wasn't sure what to do with her. Then he let out a long breath. "Okay, this is how we're going to play it. We are going to walk into that room, blow them away with our ideas and win this contract. You are not going to be distracted. You are not going to address Alexander in any way, shape or form unless he asks you a question. Play to Davide, play to the other two. But do not let Alexander shake you."

Relief flooded through her. He wasn't going to push her. She could have kissed him except that had been a bad idea. "Got it," she said firmly. "You can trust me."

His gaze singed hers. "Too bad that doesn't go both ways."

She shook her head. "It does, I swear it. This is just… different."

The furrow in his brow deepened. "Someone's done a number on you, Bailey."

How about her life? Did that count?

He made a rough sound in his throat. "We have ten minutes. We should go set up."

She nodded and found her notes.

If Jared had expected Bailey to be shaky and off her game in the presentation, he was proven wrong. Something switched on in her brain when she walked into that room. Her survival instincts, he figured. She plowed through her slides with a steely determination and enthusiasm that made everyone at the table catch the spirit and engage. He watched that sharp brain of hers ignite, gather momentum as she fed off the feedback she was getting from the table and push her ideas to an even higher creative level. Not once did she look at Alexander, except to answer his pointed and often challenging questions.

His own strategies had been solid, but they had been lacking the marketing savvy Bailey possessed. Together they made a formidable team.

Don't fight the exodus from retail, she was counseling now, pointing at the screen. Touch consumers where they work and play, *show* them what they are missing in a lifestyle setting like a yoga studio that drives it home for them, then *sell* to them on the spot with the kiosks.

"Intriguing," Alexander conceded, "if a bit sacrilegious to a retailer like me. You're asking us to focus our marketing budget *outside* of the stores?"

"Some of it, yes," Bailey said, nodding. "It's a reality that people are moving away from brick-and-mortar retail to the online space. You need to get ahead of the trend now."

Alexander got to his feet and started pacing the room, a technique Jared figured he used to intimidate. "Yoga is niche, however. How is this really going to impact our bottom line?"

"You replicate it." Bailey flipped to her next slide. "You train demo staff, send them not just to yoga studios, but to running centers, health and wellness clinics, gyms… You seed the instructors first, make them fall in love with the product, and then you capture their students."

Alexander didn't look convinced. Bailey plunged on, undeterred. When she'd finished the last of the slides and Jared had closed with a "why Stone Industries" recap, they wrapped the presentation.

Davide looked at his son. "What do you think?"

"I like it," Alexander said, nodding. "I think the direct-to-consumer ideas are the strongest, they fit with our strategy, our target markets, but I am skeptical they can be rolled out on a large scale. And," he added, dropping a file folder on the table in front of Jared, "I *am* worried from this latest consumer research that you've alienated the target female consumer with your manifesto. You've dropped ten points in intent to buy with females since it happened."

Jared eyed the file in disbelief. "They'll be back up by next week. This is a flash in the pan." *And you know it.*

"Perhaps." Gagnon lifted a brow. "But the fact remains, the female demographic is our most important to capture right now. We can't afford to partner with a company that's alienated the market segment."

"It won't last," Jared repeated on a low growl.

"Likely not," Alexander agreed. "Your ideas are creative and sound. But I'm afraid I'm going to need market research to buy into them. So we're not all having a little enthusiasm party here that isn't based on reality."

Jared folded his hands in front of him, struggling to control his anger. "That will take time." He had a board meeting in two weeks he needed this deal signed, sealed and delivered for if he wanted to maintain control of his company.

Alexander shrugged. "We'd like you to repitch next week in Paris." He lifted a brow. "You're a busy man. If you have other engagements, send Bailey back to Paris with me. I can weigh in with what I know works and we can chew away at it."

Bailey turned gray. Jared's blood heated to a dangerous level. So *this* was Alexander's game? Taking care of unfinished business with Bailey? *Whatever that was...*

He looked at Davide but the Frenchman's expression was one of deference to his son. And Jared had nothing to work with but a botched attempt at humor instigated by a slightly wounded heart and a massive complication between his CMO and Maison's soon-to-be CEO.

He gathered the papers in front of him together with

a viciously efficient movement, refusing to let the fury simmering in his veins find an outlet. "That's very kind of you. But I have a friend with a villa on the outskirts of Nice. Bailey and I will regroup there, flesh the ideas out, and we'll present in Paris."

"I should add," Davide interjected, "that Alexander has indicated he'd like to hear from Gehrig Electronics as well."

Jared felt the earth tilt beneath his feet. "You're adding another company to the mix?"

Davide nodded. "We feel we need to do due diligence given some product launches we've been made aware of."

Due diligence. Jared felt the fumes rise off him. Gehrig hadn't been a factor until Alexander Gagnon arrived on the scene. His gaze flickered to Davide's son, sitting with his elbow on the table, jaw resting in his palm as he watched Jared with the intense interest of a hawk studying its prey. Davide had been right. His son liked to win. Except this had nothing to do with business and everything to do with Bailey.

Frustration clawed at him like a knife. He needed to be back in the States massaging an antsy board. But unless he wanted to muddy the waters with everything he *didn't* know, make accusations he wasn't sure of, he had no choice but to play along.

He forced what he was sure was a poor representation of a smile to his lips and stood up. "We totally understand. No problem, gentlemen. Let the best candidate win."

They answered a few more questions from the marketing team and made arrangements to pitch in Paris the week after. Then he and Bailey left to pack.

She stopped him outside their rooms, her hand on his arm, her face devoid of color. "I'm so sorry, Jared. This is my fault. I should have taken myself out of the deal."

He lifted his head. "You heard his reasons. He thinks I've alienated the female demographic."

"Yes, but—" She hesitated, worrying her lip between her teeth.

"He's playing games, yes," he growled. "We will talk more in Nice. *Much more,* Bailey. But if he wants to make this personal? Let him. I don't intend to lose."

CHAPTER SIX

BY DAY THREE in Nice, Jared was feeling good about the progress they'd made on the presentation. They were holed up in a villa in the hills overlooking the sea owned by one of his friends, where the outside world was a distant distraction and pretty much everything else could wait.

Bailey had been in charge of scaling the creative ideas and adding in the market research data Alexander had requested. Which had, thankfully, proved them extremely viable. Jared concentrated on countering the intent-to-purchase consumer data Alexander had magically come up with, while also carrying out a full analysis of their competition, Gehrig Electronics, to uncover weak spots they could exploit. Unfortunately, Gehrig was a strong prospect with a rich technological heritage, a company going through a hot streak. And consumers loved buzz.

He tossed his pen down on Hans's desk. They would beat Gehrig, because although the other manufacturer had good products coming, he had better ones. Inspired ones that would set the world on fire. And although he'd had a whole strategic plan in place to unveil those products to the world, maybe it was time to let the cat out of the bag.

He got up and walked over to the window that overlooked the terrace. Bailey was sitting in a lounge chair in the sunshine, bent over her computer, hard at work as she had been for the past three fifteen-hour days. Invaluable to him. *And his ticking time bomb all in one beautiful package.*

She wasn't talking. She refused to address Alexander when he brought him up. It was a problem.

His mobile pealed from the corner of the desk. He walked over and retrieved it. Sam Walters. *Great.*

"Sam." He cradled the phone to his ear as he sat down and swung his feet up onto the desk.

"You didn't call. What's going on with Maison? I'm getting all sorts of questions I can't answer."

Join the crowd. His jaw came together with a resounding crunch. "Davide's passed the decision to his son, Alexander, who will become CEO next year. Alexander has decided he needs to do due diligence and give Gehrig Electronics a shot at the partnership. We're revamping the presentation to pitch against them next week."

"*Gehrig?* I thought this was a one-horse race?"

"Not anymore. Apparently my manifesto has dropped our brand rating with female consumers."

There was a long pause. Jared sighed. "Don't say it, Sam."

"You know I have to…the next time you get inspired to philosophize, Jared…*don't.*"

His lips twisted. "I would heartily agree with you, but that horse is out of the gate. Now we have to win."

"Yes, you do. You know I'm doing everything I can to shore things up for you until you get those products to market. But this will make a statement."

The muscles in his head clenched like a vise, a deep throb radiating through his skull. "I'm ultra-clear on this, Sam. Mea culpa, my mess. We will win. Meanwhile, let me know if you've got anything on Gehrig. I have a week to pull them apart."

"I'll make some calls."

"Thanks. Appreciate it."

"Jared?"

"Mmm?"

"You created Stone Industries. You're the only man who should be leading it. That's all the focus you need."

A smile curved his lips. "Thanks for having my back, Sam."

He put the phone down. Wondered what he would have done if he hadn't bumped into Sam at a start-up conference in the Valley and begun a lifelong friendship with the mentor who'd taken him under his wing when his father had gone AWOL. Who'd taught him that sometimes you *could* trust a person, that sometimes they *were* always there for you. And for a young, hotheaded Jared with an astronomically successful start-up on his hands, it had meant the difference between being a dot-com failure and the solid, profitable company Stone Industries was today.

An email brought his attention back to his computer screen. It was from his PI, Danny.

Bingo. Can I say, this one was my pleasure?

Why that made his insides twist, he didn't know. He opened the report, printed it and threw it in a folder. He also didn't know why he did that. Maybe he wanted to give Bailey a chance to tell him herself first. Maybe as he'd said from the beginning, trust was paramount to him. And maybe he knew what it was like to avoid the past because it only brought pain with it. And you couldn't change it no matter how much you wanted to.

Maybe he liked Bailey St. John far more than he was willing to admit.

Bailey was bleary-eyed by the time she dragged herself away from her computer to join Jared for dinner on the intimate little seaside terrace of the villa that overlooked the Mediterranean Sea. Smaller and cozier than Davide

Gagnon's showpiece of a home, it was luxurious but understated. The kind of place you could hide away forever in.

If only she could.

She pushed her hair away from her face and took a long sip of the full-bodied red Jared had unearthed from the cellar. You didn't actually relax when your boss looked as if he wanted to toss you off the cliff you were sitting on into the glorious azure water below. When decisions you'd made in the past suddenly seemed questionable when at the time, they'd seemed like the only way out.

Jared topped up her glass and stood up. "We're taking a break from work tonight. Both our brains are fried."

True. She stifled a surge of relief as she surveyed him in jeans and a navy T-shirt. Then thought maybe it was a bad idea because work had meant there was no space in her brain to remember *that kiss.*

"I think I might try to get some sleep," she demurred. "I haven't been doing so much of that."

He stared her down. "I built a fire in the pit. Sky's perfect for star spotting."

"And here I did not figure you for a Boy Scout."

"The wood was there," he said drily. "I piled it up. Come."

He picked up his glass and a blue folder he'd left on the chair and started walking down the hill. Hadn't he said no business? Maybe there was a detail he wanted to chew over, and that was good because then they wouldn't be diverging into the personal and Jared wouldn't be prying for information on Alexander Gagnon.

She stood up and followed him down to the fire pit with her wine. A series of big boulders with flat surfaces had been positioned around the pit to sit on. She lowered herself on one and watched as Jared lit the paper and coaxed the fire into a steady flame. "My father loved fires," he said. "Used to see how big he could make them go."

"How old were you when your father embezzled the money?"

He glanced at her, his profile hard and unyielding in the firelight. "More questions while you remain a mystery?"

She lifted a shoulder. "You brought him up."

"I was in my second year of university."

"That's why you dropped out?"

"Yes." He walked around and agitated the logs with a stick. "My parents had been helping me. I couldn't afford it after we lost everything."

"What happened to your father when it was discovered he took the money?"

He put the stick down and came to sit beside her on a neighboring rock. "He went to jail for three years."

Oh. She'd wondered if the more lenient laws on white-collar crime had kept him out of jail. "What does he do now?"

He stretched his long legs out in front of him and looked into the fire. "While he was in jail, my mother divorced him and married the head of the European Central Bank. When my father got out, he disappeared. I had him traced to the Caribbean, where he's been living in a hut on the beach ever since."

Wow. She tried to digest it all. "Do you have any idea why he did it?"

His lip curled, emphasizing the rather dangerous-looking, twisting white scar that ran across it. "Why he stole money from his employer and his closest friends? I'd have to be a psychologist to diagnose, but it might have something to do with my mother. She bled him dry every day of his life. And it was still never enough."

She pulled in a breath. Well, there you go. When you had attitudes like his, they came from somewhere. "What do you mean, bled him dry?"

He looked back at the fire. "She didn't know when to

stop. My father made a fortune in investment banking, but you could tell in the later years, he was done. He needed a break. But she never let him back off. Their wealth defined her. When she couldn't flash the latest hundred-thousand-dollar Maserati in front of her friends, when my father failed to provide, she left." His jaw hardened as he turned to her. "And if you're going to ask what happened then, my father lost the plot completely. As in his mind."

She looked over at him in the silence that followed, as big as any she'd encountered. "Still? Is he still like that?"

He kept his gaze trained on the leaping flames. "I haven't talked to him in a long time. I don't know. I send him money every month and he takes it."

She stared at him. How hard that must have been. How much it must have hurt. His manifesto made so much sense to her all of a sudden.

"Not all women are like your mother, Jared. I'm not."

"See, here's where I'm having a problem with that, Bailey." His low, tight tone sent a frisson of warning dancing across her skin. "I don't even know who you are. I have a multimillion-dollar deal tangled up in a woman with a past that could bring it crashing down around us. And you won't talk."

She flinched. "I've told you all that's relevant."

"Now you're going to tell me the real story." He picked up the folder sitting beside him and waved it at her. "This is where it ends."

She stared at the folder, her heart speeding up. "What is that?"

"It's your past, Bailey. In one convenient little package."

He was holding it with his far hand, far enough out of her reach that she never could have gotten to it. But she realized that wasn't the exercise.

"Who did it?" she demanded quietly.

"My PI. And trust me when I say he didn't miss anything."

Her blood pounded in her veins. Suddenly she felt very, very light-headed. "Jared. I can't—"

"You can. I've just told you the whole sordid story of my family. Now it's your turn. I haven't read it, Bailey. This is your chance."

She watched with big eyes as he stood up, walked to the fire and threw the folder into the flames. It sparked and licked up the paper until it turned gray and curled in on itself. Just like her stomach.

He turned back to her and stuck his hands in his pockets.

"Who is Alexander Gagnon to you, Bailey? What does he have on you?"

The flames licking the folder engulfed the remainder in a fiery glow. His gesture wasn't lost on her. He was giving her a chance to tell her side of the story. To trust him as he'd trusted her from the beginning.

A clamminess invaded her palms, a by-product of her racing heart and the adrenaline surging through her. A million thoughts filled her head. But in the end it came down to the truth.

"I met Alexander Gagnon when he came to my show at the Red Room in Las Vegas."

"The *Red Room*? Isn't that a strip joint?"

"That's right." She met his gaze. "I was a high-class stripper, Jared. I made oodles of money taking off my clothes for men."

His Adam's apple bobbed as if he was going to say something. His lips pursed as words formed, then he stopped, stared at her and waved a hand. "Go on."

She let her lashes drift down over her eyes. "When I was seventeen, I snuck into Tampa with a girlfriend of mine. We were hanging out in the big city, loitering on the street with pretty much nothing in our pockets, when a girl came up to me, a dancer from the hottest nightclub in the city. She told me I should apply for a job there. That I could make good money."

She twisted her hands in her lap and stared down at them. "You have to understand we were dirt-poor, my family. My father was an alcoholic, was off the job more than he was on. My mother was doing all she could to make ends meet, but her hair salon wasn't bringing in much. So when that girl—when she told me how much money I could make dancing, I was flabbergasted. I had dance training. It was one of the few things I was able to do because the local teacher let me study without paying because she thought I had potential."

He blinked. "So you started stripping?"

She nodded. "I made more money in a week dancing than my mother made in a month cutting hair. I took it home, paid for things. But when my father found out what I was doing, he hit the roof." Her mouth turned down. "They weren't making ends meet. My sister had no clothes but my money was *dirty* money. So he kicked me out."

A frown creased his forehead. "How old were you?"

"Seventeen. And believe me," she said bitterly, "nothing was ever so good. My father was not a nice drunk."

His gaze darkened. "God, Bailey, you were a baby. How were you even allowed to be in a bar?

"I lied. Got a fake ID."

He sat down beside her, rested his elbows on his knees and pressed his hands to his temples. "So you move from Tampa to Vegas where you go to school? And you keep stripping?"

"I moved there *to* dance. To pay my way through school. The money is fantastic in Vegas if you know what you're doing. I danced at a couple of different clubs, learned the industry, then I landed a slot at the Red Room. Every girl wanted to work there. It was very burlesque in the way we did the shows, they had the most beautiful women, and it was where all the high rollers hung out. I made a ton of money, easily paid for school every year."

He scrunched his face up. "Didn't it bother you the way men looked at you?"

"Like I belonged in the *bedroom?*" She threw his words back at him with a lift of her chin. "It was a job, Jared. Like any other occupation. I went to work, made a lot of money and got out when I could."

"*You took your clothes off in front of strangers*. That is not a normal job."

Heat rose up inside of her, headed for the surface. "My body was all I *had*. That was it. My sister, Annabelle, is *still* in Lakeland, working a ten-dollar-an-hour job and dealing with an alcoholic husband of her own." She stared at him, her frustration bubbling over. "I had dreams, Jared. Just like you had. Except you had a brain and I had my body so I used it."

His gaze darkened. "You also have an incredibly sharp brain. Why didn't you use *it?*"

"I didn't know that." Frustration grabbed at her, tore at her composure. "As far as I was concerned, I was low-income trash from the swamp. And no one ever tried to convince me differently. Not my teachers, classmates, not the girls who wouldn't let me into their cliques… I was the poor Williams girl who was never going to amount to anything. Well, dammit, I *did*."

He rubbed his hands over his eyes. "St. John is not your real name?"

She shook her head. "I changed it when I left Vegas for California."

"Is Bailey your real name?"

"Yes. My mother named me after her favorite drink."

His eyes widened at that. He was silent for a long time,

head in his hands. When he finally looked up at her, his expression was bleak. "When you say high-end stripper, what does that mean?"

Did she do favors for her clients on the side? Something inside her retracted. Curled up before it could be killed off. Before she showed him exactly how much that hurt.

"You want to know if I slept with the men I danced for?"

"Yes," he answered harshly.

"Would it make any difference if I said yes?" *Would it make the stigma of what she'd been worse?*

"*Goddammit*, Bailey, answer the question."

"I danced," she said stonily, "and then I went home and studied. Nothing more. *Ever.*"

He let out a long breath. "Where does Alexander Gagnon fit in all this?"

She laced her hands together and stared into the hissing, sparking fire. "Every week at the Red Room, the owner would have his favorite dancer do a special number at the end of the night. You were the star attraction, wore fancy red lingerie, got tons of tips for it. That week, he chose me." She registered the speculative look on Jared's face and chose to ignore it. "Alexander came to the Red Room for the first time on a Tuesday night. He gave me a huge tip and asked me to have a drink with him. For some reason, I refused. He was well-dressed, had this aura about him you couldn't ignore, but there was something I didn't trust. And in that business it was all about instinct.

"He didn't want any of the other girls. He came back two other nights after that, always tipping heavily and asking me to have a drink with him. On the third night, I said no, went to my dressing room and started taking off my makeup. I was the last girl to leave. The others were all in a rush to go out that night and I was just going home to study so I took my time. At one point, I had this feeling I wasn't alone and I turned around and there he was—Alexander," she qualified. "Just standing there."

His gaze narrowed. "How did he get past the bouncers?"

She grimaced. "I found out later he'd bribed Bruno, my manager, to make them look the other way. I don't know what Alexander had on Bruno to make him do that—Bruno was a big gambler, he owed people a lot of money so maybe that was it. Anyway," she said, waving a hand, "I was shocked, totally thrown. I told him to get out. He completely ignored me."

"Then what?" Jared growled.

"He propositioned me."

"What do you mean propositioned you?"

"He offered me fifty thousand dollars to sleep with him."

A dangerous glimmer entered his eyes. "For one night?"

"Yes."

"What happened when you turned him down?"

Her fingers tightened around her glass. "He told me everyone has a price. To name mine. I told him to get the hell out again and this time he did."

"And that was it?"

"He came back two more nights to see if I'd changed my mind. I never saw him after that."

"Jesus—Bailey—" He stood up and paced to the fire. Raked his hands through his hair. "Why didn't you tell me?"

"Tell *you?*" She gave him a disbelieving look. "You, the man who just wrote a manifesto about how women belong in the bedroom, not the boardroom? You have to be joking."

"Oh for God's sake, you know that doesn't apply to you." He gave his head a shake. "What did he say to you on the yacht? You looked shaken."

"He realized that nobody knows. That I've hidden my past."

"And?"

She shook her head. "You interrupted us then."

His gaze sharpened on her face. "You can't run away from the past forever. It always catches up with you."

Her mouth twisted. "So I should just tell everyone I was a *stripper?* Get it out of the way? I have worked my *entire life* to put my past behind me, Jared. I'm not ashamed of what I did. But others will judge me. 'Jared Stone's chief marketing officer—former stripper.' How do you think that will go over?"

He was silent. Because she was right.

"He still wants you," he muttered after a long moment. "He wants to win. That much is clear."

Bailey felt her past close like a noose around her neck. Finally it had caught up with her. She'd always thought it might. But did it have to be *now?* Right at the moment she'd thought she just might rise above it?

Tears of frustration singed the back of her eyes. She drained the rest of her wine and set the glass on the ground. "I am now a liability," she said quietly. "You need to take me out of this presentation, Jared. Eliminate me from the equation. You know it and I know it."

Blue eyes tangled with darker blue. The flicker in his was almost indiscernible, but she didn't miss it. The acknowledgment that she was right.

"Pull me out," she repeated dully, getting to her feet. "It's the right thing to do."

And then she walked away before she bawled her eyes out.

Jared watched Bailey go, so dumbstruck by what she'd just told him he was actually incapable of pursuing. *She'd been a high-end stripper in Vegas. She had taken her clothes off for total strangers every night, pocketed scads of money and put herself through school with it.*

The idea of *Bailey* putting herself on display like that, letting men drool over her like that, was so far-fetched it was almost laughable. He would have laughed if he wasn't so appalled. Here he'd been picturing her *selling shoes* at the local mall to put herself through school. *Making cappuccinos at the local café*…instead she'd been balling up the cash men shoved in her G-string to survive and sacrificing her innocence along with it.

Dear God. And then there was the image of Bailey dancing in expensive lingerie on a stage that wouldn't leave his head…how many men had gotten off seeing her like that? And why did that idea *torture* him?

He went for the whiskey then, because quite honestly, he didn't know what else to do. A sixteen-year-old Lagavulin he found in the lounge would do the trick. Might help wipe from his head the look on Bailey's face when he'd tossed that file into the fire and forced her hand.

She'd never wanted anyone to know about that part of her life. And he'd made her reveal it.

He carried the tumbler out onto the terrace and rested his palms on the railing. The sea glistened at the base of the cliffs in the moonlight. The whiskey slid down his throat, smoky and salty, a welcome heat to counter the disquiet plaguing him. He'd needed to know. *Had* to know. The ends justified the means. But now what?

He should take Bailey off the pitch. He should handle it alone for both their sakes. It was clear Alexander Gagnon had a fixation with her. He'd offered her an insane amount of money to sleep with him. And a man like that just didn't give up…he pursued until he won. To hell with his deal.

But there was also Davide to consider. Bailey was his ace in the hole when it came to the elder Gagnon, and he was still very much in the picture. He needed her thinking to win.

The whiskey slid down his throat, smooth and fiery. Bailey's words echoed in his head.

I had dreams, Jared. Just like you had. Except you had a brain and I had my body so I used it.

The look on her face when she'd given up…when she'd told him to take her off the deal.

His guts twisted. Bailey had fought her way out of a life most people would have accepted as their fate and never tried to rise above. But she had. She hadn't let it define her. She was the smartest, most composed, drop-dead beautiful woman he'd ever met. Her brilliant ideas had *made* their presentation.

He stared out at the brightly lit boats bobbing on the sea, their smooth roll telegraphing a calm night to come. And a strange kind of certainty settled over him. Bailey needed someone to believe in her. He was pretty sure she'd never had that. And he wasn't giving up on her.

It wasn't even a question.

It was then that Jared Stone realized his manifesto was the biggest piece of crap he'd ever written.

Bailey had just slipped her nightie on when a knock came at the door. Her emotions far too close to the surface, she stayed where she was.

"I'm fine, Jared. I'm good with all of it. I just need some sleep."

"I'm not leaving until I talk to you. Open the door."

His tone was hard; implacable, like Jared was. She cursed, grabbed her robe and tugged it on. Attempted to compose herself as she pulled the door open and found him standing there like a fierce warrior, filling the doorway with his broad-shouldered frame.

"I am not dropping you," he announced. "We are partners and we are doing this together."

"Jared—" She bit her lip, furiously blinking back tears.

Even after what she'd just told him, he was still backing her?

"We are a team," he said quietly, blue gaze softening. "I've told you that from the beginning. You trusted me enough to tell me about your past tonight and I know that wasn't easy. I *need* you in that room with me, Bailey. You've proven that."

A tear slid down her cheek. She couldn't help it. No one had ever shown such faith in her. She'd been going it alone since she was seventeen and suddenly, she felt so tired of it. Tired of fighting every battle by herself.

"Christ, Bailey." He took a step forward and brushed the tear away with the pad of his thumb. "Did you think I was just going to abandon you? After everything you've put into this? Those are *your* ideas Davide loves."

She looked down, anywhere but at him, but the tears kept rolling. "I thought you wouldn't respect me, that you wouldn't want me anywhere near this deal if you knew what I'd been..."

He slid his fingers under her chin and brought her gaze back up to his. "I am not going in there without you. And as for respecting you? I've never respected a woman more in my life. For who you are. For what you've done..."

Something melted inside of Bailey. Something that had been frozen for so long she'd forgotten it existed. She thought it might be her heart.

"But what about Alexander? Lord knows what he's capable of and I would never forgive myself if you lose this deal because of me."

"I'm not going to lose," he said softly. "Alexander Gagnon likes to win. I like to win more."

"But—"

He pressed his fingers against her lips. She fell silent in a sea of confusion that had only one focal point: the electricity that was so strong between them that it held her completely still as his eyes darkened with an emotion she couldn't read. He put his mouth to the hot, wet tears dampening her cheeks and kissed each one away with a slow drag of his lips that started out comforting and ended up something else entirely.

Hot. Scorching hot.

She didn't know who kissed who first. It was unspoken communication, her hands cupping his jaw, devouring him, while his found the belt to her robe, untied it and pushed it off her shoulders. She moved into him until her bare skin was molded against the hard muscles of his chest, tasting him, knowing him, until she wasn't sure where she started and he ended.

"You are so beautiful," he rasped, his mouth leaving hers to trail a path of fire down her throat. When he hit the ultrasensitive spot between her neck and shoulder, she gasped and arched to give him better access. He took full advantage, nuzzling and exploring until she dug her hands into his shoulders and demanded more.

He drew back and took her in. Color swept every centimeter of her skin. "We can't do this. You are my boss."

He shook his head. "It's never been that simple with us and you know it."

"Jared..."

He slid a finger underneath the spaghetti strap of her nightie and slipped it off her shoulder. Her heart pounded in her chest as he weighed her breast in his palm and learned the shape of her. She could have pulled away then, *should* have pulled away, but the want in her shocked her, the fact she'd never let a man touch her like this becoming inconsequential somewhere around the time he took her inside the heat of his mouth and her knees went weak.

The rush, the sweet, all-encompassing rush knocked her brain sideways. She buried her fingers in his hair and closed her eyes. And for once in her life just let herself feel. *Want.* He slid his jean-clad leg between her thighs and brought her closer. He was hard and rough against her sensitive skin and it excited her beyond belief.

She moved against him and whimpered. "Jared…"

He slid the strap off her other shoulder and flicked his tongue over her engorged nipple. Gave her what her husky entreaty hadn't been able to verbalize. And the unfamiliar throb inside her reached a fever pitch.

Somehow she was in his arms and he was striding across the room to the sofa in the lounge. He sat down, wrapped her legs around him and brought his mouth back to hers in a red-hot kiss that pulled her under again.

She should have been alarmed at how fast things were moving, *that they were moving at all* given her lack of experience, but somehow with Jared, it felt so right. She buried her mouth in the hollow of his neck and explored his musky, salty, utterly male scent.

He found the hem of her nightie and pushed it up. Her gaze tracked his movements as he trailed his fingers over the concave dip where her hip met thigh.

"You are all woman," he murmured huskily.

"Too much, I'd say."

He shook his head. "You are perfection. You know what I was thinking that night you asked me to choose the shoes?"

"What?"

He trailed his fingers along the edge of her panties, down to where she was on fire for him. "This."

His whispered answer sent a shiver down her spine. Her stomach curled into a hard, tight ball as he brought his thumb to her center and rotated it so achingly slowly she thought she might go up in flames.

"I thought that if we'd been on a date," he continued huskily, "I would have kept you there until I'd made you come…at least twice."

She lost her composure then. "Jared—"

He put his fingers to her mouth. "Better late than never, don't you think?"

Having never had an orgasm in her life, Bailey couldn't answer that question. And good thing she didn't have to, because Jared flipped their positions then, went down on his knees in front of the sofa and lifted his gaze to hers.

"Spread your legs for me, sweetheart."

Her pulse went into overdrive, tattooing itself against her veins so hard she thought she might pass out. She didn't know it was possible to feel so turned on and so excruciatingly self-conscious at the same time, but the blazing heat of his deep blue gaze spurred her on. *Lustful. Full of want. Nothing she wasn't ready to give.*

Her thighs fell apart. He worked his palms up the inside of them, arranging her to his satisfaction until she couldn't look anymore and closed her eyes. And then his hands were under her hips, urging her forward; his mouth was hot against her center, burning a trail against her damp panties, and Bailey forgot her name.

He tugged off her underwear with an impatient movement, setting his mouth to her heated flesh, where she was wet and wanting him. Hot, sweet pleasure coursed through her, curled her toes.

"Beautiful, you are so beautiful," he murmured against her skin. "Twice might not be enough."

She closed her eyes. The hot slide of his tongue against her made her whimper. And he did it again and again, varying the pressure and rhythm, asking her how she liked it. She gave him rational, honest responses at first. And then she started shaking and needing something more and she begged him to shut up.

His soft laughter flickered across the sensitive skin of her thighs. The smooth slide of his finger as he eased it inside her tore a moan from her throat. Then he brought his tongue back into play and the world went a hazy gray. This, she realized instinctively, was what she needed.

"Bailey," he murmured, "baby. Give it up."

She arched her hips and clutched the fabric of the sofa as he increased his rhythm. She begged and he gave no quarter, adding another finger, increasing the intensity until she went over the edge, her palm against her mouth the only thing preventing her scream from tearing into the night.

When her body had stopped shaking like a leaf, her brain started to function again.

So that was what all the fuss was about.

Jared leaned forward and smoothed her hair back from her face. "What did you say?"

"Nothing." OMG had she just said that out loud?

He gave her a curious look, then a slow smile curved his lips as he rose to his feet, worked his palms beneath her and swung her up in his arms. "That was *one*."

Bailey's heart pounded with every step he took toward the gorgeous turquoise-blue bedroom. She had to tell him. *Now.*

"Jared." She poked a finger into his shoulder. "Stop for a second. I need to tell you something."

He halted midstride, his gaze flicking to her face. "What?"

Color rushed to her cheeks, rendering them a red-hot mess. "I've never—I mean you should know that I am a—"

The words died in her throat as he went as gray as she was red.

"You are goddamn joking."

CHAPTER SEVEN

THE LOOK ON Bailey's face sent a cold rush through Jared, like the mistral gone awry right up the center of him. He dropped her to the floor so fast she didn't have time to brace herself, and his hands at her waist were the only thing that held her up.

"Tell me you're joking," he repeated harshly.

She pushed a hand against his chest and stood back, her chin lifting to a defiant angle. "What's the big deal?"

His eyes rounded. "You're a twenty-nine-year-old, former stripper, *virgin?*"

Her face went even hotter. "Are you going to tag that description on every time you talk about me now? Because I'm afraid that doesn't work for me."

He closed his eyes and raked his hair back from his face. "I don't understand how this could happen."

Her mouth flattened. "Simple. I haven't gotten into bed with a man. Not that you'd understand anything about that. Half the women in the Valley are walking around with your cute little diamond charm bracelets on as if they were the Medal of Honor."

He let out a harsh breath and opened his eyes. "It was the combination of your age and background, Bailey. You haven't exactly been living in a nunnery."

She put her hands on her hips and stared at him. "What

were you hoping? That I'd have all sorts of tricks up my sleeve, *living the life?*"

His gaze narrowed. "I wasn't actually thinking, Bailey. As you can imagine after what just happened."

Taking her to bed and having her until sunrise had been the only thing in his head...no thinking involved there.

His mouth twisted in a scowl. Not happening now, that was for sure. Virgins wanted rings on their fingers. Assurances of undying love. That part of his manifesto hadn't been wrong.

"Why?" His frustrated, sexually aroused body wanted to know. "Why would you be twenty-nine and a virgin?"

She wrapped her arms around herself. "I dunno, Jared. I'd have to be a psychologist to say." His scowl grew as she tossed his words back at him. "I didn't date in Vegas. The men who asked me out were only after one thing, given my profession. They didn't exactly want to court me. Then when I came to the Valley I was just too busy working."

"And your father," he pointed out. "He can't have given you a very good picture of men to work with."

No. He'd broken her heart. Her mother's heart. *All of their hearts* again and again to match his own broken one. Twenty years of wanting to be the hero you once were.

She brushed her hair out of her face. "I'm sure that had something to do with it."

He frowned. "I don't buy that you were too busy to date in the Valley. I've seen the men pursue you."

"Because I'm a challenge," she pointed out. "You think I don't know what they say about me? The wagers they make? The minute I go to bed with one of them it's going to be all over the airwaves faster than your manifesto." She wrinkled her nose. "I'd rather not bother."

"So what was that?" He jerked his head toward the sofa. "You were all in there, Bailey."

"Stupid me." She rolled her eyes. "We do have this

chemistry, you and I. And for one second, *five minutes*," she amended sarcastically, "I was doing what I wanted. I wasn't holding back."

His heart stuttered. The urge to pick her up, walk into that bedroom and finish what they'd started made him shove his hands in his pockets. Because while he liked Bailey, might even be *fond* of her, despite the fact that he wanted to take her to bed more than he'd ever wanted a woman in his life, he didn't do the big *V*. Wasn't capable of it. It would be like asking him to vote Republican. To suggest he leave a big messy pile in the middle of his impeccably clean desk.

Clean desk, clean mind, his Zen master had told him on that thirty-day search to find his soul. If he slept with Bailey, there might never be enough meditation for that.

He lifted his gaze to her rather glazed one, resolute despite his screaming body. "I just have one question for you."

She gave him a wary look. "What?"

"Don't you ever get…*frustrated*?"

Her eyes darkened. "Get out of my room, Jared."

How were you supposed to greet the day when you'd just spent the night before getting down and dirty with your boss? It wasn't a particular skill Bailey had arrived in France with, and the thought of facing him across a plate of croissants while she remembered him on his knees between her thighs, *devouring* her, wasn't going to fly.

She yanked a pillow over her face and lay back in the big king-size bed. Her only saving grace was she hadn't screamed out loud. But even that was tempered by the fact that her moans of approval *had* been loud and clear. And *if* he'd taken her to bed, she would have let him take her virginity. She would have let *Jared Stone* take her virginity. Because for a moment there, she'd thought she'd seen the real Jared. The man behind the manifesto. The man who thought enough of her that he was backing her when he shouldn't be…

Who had called her the smartest marketing person he'd ever worked with.

I've never respected a woman more in my life. For who you are. For what you've done.

Ugh. She pressed the pillow harder against her face. Had he just been trying to get her into bed? Had he been intrigued by her past and wondering how hot she was? How skilled? But even as she thought it, she knew it wasn't right. Jared was risking too much standing behind her to just be out for sex. His Achilles' heel was his utter and complete inability to commit. This was right within character. A virgin must be an intensely scary, disconcerting phenomenon to him. *What had she expected him to do?*

She threw the pillow off, fury at herself coursing through her. He might respect her even after all she'd told him, but he was still Jared—a man no female should get anywhere near unless she was as shallow as he was when it came to the art of the casual hookup.

It made her wonder about the rest of the manifesto she hadn't read…

She swung her legs over the side of the bed, padded into the lounge and woke up her computer. Gave the scattered sofa pillows a grimace. His manifesto now had five million views. She typed in the word *virgin* and pressed Find. And there it was. Bolded.

Never, ever take a virgin home with you unless you're prepared to open up the homestead to her. Lock, stock and barrel. There is no "see how it goes" with a virgin. I've seen better men than me crash and burn. Hard.

Her vision misted over. What was wrong with her? When had she forgotten exactly who Jared was? *About the same time he had kissed her brain into some sort of ancient and useless artifact.* Because let's face it. Some women would trade their self-respect for that skill in the bedroom.

If she'd kept her mouth shut last night, she would have.

She got to her feet with a jerky movement, strode into the bathroom and pushed her obviously cloudy head under the hot spray of the shower. She was going to pretend last night had never happened. Appreciate what Jared was doing for her because he *was* risking a great deal by keeping her in this pitch, she knew that. And she was going to win it for him. Then she was going to get far away from Jared Stone while she still had her wits about her.

Jared was eating breakfast on the terrace when she arrived downstairs, newspaper spread out in front of him, undoubtedly having already inhaled a couple of the croissants from the basket as he did every morning. He had the highest metabolism of anyone she'd ever encountered, which she had to admit was likely stoked by all the *muscle* on display for her this morning. Athletic shorts and a gray T-shirt left little of it to the imagination.

Not helping.

Heat rushed to her face as he glanced up at her, and the night before slammed into her brain like an unavoidable fact. But this was cool and controlled Bailey in charge now. She could do this.

She sat down opposite him at the little table. His gaze traveled over her face. "Good morning."

She tried to ignore how sexy and rusty his voice sounded before he'd put it to use for the day and muttered a greeting back. Refused to imagine how superhot it would be if she was *still* in his bed at this time of the morning, which of course she was not, because he'd walked out on her as though she was a communicable disease.

Not that she was bitter about it or anything.

She reached for the croissants, still warm from the oven, her fingers closing over one with chocolate oozing out of it. "Georgina outdid herself this morning."

He gave the croissant a hard look. "I've been trying to figure out how they get the chocolate in the center."

"You roll them this way." She spread her napkin on the table and demonstrated.

He lifted a brow. "You're handy in the kitchen, too. That's a big turn-on."

Apparently not when combined with her virgin status. She picked up a knife and sliced through the croissant with a vicious movement. "But then I would want to commandeer all your baking supplies at the homestead. How horrific..."

A smile edged his lips. "I knew you were going to look that up. And actually, Bailey, I love nothing more than when a woman cooks for me. As long as she shuts the door after her when she leaves."

She closed her eyes against the oh-so-tempting vision of him with the chocolate pastry smeared all over his face.

"I don't know if I can do this."

"What? Live with me for another week?" His tone was overtly amused. "Feel free to speak openly."

She shook her head. *No. No thanks.* She was not letting him draw her in again. He was a professional instigator—head and shoulders more skilled than her in that department. She picked up the coffeepot, poured herself a cup of the steaming brew and set the tall silver canister back on the table so it effectively blocked him from view. He reached out and slid it aside, laughter dancing in his eyes. "You think you can block me out with a coffeepot?"

"Not really." She gave him an even look as she stirred milk into her coffee. "But what's the alternative? We talk about last night?"

He shrugged. "At least you had some sort of relief. Me? It took a five-mile run this morning to work it out."

Her already-hot face incinerated. "I am so not talking to you about this. In fact, I suggest we never reference it again."

A wide smile curved his lips. "Fine. I'm just saying you aren't the only cranky one this morning."

Her eyes widened. "I'm not cranky." Angry, more like it. "Reading the rest of your manifesto was a good wake-up call. Stupid me for thinking my virginity wouldn't make a difference to a Lothario like you."

His smile faded. "First, I think that's an exaggeration. And second, there's only one reason I walked away from you last night, Bailey. I don't make promises I can't keep. I don't like taking women for a ride like some guys do. And if that makes me a jerk then so be it."

"Who was asking you for a promise?" She shook her head in amazement. "You're so caught up in yourself, in what you *think* you know about people, you haven't got a clue, do you?"

He leaned forward and rested his elbows on the table, his gaze spearing hers. "Tell me you don't want the full deal. A man who loves you. A diamond ring…everything that goes with it."

She sank her teeth into her bottom lip, knowing he was sucking her in again but too stung to care. "You want the truth, Jared? I don't know what love is. I've never had it so how would I? My parents kicked me out when I was seventeen…dancing pretty much ruined my trust in men…" She lifted her shoulders. "I've been fighting my own battles for so long, I'd settle for a man who respects me. A man who tells me the truth." She angled her chin at him. "One who wants me for who I am."

His lips tightened. "This is about *my rules*, Bailey. Not you. If you hadn't been the last virgin on the face of the planet last night we'd be acting out my deepest, darkest fantasies about you—and believe me, I have many."

Her breath caught in her throat, heat searing through her in a potent combination of lust and humiliation. "You are such a jerk, you know that?" She pulled in a breath and stared at the hard, uncompromising lines of his face. "You know what I think? I think your rules are a cop-out. Your parents' marriage was a disaster so you think all relationships are like that. You avoid ties to anyone so you don't have to face the reality of being in one yourself." She lifted a brow. "I think you're scared."

His face took on a gray tinge. "Look who's talking."

"You're right." She abandoned her croissant and pushed away from the table. "But at least I admit it."

"Where are you going?" he barked. "We aren't finished here."

"I need a walk. All of this denial is making me lose my appetite."

Jared had been trying to avoid the truth the entire two hours he'd been up and Bailey had been in bed. Kissing her, touching her like that last night, had almost been an inevitability. He got that. *Bailey's being a virgin had not.* How did *anyone* reach the age of twenty-nine and be a virgin? Honestly?

He watched her walk down the path toward the beach, back ramrod straight, her shoulders up around her ears.

For once I wasn't holding back. For once I was doing what I wanted.

He scowled and tossed his napkin on the table. How was he supposed to interpret that? What was he supposed to *do* with that? He needed to stay away from Bailey. She was like a flashing neon danger sign for him. A weakness he couldn't afford to indulge at a time when winning this deal was all that mattered. So why was he now striding down the path after her like a raging bull intent on having his way?

She looked warily at him as he fell into step beside her. "Go away, Jared."

"When you said dancing destroyed your trust in men, what did you mean?"

She gave him a long look. "You wouldn't ask that if you'd spent any amount of time in a strip club."

He shrugged. "It's not my thing."

"I don't imagine. Not when the women are beating down your door for a night with the *lion*."

"Bailey…"

"Why are you asking this?"

"I want to know."

She looked as though she was going to tell him to mind his own business. He wasn't sure what was going on in those cool blue eyes. Embarrassment? The need to protect herself? But then she lifted her shoulders. "There are four types of men who come to a strip club. The jokers, the guys who come in with a bachelor party or to party with their friends, they drink too much, leave you nice tips and go on their way. Then there's the regulars. Some of them become friends, they pay you to dance for them, sit with them, listen to the things their wives won't because their marriage is so far gone, they don't listen to them at all anymore."

His mouth twisted. "You realize you're proving my point."

She ignored him. "Those are the good regulars. Who can become bad regulars if they fall for you. Then they decide you need to be rescued. That you shouldn't be living this life and they want to marry you. If you're unlucky, they become stalkers and then they're a real problem."

"Did that happen to you?"

"Once. The club saw him follow me to my car and called the police."

He looked horrified. “And the final kind?”

“The men who want to degrade you. The ones who are unsuccessful in life, feel they aren’t appreciated enough at home—the ones who don’t feel *manly* enough. They come in to put themselves on a power trip. They’ll call you names, call you stupid, whatever makes them feel better about themselves by making *you* feel like you’re about an inch tall.”

“So how did you deal with that?” A wry smile curved his mouth. “I can’t imagine you took it well.”

“I didn’t. One night when a guy grabbed my butt, I slapped him across the face.” Her mouth pursed. “He hit me back, only, much harder.”

Jared’s heart lurched. “What happened after that?”

“The bouncers threw him out. He came back the next night.”

“They let him back *in*?”

“He was spending. That’s all they care about.”

“Did that happen often?”

“No. It was more verbal abuse. You got used to it, you developed a thick skin, but it still wears away at your self-confidence.”

She looked so vulnerable, so tiny beside him when some of those guys must have been twice her size, it made his skin burn just thinking about it.

“What were the rules on personal contact?”

Her gaze skipped away from his. “To make the really good money, you had to do private dances.”

“Lap dances?”

“Yes.”

He’d never had a lap dance. He’d watched his groom-to-be buddy have one and hadn’t felt any desire to do that with a stranger. Hadn’t seen the sexiness in it. His buddy had, though. He’d loved having the beautiful girl intimately plastered across his lap.

"Was this," he asked Bailey, his voice a little on the rough side, "all done with or without clothes?"

Rosy color stained her delicate cheekbones. "We had to wear bottoms. We wore two, in fact. I'm not even sure why. It might have been more of a fashion statement."

The thought of Bailey dressed like that, dancing on a guy's lap, had him asking, "Didn't it bother you, doing that?"

"Of course it bothered me," she snapped. "It wasn't Sunday school, Jared. It was a job—a very lucrative job where men paid me a lot of money to take off my clothes. And maybe if I hadn't had to worry about money my entire life, hadn't had to wear hand-me-downs every day to school, I would have chosen differently. But I didn't have that luxury and I wanted to make a better life for myself."

Point taken.

She looked out at the sea, the sun slanting over her alabaster skin. "Most of the men were fine. Most of them respected the line and didn't cross it."

"Except for the ones like Alexander."

She looked back at him, the remnants of a memory in her eyes. "Do you know what he said to me that night in my dressing room?"

He was pretty sure he didn't, but he nodded anyway.

"He said he would respect my hard limits."

Jared's hands clenched into fists by his sides. "You stay away from him in Paris," he said harshly. "I don't want you interacting with him."

She nodded. "I will."

He didn't want Gagnon anywhere near her. He was also sure he never wanted a man to raise a hand to her again. *Put* a hand on her. *Ever.*

He raked a hand through his hair and blinked against the sunshine breaking through the clouds as they stepped down onto the beach. Absorbed the uneasy feeling in his gut as he worried he was seriously losing his edge. Protecting Bailey against Alexander Gagnon was a given. The rest of it—the urge to keep her for himself—that was something he could never, ever do. He wasn't even sure where such a crazy thought had come from.

CHAPTER EIGHT

AN UTTERLY BRILLIANT, rock-solid presentation under their belt, Jared and Bailey landed in Paris on Sunday night after a quick hour-and-a-half flight north from Nice in the Stone Industries jet. A car picked them up from the terminal and whisked them into the city, lights sparkling from every vantage point as dusk fell.

Jared studied the play of color across the Seine as they neared their hotel in the Left Bank, thinking the City of Light was so much more appropriate a descriptor than the City of Love. For one thing, he thought, mouth twisting, love was a myth perpetuated by all the romantics of the world. Secondly, there was no city as gorgeous as Paris at night.

He watched Bailey once again play twenty questions with their driver, asking him about the city landmarks.

I don't know what love is, she'd said. *I've never had it so how would I? I'd settle for a man who respects me. A man who tells me the truth. One who wants me for who I am.*

He pursed his lips and stared out at the elegant facades of the historic buildings that lined the river. Bailey was everything a man in his right mind would want in a woman. Intelligent, stunningly beautiful, interesting and desirable… How had one not snapped her up, pushed his way past that impenetrable facade? Tapped into that wistfulness she kept hidden so well? Had the life she'd led made her bury it that deep?

He put it out of his head as the car whipped around a corner and pulled to a halt in front of their elegant old hotel. It was exactly that vulnerability, the fact that she was untouched, that was going to keep him a hundred paces from her at all times if he knew what was good for him.

Their takeoff spot had been delayed in Nice, which meant they had less than an hour before they were due at the dinner that had been organized for them and their Gehrig counterparts. Enough time to check in to their hotel, change and go. Jared left Bailey to shower and dress in the suite that adjoined his and did the same.

He had showered and was pulling on his shirt when a knock came at the connecting door. He strode over and pulled it open, finding a fully dressed, toe-tapping Bailey on the other side. Her gaze moved over his chest, down over the muscles of his abdomen in a caught-off-guard perusal that couldn't be mistaken for anything but total appreciation.

It made his vow to avoid anything that constituted lust between them snag in his throat.

"I just need a tie," he muttered, turning around and putting distance between them.

Bailey walked in and strolled to the Juliet balcony to look out at the lights. "It's so beautiful at night."

Jared did the buttons of his shirt up. "One of my favorite cities in the world."

"Which you will never enjoy on your honeymoon because you're never getting married. How sad for you."

"How forward-thinking of me," he retorted. "I can bring my girlfriend here instead of paying for divorce proceedings."

Her throaty laugh did strange things to his stomach. "You think you're so tough, Jared Stone," she murmured as she turned around. "But you're really not. You know that?"

He elected not to respond. She was in white tonight, a simple classy knee-length dress that made the most of her curvaceous figure, hair up in a sleek chignon that left her beautiful neck bare. His strict no-virgin policy should have shielded him from the desire to bury his mouth in the exposed hollow between neck and shoulder. Unfortunately, his body wasn't following his strategic plan.

Biting out a curse, he whipped the tie around his neck and tied it with the quick efficiency of a man who hated that particular accessory. *He was not having her.*

Bailey surveyed him with a critical eye. Walked toward him with a purposeful movement that sent his pulse into overdrive. He yanked in a breath as she came to a halt in front of him and pushed his hands aside.

"Your tie is crooked."

As disheveled as his mind.

He kept his hands by his sides while she undid the tie, set it back around his neck and retied it, her technique smooth and flawless. Her perfume drifted into his nostrils, the curves he was almost going crazy not touching so close he would only have had to take a step to feel her against him.

"How did you," he murmured roughly, "learn to tie a tie so well with no lovers in your life?"

She pursed her lips as she finished it off. "Etiquette training."

"*Etiquette* training?" He stared at her as if he hadn't heard right. "As in Pygmalion?"

She smiled. "If you want to put it like that."

"*Why?*"

Rosy color stained her cheeks. "I grew up dirt-poor with no idea of how to function in society, Jared. I was a stripper. Where was I going to learn what to say over a business dinner? What fork to use? I might have gotten an MBA, but it in no way prepared me for any of that. So I had someone teach me."

"Right." His heart contracted. Just a bit.

Every time he built a wall against her, she disarmed him. She said something like that and reminded him just how vulnerable she was under that tough exterior. It made him want to hold her and never let go.

"Jared—" She bit her lip and stared up at him and God help him, he almost snared that luscious mouth under his and did what he wanted to do. But that was absolutely, definitely not happening. Not tonight when he needed his wits about him. When he needed to *win this deal*.

"We need to go," he announced abruptly, stepping back. "We're already late."

The hurt he seemed to be a professional at putting in her eyes gleamed bright. He ignored it and shoved his wallet into his pocket.

"The car's waiting. Let's go."

The seafood restaurant on the Rue de Rivoli was packed with people on the warm, steamy Paris night. The maître d' led them to the chef's table at the back of the restaurant with its much-in-demand view of the bustling, sparkling kitchen in which white-coated chefs worked in symphonic precision.

They were the last in the group of seven to arrive. Their competition, John Gehrig, the CEO of Gehrig Electronics, rose to introduce himself, his wife, Barbara, and his vice president of marketing. Gehrig was a warm, friendly Midwesterner in his early fifties whom Bailey couldn't help but instantly like. As was Barbara, who was utterly charming as his feminine counterpart, and apparently whip-smart as Gehrig's legal counsel.

She moved to greet Davide, then Alexander, who was superbly dressed in a gray suit and navy shirt and drawing more than one set of female eyes as he stood. He bent to press a kiss to each of her cheeks, the touch of his lips sending an involuntary shiver through her. "You look outrageously beautiful," he murmured in her ear as he brushed the other cheek. "Unfortunate Stone had the pleasure of escorting you."

Bailey stepped back, firmly disengaging his hands. "So lovely to see you again."

Jared made a point of sitting in the seat beside Alexander at the round table designed for conversation, which left Bailey to his left and Barbara beside her. A potent predinner cocktail Barbara suggested was a fine method of relaxation, and before long, the two of them had hit it off.

"So," Barbara murmured as the fish course was being removed, "are you and the delectable Jared together?"

She shook her head. "What made you think that?"

"The way he looks at you. Like he'd like to have you for the main course…you might want to address that."

Or not.

"And then there's the dark and dangerous Alexander…" Barbara mused. "Uncatchable, say the tabloids."

Bailey wondered, for the millionth time, why he was fixated on *her*. Surely the man could have any woman with his looks and fortune?

Jared asked her a question, claiming her attention with a touch of his hand on her arm. It was a gesture that did not escape Alexander's attention because he had been watching her like a hawk all night. Bailey leaned into Jared and contributed her thoughts on the changing retail climate. Alexander tracked the movement. That she heartily enjoyed the constant touching when she was supposed to be hating Jared was a matter she didn't care too examine too closely. It was all an act for Alexander's benefit, of course.

Dinner stretched on, Parisian-style, with course after course of delectable French food. More bottles of twenty-year-old wine were consumed than Bailey could count, accompanied by enough business talk to make the night worthwhile, but not so much it impinged on the very civilized French way of taking the time to truly savor a meal. Talk turned to port when a cheese plate was placed on the table to finish. Davide and Jared, both huge fans of the intensely flavored wine, were invited down to the cellar by the owner to choose their selection. While the Gehrigs went out for a smoke, and their VP left to make a call, Bailey excused herself to use the ladies' room rather than be alone with Alexander.

She took her time, but when she returned to the table, Alexander was still its only occupant. Jerking her head around, she found the Gehrigs chatting to a couple at another table.

Alexander stood. "Sit down, Bailey. I don't bite."

Yes, you do, she wanted to say. But rather than cause a scene, she did. Alexander picked up his wine, lowered himself into his chair, and took a sip. "How did your strategy session go? Ready for Tuesday?"

She nodded. "I think you'll be very happy with the final plan."

"Good." He set the glass down. "Jared may be a maverick but his vision is right."

Her gaze met his warily. "I'm glad you realize that."

His slate-gray eyes glittered. "Why didn't you take me up on that offer in Vegas, Bailey?"

She swallowed. "It wasn't personal. I never fraternized with customers."

"Yet you fraternize with your boss."

Warmth flooded her cheeks. "Jared and I don't have a relationship."

"Oh, come on, Bailey. You're infatuated with him. If you're not sleeping with him now, you will be."

Her blood pressure skyrocketed. "Pick a more appropriate topic or I will leave the table."

"It's fine, you know," he continued. "I only want one night. Think of it like this, my Vegas proposal, except this time, you don't get fifty thousand dollars, you get to save your boyfriend's deal."

Her jaw dropped open. "*Why?* Why me, Alexander? You could have any woman you wanted."

He nodded his head toward Jared's chair. "I want what *he* has. I want what I've wanted from the beginning."

She shook her head at the direct, unhesitating stare he leveled at her. The man was a sociopath.

His gaze narrowed. "For a woman who stripped for a living you are very naive, Bailey. I want the fantasy. I want what you were selling on that stage—but I want it for me. To know when I sink myself into you, I have what none of them had."

Bailey stood up on shaking legs. "You are insane."

"No," he said underlining the word, "I know what I want." He nodded his head toward the back of the restaurant. "Sit down. They're coming back."

She turned and saw Jared and Davide winding their way through the tables, Jared's gaze pinned on her. She sank back into her chair.

"Don't make a mess of this for Jared," Alexander murmured as the din of the restaurant buzzed on around them. "Think about it."

She wasn't actually sure what happened the last hour she sat there in a frozen state. The port was consumed, the cheese eaten by connoisseurs other than herself, and somehow the evening ended.

Alexander offered to drive them back to their hotel and rather than be rude, Jared accepted. When the Frenchman had dropped them off and they were in the elevator riding up to their rooms, Jared crossed his arms over his chest, the hot and bothered look to him suggesting he wasn't so under control.

"What happened with Alexander at the table?"

She leaned back against the wall of the lift, her head

spinning. "He told me if I took him up on his offer from Vegas, I could save your deal."

His head jerked back. "*What?*"

She swallowed hard. "He said your vision was the future and we were the right choice. But that I could seal the deal by sleeping with him. That he only wanted one night."

His nostrils flared, his fingers flexing around the metal bar that surrounded the lift. She was half terrified he would stop the car and go after Alexander from the coldly furious look on his face. Instead, as the lift stopped at their floor, he stepped out, held the door for her and stalked toward their rooms.

"Your card," he barked, taking it and opening the door. It was a good two or three moments before he spoke.

"What else did he say?"

She lifted a trembling hand to her cheek. "I asked him why. He said he wanted the fantasy. That when he was *deep inside me* he would have what none of the others had." She stared at him. "God, Jared. He's sick."

He was so still, so absolutely still, she could feel her heart pounding in her chest. It throbbed once, twice, three times before he took a deep breath and started toward her, his hands cupping her jaw. "He's a megalomaniac who thinks he can have anything he wants, Bailey. But he will never put his hands on you. I promise you that."

She was shaking. He folded her against his chest and held her there, his hands in her hair. "He's bluffing."

She shook her head. "He brought in Gehrig."

"Gehrig was a natural choice. They're an extremely hot brand. I'm surprised they didn't include them from the beginning. It was a smart move on Alexander's part."

She pushed away. "You need to send me home, Jared. This is crazy."

"Not happening. We have Project X. It's going to win this for us. We stay the course, Bailey."

But he'd never wanted to use his secret launch. They had a whole strategic plan built around the products that involved an array of global partners. And now he was messing with that because of *her* past.

She stalked past him to the closet, pulled her suitcase out and started throwing clothes in.

"What the *hell* are you doing?"

She spun around. "I have to go. It's the only way. If I'm gone, Alexander might lose interest and play fairly."

Hot color stained his cheekbones. "Have you been listening to anything I've said? *He doesn't care*, Bailey. You are not a deciding factor. You are a pawn in his game. So forget anything but us going in there and winning the entire committee over. *Making* him make the right decision."

But what if Alexander didn't do the right thing? She shook her head. "I can't take that chance. I will not lose this deal for you." She turned and started dumping her shoes into the bag, tears stinging the back of her eyes. Jared's hands sank into her waist and spun her around.

"How many times do I have to tell you I'm not doing this alone? We're pitching this together and we're winning."

Her gaze dropped to his perfectly knotted tie. A Windsor knot. Her favorite. And she wondered why, why was he doing this? Why was he backing her to his own detriment?

Her mouth twisted. "He told me he wanted to have what you have. Ironic, isn't it, when you don't even want what I'm offering?"

His gaze darkened to a deep, stormy blue. "You know that isn't true."

"How?" She practically yelled the word at him. "I put myself out there for the first time in my life, we share what we shared and then you shut it down as if I'm totally expendable. A dime a dozen...because of your stupid rules."

His face tightened. "They aren't stupid rules. They're designed to ensure you don't get hurt."

"They're designed to ensure *you* don't get hurt."

He lifted a shoulder. "They are what they are."

"Coward." She hurled the word at him with all the hurt and confusion surging through her. "You talk about trust. You want me to trust you on this, to walk into this pitch with you when you won't even be honest with yourself?"

His cheeks stained deeper. "You want the *truth*, Bailey? You want to know what's been eating at me? I've spent the entire evening, the entire *week* telling myself I can't have you. Telling myself I will hurt you. When all I can think of is *having* you. Teaching you what it's like to be with a man and pleasuring you so much you'll never want another." His blue eyes blazed into hers. *"How messed up is that?"*

Her stomach contracted. Dammit, she wanted that. Jared had *seen* her, the real her, in Nice, and he still wanted her. She'd never felt so stripped down, so vulnerable, so needy of what another person had to offer in her life. And she wasn't questioning it. Not anymore.

"Then do it," she murmured. "Forget about your rules."

"Bailey—"

She silenced him with a finger to his lips. "I don't *want anything* from you, Jared. I don't want promises. I don't want the homestead. But I do want to know what it's like between us. It's burning me up…"

He went so still she wondered if he was still breathing. She stepped into him before he regained the control he always found and cupped his jaw with her palm. "Not one more word. I swear if you say one more word about your rules I'll scream."

Those long lashes settled down over his eyes. Then he opened them and rested his gaze on her. "You sure you can handle this?"

She stood up on tiptoe, balancing her palm against his chest. "You sure you can?"

"No," he muttered. "I am not."

He backed her up against the wardrobe, his suit-clad thigh sliding between hers, his hard gaze full of intent. Thought ceased as he rocked his mouth over hers and took it in a kiss that made her knees go weak. Over and over again, he tasted her, commanded her response until he was the only thing in her head. Until she moved against him and surrendered more of herself. As if he knew exactly what she needed in the way her body softened against his. In the way she accepted his tongue into her mouth and met the erotic slide of it against hers with a low, soft moan that told him she was fully his.

When she was there, fully in step with him, he tangled his hand in her hair, arched her head back and took the kiss deeper, his insistent, bold strokes as he explored her mouth sending a hot, honeyed warmth through her. If he'd lifted his head and told her in that raspy voice of his how he would take her, he couldn't have demonstrated more clearly. She moved against him again, needing more, and this time he dropped his hands down her back, cupped her bottom through the filmy material of her dress and brought her firmly against the hard length of him outlined against the fine material of his pants.

Her half gasp, half sigh reverberated against his lips. His mouth left hers to trail a line of fire across her cheek to her ear. "Be careful what you wish for, sweetheart… you just might get it."

His fingers splayed across her bottom and moved her against him in a delicious slide against the hard, thick length of him, and intimidation faded on a wave of pure, unadulterated lust. She'd heard the other girls in the club going on about their sexual escapades as they'd dressed before a shift, but the way Jared made her feel was…*insane.*

He trailed kisses down the length of her neck to the spot at the base that made her crazy. Made her squirm. Jared lifted his head with a curse, sank his hands into her waist and turned her around so her palms were flat against the wardrobe.

"Enough of that if we're making it anywhere near where we're supposed to."

The rough tone of his voice sent a tremor through her. Being pressed up against the wardrobe made it tunnel deep inside. He lifted her hair away from her neck and resumed his kisses with a slide of his lips against her nape. The soft rasp of her zipper as he multitasked filled the air.

The warm breeze from the French doors slid across her skin as he pushed the dress off her shoulders and let it fall in a swish of fabric to the floor. But it was Jared's hands and lips as they worked their way down her back that had her full attention, making her arch into them and plead for more.

She drew in a breath as he sank to his knees and pressed kisses against the rounded curve of her bottom. His hands were reverent, sure on her skin, as if he wanted to memorize every inch of her. Fire lit her belly, licked at her nerve endings. She was sure she wanted him to. And then he turned her around…

His gaze swept up the length of her, from her legs still clad in high heels, over the curves of her hips and breasts encased in the barest hint of lace, and finally to her face. By the time he got there, she was flushed with self-consciousness and excitement so intense, her breath came in short pulls. Which deteriorated into no breath at all when he slid his fingers underneath the thin strips of silk that held her barely there panties in place and stripped them off.

Her legs went another step toward jelly. If she'd hoped he'd lavish the same attention on her that he had on his knees in Nice, it wasn't to be found as he stood, anchored her against the door and brought his mouth back to hers.

"You are so gorgeous," he murmured against her lips. "My words aren't working."

She melted. Figuratively, of course, because she was still standing when he slid his palm up the inside of her thighs and pushed them apart. Still standing when he cupped the heat of her in his palm in an overt claim of ownership that had her pressing her hands against the wood to keep upright. Her mouth stilled against his, her gasp filling the air as he stroked her. She was hot and wet for him, so turned on she thought she might come apart with the lightest touch. But he claimed her with the slide of his finger instead.

"You'll come with me inside of you this time," he muttered. "And not before."

Bailey tried to keep her head but there was no fighting the mind-numbing pleasure he gave her with the firm strokes of his hand. He urged her thighs wider and slid another finger inside her, stretching her, preparing her. It was so good she could have screamed with the pleasure of it. But he stopped before she could.

"There will be a bed this time." He slid his palm to the small of her back and gave her a gentle push toward it. "Maybe not the next."

She sat on the queen-size bed as he stripped off his clothes and revealed the incredible body she'd seen in swim trunks, but never in tight black boxers that emphasized how very well-endowed he was. Apparently the jokes had been true, she acknowledged with a hellishly dry mouth. Maybe she wasn't so wise to choose him as her first....

If there was any way Jared could have gotten his clothes off faster, he would have. Bailey's unabashedly intent look as he undressed, as if he was putting on a show for her pleasure, did something serious to his insides...left his composure hanging by a thread. And if he'd ever needed composure, now was the time. He'd never taken a virgin. Had no idea what made it a better experience for a woman. Add that to the fact that he'd never wanted anyone as much in his life as he wanted Bailey right now and there were all sorts of ways this could go.

Blocking his mind to anything but her, he moved to the bed and took in how outrageously, spectacularly beautiful she was clad only in a lace bra, curled up with those never-ending legs beneath her. But it was her face that held him. Utterly vulnerable, yet tough at the same time. It was a combination he found irresistible.

He sat down on the bed and pulled her into his lap. Turned her so her knees were on either side of him and they were face-to-face. "I have no idea how some man hasn't persuaded you into bed with him before now, but at this moment, I'm glad of it."

She blinked. "That's quite an admission, Mr. Manifesto."

His lips curved in a wry smile. "I think my rule book's been gone for a while."

He watched her process that. Lifted her hair away from her shoulder and took a mouthful of smooth, silky skin, scoring the surface of the elegant curve with his teeth. He was so hard, so hot for her it took all his willpower to go slow. But that was what she needed and that was what he was going to give her. Even if it killed him.

He slid his lips lower to the swell of her breasts above the lace. She moved her shoulders to help him as he slid the straps of her bra down and stripped it off. His hands moved over the weight of her silky, creamy flesh and cupped her breasts in his palms. She was so perfect, so exquisite, her shaky sigh as he brushed the pads of his thumbs over her rose-tipped nipples almost undid him.

"You ready for me?" he murmured against her mouth. "Because I need to have you *now*."

The way she blindly sought his mouth, wound her fingers in the hair at the nape of his neck, was all the impetus he needed to turn and push her back on the bed. Her gaze was steady, trusting him completely as he ran his palm down her stomach and reclaimed the heat between her thighs.

"I need a condom," he rasped, a last sane thought entering his head. "I'll be right back."

Her delicate fingers grasped his arm. "I've been on the Pill for years for cramps."

That was all the incentive he needed to slide his fingers inside her again, his smooth, rhythmical movements increasing in tempo as he brought her to a feverish, desperate state that would make his possession better for her. When she was twisting, writhing under him and begging for more, he stripped off his boxers and moved between her thighs.

He captured her hands in his and pressed them back against the bed above her head so their fingers were entwined and their eyes locked. "I'm right here," he murmured. "Every step of the way. Guide me."

She nodded. Her gaze clung to his as he brought the hard length of himself against her and teased her with it, back and forth until she closed her eyes and gave a soft moan. "Jared—"

He eased inside her, just the tip to allow her to get used to his possession. She was tight, incredibly tight, and he shook with the control it took to stay there and not move. "Breathe," he instructed huskily. Her chest rose as she did, depressed and rose as she took in another puff of air. And he felt her relax around him. He eased deeper, her flesh clenching him; accepting him and rejecting him all at the same time.

"Bailey—" he demanded roughly, "you okay?"

She nodded. "You feel…amazing."

His soft curse split the air. "Wrap your legs around me, sweetheart. I need more."

She did and he pushed deeper, a fraction at a time, stopping to let her adjust as he went. Finally, he reached the barrier he'd been waiting for, felt her flinch beneath him. He brought his mouth to hers. "I've got to hurt you for just a second and it'll be over."

She nodded and closed her eyes. He claimed her fully, pushing through the barrier with a smooth, sure stroke that made her gasp and twist beneath him. He kissed her through it, holding himself completely, agonizingly still until her body relaxed around his and she sighed into his mouth.

"That's it," he encouraged huskily, "stay with me. You're good now."

He started to move, excruciatingly slowly although his rock-hard body was begging him to go faster. Their hands were still laced together, her eyes glued to his as he caressed her with his pulsing flesh, her muscles clenching him as he withdrew and entered her again and again until she was arching against him and taking him deep.

"You feel so good," he told her, her incredibly tight body fitting him like a glove, making him swell even bigger. "Tell me how you like it. How it feels..."

Her eyes were glazed; she was just this side of incoherent. "So good," she muttered. "So good. God, Jared, don't stop—*please*..."

He released a hand to cup the sexy curve of her hip. To anchor her to him so he could put more power behind his thrusts, hit her in that place that gave a woman the deepest, most powerful orgasm.

"Talk to me," he urged, dangerously close to the edge. "Tell me, Bailey."

"*Amazing*. It feels amazing. Jared—I don't think I can—"

He released her hands and reached between them, setting his thumb against the hard nub of her just above where their bodies were joined. Slowly, deliberately rotated it against her until her hips were writhing against his thumb. She threw her head back and came for him, her body clenching around his so fiercely, it took him only a few strokes to push himself into oblivion. His body exploded inside her, a hoarse cry tearing itself from his lungs as a shattering release swept over him.

It was minutes, long minutes later before his body stopped shaking. Before the chill in the air stole over him. Bailey shivered, her legs still wrapped around him, his flesh buried in hers. And he wondered how he could still be semi-hard after *that*.

He left the warmth of her body to push back the comforter and tuck her beneath it. Bailey protested, a tiny whimper that made him smile. "One second," he murmured, pressing a kiss to her lips. "I am not nearly done with you yet."

He found a bottle of water on the dresser and drank half of it down while he quite frankly tried to compose himself. Because that hadn't been just sex. He felt open, raw, as if someone had stripped off his layers and left him exposed. And the instinct to roll over, to reclaim his power, pulsed through every cell.

Bailey lay there sultry and replete, platinum hair spread across the pillow, gaze tracking him as he drank. Oblivious to the storm in his head. Watching her there, strong, sexy, *unforgettable*, the thought crossed his mind that he could have her a million times and it would never be enough.

His hand tightened around the bottle. *That was truly crazy talk.* No matter how much he'd wanted a woman in the past, it had always faded. Soured. Relationships ended. People got bored. It was just the way it was.

He set the bottle down. Reached for her. Bailey studied his face as he took her in his arms. "You're regretting this?"

He shook his head. *Lied.* "I want more. And I'm not sure you're ready."

She pulled his head down to hers and gave him a long, lingering kiss as her answer. It was all the encouragement he needed to stir to life. He curved his hand around her shoulder, slid it down to press against her shoulder blade and turned her over.

“Jared—” she murmured, a question in her voice.

“I want you this way,” he told her softly, pushing her hands apart and moving over her. It was testament to the trust they’d built that she stayed there, her breath picking up in rhythm as he nudged her knees apart, moved between them and pressed openmouthed kisses from the top of her spine to her waist. When she was fully relaxed and supple beneath him, he slid his hand between her legs and stroked her damp flesh.

“Okay?”

“Yes,” she moaned, shifting her legs farther apart, pushing up against his touch. It was all the invitation he needed to slide an arm beneath her, lift her and push inside her hot, welcoming flesh with a smooth thrust.

This time he could move slower, build it up, enjoy every centimeter of her undeniably sweet body. When she dug her fingers into the comforter and came with a guttural moan, as if the control he was exerting over her turned her on as much as it turned him on, it destroyed him completely. She was more than a match for him in every way.

He set a palm to the small of her back, held her where he wanted her and chased his own blindingly good release. When it came, tightening his limbs, sweeping through him like the lazy aftershock of a powerful tremor, he knew he’d never experienced such pleasure.

Bailey tucked into his side, curved against his warm body as the filtered Paris moonlight carried them off to sleep, his denial grew weaker. It was useless to pretend even for a second that nothing had changed. Because everything had.

CHAPTER NINE

THE PEAL OF his cell phone in the adjoining room woke Jared at six the next morning. Blinking against the light filtering through the windows, he slid out of bed, grabbed his boxers from the floor and hightailed it into his room in the hopes of catching it before it woke Bailey.

A glance at the call display told him it was Danny, his PI. Kicking the connecting door closed, he took the call.

"Stone."

"You sound half-asleep. Thought you'd be halfway down the Champs-Elysées by now, running your little heart out."

"Eventful night last night." Jared crossed to the French doors and squinted out at the empty Paris streets. "You have something for me or did you just call to pay me back?"

"It's your father. I had my contact do the usual check-in this week. He said he wants to talk to you."

His father wanted to talk to him? He pressed his palm against the elegantly carved mahogany casing of the door. It had been, what, a year and a half, two years, since he'd talked to Graham Stone in a short, curt conversation to sort out some legalities.

"What does he want? Is he okay?"

"He wouldn't say. Says you need to come to him."

His shoulders stiffened. Why should *he* go running when his father had shut him out for almost a decade?

Danny read the pause. "He doesn't look great, Jared. Pretty haggard from what my guy says."

His chest tightened. This was *not* what he needed right now. "I can't go for a couple of weeks."

"I'm just relaying the message. Oh and Jared?" His PI's voice deepened to a satisfied purr. "That dirt you wanted on Michael Craig's proclivity to abuse his expense accounts? I have it. It's bigger and better than you could have imagined."

A twist of satisfaction curled through him. "Send it through. All of it."

He ended the call and tossed his cell phone on the desk. Michael Craig deserved what he had coming to him. What caused an ache to sit low in his chest, ever-present but more pronounced now, was how much he loved his father. Graham Stone had never been too busy, even with his insane hours as a banker, to spend time with his son. Whether it had been building a car or throwing a football around, he'd always been there, even if it wasn't as much as Jared would have liked. Then slowly, in the later years, his father had begun to sink. The massive amounts of stress had finally gotten to him, sending him to a place his youthful son couldn't understand or help him out of.

A fist squeezed his chest, growing larger with every breath. When his father had made his biggest mistake, had stolen that money, it had been too late, far too late to do anything to save his soul. There likely would never be a day on this earth when Jared wouldn't wonder what else he could have done to prevent it. He'd just learned to live with the guilt.

Or had he? The slow burn consuming him didn't make him think so. He'd always thought that walking away, distancing himself from the shame that had enveloped his family, was the right thing to do for his own survival. For his business, where reputation was everything. His father hadn't wanted his help, so what choice had he had?

Light slanted across his face as the sun rose higher in the sky. He had a decision to make. Did he stop running and see what the man who had once been his hero wanted? Or did he wait until it was too late?

Rather than contemplate a question he wasn't prepared to answer, he headed for the shower. It was too late to go back to bed and really, it was the last place he should be. Why he'd thought he could take Bailey to bed in a no-strings arrangement as she'd offered was the joke of the century.

He turned the shower on and stepped under a steaming hot spray. *No strings.* He might as well have handed Bailey the rope and asked her to tie him up in knots. Because if his Zen master had cornered him now and ordered self-awareness, he would have had to admit the only word for last night was...*emotional.* He struggled to get his mouth around the word because it was so foreign to his vocabulary. Emotion didn't figure into his work or relationships. It was an unwise word that made people do stupid things. But he could not deny the truth. He had never felt so connected to another person in his life. And not just because Bailey had been a virgin. It'd been as if he was in her head and she'd been in his.

God. He tipped his head back and sluiced the water out of his face. He'd told himself not to do it. Had warned himself it was a mistake. Why did he continue to let himself want what he couldn't have? How could he be tangling himself up in a woman who was not only the obsession of Alexander Gagnon, she was rapidly becoming *his?*

He tipped shampoo over his head and attempted to scrub some sense back into his brain. He needed to focus on this presentation and win. Take Bailey at her word. It had been one night of ridiculously good sex agreed upon by two consenting adults.

The fact that Bailey had stolen a piece of his heart last night, had been stealing pieces of it for the past week, was inconsequential. He would never be the kind of man who connected on a permanent basis. He didn't have it in him.

It was time he started acting like it.

Bailey leaned back against the bathroom door, nail in her mouth in an absentminded chew as she contemplated an in-the-shower Jared from the perspective of a woman he'd just taken to heaven and back. She was sure no other man would equal his outrageously good body and technique, and had a newfound appreciation for the tennis bracelet club in the Valley.

She replaced the thoroughly chewed nail with another. Last night had been exactly what she'd needed to take her mind off Alexander Gagnon. Except she wasn't sure it'd just been sex. She could have stayed in Jared's arms forever. And *that* was the problem. Not that he'd sneaked out of her bed.

She swallowed hard. Last night had been unforgettable. The heartbreakingly beautiful way Jared taken her virginity, so in tune with her every emotion…how treasured he'd made her feel…how desired.

Oh, Lord. She snaked a hand through her tangled hair. She'd told herself she wasn't getting emotional about this. *Enough.*

She cleared her throat. "Could you tell me where that research is? I want to read it before our meeting."

The click of the shower shutting off should have been her first clue he was getting out. Why she stood there frozen as he shoved the curtain aside and reached for a towel, water dripping off his utterly delicious masculinity, she wasn't sure.

"Sorry, I—" She took a step backward. "I'll wait for you in the bedroom."

"For God's sake, Bailey." He ran the towel over his hair. "You had your legs wrapped around me last night. It's a little late to be embarrassed."

Yes, well, that was last night and this was now. She bit her lip. "Was that your phone I heard earlier?"

He nodded, relieving her immensely by wrapping the towel around his hips. The hard set of his angular face didn't do a great job of reinforcing that comfort, however. His blue gaze was laser-focused and impersonal as he waved his hand toward the bedroom. "It's on the table by the window. Help yourself."

She shifted her weight to the other foot, studied him. *Regret. Definitely regret.* Fine.

"I ordered us coffee and croissants. I'll go read it."

"Thanks."

She waited, a fraction of a second, just to see if he'd have anything to say about last night. Anything that might make today a little less awkward.

The silence was deafening.

She dug her toe into the tile and looked up at him. "It's clear you regret what happened last night."

He gave her an even look. "I don't regret it."

"Then why do you look li—"

"*Bailey.*" His gaze narrowed. "It was great. It was hot. *You* were hot. Absolutely worth it. What else can I say?"

She squinted at him. Had he *actually* just said that?

A sharp pain gouged her insides. "Right," she said, clenching her stomach and pushing past it. "Good to know. And in case you're running a little scared which is wholly possible, you're absolutely right. I meant what I said. It was one night. We're good."

She turned on her heel and left before she became certified dangerous.

* * *

They spent the morning hearing presentations from the marketing and sales groups at Maison headquarters in the Montparnasse district of Paris. Jared thought it interesting that Bailey sat on the other side of the room from him beside an attractive, very young French marketing executive who flirted with her at every possible opportunity. He told himself it was a smart, strategic move on her part, positioning herself as part of the Maison team.

That was before, however, she walked away from him midsentence during a break. Before she blew off his request to get her a coffee.

"Bailey." He kept his voice low as he cornered her on the way back from the machine, coffee in hand. "You know this can't happen between us. It's a bad idea."

She looked up at him, the only sign there was anything going on behind that ice-cold expression of hers the quivering of her bottom lip. "I told you this morning, I *get* it. Hang on to that impressive set of rules, Jared. It's all good."

He stood there, speechless, as she ducked around him and set the coffee down. *Really? She was going to be like that about it?*

The deep freeze continued throughout the afternoon as they toured three of Maison's stores in Paris. Through the cocktails that preceded the French company's annual summer party they'd been invited to attend along with the Gehrig team. He held it together through it all, until they were speaking to the CEO of a Parisian cosmetics company Maison had a partnership with, Jared laying on the charm because the CEO was a great contact to have. Then Bailey rolled her eyes at him. *Rolled her eyes at him* and muttered something about needing to use the ladies' room.

He stared after her, a dangerous heat filling his head. What was wrong with her? *They had the biggest deal of his life to win tomorrow, he had backed her without fail this entire time, and she was acting like a girl over one night together?*

He made it through the rest of his conversation with the CEO, scouted out the washrooms and found them in a hallway off the restaurant. They were one-person affairs, and there were multiples of them. He eyed the one marked women with the door closed, stuck his hand against the wall and waited.

When the door swung open and Bailey stepped out, he pounced.

"Give me a minute, will you?" He bit the words out as he shoved her back into the washroom and shut the door.

"Jared—" She looked up at him with wide eyes. "This is not the place."

"You're *making* it the place." He jammed his hands in his pockets and stared at her. "You told me last night there were no strings. So for God's sake what is *wrong* with you?"

"Nothing." She bit her lip and made a study of the intricate pattern of the floor tiles.

His curse split the air. He slid his fingers under her chin and brought her gaze up to his. The brightness in her eyes made his stomach clench. "Don't you do this to me, Bailey. You promised me you'd be okay with this."

"I am." She pulled out of his grasp and backed up against the vanity. "I guess I'm just not made of stone like you are. Funny," she derided, forcing out a harsh bark of laughter, "women like to use that to refer to a certain body part of yours, but I think it better describes your heart. You can just turn it off and on at will, can't you?"

He looked at her nonplussed. "Apparently not with you, because here I am when I should be schmoozing executives."

"Oh," she choked out. "I think you were doing an excellent job of that."

"Jealous, Bailey?"

She stared him down for a moment, then leaned back against the vanity and ran her hands through her hair. "I just—I don't...I'm just finding it hard to put last night aside. To pretend it wasn't special when to *me*, it was."

He felt his carefully engineered defenses dissolve into dust. Bailey was like a flaw in his perfectly designed ability not to care. A weakness that would surely dismantle him completely if he let it.

"It was...*special* to me too," he admitted, choosing his words carefully. 'I just don't want us to get too carried away here."

"Why?" She poked him in the chest, and *God*, didn't she know by now how much that antagonized him? "What do you think might happen if you let yourself feel? The earth might open up and swallow you whole?"

"No, Bailey..."

"Then *what*? What do you think's going to happen?"

He reached for her then, his hands purposeful as he sank them into her waist and deposited her on the marble counter. "I might do this."

He brought his mouth down on hers in a hot, hungry kiss that was equal parts punishment and absolution. She pushed her hands against his shoulders as if to reject him, but if he was jumping into the fire, then so was she. He cupped her jaw, gentled the kiss and called himself a complete and absolute fool. A sigh racked her as she buried her fingers in his hair and kissed him back, heated and without reserve.

When he finally lifted his head, it was to nudge her thighs apart, step between them and draw her closer. "You are pulling me apart, piece by piece," he admitted huskily. "And I don't like it."

"I don't, either." She reached up and cradled his jaw in

her palms. "But you hurt me this morning, Jared. Be honest with me, yes, but at least explain where it's coming from."

"I'm sorry." He whispered the words against her mouth. Against the velvety softness of her cheek. Against the perfectly shaped earlobe he bit into, sending a shiver through her. It moved through him, made his heart race as his hands went to the hem of her dress and pushed it up, allowing his palms access to the smooth, voluptuous curve of her hip. The scent of her warm, heated flesh filled his head. He slid his hands under her bottom and dragged her to the edge of the vanity. He wouldn't take her here…he just needed to feel her against him.

"Jared—" She moaned his name as if they should stop and start all at the same time. He pulled her hips into his and kissed her. Bailey whimpered and wound her legs around him, and if he'd been inside her it couldn't have felt better than the sweet torture he was inflicting upon himself now.

He lifted his mouth from hers and framed her face with his palms. "As much as I want this, it's not happening here."

She nodded.

He lifted her off the counter and straightened her clothes, then his own.

"I need to fix my lipstick," she murmured, looking a bit shattered. "You go."

He nodded and pulled open the door. Was halfway through it, when he turned back, pulled her into his arms and stole one last kiss. She wound her arms around his neck and kissed him back. He indulged it for a few seconds, then set her away from him.

"We talk when we get back to the hotel, okay?"

"Okay."

He released her and left. He did not see Alexander until

he just about walked into him. Stopping short, his gaze flickered back to the door he'd just exited from.

"Oh, I caught the whole touching kiss." The Frenchman's smile didn't reach his eyes. "Am I allowed to say I'm jealous? Because I am, Stone."

"Why don't we say we're overdue for a drink instead?" Jared resisted the urge to deck him. He was shutting Alexander Gagnon down and he was shutting him down now.

Alexander lifted his shoulders. "If you say so."

Jared led the way to the bar by way of answer, ordered two scotches and took a deep pull of his before he deigned to speak. "Here's how this is going to go, Gagnon. You're going to stay away from Bailey, you're never going to say another sideways word to her, and if you do, I will take you out at the knees."

Alexander smiled, a lazy, loose twist of the lips that wasn't at all concerned. "You have it bad, you know that, Stone?"

He did. He was only beginning to realize how bad.

Alexander eyed him over the top of his glass. "She said you weren't sleeping together."

"Things change." Jared set his drink down, flattened his palms on the bar and leaned forward until the far-too-smooth soon-to-be CEO filled his field of vision. "You aren't ever having her. Get that through your head."

Alexander took a sip of his scotch. "*No* isn't a word I tend to take very seriously. It only makes me want something more."

His mouth twisted. "You couldn't even *buy* her. What makes you think you could ever have her?"

A warning light flickered in those slate-gray eyes, but his shrug was elegantly dismissive. "This deal will make or break you, Stone. Decide your future at a very rocky point in your company's history. Why not set Bailey free for a night? Donate her to the cause? You can put her in the shower afterward and pretend I never happened."

He froze. Clenched his hands by his sides. A fury like he'd never known blanketed him. "You are a sick bastard, you know that?" he gritted out. "She told me you wanted what I have. Well, you will never have what I have, Gagnon. Ever."

Alexander's face tightened. "You are walking a thin, thin line Stone."

"As are you," he bit out, shoving his drink on the bar and pushing to his feet. "I should have taken her under your nose tonight. That would have given me a deep sense of satisfaction."

He walked away before he lost his mind. Then thought he might already have. Because he shouldn't have said that. He should not have gone there.

Bailey reentered the restaurant just as Jared got up from the bar, a coldly furious look on his face, and walked away from Alexander. The matching look the Maison heir wore sent alarm bells ringing through her. What could possibly have happened in the last ten minutes?

Before she could snare Jared and find out, Davide was flagging him down to introduce him to someone. Then they were being rounded up for dinner with both Gagnons, the Gehrig team and several marketing executives from Maison. Jared sat beside her at the round table of ten, quietly seething, leaving Bailey to carry the conversation from their end.

"So," she offered valiantly, "you must all love living in Paris. It's so gorgeous."

Davide nodded. "Although I intend on retiring to the house in the Cap. To me it's *le paradis sur terre.* Heaven on earth."

"Agreed," Bailey nodded. "I love the climate. Perfectly temperate."

"But you must like the extreme heat," Alexander interjected. "Given that you lived in Las Vegas."

The edge to his tone made Bailey set her wineglass down with a jerky movement. "I do," she agreed evenly. "But I much prefer the more moderate Northern California climate."

"Speaking of Vegas," Alexander waved an elegant long-fingered hand at her, "I remembered last night where I met you. I usually have such an impeccable memory…it was driving me crazy."

Bailey froze. Jared's gaze flickered to Alexander, a warning glint in it. "Gagnon—

"It was the Red Room," Alexander continued. "How I could have forgotten when you were so *memorable* I don't know."

John Gehrig's mouth dropped open. The room began to spin.

"Do you know the Red Room?" Alexander turned to one of his marketing executives. The perfectly put together Frenchman shook his head. His boss sat back in his chair and folded his arms over his chest. "You must go the next time you're there. They have the most drop-dead beautiful women on stage; my clients used to salivate. But there was one dancer," he commented, looking over at Bailey, a dark glitter in his silver eyes, "who called herself Kate Delaney who held us all spellbound. We couldn't take our eyes off her."

A buzzing sound filled Bailey's head. Davide gave his son a confused look. "What does this have to do with Bailey?"

"Kate Delaney was Bailey's stage name."

"*Oh*." Davide ran a hand over his jaw and looked at Bailey. "So you were one of those…what do they call them? *Burlesque* dancers?"

"No," Bailey corrected quietly, bile climbing her throat at an alarming rate. "The Red Room is a high-end strip club."

Davide's eyes widened. "A strip club?"

The couple of execs who'd had their heads buried in their smartphones the entire meal looked up, eyes fastening on her. Bailey swallowed hard, heat flooding every inch of her skin. "Yes. It was how I paid my way through school."

A frown creased the elder Frenchman's brow. "That must have been…"

"Lucrative." Bailey dropped her gaze to the candle flickering in the center of the table and absorbed the total and complete silence. Wished she could disappear into the red-hot flame.

John Gehrig cleared his throat. "Well, I for one love the Red Room. The ladies are all just beautiful and I'm sure," he said, shooting a red-faced look at Bailey, "you looked just…lovely."

"There wasn't an unaffected man in the room," Alexander agreed. "Isn't it great to see the American dream alive and well? From stripper to CMO…how *inspiring*."

The bile in her throat threatened to make an immediate appearance. She pressed a hand to her mouth and swallowed hard. Jared made a sound and pressed his palms into the table. Bailey covered his hand with hers. "Don't."

He stared at her hand for a long, hard moment, then lowered himself back into his seat. Davide flicked his son a reprimanding look.

"If you were a gentleman you would pick another line of conversation, Alexander, but since your manners often escape you, *I* will."

Davide started a discussion about foreign exchange rates. John Gehrig hurriedly joined in. Bailey drew in a breath, then another. Told herself walking away from the table right now wasn't an option. But it was painful, physically uncomfortable to sit there with the young executives shooting speculative glances across the table at her. One of them was tapping away on his phone, then slid it discreetly toward his coworker. Photos of her as Kate Delaney no doubt. She'd tried to get the club to sell the promotional photos to her, to take them off the website, and they'd agreed, but nothing ever really disappeared from the internet. It just pretended to.

Jared laid his palm on her thigh. "Breathe."

She pushed his hand away and stared sightlessly out the window at the glittering Eiffel Tower. Felt everything go gray around her as she retreated. She knew the routine. Knew this humiliation like a second skin. It was a familiar, hateful feeling she'd never wanted to feel again.

She drained her wineglass. Smiled tightly at the waiter as he appeared to refill it. Growing up in her house, it had been taboo to say the word *alcoholic*, even though her father had clearly been one and his booze-induced rages had been a monthly fixture. As if none of them said it, it didn't exist.

Apparently she'd also decided to live her life in denial. If she didn't acknowledge the past and the choices she'd made, it could never hurt her. She could go on pretending she was something she wasn't.

But that was all over now. With those men looking at her like this, she felt like a Jenga puzzle someone had pulled the last piece out of.

"I need to go," she muttered in a low, harsh voice to Jared as their dessert plates were cleared. "Tell them I have a headache, tell them I'm exhausted…tell them whatever you want."

She stood up, grabbed her wrap and skirted her way

through the tables to the exit. On the street, she flagged a cab. Jared caught up with her as she was about to slide in.

"Get in," he said grimly, climbing in behind her when she did.

Neither of them spoke until they were in Bailey's hotel suite. She tossed her bag on a chair and turned on him. "Why would he do it? Why would he humiliate me like that? What happened between the two of you?"

Jared sat down on the sofa near the windows. The guilty schoolboy look he wore as he raked his hands through his hair made her heart sink into the ground.

"Alexander saw me coming out of the washroom. He made some comments I couldn't let pass. I figured it was time we had a chat."

She felt the color drain from her face. "We weren't going to do that."

"I changed my mind. I said some things I shouldn't have."

"Like *what?*"

His mouth flattened. "When I made it clear you were with me, he said he didn't care. He said I should take one for the deal. Give you to him for a night then put you in the shower afterward and forget it happened." He pressed his fingers to his temples. "I lost my mind. I went too far."

A wave of nausea flashed over her. "What else did you say?"

"I told him I wished I'd taken you right there under his nose so he would know what he could never have."

Her breath left her. "You didn't."

"I did."

Her hands curled by her sides. "You…."

He stood up. "Bailey—"

"No." She hurled the word at him. "You do not get to be excused for this, Jared. You do not get to be excused for egging him on in some testosterone-fueled duel when

you *knew* what he was capable of. You *knew* he would not hesitate to throw my past in my face."

His face grayed. "I wasn't thinking."

"No—no, you weren't. You were too busy *bragging* about being the one to get me into bed. Making it impossible for him to not retaliate..." She threw her hands up in the air. "My God, Jared, I'm falling for you. *Falling for you*. How could you do this?"

He covered the ground between them with swift steps. The fire in his eyes set her back on her heels. "I have put this deal, this *must-win deal*, on the line for you this entire time, Bailey, because of my feelings for you. So *do not* question my intentions. Yes, I made a mistake tonight...I let my temper get the best of me, and I'm sorry for that. But it's done. And maybe it's a good thing, because you need to move on, you need to stop letting the past hold you captive."

Her eyes widened. "You're kidding, right? You think it's a good thing that the entire table of men I have to present to tomorrow will now be picturing me naked on a stage rather than listening to what I have to say?"

He lifted a brow. "So what? Who cares what they think? You're brilliant. Your ideas are brilliant. You want to defy the naysayers? Prove my manifesto is crap? Then get tougher, Bailey. Get a whole lot tougher than that."

The fists she had clenched by her sides tightened. She thought she might hit him then, and he eyed her as if he would take it. Instead, she felt big, huge, fat tears burning the backs of her eyes and backed away from him before she gave in to them.

"You said earlier you wanted to talk. Let's talk then. This is proving very illuminating."

He shook his head. "I don't think now is the right time."

His eyes said more than his words, the grim look stretching his face making her chest go tight. He was second-guessing what he'd said earlier. Second-guessing his feelings for her after what had happened tonight. After he'd watched an entire table of men react to what she'd been just as he had the first time she'd told him. Shocked. Appalled. She could *see* it on his face.

Anger built inside her, a white-hot storm that was impossible to control. She clenched her hands by her sides. How was it that every man in her life eventually rejected her? Her father, who'd thrown her out? The man she'd liked in Vegas who'd wanted only one thing? Now Jared.

Shame washed over her, stained her skin like a brand. He had treated her like a power play with Alexander because that's what she was to him—expendable.

"Now that you have me," she lashed out, so hurt she couldn't see straight, "why not enjoy the full benefits?" She reached down and yanked her shoe off and threw it at him, a silver missile he plucked out of the air with catlike reflexes. "I know you're curious," she continued. "You asked me about it in Nice…why not sit back and let me demonstrate?"

His gaze tracked her as she bent her leg and reached for the other shoe. "Bailey—"

Wham. The shoe smacked his outstretched palm and fell to the floor. He took a step forward and reached for her, but she backed away, flashing him a furious look. "*Sit.*"

He sat. Likely because he didn't know what else to do with a crazy woman on the loose. Bailey's fingers moved to the buttons of her shirt, stumbling as she undid them. "That was hot, right, on the sink in the washroom? I'll make it hotter."

He shook his head. "Stop it."

"Oh, come on, you'll love it." She tore at the last button and yanked the shirt off. "Get in the spirit, Jared."

"Bailey." His eyes flashed a warning. "Put your shirt back on."

"Why? All you want is this. You made that clear this morning." She eased her skirt over her hips in a seductive, admittedly angry twist. "All men ever want is this."

He shook his head. "I care about you. You know I do."

She stalked toward him, sank her hands into his shoulders and straddled him. "You wanted to know how I danced for them? How I touched them?" She settled herself into his hard thighs. "Like this…"

He kept his hands stiffly by his sides, anger darkening his face. It made her furious. Made her push her breasts into his chest and rotate her hips against him in a much more intimate caress than she would ever have given a customer. A harsh breath left his lungs.

"You see," she derided, "you can't deny you like it."

"Of course I like it." He clamped his hands around her hips and held her still. "There isn't a second I don't want you. But you are worth more than this."

She shook her head, tears burning the back of her eyes in a glittering prelude to total breakdown. "I saw your face when I told you what I was. You were horrified."

"I was shocked."

"Shocked, horrified…what's the difference?"

He grimaced. "A big one."

She swallowed hard. Dared herself to ask the question that might break her, because how much worse could she feel about herself?

"Could you ever imagine yourself with me, Jared? With all my flaws?"

His jaw hardened. "I've told you I care about you. Stop pushing me."

The warning in his eyes scared her. The sudden, earth-shattering realization that she was undeniably, unmistakably in love with him was worse.

She reached for old habits, old powers as she pressed a kiss to the corner of his mouth. Slid her palm across his thigh to where he lay stiff and thick beneath his trousers. He jerked against her hand and the triumph rocketed through her like a drug she'd been denied too long.

"No."

He dumped her on the sofa so fast it made her head spin. Stepped back. The rebuke in his face made her heart shrivel. "We have a presentation to do tomorrow. We are going in there as a team, Bailey, and we are winning. We are doing what we came here to do. *This*," he said, glaring at her, "is not happening."

Her lips trembled. "You don't want me."

"You're right," he said harshly. "I want the Bailey I know. The woman who let me look into her soul last night. Not *this*."

He turned on his heel and left, slamming the connecting door behind him. Bailey curled up in a ball on the sofa and cried. Cried for the girl she'd been. For what she wished she hadn't had to do.

At Jared for being so cruel.

At herself for ruining everything.

CHAPTER TEN

BAILEY WOKE WITH the birds. At some point, after Jared had left, she'd stumbled into bed and slept. Given herself over to a seemingly endless series of dreams whose characters and content overlapped without rhyme or reason, which sent her spiraling into the past, then hurtling forward into the present again in a dizzying journey that ended only with the arrival of the first light of day.

And perhaps the appearance of the loud, squeaky garbage truck that parked outside her window. She winced at the piercing, grinding sound, thinking maybe it wasn't as early as she'd thought, and levered herself into a sitting position. Somehow Paris seemed too elegant a city for garbage trucks…but apparently it too had its baggage it needed to get rid of.

She slid her legs over the side of the bed and padded to the window in time to see the very inelegant green garbage truck move on to the next storefront, hogging most of the narrow street with its robust, squat girth. Watching it made her think. Was Jared right? Was her determination to distance herself from her past destroying her instead of saving her?

She opened the French doors, walked out onto the balcony and braced her palms on the railing. She was proud, extremely proud of what she'd accomplished. Of whom she'd become. If she'd hadn't had the past she'd had, she wouldn't be the person she was now. And maybe that was the way she needed to look at herself: accept the parts she didn't like, the parts she was ashamed of, because they were part of the whole package like it or not.

The cold light of day was telling, exposing, and she shivered against the glare of it. Last night as the world had learned the truth of her, she'd felt as if she'd disintegrated into a million pieces. Funny how you could wake up the next morning and still be here. Could still hurt. Could still be angry.

Could discover that even though you thought the past had the power to destroy you, it really didn't. Not unless you let it.

The graffiti-emblazoned garbage truck turned the corner to meander down the next street, leaving only Jared's stark rejection of her in its wake. She'd spent her life being tougher than all the rest. Refusing to give in when the odds were stacked against her. Which explained why his words had hurt so much last night. She couldn't stand to be a quitter. She couldn't stand for *him* to think she was a quitter.

Couldn't stand for him not to love her.

Her heart squeezed hard in her chest. She hadn't even known she wanted to be loved. Hadn't known she craved it, needed it, like some missing piece of the puzzle that was her until now. It was frightening, *terrifying*, and it had made her drive him away last night—perhaps for good.

She pressed her fingers to the pounding pulse at her temples. Jared wanted a woman *she* didn't even know yet. It was a vulnerable, open version of herself he brought out. Not the old or the new Bailey, something else entirely. It occurred to her that maybe that's who she needed to be. A product of her past but in command of her future.

Increased activity on the street told her it was time to go inside and dress. The pitch was today. And the only thing she *was* certain about this morning was that she had to win this for Jared. Support him as he'd supported her this entire time.

She was dressed in a conservative gray pantsuit when she stopped, high heels in hand. No way was she doing this. Downplaying her femininity just because those men now thought she was entertainment for hire.

That would be letting them win.

She shrugged out of the suit and reached for the new chic mauve one she'd purchased on a whim on the Champs-Elysées. The material was gorgeous and the skirt showed a lot of leg.

Jared knocked on the door just as she'd finished dressing. His mouth curved as he looked her over. "That your battle gear?"

"Something like that."

He stepped closer and tucked a chunk of her hair behind her ear. "There isn't another person I'd want by my side today."

The dark glimmer of emotion in his eyes sent a flicker of hope through her. "Nor I."

She led the way out of the room. Today wasn't about emotion. Today was about getting the job done.

Jared spent the short ride from their hotel to the Maison offices finding his center. He'd spent the night sleepless and keyed up, not just because of what had happened with Bailey, but because this was it. One way or another his future would be determined today. He was done romancing the board, done proving himself when that's all he'd done over the past ten years to make money for his shareholders. They had to climb aboard his vision, understand where the future was, or he was out.

He stared out the window, watching the mad drivers dart in and out of traffic with an early-morning fervor that was just this side of frightening. Winning the Maison partnership would be an incredible achievement. He could transform the consumer electronics industry with it. But he could no longer sacrifice his soul for the company he'd built. Maybe it was the summons from his father that had done it, the knowledge that life was finite. But he knew the path and it wasn't this.

He didn't need a trek to the Himalayas to find peace. He needed to trust himself. And he wanted to be back in his labs creating with the engineers.

The car rolled to a halt in front of the skyscraper containing the Maison offices. The Gehrig team had already pitched when they walked into the metal-and-chrome boardroom, filled to the brim with the marketing, PR and sales teams. He read the atmosphere: alive but not buzzing. And knew they just had to set the room on fire and the deal was theirs.

If Alexander Gagnon played fairly. Gagnon was uncharacteristically subdued as he introduced them to the heads of the key departments. They socialized for a few minutes, then began. Adrenaline surged through him as he walked to the front of the room and opened with the history of Stone Industries, the "why us" argument and the successful alliances his company had forged around the world.

By the time he'd laid the groundwork, given an impassioned speech about vision, the room was noticeably energized. He handed the clicker over to Bailey, who looked calm and composed. Gobsmackingly stunning. "We've got this," he murmured. "Bring it home."

She nodded and walked to the front of the room. There wasn't a male eye that wasn't on her behind in the beautifully tailored suit as she stopped and turned around. He was pretty sure the hushed whispers had more to do with the gossip from last night than the subject at hand, and apparently Bailey had figured that out too, a shadow falling across her face. He watched her blink, then visibly check herself. Pull her shoulders back. And begin.

She launched into her slides with an easy, firm command of her ideas. Laid them down as if everyone in the room better be in the game or they were missing something special. Head thrown back, she roamed the room, keeping their interest, soliciting their response. And when the arrogant young marketer who'd passed her photo around last night started a side conversation with a coworker that clearly had nothing to do with the presentation and everything to do with Bailey's assets, she stopped by his chair and asked him if he had a question. Davide's mouth twitched, the marketer shut his and sank back into his chair, and Bailey moved on.

Jared leaned back and simply watched. He didn't sit poised to jump in and help her. Wasn't concerned a fact might be wrong. He knew Bailey now, knew he could trust her. What he was fascinated with, however, was *this* Bailey. He'd seen her confident before, seen her unsure in her own shoes and overcompensating. But he had never seen this version. *Commanding. Fierce. Combative.* And he knew in that moment he'd been wrong the day they'd driven in from the airport into Paris. Bailey was *more* than any man had a right to expect in a woman. She was courageous and vulnerable and stunningly brilliant, everything he'd been convinced didn't exist in a female.

She made him feel things he'd thought he'd never experience for another human being. Realize he was capable of it. And knew she'd been right; he was afraid. Afraid of making the same mistakes his father had made. Afraid of loving a woman who might leave.

Afraid of facing the truth of himself.

He shifted in the chair, his clarity unsettling. Bailey had never had love in her life, never had someone to protect her. Yet she was courageous enough to open herself up in the hopes she might someday have it. He was pretty sure he wanted to be that for her. To be the one to protect her. To believe in her.

He was scared he wanted all of her. Frightened it wasn't within his realm.

He raked a hand through his hair, his guts doing a fine job of rearranging themselves as Bailey sat down beside him, a rosy glow in her cheeks.

He gave her a sideways look. "Where did *that* come from?"

"Garbage trucks."

"Garbage trucks?"

Her mouth curved. "I'll tell you later."

Alexander opened the room to Q&A. There was a spirited debate about their direct-to-consumer ideas, their unorthodox retail strategy. But a seemingly general agreement the ideas were inspired. Alexander spoke last, directing a hard look at Jared. "All very impressive, Stone. We'd no doubt make a great partnership together. But when it comes down to it, it's the products that will win, not the marketing. And to me, you and Gehrig are neck and neck."

Fair point, Jared conceded. If you looked at the here and now. He stood up and walked to the front of the room to advance the slides.

"I'd like," he said, pausing for emphasis, "to introduce you to Project X."

The room buzzed as he unveiled his next generation product line: phones, tablets, computers, home alarms, thermostats all linked by a common platform—the connected home realized. No company, anywhere, had anything like it, and he felt the energy of the room skyrocket as the questions came fast and furious. *How quickly can you bring it to market? Would people really pay that much for a thermostat that controlled their house? Can it really do that?*

Alexander watched it all, a smile playing about his lips. As if he knew Jared had won. As if he wasn't sure he had a choice anymore.

He said nothing until it was just them and Davide in the room. "You didn't deign to enlighten us about Project X before now?"

"No," Jared said deliberately, "I didn't."

Alexander's eyes glittered. "I'll give you a decision within the week, then."

Jared nodded. Said his goodbyes to Davide. The older Frenchman looked heartsick as he kissed Bailey goodbye, and Jared had to smile. She had that effect on men. Now what was he going to do about it?

CHAPTER ELEVEN

FOR THE FIRST hour and a half of their flight back to San Francisco, Jared tore through the wrap-up from their presentation with quick efficiency. He fired a list of to-dos at Bailey, marked items for follow-up and outlined his vision for how he saw their marketing evolving. He wanted to expand her ideas to other partners, make them a cornerstone of their strategy, and although she loved the idea, she was too tired, too emotionally exhausted and too wary of him to really take any of it in.

Were they ever going to have that talk or was he just planning on forgetting they had ever happened?

Her stomach rolled. Had she turned him off that badly?

Jared repeated something in that relentless, authoritative tone that was getting on her nerves.

"What?"

He gave her a long look. "Need a break?"

She threw her notebook on the table in answer, stood and crossed to the tiny windows to stare out at the inky darkness. The snap of his laptop closing cut across the silence.

"Consider our business concluded for the evening, then."

Something, some edge to his voice made her turn around. He was watching her with that strange, contemplative look he'd been giving her all day since they'd walked out of the Maison building, their presentation behind them.

He pressed a button on the console and asked the attendant to serve the champagne.

She lifted a brow. “We haven’t won yet.”

“You need to be a more positive thinker.”

Her chest tightened, lifting her shoulders. “Alexander could still follow through on his threats, Jared. Choose Gehrig.”

“He won’t. He wants Project X.”

“And if he continues to play games for the sake of it?”

He lifted a shoulder. “Then I’ll reinvent myself. Frankly, I’m very much in the mood.”

He was in *some* kind of mood, that was for sure. Another side of him she couldn’t read.

Betty, a young, attractive twenty-something brunette with an eye for Jared, bustled in with the champagne and poured it into two flutes.

“Get some rest,” Jared told her. “We won’t be needing you anymore.”

The brunette put the champagne bottle in the ice bucket, flashed Bailey an “I am so jealous” look and disappeared.

Jared picked up the glasses and crossed over to hand one to her. Warmth seeped into her cheeks as his fingers brushed hers. “You know what she was thinking.”

His blue eyes glittered with intent. “Then she’d be right wouldn’t she? I don’t intend to spend the next thirteen hours studying our stock price.”

Her pulse sped into overdrive. “We haven’t even talked yet.”

“So let’s talk.” He lifted his glass and tipped it at her. “You were magnificent in that room today, Bailey. Absolutely brilliant. You have earned my trust, earned my respect. You can stand by my side any time and I would be lucky to have you there.”

Oh. She rocked back on her heels. His gaze remained on her, purposeful, intent. "You had the room in the palm of your hand. Including me."

Her stomach contracted. "I don't know about that." She rested her glass against her chin, "The garbage trucks woke me up this morning. And there I was standing at the window watching them and I knew you were right. If I don't deal with *my* garbage, with my past, and accept that it's a part of me, I will never truly move forward." She looked up at the man who had never doubted her, not even once, when so many people in her life had. "I wanted to win this for you. That's all I knew."

He captured her free hand in his and tugged her forward. "I didn't walk away from you last night because I didn't want you, Bailey. I walked away because I wanted *that* woman, the woman who blew my mind in that boardroom today."

She pulled her bottom lip between her teeth. "I'm still figuring out who she is."

"I know," he said softly. "Every time I watch you struggle and triumph, it touches something inside of me. I can no more remain immune to you than I can stop the sun from rising in the morning. And that terrifies me."

Her heart slammed against her chest, loud and insistent.

"Last night," he admitted, tracing his thumb over her cheek, "the thought of Alexander getting anywhere near you made me crazy. I had to tell him he would never have you because *I* want you. I don't want anyone else to have you. But I've never been *that* man, Bailey, the man who sticks. I don't even know if I'm capable of it."

She pulled in a breath, but the air in the tiny plane suddenly seemed nonexistent. The joy exploding inside her that she hadn't ruined everything was almost overwhelming. "Maybe we both need to try..." she managed to get out. "Try to move beyond our pasts."

His mouth twisted. "We're quite a pair, no?" He hooked his fingers in the waistband of her skirt and pulled her flush against him.

Her lashes drifted down as heat ignited inside her. "We make a good one, though."

He nodded, his gaze resting on hers. "You said you'd settle for a man who respects you. A man who tells the truth. A man who wants you for who you are. I cannot, will not, make promises I'm not sure I can keep. But I can promise you those things, Bailey. And I'm willing to try with the rest."

Emotion clogged her throat, so big, so huge, she felt as if she might choke on it. She didn't need his promises. It had never been about that with them. It had been about trust. And for the first time in her life, she trusted a man explicitly, without reservation.

"Last night might not have been the last time you need to pick me up," she murmured, offering him an out. "I am definitely a work in progress."

He brought his mouth down to brush against hers. "Consider me on board."

He kissed her then, a long, lingering promise of a kiss that lit her from the inside out. Her arms crept around his neck. He ditched their glasses, swung her up in his arms and carried her into the bedroom at the back of the plane. It was tiny, dominated by a king-size bed and a chest of drawers, and when he set her down on the soft carpet and sat on the bed, her pulse rate skyrocketed.

"Last night," he murmured, leaning back on his palms, "I didn't want sex between us to be about anger. I didn't want you lowering yourself to that. But tonight," he amended huskily, his gaze on hers, "feel free to demonstrate."

She stared at him. "Jared—"

He shook his head. "I don't want that memory between

us. The thought of you doing this for me is a massive turn-on, Bailey. For no other reason than you are you and you do that to me. Not because you did it for hundreds of other men who couldn't have you and I can."

The heat in his gaze got her. The deep, powerful throb of the jet beneath her feet mirrored the one pulsing between them. Her head went there and then her body followed. She *wanted* to do this for him. She wanted to wipe away the memory of last night.

She bent her leg and tugged a shoe off. He held up his hands, eyes glittering. "No missiles, please."

She tossed the shoe on the floor. Reached for the second. Then she moved forward to stand in front of him. His electric-blue eyes darkened into deep metallic as she reached for the top button of her blouse.

"There are rules," she murmured. "No kissing and no touching."

His gaze narrowed. "I think I've changed my mind."

"No, you haven't." She took her time, working her way down the buttons. Watched him as she stripped off the shirt and dropped it to the floor. His gaze fell to her breasts encased in cream-colored lace, her nipples already hard and pressing insistently against the confining material. He swallowed hard.

"Still want to change your mind?"

"No," he rasped. "I'm good."

She straddled him. Waited for the detached feeling that always came with this. But his eyes wouldn't let her; they held hers firm and forced her to connect. With Jared there was only the truth. There only ever had been.

His heavy-lidded stare dropped to her erect, pink-tipped nipples. "I'm not sure why they call this a lap dance. Feels more like torture to me."

"Yes," she agreed, "it could be described that way. Except," she murmured, rotating her hips in a seductive circle against him, "if you're a very good boy you might get more."

He muttered something under his breath she thought she deciphered as, "I sure hope so," and closed his eyes.

He was hard beneath her, thick and long under his suit pants, and this time it was she who swallowed. She remembered how he had filled her. Remembered how her muscles had clenched around him and how powerful her release had been. *Lord.*

She kept up her sinuous rotations. His thighs tensed beneath her, his hands fisting at his sides. "This better be special treatment, Bailey. Because if you did this for another man, I might have to kill him. Kill them all."

She leaned down and gave him a kiss. "Easy, tiger. It is."

He slid his hands over her hips. She removed them. "No hands."

"But you just kissed me…"

"That's because I'm in charge."

Ruddy color dusted his cheekbones. "Go ahead, convince yourself of that."

"No hands," she repeated, swaying closer. "Lips, however, are allowed."

He dipped his head and took her engorged nipple in his mouth. The hot warmth of his lips around her sent a bolt of heat to her core. She arched her back on a low moan and gave herself to him, wholly, sinfully, rocking against him.

He transferred his attention to the other hard peak and took her higher. She felt herself unraveling under his touch, losing the control she'd once so desperately craved. But this was Jared, and she was mad about him.

"Goddammit, Bailey." He lifted his head, eyes glittering. "I'm waving the white flag, whatever you need."

She stood up and slid her skirt off. Her panties. His gaze tracked her every movement, hot, hungry. She came back to him, moved her fingers to the button of his trousers and slid it out of the material. Then she eased his zipper down.

"Please," he was begging now. "Hands are good. I do good things with them."

She freed him from his boxers. Lowered herself to brush against the hard, hot length of him. "No hands."

She was slick and fully aroused, but he was a lot to handle. It took all her concentration to take him inside her, ease herself down on the potent length of him. She hadn't taken half of him when a low groan escaped her lips. "Jared—"

"Oh yes you can," he rasped, reading the look. "But you need to let me use my hands."

She nodded. Closed her eyes as his palms took the weight of her hips and held her over him, sliding farther inside her. He held her there while her body adjusted to him, his superior strength sending a surge of lust through her.

"More," she groaned.

He gave it to her, slowly, inch by inch, whispering in her ear how much he wanted her, how good she felt. His sexy voice excited her, inflamed her, softening her body until she took him all. It was all she could do to breathe with him buried inside her, but his hands supported her hips, controlling the rhythm, easing her into it.

The feeling of intense fullness morphed into a slow, hot burn every time he took her. The angle, the spot he was reaching deep inside her, promised extreme pleasure. Higher and higher he led her until it wasn't enough anymore—until she wanted to scream. She buried her hands in his hair and pleaded in a husky tone she didn't recognize as her own.

He slid his hand between them and pressed his thumb against the throbbing center of her. She looked down, watched him, the erotic sight of the rough passes of his thumb over her throbbing center summoning a wild, shattering release within seconds, her love for him escaping her lips as the white-hot intensity tore her apart.

He heard her, she knew, from the way he froze beneath her. Then the tight convulsions of her body around him pushed him over the edge, an animalistic groan tearing itself from his throat. And then there was no room for thought. Only pleasure.

The fact that he didn't repeat her words as he settled her against his chest and put his lips to her hair, his breathing hard and uneven, didn't completely throw her. This was Jared, after all, who'd just taken a huge step in telling her how he felt. She was going to focus on that and nothing else. Not on the very real possibility he would never get there.

She woke by the light of the moon, by herself in the bed. A glance at the clock told her it was almost eleven, another couple of hours before they would land. She sat up, looking for water, figuring Jared had left her to work. As her eyes adjusted to the darkness, she saw him sitting in a chair by the windows, dressed only in jeans. He looked lost, distant, in his own world.

"Couldn't sleep?"

He lifted his head. Blinked. "No." He didn't invite her over but she went anyway, setting her hand on his shoulder. His stiffness beneath her fingers made her hand still. The utter remoteness on his face made her consider retreating, until he reached up and pulled her down on his lap. Her heart squeezed at the near rejection. He was such a complex, multifaceted man. She was sure she only knew pieces of him.

She stayed there, curled against his chest, until the restlessness emanating from him made her draw back. She traced the hard line of his jaw, the unyielding curve of his mouth, the jagged white scar that bisected his upper lip. "How did you get this?"

He frowned, as if he had to pull the memory from the deep recesses of his mind. "The son of one of our friends my father embezzled the money from went to Stanford with me. After my father was sent to jail, he confronted me in one of the campus bars. He was angry, said some things about my father I couldn't let pass, and we got into a fight." His mouth twisted. "I thought it was a fistfight, but when Taylor started to lose, he added a beer bottle to the mix."

She shivered as she looked at the vicious-looking inch-long scar. "He could have done much worse."

His shoulder lifted. "He was hurting. His family was ruined. I got it."

She ran her fingers across the heavy dark stubble on his cheek. "You were too. Couldn't he see that you weren't to blame for your father's actions?"

"When you're angry and sad, you lash out."

Yes, but it hadn't been his burden to carry. Her heart squeezed. How hard must it have been for a college-aged boy to have to defend his hero.

He pulled her tight against his chest, his hand smoothing her hair. "My father wants to see me. That call you heard yesterday morning was my PI saying he'd done his usual check on him, that he didn't look great and he wants to see me."

The call that had come right before he'd gone ice-cold on her…it made sense now.

"Do you know why?"

"No."

"Are you going to go?"

"I don't know. When he got out of jail, he told me he needed time to get his head together, to figure out what he wanted to do. My mom had already remarried, and many of his friends wanted nothing to do with him. I was it really for him, but he didn't even want to see me. He disappeared, showed up in the islands. I told myself distancing myself from him was the best thing for me. I was hurting so badly, *I* needed space. But we never really reconnected after that, except over legalities. Every time I tried, he pushed me away."

"I'm sure he felt a lot of shame."

His fingers traced the curve of her ear. "I think I was afraid to face what had become of him. He was such a strong, proud man. Afterward…it was like seeing a ghost of him."

Her heart contracted in another long pull. She took his hand in hers and laced her fingers through his. "That could never happen to you. You are self-possessed in a way I have rarely seen, Jared. You know who you are."

His fingers tensed beneath hers as if he might pull them away, then he let out a breath and curled them tightly around hers. "I should have gone to see him. I should have insisted on it instead of just having him watched over. He's my father, for God's sake. He's not well and I've let him become a virtual hermit."

She shook her head. "You were hardly more than a boy when he left. You were sad and angry because he was supposed to take care of you."

"It doesn't excuse my behavior."

"It's never too late to make it right."

There was a long pause. Her fingers tightened around his. "Go, Jared. Talk to him. You won't forgive yourself if you don't."

He was silent then. She curled into his chest and tried to absorb his tension. But this part of Jared, this haunted part, was one only he could deliver himself from. Forgive himself for. She felt it rise up between them like a physical presence as the minutes wore on, creating a distance she couldn't bridge.

She got the message. Dressed and went back into the cabin and asked Betty for a cup of tea. Then sat watching the night as it sped by. Did people ever truly slay their demons? Or was it just easier to accept them as a part of you? She had always done that, but Jared had convinced her to try harder. Now if he could only do that for himself.

CHAPTER TWELVE

THEY NEEDED GLAMMING up.

Bailey came to that decisive conclusion about her slides for the executive committee meeting about the same time she remembered that the steaming Americano her colleague had brought her as reinforcement was sitting untouched on her desk. Tugging the top off the coffee, she brought the steaming brew to her lips. Maybe she needed some graphs. Clip art? Or maybe a joke…those meetings always needed livening up, didn't they?

And where had her concentration gone? She'd been doing so well all morning, ignoring the fact that Jared returned from the Caribbean today. Ignoring the fact that she was dying to see him to the point she really had to wonder about herself. She wanted to know how things had gone with his father. She wanted to know if he'd heard from Alexander. *And shouldn't he be in by now?*

A smile curved her lips. She hadn't needed to convince herself things could be different since she'd returned from France a week ago. They *were* different. She was the CMO of this vibrant, innovative company, she had a gazillion ideas in her head she couldn't wait to execute and yes, there was that little detail that she was in love with her boss.

A zing of anticipation ratcheted through her, sparking a warm glow in her cheeks. She'd spent two nights at Jared's place before he'd left. Two perfect nights in his stunning Pacific Heights mansion cooking together, getting to know each other and finishing off whatever work they'd had. And yes, countless hours in Jared's bed learning each other in different ways. It had been so good, so intimate, she'd laughingly threatened to bake the next time she'd come over. Except the next time hadn't come until the night before Jared had left to visit his father, and he'd been so keyed up about it, it had been a certified disaster.

In the days leading up to the trip, she'd watched him grow increasingly agitated. About everything, she suspected: the board meeting, the deal, the trip. She'd offered to cook for him that night thinking maybe she could distract him. Tempt him with a passionate night in bed. But he hadn't been there, not really. He'd toyed with his dinner, a distant look on his face, and cut the night short after they'd finished, pleading an early flight.

She'd tried not to remember his sarcastic line in Nice about kicking a woman out after they'd cooked for him, but that's exactly what had happened. And she, who wasn't at all sure what being in a relationship entailed, hadn't really known how to analyze it.

Was he pulling back? Did she just need to give him space because of his father? Was she supposed to be unnerved he hadn't returned any of her texts while he was away except to say that, yes, he'd landed fine?

Her heart thumped nervously in her chest. She supposed she was about to find out when he did come in. Which was a good thing because she needed to ground herself. Being with Jared had made it clear her job wasn't enough anymore. That being with someone as she was with him was something she'd been missing her entire adulthood. She *did* want the house and the white picket fence, as long as he was in it. As long as they were equals. And although she knew she needed to take it step-by-step with him, although the idea terrified her as much as it did him, she wanted to know she could have it. That this was real.

The slides stared back at her—clearly lacking. She needed to have them done for Jared so he could review them before they presented at tomorrow's board meeting. With a sigh, she put her coffee down and went searching for clip art.

Tate Davidson waltzed by her desk, leaving a trail of his sleazy cologne. "Big guy's in fine form."

Her gaze whipped to him. "Jared's back?"

"Sure is." He lifted a brow. "Surely he's checked in with his *CMO*?"

She lowered her head and ignored the dig. Tate was insanely jealous she'd been promoted over his head. And more importantly, her brain whirred, Jared was back. How long had he been in? Why hadn't he come to see her?

Her phone rang. She barked a greeting into it. It was Nancy from HR, wanting to schedule a meeting. "Sorry, what is this for?"

"Your sixty-day check-in."

She frowned. "What sixty-day check-in?"

"The one that's in your contract," Nancy said patiently. "Jared wanted to review things at the sixty-day mark."

He did? Wasn't it usually ninety days? Having signed the contract and not read it thoroughly before they'd left for France, she wouldn't know. She whipped it out of her drawer and scanned it. There it was on page eight in the fine detail. *Employee Trial Period*: *Employee's performance in the role to be reviewed at the sixty-day mark.*

"Isn't it usually ninety days?" she asked Nancy.

"Often, yes, but this is a high-profile role. Jared wanted to make sure he wasn't making any mistakes."

Mistakes? Her blood flashed hot in her veins as she kept reading, scanning through the legalese. *This position can be terminated for any reason determined by the employer, not limited by underperformance.*

"And *this* termination clause…*can be terminated for any reason?* Is this normal?"

There was a pause. "That's a little more…stringent than usual. But again, a high-profile position."

Bailey stared at the words. That clause said Jared could demote her for any reason after two months regardless of her performance on the job. Any clause she'd ever had in a contract had been based on performance.

She pulled in a breath. "You know what, Nancy? I'm going to schedule this check-in myself. Consider it done."

"Yes, but Bailey we don't do it that wa—"

Slam. She whacked the earpiece on the base. Shot to her feet. The hallways flashed by in a stream of silver as she made her way to the elevator and up to the executive floor. Mary, Jared's PA, gave her a bemused look as she stormed past her, knocked once on his door and flung it open.

Jared was bent over a pile of papers, a frown on his face. He looked up in surprise, flicked his gaze over her and rose to close the door.

"What's wrong?"

"First of all," she bit out, "it's nice that Tate Davidson knows you're back. It would also have been nice to get an answer to one of my texts. I know you're a very busy, important man but I would have enjoyed that courtesy."

His face softened, and now she could see the lines of fatigue crisscrossing it. "I'm sorry. I was on my way down after lunch."

"Two." She waved the contract at him. "Did you instruct HR to put that clause in my contract? The one that allows you to demote me *for any reason*, regardless of my performance?"

His frown deepened. "Yes. But that was before I knew what you were capable of."

She crinkled up her face. "You stood here and agreed to my terms. You asked me to come to France, to *save* your reputation and win that contract, when you weren't intending on *honoring* our deal?"

He walked toward her, his hands raised as if she were a child who needed to be calmed. "You were an unknown quantity, Bailey. I could hardly make you CMO without an opt-out. Be reasonable."

"An opt-out?" Her voice lifted a notch. "That clause is way beyond an opt-out. It's an ironclad opportunity to get rid of me whenever you so choose. Even Nancy said it was unusually…what did she say? Oh, *stringent*, that was the word."

"Bailey," he said quietly, holding her gaze, "that clause has nothing to do with the here and now. You have proven yourself to me. The job is yours. If you like, I'll have another contract drawn up."

"What I'd *like* is to know that you believed in me from the beginning. That you are a man of your word and you were going to honor our agreement."

He blanched. "Trust is earned."

"And I gave it to you *every step of the way*." She flung the words at him as she brought herself within inches of his tall, imposing figure. "I opened myself up completely to you, Jared. I let you break me down. And all I required in return was the honesty you promised me."

He shook his head, eyes flashing. "Everything I said to you, promised you over the past couple of weeks, is true, Bailey. Do not let *this*, do not let your insecurities, ruin a good thing."

"A good thing." She barked the words out, hands on her hips. "How long should I expect this *good thing* to last, Jared? A couple months? Three? Four? You were already backing off the other night as per usual. Then you go completely incommunicado."

He shook his head. "I've been up to my ears, stressed about my father..."

"So you shut me out?" She pressed her lips together, the insecurity, the hurt she'd felt over the past few days, sitting like the devil on her shoulder. "I'm no expert but I'm pretty sure this is where we're supposed to lean on each other. Be there for each other."

His mouth tightened. "I've been trying. You push too much, Bailey."

The stubborn tilt of his chin, the forbidding line of his mouth, did her in. "I know you heard me say I love you on the plane, Jared. You ignored it completely."

He shook his head, his face losing color. "I told you I don't make promises I can't keep. It isn't in my DNA. You knew that."

He could have said anything, *anything* but that and she might have been okay with it. But a cop-out like that? It made her chest feel so tight she couldn't breathe. Because it wasn't enough anymore. Not when she'd handed him her heart.

She nodded sagely. "Now there's the honesty I need. Because I've decided I can't do this, Jared. You asked me to open up, to trust you. Well here I am. And if you can't do the same, I think we should end it now."

His gaze flashed. "You're using this as an excuse to end things before it's started."

She shook her head. "This is me not wanting to be another casualty of the cult of Jared. I guess it's not in *my* DNA to expect anything less than everything."

"Bailey—" He reached for her, but she shook him off, stalked to the door and left. Enough of this emotional roller coaster.

Jared was debating whether to go after Bailey when Mary stuck her head in his office. "Alexander Gagnon is on the line."

He cursed. If there was a person he did not want to talk to at this moment in time, it was Alexander. However, as the fate of his company lay in the man's hands, he had no choice but to.

He shut the door, walked to his desk, sat down and took a deep breath. Then he hit the blinking line.

"Gagnon."

"Bonjour, Stone." Alexander's smooth, silky voice slid over the phone line. "Good news for you. We have decided we would like to offer Stone Industries the partnership."

The rush of satisfaction that ran through him at Gagnon's words was swift and sharp. But the burn that stung his eyes, the tremor in his hands as he pressed them against his desk, came from a deeper place. A place he'd been loath to acknowledge. He would have walked, he'd been prepared to walk, but *this* was his company. To restore what he'd built with his heart and soul to its former brilliance—he wanted it with every fiber of his being.

"Thank you," he rasped. "I'm very happy to hear that."

"This is dependent, of course," Gagnon said, "on Project X being exclusive to our stores."

"Certain product lines, yes, but not all."

"We can come to some kind of an agreement on that, *oui*. We will need to work very closely together in the beginning. The planning will be key. I want Bailey in Paris for quarterly meetings. How is your beautiful CMO, by the way?"

Jared sat up straight. "Bailey is not part of this deal, Gagnon."

"So vehement," the Frenchman chided. "I merely want her brain. What are you going to do, Stone? Marry her? That would certainly keep the dinner conversation interesting."

His blood bubbled dangerously close to the surface. He

thought he might, actually. Want to marry her. Watching her walk out of his life could do that.

He stared viciously at the phone. "Send the contract over, Gagnon. And forget about Bailey in Paris. You'll have Tate Davidson, my VP."

He ended the call before he said something to trash the deal. Sat back and tried to digest. He was overwhelmingly relieved to be walking into that board meeting tomorrow with Maison in his pocket. Michael Craig's massive abuse of his expenses as CEO had been splashed across the news this morning in a carefully executed plan to discredit him and oust him from the Stone Industries board, thanks to a friendship Jared had with a high-placed reporter at a daily newspaper. Everything was falling into place. But it was Bailey who occupied his head. He'd had to put that clause in her contract. He was running a multibillion-dollar company. He didn't put someone whose ability he'd questioned into a C-suite position without a backup plan.

His chin jutted out, his resolve fierce. Except she was right. He'd promised her the job. The clause should have been about performance. Instead he'd been intent on manipulating the situation to his advantage. That was the real truth. He'd been running as fast as his legs could carry him the last few days.

Bailey was right.

His time in the Caribbean had been mind-altering. Just as terrifying as he'd anticipated. His father was a shadow of his former self; old, suffering from debilitating diabetes and wanting his son to know the truth after reading his manifesto. It had not just been his marriage that had brought him to his knees, his father had told him, but his lack of faith in himself. His inability to follow his dreams. But Jared, he'd counseled, a wisdom in his eyes that seemed out of place in such a weak, frail man, had done just that. He had followed his heart, and that's all a man could do.

You cannot, his father had warned him, *take on my legacy, or you will destroy yourself.*

Achingly honest, frighteningly intense, his conversations with his father had nearly undone him. Had left him shaken and angrier than ever at himself. He should have done more. He should have done something sooner. *He* should have been braver.

The burn in his eyes brought a hot glitter to his vision. He was not his father. He knew that. And Bailey wasn't his mother. He had spent the flight home thinking about the two of them, how very different they were. His mother was brittle, power-hungry, content to live life on the coattails of each successive powerful man she conquered, whereas Bailey was strong in a beautiful, courageous way. Independence personified. You could see how much she cared in her eyes just now. Funnily enough, what he'd thought would never work for him was now the only thing he knew would. To have a woman that strong. His equal.

I know you heard me say I love you on the plane, Jared. Why hadn't he had the courage to tell her? He loved her. Of course he did. He'd been half on his way that night in Nice when he'd learned the truth of her. Fully so after the night she'd given herself to him. And all he'd done since was deny it.

He leaned back and stared at the ceiling. He'd broken Bailey's trust with that clause. The one thing sure to drive her away. And even though he'd had his reasons, they seemed blindingly inappropriate right about now. Not when she was everything he'd never known he wanted.

An idea that might be the product of his jet-lagged brain or pure brilliance, he wasn't sure which, entered his head. He wasn't letting her go. Not a chance.

CHAPTER THIRTEEN

WHEN BAILEY HAD left Las Vegas for California, a freshly minted business degree in her pocket and a lifetime of wisdom garnered from her very real job and her less-than-ideal family background, she'd thought she had it all figured out. Rely on yourself, don't expect too much and keep your eye on the ball, and you'd get where you were going. That mentality, she decided, driving to work the day after that scene with Jared, would have served her well if she'd actually *employed* it with her boss as well as the job. If she hadn't let herself fall in love with a man with a heart of stone. But somewhere along the way, she'd allowed herself to believe, to want far more than her destiny had ever been when it came to him. And suffered the glaring truth of her life-learned rule: wanting more than what you were destined to have was a recipe for heartbreak.

She peeled herself out of her car and walked into her favorite coffee shop in San Jose. Their argument hadn't really been about the clause. It had been about her loving him and being afraid he would never return it.

The lineup of slouchily dressed students, computer nerds and suits was three deep on either side. She chose the typically faster one and tapped her foot impatiently on the faux hardwood floor. Maybe Jared was right, maybe she was running. Maybe it was just easier that way when you wanted what you couldn't have.

The line finally cleared. Christian, the jean-clad, scruffy-looking barista who served her every morning, gave her a curious look as she slid a bill toward him. "Didn't expect to see you here this morning."

"Because this morning is any different from the last five years?" Her attempted humor came out bitter and unattractive. "Sorry," she winced. "Bad morning."

He pushed his funky glasses farther up his nose. "Have you read the paper this morning?"

She shook her head. That was part of her Americano ritual *after* she'd triaged her email. "Why?"

He yelled her order to the barista mixing the drinks. "It's been the talk of the place this morning. You should get on that."

She lifted a brow. "Anything in particular I should be looking for?"

"You'll know it when you see it." He pushed her money back at her. "Drink's on the house, by the way. You look like you need it."

He took the next customer's order. Bailey shook her head, picked up her Americano and drove to work, her re-created resignation burning a hole in her pocket.

Aria called as she was walking through the front doors of the office.

"I gotta admit, even with all his imperfections, *that* would do it for me."

Bailey frowned, using her elbows to negotiate the doors. "What *are* you talking about?"

"Have you read the paper this morning?"

"Why does everyone keep asking me that? What earth-shattering thing has happened? Did Jared make an announcement about Maison?"

"Oh my," Aria sighed. "You really haven't read it. He has certainly made a statement, but it wasn't about Maison."

"Great," Bailey muttered. Another illuminating Jaredism to set the internet ablaze.

"Did you say you have your first executive committee meeting this morning?" Aria asked.

Bailey cradled the phone against her ear and jabbed the call button for the elevator. "I do. If I don't resign first."

"I suggest you read page five of the *Chronicle* before you do that. Then call me. I will kill you if you don't call me."

"Aria." She stepped onto the elevator. "What's going on?"

The iron box swallowed up her call. She hit the button for the twenty-sixth floor, and thought about what Christian had said. *Didn't expect you to be in today...* What did that mean?

She exited the elevator, went straight to the PR department where she collected the *Chronicle* and took it back to her desk. Coffee in hand, she flipped to page five. An open letter from Jared took up the entire page. It was headlined, The Truth about Women—A Rebuttal.

Oh. My. God. He had not. Eyes glued to the page, she started reading.

A few weeks ago, I wrote a manifesto titled "The Truth about Women." Intended as an honest if tongue-in-cheek summary of my views of women both in the boardroom and bedroom, it has provoked a great deal of debate, resonating with some of you and provoking anger in others.

At the time I wrote it I honestly believed everything I said. Experience had taught me that many women do not want the career life we as a society have insisted they do. That cries of a glass ceiling were perpetuated by females caught up in their own self-deception. And if the truth be known, I was not overly sold on a woman's place in the boardroom, nor her ability to stand toe-to-toe with a man.

Then I had the chance to work with a woman I have admired for years, my chief marketing officer, Bailey St. John. In keeping with my theme of nothing but the truth here, I have to admit I severely underestimated her talent. I did not give credit where credit was due. She is not only a superior thinker to any other marketer I have ever had the opportunity to work with, male or female, she could likely wipe the floor with most of them.

This extraordinary woman also taught me something else. Something far more important than the value of a woman in the boardroom. She has proven me wrong about a woman's place in my life. Hers. She has taught me that I can connect with another person on a deeper level, that I do want someone in my life in a forever sense, not just for the sake of the nuclear family, but because I love her. For who she is. For her courage. For what she's taught me. She has made me a better man.

So here is my offer, Bailey, with all my imperfections as previously noted:

I offer you the homestead, and all the baking supplies in it, minus the white picket fence because Pacific Heights does not consider this fashionable.

I offer you a ring and a lifetime commitment.

I offer you a lion in the bedroom because that part is still true and I know you like it. Love it, actually.

And most importantly, if I am lucky enough to have you I am offering you complete honesty—after a mistake I swear I will never make again. Even when it's hard. Even when it hurts because that works for us.

If you're interested in all I have to offer, you know where to find me.
All my love,
Jared

Her eyes blurred as she read the last sentence. Hot tears spilled down her cheeks in a wet line that dripped into her Americano. She reread the whole thing. Stared at it hard. Vaguely registered the arrival of Tate Davidson and the fact that her executive meeting started in five minutes.

She blew her nose. Fixed her lipstick. Clutched her notebook and letter of resignation to her chest and followed Tate upstairs to the boardroom. It was packed with a full contingent of board members as well as executives at the vice president level and above, presided over by the chairman of the board, Sam Walters.

And Jared. Seated at the head of the table beside Sam, his gaze, which might be described as distinctly hostile, was trained on her. As was every set of eyes in the room, for that matter, and honestly, she could do without that.

Sam waved her and Tate into two chairs at the front. Bailey sat down, glad for the seat given her knocking knees. Tate opened the meeting, and began going through the financials. Jared took off his jacket and loosened his tie. Started drumming his fingers on the table. Tate announced the Maison deal to much applause, the buzz in the room palpable. He waited while the other directors congratulated Jared, then turned to the CEO for a word.

"I'm sorry," Jared said, waving a hand at Tate, his gaze still pinned on Bailey, "but did you read the paper this morning?"

Her lips curved, his disheveled appearance, the agitated air about him, solidifying what she already knew. Jared Stone was irresistible. "Five minutes ago," she said evenly. "I was late this morning."

The scowl on his face grew. “You have anything you’d like to share?”

“Yes,” she said softly, because you could hear a pin drop in the room, it was that quiet. “But I’d prefer to do it in private.”

He sat back, blue eyes stormy. Julie Walcott, his VP of PR, raised her hand. “Can I make a request? Can we make this the last manifesto? It’s such a work of art we should allow it to become infamous.”

“Considering this one just about killed me,” Jared growled, “that would be a definitive yes.”

Sam took control of the meeting after that. Somewhere near the end, she found herself the bewildered owner of a whole new set of responsibilities Jared bestowed on her in a bid to go back to doing what he did best. He relinquished the “first look” privileges he had over Stone Industries’ marketing and handed them to her. From now on everyone on the PR, advertising and marketing teams would report to her. He did not, Jared stressed, want to spend his time approving ad campaigns.

She stared shocked at him while Tate Davidson nearly lost his breakfast. It was a controversial call, no doubt, but given the stormy nature of her boss at the moment, no one was saying a word.

Lunchtime arrived. She stood up with everyone else, snatching her resignation off the table. Jared appeared at her elbow. “My office,” he growled and propelled her down the hall into his minimalistic haven. Bailey stood, paper clutched in her hands, as he shut the door and leaned against it, his stance turning predatory.

“What *is* that in your hands?”

“My resignation.”

His gaze narrowed. “You aren’t resigning. I feel a sense of déjà vu here.”

She drank him in, the same fierce warrior in evidence

as the one in her bedroom that night in Nice when he'd promised to back her no matter what.

"Did you mean everything you said in that rebuttal?"

He nodded. "Every word. Including the part where I declared my love for you in a national newspaper."

Her heart melted, so full of emotion she didn't know where to start. "Promises aren't in your DNA."

"I didn't think love was in my DNA either," he countered roughly, snagging her sleeve and tugging her closer. "And now look at me."

She was. He was everything she'd never dreamed she could have. And so much more.

"Seeing my father threw me. I needed time to process. To understand my feelings. But never for one minute did I change my mind about you. About what I said on the plane." He ran his thumb across her cheek. "I will always tell you the truth, even when you don't want to hear it."

"I know," she whispered. "I just needed to hear you say it. Write it. Whatever. Actually can you say it?"

He lowered his head to hers. "I love you. I've loved you from that night in Nice."

He kissed her then, slow and deep. She was ready to sink into it completely, into *him* completely, when he set her away from him with a determined movement.

"Hey," she protested. "That wasn't—"

The words died in her throat as he pulled a jeweler's box from his inside pocket. "You weren't supposed to be late this morning. I was going to give you this."

Her heart jumped into her mouth as he flipped the box open. Nestled inside the blue jeweler's box sat a diamond eternity band that sparkled in the light. "You can have another if you like," he said huskily, "you can have ten. But this is my promise to be your constant, Bailey St. John. Marry me."

She shoved her hand at him. He slipped the ring on.

The diamonds, hugging her finger in an unending circle of fire, made her heart take flight.

He brought her hand to his lips. “Is that a yes?”

“Yes.”

“Good. After this meeting, I’m taking you home to celebrate.”

“After?” she pouted.

“I just gave you direct responsibility for all marketing activity. You’d better take the helm while you can.”

“True,” she murmured. “I do love you, Jared Stone. I’m not afraid to say it.”

His gaze darkened. “You can tell me that again tonight. Over and over.”

She did. Many times as he proved his nickname All-Night Jared Stone was aptly earned. The ring sparkling on her finger made that just fine with her. He was hers; he would always be hers, she knew that. And in his arms, Bailey finally found herself. Not the old Bailey, not the new Bailey, just the Bailey she was destined to be.

* * * * *